THE GLITTER BABY—ONCE THEY ALL OWNED A PIECE OF HER.

FLEUR SAVAGAR—America's #1 Cover Girl. Sweet, funny, outrageously beautiful. Her mother's dreams carried her to the top. But in the glamorous fast lane even a Glitter Baby has to become a woman someday.

BELINDA—Fleur's bewitching mother. She came to Hollywood in search of James Dean and met Errol Flynn instead. Their passion-drenched nights at the Garden of Allah changed her life forever.

JAKE KORANDA—Hollywood's hottest actor, America's most brilliant playwright. Sexy, sensual, he was every woman's favorite tough guy. Now he had to teach a tender baby the grown-up rules of love.

ALEXI—A European aristocrat with a gift for turning old money into new. He collected priceless Bugattis and innocent women. What he couldn't have he tried to destroy . . . including Belinda's beautiful daughter.

THEN SHE GREW UP AND SWORE NO ONE WOULD EVER OWN HER AGAIN!

4/21/90

Also by Susan Elizabeth Phillips
RISEN GLORY

To Lydia, with love

ACKNOWLEDGMENTS

So many people have helped directly and indirectly with this book. My special thanks to the following:

Those in fashion and film who answered my questions so graciously: David Price, Calvin Klein Ltd., Ford Models, Inc., and the production staff and cast of *Flanagan*.

My editor Maggie Lichota and my agent Steven Axelrod, two people who really like writers.

"The Group," Dionne Brennan Polk and Mary Shukis, who were with me all the way. Rosanne Kohake and Ann Rinaldi, for their wise counsel. Barbara Bretton and Joi Nobisso, for helping out.

Friends and neighbors who shared their specialized knowledge with me: Simone Baldeon, Thelma Canty, Don Cucurello, Dr. Robert Pallay, Joe Phillips, and the staff of the Hillsborough Public Library.

Ty and Zachary Phillips, the world's best kids.

And to Bill and Dr. J.—thanks for the inspiration.

Susan Elizabeth Phillips

CHAPTER 1

The Glitter Baby was back. She paused inside the arched entrance to the gallery so that the opening night guests would have time to recognize her. A low buzz of polite party conversation mixed with the street noises outside as the patrons studied with varying degrees of interest the new collection of African primitives that hung on the stuccoed walls of the prestigious Orlani Gallery. The air was full of the scent of Joy, imported *pâté de foie gras,* and money. Six years had passed since hers was one of the most famous faces in America. The Glitter Baby wondered if they would still remember and what she would do if they didn't.

She gazed straight ahead with studied ennui, lips slightly parted, her ringless hands relaxed at her sides. In her black ankle-strapped stiletto heels she stood over six feet tall, a beautiful Amazon with a thick mane of hair that fell past her shoulders. It used to be a game among New York's one-name hairdressers to try to identify the color, using only a single word. They offered up "champagne" and "butterscotch" and "taffy," but they never felt they'd got it quite right, and since each considered himself a creative genius, the word "blond" was never mentioned.

Actually, her hair was all those colors, interwoven threads of every shade of blond—hair that changed color with the light. It wasn't just her hair, however, that inspired the poetic; everything about the Glitter Baby seemed to encourage superlatives. A famous fashion editor was once said to have fired an assistant editor who made the mistake of referring to the famous eyes as "hazel." The editor herself rewrote the copy, describing the irises of Fleur Savagar's eyes as being "marbled with gold, tortoise, and startling sluices of emerald green."

Six years later, on that September evening in 1982, as the Glitter Baby gazed out on the crowd, she looked more beautiful

9

than ever. She also looked bored and just a little condescending. There was a trace of hauteur in the not-quite-hazel eyes, an arrogant tilt to the sculptured chin. But the pose was merely that—a pose—for inside, Fleur Savagar was badly frightened, and at that moment she wanted nothing more than to turn her back on all of them and run away. Instead, she took a deep, steadying breath. She was through with running. She had been running for six years, and that was enough. She wasn't nineteen anymore. The Glitter Baby was all grown up, and they weren't ever going to hurt her again.

She watched the crowd for several minutes. A few of the people present she had known rather well, others only slightly. Diana Vreeland, impeccably dressed in an Yves Saint Laurent evening cape worn over black silk pants, was studying a bronze Benin head, while Mikhail Baryshnikov, all cheeks and dimples, stood at the center of a small group of women who were obviously more interested in Russian charm than African primitives. In one corner a television anchorman and his socialite wife chatted with a fortyish French actress making her first public appearance since a not so hush-hush face-lift; while across from them, the pretty showpiece wife of a notoriously homosexual Broadway producer stood alone in a Mollie Parnis she had unwisely left unbuttoned to the waist. Fleur felt a flash of pity for her. According to Kissy, who made it her business to keep up with such things, the showpiece wife was losing a battle with an eight-hundred-dollar-a-day cocaine habit.

Although there were a few backless high heels with disco dresses left over from the previous season, Fleur observed that most of the younger women in the crowd were dressed in what was currently passing for chic—female versions of the male tuxedo, a fashion look that the man who had designed her dress labeled "Butch-Gone-Bad." Of course, at the Orlani Gallery, the tuxedos were accessorized with Russian lynx jackets and Tiffany twenty-karat gold-mesh Peretti-designed evening purses.

Fleur's dress was quite different. Her designer had seen to that. "You must be elegant, Fleur. Elegance, elegance, elegance in the Dismal Era of the Drab." He had cut black velvet on the bias and constructed a cleanly sculptured gown with a high neck and bare arms. At midthigh, he had slashed across the skirt, opening it in a long, diagonal cut to the opposite ankle, then he had filled in the space with a waterfall flounce of the thinnest black point d'esprit. Fleur remembered how he had teased her about the flounce, saying he had been forced to design it as camouflage for her size-ten feet.

And then she forgot about her dress and her feet as the heads began to turn in her direction. She could see the instant when their curiosity about who she was changed to recognition, and she slowly let out her breath. There was a small hush, and then a bearded photographer abruptly turned his Hasselblad from the French actress to Fleur and caught the picture that was to take up the entire front page of *Women's Wear Daily* the next morning.

Across the room, Adelaide Abrams, New York's most widely read gossip columnist, squinted toward the arched doorway. It couldn't be! Had she finally been flushed out? God, if she was wrong about this, she was going to kill herself. She took a quick step forward, and then another, cursing the optometrist who couldn't get her new contact lenses to fit right, cursing her long-dead mother who had passed on her bad eyesight to a daughter who already had a *goyisher* husband and a flat chest, cursing the schmucks who were standing in her way. . . .

She bumped into a multimillionaire real estate developer and rushed on without apology, glancing wildly about for her own photographer. Where was he? She was going to kill him when she found him. She was going to kill him, and then she was going to kill herself. Son of a bitch. She had heard a rumor that he was a Presbyterian. What else could you expect from a Presbyterian? Shit. That *nafka* from *Harper's Bazaar* was already bearing down on the doorway. Adelaide Abrams took a deep breath, plunged past two startled socialites, and like Secretariat going for the Triple Crown, made the final dash to Fleur Savagar's side.

Fleur had been watching the race between *Harper's* and Adelaide Abrams, and she didn't know whether she was relieved or not to see that Adelaide was winning. Adelaide was a shrewd old bird, and it wasn't going to be easy to put her off with half-truths and vague answers, especially after all the gossip.

"Fleur my God it really is you I can't believe what I see with my very own eyes my God you look wonderful!" Adelaide exclaimed.

"Hello, Adelaide." Her speech was musical, vaguely midwestern, and no one listening to her would have guessed that English was not her first language. She leaned down, and the two women pressed their cheeks together. When she straightened, the bottom of her chin was level with the top of Adelaide's skillfully hennaed hair.

Adelaide determinedly pulled her toward the back corner of the room, effectively cutting her off from the other members of the press, and then she looked at her reproachfully. "Nineteen seventy-six was a bad year for me, Fleur. I went through menopause. God forbid you should ever go through what I did. It would have made a difference if you'd given me the story. Dropped me a little note telling me what was what. Let me know why the most famous model in the world with her whole life ahead of her should run away all of a sudden. It would have made a difference. At least if I'd had the story, I could have been happy during the hot flashes."

Fleur laughed and took a glass of champagne from a passing waiter. It was crisp and dry, and she held it in her mouth for a fraction of a second before she swallowed. "You haven't changed a bit, Adelaide," she said. "And you're not going to force any secrets out of me with the Jewish mother routine, either."

"What the hell," Adelaide shrugged. "It's always worth a try. You'd be surprised how many people who should know better get suckered in that way." She grabbed a glass of her own from the tray.

"My days of getting suckered in are over."

Adelaide looked at her speculatively. "You're no fool, Fleur. You never were. I remember the first story I ever did on you. You were seventeen years old, and you'd just been on your first *Vogue* cover. If I live to be a hundred, I'll never forget that picture. It was ageless. Those bones of yours . . . and those great, big hands—no rings, no nail polish—holding up your hair. They were shooting you in furs the day I met you. When they stopped to adjust the lights, you went into the corner to study geometry or biology or something like that. I'll never forget it. Only seventeen, and you had on a chinchilla coat I should live so long to own and a diamond choker from Harry Winston that had to cost a quarter of a million. You were sitting in the corner with a schoolbook in your lap and a big wad of bubble gum in your mouth. I remember Belinda that day, too.

12

The second she spotted that gum, she reached right into your mouth after it. I'll never forget that."

The last thing Fleur wanted to talk about was Belinda, even though she knew it was inevitable. Still, she could postpone it for a while. "I was in Europe most of the time, Adelaide. There were some things I needed to sort out."

"Sorting out I can understand. You were a young girl. You'd hardly had a normal childhood, and it was your first movie. Hollywood people aren't always sensitive, not like us New Yorkers. But when you finally came back, you wouldn't say anything to anybody. Six years, Fleur. What kind of sorting takes six years?"

"The kind of sorting I had to do."

Her tone was light, but there was something closed about her expression that Adelaide recognized from years of experience. She had hit a dead end. Quickly, she switched direction. "So tell me, mystery lady, what's your secret? I would have sworn you couldn't improve, which just goes to show what I know. You're looking better now than you did at nineteen, we should all be so lucky."

Fleur smiled, accepting the compliment gracefully. It gave her no particular pleasure, but it interested her. Sometimes when she looked at her photographs, she could see her own beauty, but in general she had learned to rely on other people's judgments. She knew the years had changed her face, bringing to it a greater strength and maturity, but until she'd heard Adelaide's comment she hadn't been certain how others would view the changes.

Fleur possessed almost no personal vanity, simply because she had never been able to see what all the fuss was about. She found her own face too strong. The bones that photographers and fashion editors had always raved about looked masculine to her. As for her height and the large hands and feet that accompanied it—they were simply impossible.

Adelaide's next question seemed to come out of nowhere. "Have you seen Belinda?"

"I'm sorry, Adelaide; I won't talk about Belinda. What happened between us is personal, and you can make whatever you want of that. I won't talk about *Sunday Morning Eclipse* either, or anything else that happened six years ago. I'm done with the past."

13

Adelaide gave a deep, martyred sigh. "You were such a sweet child, Fleur. I don't know what's happened to you. All right, if that's the way you want it, we'll talk about something else, like what you're planning to do with the rest of your life and where you got that gown. Nobody's worn anything like it in years. It reminds me of what fashion used to be all about." She jerked her head vaguely in the direction of those behind her and sniffed disdainfully. "Women in tuxedos. I should have lived so long to see such a thing. And God forbid you should criticize. They tell you you're an old fuddy-duddy who doesn't know what's what."

Fleur grinned. "It'll be a cold day in hell, Adelaide, when you don't know what's what. And thank you for the compliments on my gown. It *is* beautiful, isn't it? The man who designed it will be here later tonight if you'd like to meet him. Now, if you'll excuse me, there are some people I have to speak to. And I think I'd better talk to *Harper's* before she burns a hole in your back glaring at you."

She was just about to move away when Adelaide caught her arm. This time her concern was genuine. "Fleur, stop a minute. Before you turn around, you should know that Belinda just walked in."

Fleur felt a queer, dizzy sensation, as if she had stood up too quickly. She hadn't expected this. How stupid of her. Damn! She wasn't ready . . . it was too soon. She turned around slowly, knowing without having to look that most of the eyes in the room would be on them.

Belinda was loosening the scarf that lay just inside the collar of her golden sable when she saw Fleur. She froze, her fingers paralyzed awkwardly at the knot, her mouth slightly open, the unforgettable hyacinth-blue eyes widening.

Belinda. She was forty-five and still lovely, even though her appearance now bore a subtle air of careful preparation. Her hair was a lighter shade of blond, but she wore it as she always had, cut just below her jawline in Grace Kelly's sophisticated *Dial M for Murder* side-parted arrangement, a hairstyle from the fifties that had always managed to look just right because Belinda wore it. Even though she was cocooned in sable, Fleur could see that she was as slim as ever. There was no loose flesh under her chin, and her knee-high soft leather boots clung to calves that were still small and shapely.

14

Belinda's fingers fluttered in that curious, nervous gesture that had become so characteristic of her. Without even a cursory acknowledgment of the people standing near her, she walked straight toward Fleur. She pulled off her gloves and stuffed them in her pockets, not even noticing when one fell to the floor. Then she reached out her hand.

"Fleur."

There was a small moment of quiet, the kind that sometimes falls over a large gathering.

"Hello, Belinda." Fleur kept her arms at her sides.

But Belinda was stubborn. She refused to retreat. Even though her hand had begun to tremble, she extended it a fraction further. "There are people watching, darling," she said softly. "For appearances, at least."

"I don't play to the crowd anymore, Mother." Fleur turned and walked away.

Belinda was left standing alone, her hand awkwardly extended, but she was not even conscious of the fact that she had been made to look foolish. All she could think about was her daughter.

The Glitter Baby.

It was a name she had invented. How perfect it was for her beautiful Fleur, the creature she had created. The creature Alexi had wanted to destroy. But Fleur had never been Alexi's daughter. Fleur had been Flynn's daughter . . . her daughter . . . and in some special way, Jimmy's too.

Her fingers reached inside her coat and touched the small spinning charm that she had begun to wear again on a chain beneath her clothing. Flynn had given it to her during those golden days at the Garden of Allah, but that hadn't really been the beginning.

The beginning . . . She remembered it as clearly as she remembered this morning's newspaper. The day it had all started.

It had been a Thursday in September, hot even by Southern California standards. It was the day she met James Dean. . . .

The Baron's Baby

"There I am, unable to understand myself. Still not knowing who I am. Still hunting for my soul."

Errol Flynn:
My Wicked, Wicked Ways

CHAPTER 2

It was 1955 and Jonas Salk was the most beloved man in America. Children could swim in city pools again and go to summer camp without the threat of polio striking terror in their parents' hearts. God-bless-him Jonas Salk had freed America from fear.

Ike and Mamie were in the White House, Anthony Eden at No. 10 Downing Street (it didn't seem quite right to most people that Churchill was no longer there) and Juan Peron was hiding out in Paraguay.

Walt Disney introduced mouse-ears and coonskin caps while Madison Avenue extolled the merits of roll-on deodorants and filter-tip cigarettes. America cleaned its teeth with Ipana, bought Polaroid Land cameras, and used Modess . . . because.

It wasn't the best time for marriage. Princess Margaret decided not to give it all up for the man she loved, thus sparing Group Captain Peter Townsend a life of almost certain misery, and the Yankee Clipper and the Blond Bombshell made up their minds to call it quits. The mausoleum and Joe's sad roses were still far ahead.

It was of Marilyn that Belinda Britton was thinking as she lifted a copy of *Modern Screen* from the magazine rack at Schwab's Sunset Boulevard drugstore. She couldn't wait to see Marilyn's new picture, *The Seven Year Itch*. As she thumbed through the magazine, she found herself wishing that Marilyn weren't making it with Tom Ewell. He wasn't very handsome. She would rather see her with Bob Mitchum again, like in *River of No Return,* or Rock Hudson, or, even better, Burt Lancaster.

A year ago she had had a terrible crush on Burt Lancaster. When she had seen *From Here to Eternity,* she'd felt as if it were her body, not Deborah Kerr's, that he had held beneath his own as the waves crashed around them, and her lips he had kissed. She wondered if Deborah Kerr had opened her mouth when Burt kissed her. Somehow she doubted it. Deborah didn't seem the type. If she had been playing the part, she would have opened her mouth for Burt Lancaster's tongue, you could bet on that.

For weeks after, the fantasy had slowly unwound inside her head. For some reason—the light wasn't right or the director had gotten distracted—for some reason the camera wouldn't stop and neither would Burt. He would peel down the top of her sandy one-piece bathing suit until he freed her breasts. And then he would stroke them, calling her Karen because that was her name in the movie. But she and Burt both knew it wasn't Karen he was making love to, but Belinda. And when Burt Lancaster bent his head to her nipples . . .

"Excuse me, miss, but could you hand me a copy of *Reader's Digest?*"

Fade to wave's pounding, just like in the movies . . .

Belinda passed over the requested copy of a *Reader's Digest* and then traded her *Modern Screen* for a *Photoplay* with Kim Novak on the cover. As she walked to the counter to pay the cashier, she realized that it had been a long time since she'd daydreamed about Burt Lancaster or Tony Curtis or any of the rest of them. Six months to be exact. Six months since she had seen the magical face that had made all the rest of those handsome faces fade into unimportance.

She had left for Hollywood two weeks after she had first seen that face, not bothering to finish her senior year in high school, even though she was third in her class. A high school diploma didn't seem important when all you wanted in life was to be a movie star. *He* had given her the courage to find the way.

As she waited in line behind the woman who was buying the *Reader's Digest,* she wondered if her parents missed her at all. It was a stupid question. They might miss her in public in front of their friends, but in private they were glad to have her gone. Still, she couldn't complain. They sent her one hundred dollars a month to keep her from having to work at the sort of menial job that would disgrace them if anyone they knew ever found out about it.

Her parents had both been past forty when she was born. Dr. Britton had his prosperous Indianapolis medical practice, Mrs. Britton her hospital charities. Edna Cornelia, as they'd named their daughter, was a great inconvenience to both of them. They weren't cruel people. They bought her beautiful doll houses and china tea sets and every game she asked for. When she grew older, they were generous with spending money and let her walk the two blocks to the movies whenever she wanted, but they didn't talk to her very much, or play with her at all.

As a result she grew up with a faint sense of panic, the feeling that she was somehow invisible. Other people told her she was unusually pretty, her teachers told her she was smart, but their compliments didn't mean anything to her. How could someone who was invisible be special?

Belinda made a magical discovery when she was nine. The bad feelings went away when she was sitting in the back row of the Palace Theater. All she had to do was pretend she was one of the magical women who shone before her on the screen, their faces and bodies enlarged once, twice, a hundred times bigger than life. They bore no resemblance to ordinary women. Instead, they were dazzling goddesses, special in a way that only a few chosen ones can ever be.

She vowed that someday she would make it happen for herself and become one of the beautiful, adored women. She was going to take her place on that same screen, be magnified as they were magnified until she could never feel invisible again. Nothing was going to stand in her way.

Except, of course, everything did because she was still a child and children stay with their parents until they are grown, even when their parents don't care for them very much.

"That'll be twenty-five cents, beautiful." The cashier was a handsome, Chiclet-toothed blond who was too obviously an unemployed actor. His gaze slid appraisingly down over Belinda's figure, fashionably clad in a pencil-slim navy blue cotton sheath trimmed in white and cinched at the waist with a poppy red patent leather belt. It was one of Belinda's favorite dresses, reminding her of something Audrey Hepburn would wear, although she actually thought of herself more as the Grace Kelly type, since so many people told her she looked like Grace. She had even had her hair cut to make the resemblance more pronounced.

She didn't always dress in such a ladylike fashion when she came to Schwab's, however. Sometimes she wore her tightest pair of black pedal pushers, a shocking-pink halter that left her midriff bare, and dark glasses, all with her very highest heels.

21

Whenever she wore this outfit, she pushed her hair back on the right side and secured it with a small pink comb just above her ear. Directors were always looking for different types, and she wanted to make certain she was ready for them.

Her features were small and fine, and she was meticulous about applying her makeup to enhance them. Today, in deference to the poppy red belt, she was wearing Tangee's Red Majesty on her lips, drawing them a little larger than they actually were. She had also blended a few dabs of Revlon's newest cream rouge just below the line of her cheekbones to emphasize the contour, a trick she had learned in a *Movie Mirror* article by Bud Westmore, makeup man to the stars. She kept her pale lashes touched up with dark brown mascara to highlight her very best feature, a pair of exceptionally startling hyacinth-blue eyes, so saturated with color and innocence that it was difficult to forget them.

The Chiclet-toothed blond, obviously approving of everything he saw, leaned forward over the counter. "I get off work in about an hour. How about waiting around for me? *Not as a Stranger* is playing down the street."

"No, thank you." Belinda picked up one of the Bavarian chocolate mint bars that Schwab's kept displayed on the counter and handed over a dollar bill. Ever since she had read that the candy bar was Sheilah Graham's favorite, she had decided it was her favorite, too. They were her special treat, along with a new movie magazine, on her twice-weekly trips to the Sunset Boulevard drugstore. So far, she had seen Rhonda Fleming at the counter buying a bottle of Lustre-Creme shampoo and Victor Mature walking out the front door.

"How about this weekend?" the cashier persisted.

"Sorry." Belinda took her change and gave him a sad, regretful smile that somehow managed to restore his masculine ego and make him feel as if she would remember him forever with bittersweet regret. She had long ago grown accustomed to the effect she had on men. She enjoyed it, although she had never understood how it happened, especially since she was too captivated by her fantasies to be interested in ordinary men. She assumed their attraction to her was based on her uncommon looks, but in fact it sprang from something quite different.

Belinda had the ability to make a man feel better than he was —stronger, more intelligent, more masculine. Even those she

22

rejected were left with the feeling that she secretly adored them. It was a talent many women would have been able to turn to their own advantage, but somehow Belinda never had. Her failure had nothing to do with a lack of intelligence. Instead, it was rooted in the simple fact that she thought too little of herself to put her special talent to good use.

As she turned away from the cashier, her gaze fell on a young man sitting in a back booth, shoulders hunched forward over a book and a cup of coffee. Her heart turned over in her chest, even as she told herself she was only going to be disappointed again.

It wasn't unusual for her to see someone who looked like *him.* She thought about him so much that it happened all the time. Once she had followed a man for nearly a mile only to discover that he had a big, ugly nose that had no place on the face of her dreams.

She walked slowly toward the back booth, excitement, anticipation, and almost certain disappointment churning inside her. His hand, fingernails bitten to the quick, reached for a pack of Chesterfields that lay open in front of him, and he tapped a cigarette out. Belinda held her breath, waiting for him to look up, her heart thumping so loudly it seemed to be drowning out everything except the sight of the man before her.

He turned a page of the book, the cigarette dangling unlit from the corner of his mouth, and flicked open the match pack with his index finger. She was nearly beside the booth when he set down his book, spine upward, and struck the match. As he lit the cigarette, he looked up, and Belinda found herself staring through a cloud of gray smoke into the cool blue eyes of James Dean.

In that instant she was back in Indianapolis at the Palace Theater. The movie was *East of Eden.* She was sitting in the last row when the same face that was now before her had exploded on the screen. With its high, intelligent forehead and restless blue eyes, it roared into her life larger than all the other larger-than-life faces that she had seen over the years in the same theater. Fireworks burst inside her and catherine wheels spun, and she felt as if all the air had been punched from her body.

Bad Boy Jimmy Dean, with the smoldering eyes and crooked grin; Bad Boy Jimmy, who snapped his fingers at the world and laughed when he told it to go to hell. From the moment she saw him on the screen of the Palace Theater, he was everything to her. The shining beacon, the rebel, the call, the spirit. In the tilt of his head, the slouch of his shoulders, he said that a man is his own man. She had taken the message, transformed it within herself, and walked out of the theater her own woman. Two weeks later she lost her virginity in the back seat of an Olds 88 to a boy whose sulky mouth reminded her of Jimmy's. Then she left for Hollywood, changing her name to Belinda on the way in an effort to put Edna Cornelia behind her forever.

Now she was standing in front of him, not even remembering how she got there. Her heart was thumping in a crazy dance as she wildly wished for the black pedal pushers and the pink halter instead of her prim, navy blue cotton. "I—I loved your movie, Jimmy," she said softly, her voice quivering like a violin string that had been drawn too tight. *"East of Eden. I loved it." And I love you. More than you can imagine.*

The heavy-lidded eyes squinted against the smoke from the cigarette, an exclamation point to the sulky lips that held it. "Yeah?"

He had spoken to her! She could hardly believe it. "I'm your biggest fan," she stammered. "I've lost count of how many times I've seen *East of Eden.*" *Oh, Jimmy, you're everything to me! You're all I have.* "It was wonderful. You were wonderful." She stared worshipfully at him, her hyacinth-blue eyes sending ageless messages of love and adoration.

Dean shrugged his fine, narrow shoulders, which were still hunched forward over his book.

"I can't wait for *Rebel Without a Cause.* It opens next month, doesn't it?" *Get up and take me home with you, Jimmy. Please. Take me home and make love to me.*

"Yeah."

Her heart was racing so fast she felt dizzy. No one understood him like she did. "I heard *Giant*'s really going to be something." *Love me, Jimmy. I'll give everything to you.*

He grunted unintelligibly and looked back down at the book he was reading. Success had made him immune to hyacinth-eyed blondes with star worship emblazoned across their pretty faces.

She backed slowly away. It didn't occur to her that his behavior was rude. To her, he was a giant, a god. Rules that applied to others didn't apply to him. "Thank you," she murmured, and then, in a whisper, "I love you, Jimmy."

Dean hadn't heard. Or if he had, it didn't matter. He'd heard it too many times before.

Belinda spent the rest of the week reliving the magical encounter—what she had said, what she should have said, what she would say the next time. There would be a next time, she knew it. His location shooting in Texas was over, so he was sure to be at Schwab's again, and she would go there every day until she saw him. When that finally happened, she would slide right into the booth across from him. She wouldn't stammer like an idiot, either; she would have a better idea of what to say. Men had always liked her, and Jimmy would be no different. She would also make certain she was wearing her sexiest outfit.

But it was the respectable navy blue sheath she was wearing the following Friday evening as she opened the door of the small shabby apartment she shared with two other girls to admit her date. She had chosen to wear the dress, not because it flattered her, but because it had a long row of small, unwieldy buttons running up the back, and she intended to make things as difficult as she could for the octopus who was taking her out.

Belinda had gotten her first break the month before. She and several dozen other girls had been auditioned by the assistant casting director at Paramount. A few of them, including her, had been asked to read a short scene about a young girl whose boyfriend was leaving her to go to college, and since the audition she had alternated between high hopes and awful, crushing despair. She had been one of the prettiest girls there, but she hadn't been able to tell if the man had liked her. Leaving the interview, she had met Billy Greenway.

Billy was the head messenger for the casting department at Paramount, so she had agreed to go out with him, despite the fact that she didn't like him very much or think he was very good-looking. It wasn't that he was ugly, exactly. His light brown hair was clean and combed into a neat d.a. He had a few acne scars on his cheeks, but they weren't disfiguring and actually managed to give a little character to his face. It was just that he was so ordinary, and she couldn't help but compare him to Jimmy. So far, she had gone out with him three times and let him play with her titties once. In return, he had promised to get her a copy of the memo that recorded the outcome of the audition. Yesterday he had called her and told her he had what she wanted.

"Hi, babe."

He came into the apartment, and pulled her against him for a long, too-familiar kiss. As she pushed herself away, she heard the rustle of paper in the breast pocket of his checked sports shirt. "Is that the memo in your pocket, Billy?"

He pulled her back and kissed her neck, his breathing loud and heavy in her ear, just like all the raw Indiana boys she had left behind. "I told you I'd bring it, didn't I? Your roommates home tonight?"

"Yes, they're in the kitchen. Let me see the memo, Billy."

"Later, babe." His hands moved down her back to her hips.

She pushed herself further away this time and gave him her coldest look. "I don't appreciate being mauled. I wish you would remember that you're going out with a lady."

She had the satisfaction of seeing him look uncomfortable. He came from a poor family, and one of the things he most liked about her was what he called her "classy air." Still, she knew she didn't have much chance of getting the paper from him until she'd paid some sort of price. She walked over to the chipped blond veneer coffee table and picked up her purse. "Where are we going tonight? You didn't tell me."

"I wanted it to be a surprise. How'd you like to go to a little blast at the Garden of Allah?"

"The Garden of Allah?" Belinda was immediately attentive. During the forties the Garden had been one of the most famous hotels in Hollywood. Even now stars stayed there. "How did you get an invitation to a party at the Garden?"

"I got my ways. I also borrowed my buddy's wheels. It's a great big car with soft seats, you dig me?"

"Depends."

"On what?"

"Depends on what you have for me in your pocket, Billy."

His smile was sly. I'll show it to you after we make a little stop in the Canyon."

He drove with one hand on the plush-covered steering wheel and the other draped over her shoulder, winding through the side streets off Laurel Canyon until he found a place that was deserted, then he turned off the ignition and flicked the key over so they could hear the radio. Perez Prado was playing "Cherry

Pink and Apple Blossom White." "Belinda, you know I'm real crazy about you." He nuzzled his face in her neck.

She wished he would just give her the memo and then take her to the party at the Garden without making her go through all this, but she knew it wouldn't happen. Billy was going to give her the memo, but first she had to give him at least a little bit of what he wanted. Besides, it hadn't been so bad the last time. She had just closed her eyes and pretended he was Jimmy.

"I'm crazy about you, babe," he muttered against her neck. "Crazy about you."

His kisses moved up the line of her jaw to her lips, and then he thrust his tongue in her mouth before she had time to catch her breath.

Jimmy's face imprinted itself on the back of her eyelids, and some of the tension left her. *Bad Boy Jimmy, taking what you want without asking.* A small moan escaped her at the feel of the rough, invading tongue. *Bad Boy Jimmy, tongue so sweet. Do me with your tongue, Jimmy. Do me.*

His hands were on top of her clothes, kneading at her breasts, burning her skin through her dress and through her white cotton bra. Then they were tugging at the buttons. "Shit, Belinda . . ."

"Shhh, don't talk. Please, don't talk."

He worked at the buttons, tongue stuck deep in her mouth. She felt cold air on her back and shoulders as he peeled the dress down to her waist. Then the bra fell to her waist, too, and he moved back.

She knew he was looking at her, and she pressed her eyes more tightly shut. *Are my titties beautiful for you, Jimmy? I like it when you look at them. I like it when you touch them.*

His breath was warm on her skin, then his mouth hot and wet on her nipples. She felt a hand on her knee, sliding upward along her stocking, moving over her garter and onto bare flesh. He touched the skin at the inside of her thigh, and she eased her legs open for him. A finger stroked her through the nylon, back and forth, setting her on fire, and then slowly slipped beneath the elastic leg band. *Yes.*

Touch me, Jimmy. Touch me there. Beautiful Jimmy. Oh, yes. He was grabbing at her hand, pulling it onto his lap, rubbing it up against him. Her eyes flew open. "No!"

Billy groaned. "Come on, Belinda. Just touch it."

"No." She pulled herself away from him and began straightening her clothes. "You don't really think I'd go that far, do you, Billy? I'm not like those other trampy girls you date." She reached behind her to do up the buttons of her dress.

"I know that, babe," he said tightly. "You've got a lot of class. But I don't like it when you get me all worked up and then turn off."

"You got yourself all worked up, Billy. And if it bothers you, you can just stop dating me."

He didn't like that, as she'd known he wouldn't. He turned on the ignition and peeled out onto the dark street. The music on the radio ended and the news came on. Angrily, he flicked off the dial. She ignored him. Turning the rearview mirror toward her, she combed her hair and fixed her lipstick. He sulked in silence all the way down Laurel Canyon and was still sulking as he swung right onto Sunset Boulevard. Only when he'd eased the car into the space in the parking lot at the Garden of Allah did he look at her. Reaching into his pocket, he pulled out the paper she wanted and unfolded it. "You're not going to like this, babe."

Belinda could feel a hollowness growing in the pit of her stomach. She snatched the paper from him and ran her eyes down the typed list of names, noticing as she did that there were comments penciled in after some of them.

She scanned the list twice before she found her own name at the bottom of the page, but it still took her a few moments to absorb the words.

Belinda Britton, she read. *Great eyes, great tits, no talent.*

CHAPTER 3

The Garden of Allah was once Hollywood's favorite playground of the stars. Originally the home of Alla Nazimova, the great Russian film star, it had been a hotel since the late twenties. Unlike the Beverly Hills or the Bel Air, it had never been completely respectable, not even when it first opened. There was something slightly seedy about it. But still the stars came, drawn like magnets to the twenty-five Spanish bungalows and the party that was always going on.

Tallulah Bankhead cavorted naked around the pool shaped like Nazimova's Black Sea. Scott Fitzgerald met Sheilah Graham in one of the bungalows. The men lived there between marriages: Ronald Reagan when it was over with Jane Wyman, Fernando Lamas after Arlene Dahl. During the Golden Age, they could all be found at the Garden: Bogart and his Baby, Ty Power, Ava Gardner. Sinatra was there, and Ginger Rogers. The Marx brothers. Dorothy Parker and Robert Benchley. Screenwriters sat on white slat chairs by their front doors and typed during the day. There was music. Rachmaninoff rehearsed in one bungalow, Benny Goodman in another. Woody Herman lived there, and Stravinsky, and Leopold Stokowski. And always, there was a party.

By that September night in 1955, the Garden was in its death throes. The white stucco walls were streaked with dirt and rust from the wrought-iron lamp brackets, the furniture in the bungalows was shabby, and just the day before, a dead mouse had been found floating in the pool. Ironically, it still cost the same to rent a bungalow there as it did at the Beverly Hills, although within four years it would all fall to the wrecker's ball. But on that September night in 1955, the Garden was still the Garden, and some of the stars were still around.

Billy opened the car door for Belinda. "Come on, babe. The party will cheer you up. A few of the guys from Paramount will

29

be here. Probably some of the other studios, too. I'll introduce you around."

Her hands were clasped in tight fists on top of the paper that lay in her lap. "Leave me alone for a little bit, will you, Billy? I'll meet you inside."

"Okay, babe." He shut the door and then leaned down to the open window. "Hey, there are other studios. You'll knock 'em dead yet."

His footsteps crunched in the gravel of the parking lot as he moved away. When the sound had faded, she angrily wadded the memo into a ball. Billy was right. There *were* other studios! Paramount was getting to be second-rate anyway. She'd show them! How could they say she didn't have any talent? And then she sagged back against the seat. What if it were true? When she'd dreamed about being a movie star she'd never thought much about the acting part of it. If she were going to be honest with herself, she would have to admit that it hadn't really interested her. She'd imagined they would give her acting lessons or something.

A car pulled into the space next to her with the radio blaring. Belinda glanced over. The couple hadn't even bothered to turn off the engine before they started necking. High school kids, hiding out in the parking lot at the Garden of Allah.

And then the music was over and the news came on.

It was the first story.

The announcer repeated the information calmly, as if it were an everyday occurrence, as if it were not an outrage, not the end of Belinda's life, the end of everything. She screamed, a horrible, long cry, all the more terrible because it happened inside her head.

James Dean was dead.

Without knowing how it happened, she was racing across the parking lot, not looking where she was going, not caring. She tore through the shrubbery and down one of the paths, trying to outrace the awful anguish that was suffocating her. She ran past the swimming pool shaped like Azimova's Black Sea, past a big oak at the end of the pool that held a telephone box with a sign, FOR CENTRAL CASTING ONLY. She ran until she came to a long stucco wall at the side of one of the bungalows. It was dark, the music of the party was distant, and she sagged against the wall, crying until she thought her heart would break, crying out for the death of her dreams.

Jimmy was gone. Killed on the road to Salinas driving a silver Porsche he called Little Bastard. How could it have happened? Jimmy was from Indiana, just like she was. He had said that anything was possible, and now he was dead. A man was his own man; a woman her own woman. Without Jimmy, her dreams no longer seemed possible.

"My dear, you're making a frightful noise. Would you mind terribly taking your troubles somewhere else? Unless, of course, you're very pretty, in which case you're invited to come through the gate and have a drink with me." The voice, deep and faintly British, drifted over the top of the stucco wall.

Belinda's head jerked up. "Who are you?"

"An interesting question." There was a short silence, punctuated by the distant splashes of the swimming pool. "Let's just say that I'm a man of contradictions. A lover of adventure and women and vodka. Not necessarily in that order."

There was something about the voice . . . Belinda wiped her tears with the back of her hand and looked along the wall for the gate. She could dimly make out its shape about twelve feet away from where she was standing. She went to it without hesitation, drawn by the voice and by the possibility of some small distraction from her awful pain.

The center of the patio was awash in a pool of pale yellow light that emanated from the interior of the bungalow. She stopped in the middle of it and looked toward the dark figure of the man sitting off to the side, alone in the night shadows. "James Dean is dead," she said. "He was killed in a car accident."

"Dean?" She heard the soft clink of ice cubes as the man raised his arm. "Oh, yes, Dean. Undisciplined sort of chap. Always raising a ruckus. Not that I hold that against him, mind you. I've raised a few in my time. Sit down, my dear, and have a drink."

She didn't move. "I loved him."

He snorted. "Love is a transient emotion that I've discovered over the years is best satisfied by a good fuck."

She was deeply shocked. No one had ever used that word in her presence. She said the first thing that came to her mind. "I didn't even get that."

31

He laughed. "Now, that, my dear, is the real tragedy."

There was a soft creak, and then he stood and walked toward her. His silhouette was that of a tall man, probably over six feet, a little thick around the middle, with wide shoulders and a straight carriage. He was wearing white duck trousers and a pale yellow shirt filled in at the neck with a loosely knotted ascot. She took in the small details—a pair of canvas deck shoes, a watch with a leather band, a webbed khaki belt. And then her gaze lifted, and she found herself looking into the world-weary eyes of Errol Flynn.

By the night Belinda met him, Flynn had already gone through three wives and several fortunes. He was forty-six, although he looked twenty years older. The famous moustache was grizzled; the handsome face with its chiseled bones and sculptured nose had grown jowly and lined from excesses of vodka, drugs, and cynicism. The face was a road map of his life. In four years he would be dead of a long list of ailments that would have killed most men much earlier. But most men weren't Flynn.

He had swashbuckled his way across the screen for two decades, fighting villains, winning wars, and saving damsels. Captain Blood, Robin Hood, Don Juan—Flynn had played them all. Sometimes, if the mood struck him, he had even played them well.

Long before he came to Hollywood, Errol Flynn had taken part in adventures every bit as dangerous as those he had played on the screen. He had been an explorer, a sailor, a gold prospector. He had traded for slaves in New Guinea. There was a scar on his heel where he had been shot by a party of headhunters, another on his abdomen from a scuffle with a rickshaw driver in India. At least that's what he said. With Flynn, no one could ever be sure.

And always, there were women in his life. They couldn't get enough of him, and Flynn felt the same about them. He especially liked them young. The younger the better. It was as if looking into a fresh young face and plunging into a fresh young body could bring back some measure of his lost innocence. It also brought him trouble.

In 1942 he was arrested for statutory rape and went to trial. The key word was "statutory." As the trial progressed, it became obvious the girls were willing, but in California in 1942, it was illegal to have sexual intercourse with anyone under the age of eighteen, willing or not. There were nine women on the jury, however, and Flynn was acquitted. Even so, he never quite got over becoming a phallic joke, and he hated it, even as he worked hard at perpetuating the myth of his own prowess.

The trial did not end his fascination with young girls. It did, however, make him more careful, for even at forty-six, alcoholic and dissipated, they found him irresistible.

"Come over here, my dear, and sit next to me."

He touched her arm and Belinda felt as if the world had suddenly come to a screeching halt. She sagged gratefully into the chair he led her to, knowing that if she had been forced to stand an instant longer, her knees would have given out under her. He pressed a glass toward her, and her hand shook as she took it from him. This wasn't a dream! It was real. It was happening to her right this minute. She and Errol Flynn were alone together. She looked over at him to make certain she wasn't imagining it all.

He smiled at her, a crooked smile, roguish, urbane, the famous left eyebrow slightly higher than the right. "How old are you, my dear?"

It took her a moment to find her voice. "Eighteen."

"Eighteen. I see." His left eyebrow rose a little higher. "I don't suppose— No, of course not."

"What?"

He tugged on the corner of his moustache and gave her an apologetic chuckle, which was both charming and disarming. "You wouldn't happen to have your birth certificate on you?"

"My birth certificate?" She looked at him quizzically. It seemed like such a strange question. And then the old stories of the trial clicked into place in her mind, and she laughed. "I don't have my birth certificate on me, Mr. Flynn, but I truly am eighteen." Her laughter turned darlingly mischievous. "Would it make any difference if I weren't?"

His answering grin was vintage Flynn. "Of course not."

For the next hour they observed the amenities. Flynn told her a story about John Barrymore and several anecdotes concerning his leading ladies. She told him about Paramount. He asked her to call him Baron, a nickname of which he was especially fond. She said she would, but she called him Mr. Flynn just the same. At the end of the hour, he took her by the hand and led her inside. With some embarrassment, she asked to use the bathroom.

After she had flushed the toilet and washed her hands, she sneaked a peak at the contents of his medicine cabinet. Errol Flynn's toothbrush. Errol Flynn's razor. Errol Flynn's shaving cream. Her eyes skipped over the pills and Errol Flynn's suppositories. When she shut the cabinet, her face, reflected in the mirror, was flushed and her eyes bright with excitement. She was in the presence of a great star. Two years ago she had seen him in *The Master of Ballantrae* and right after that, *Crossed Swords,* with Gina Lollobrigida. No one wore a costume like Errol Flynn.

He was waiting for her in the bedroom, wearing a burgundy-colored dressing gown and smoking a cigarette from a short amber holder. A fresh bottle of vodka was on the table at his side. She smiled tentatively at him, not sure what she should do next. He seemed amused and, in some way she couldn't quite define, pleased with her. "Contrary to what you may have read, my dear, I am not a ravisher of young women."

"I didn't think you were, Mr. Flynn . . . Baron."

"Well, then, are you absolutely certain you know what you're doing here?"

"Oh, yes."

"Good." He took a last drag on the cigarette holder and then set it down in the ashtray next to him. "Perhaps you'd like to get undressed for me."

She swallowed hard. She'd never been completely naked with a man. She'd had her panties off or her dress unbuttoned, like tonight with Billy, but the boys had always done that. She'd never personally gotten undressed for anybody. Of course, Errol Flynn wasn't just anybody. He was a very famous movie star.

Reaching behind her, she fumbled with the long row of buttons. When she finally had them unfastened, she slipped the dress down over her hips, not daring to look at him. Instead, she thought of his wonderful movies—*The Dawn Patrol, Objective, Burma!, The Charge of the Light Brigade,* with Olivia De Havilland. She'd seen that one on television. She realized her dress was dangling from her hand, and she looked nervously around for someplace to put it. There was a closet on the far side of the room. She went over to it and pulled out a hanger. After she hung up her dress, she stepped out of her shoes.

She tried to think what she should take off next. Darting a quick glance at him, she felt a little shiver of pleasure as she saw that he was watching her intently. Her eyes lovingly erased his wrinkles and jowls until he looked the same sitting before her as he did on the screen. She remembered how handsome he was in *Against All Flags.* He had played a British naval officer, and Maureen O'Hara had been a pirate named Spitfire. Reaching beneath the lace hem of her slip, she unfastened her garters. Then she slipped her stockings off and, folding them neatly, set them on a chair next to the closet door. After that, she took off her garter belt. *Santa Fe Trail* had been on television not long ago. He had starred with Olivia De Havilland again. They were wonderful together. He was so masculine, and Olivia was always such a lady.

Belinda realized she was almost naked. All she had left to take off was a slip, her bra and panties, and her charm bracelet. She unfastened the small gold clasp. It took her a while because her hands were shaking. When it was off, she set it next to her stockings.

"Are you nervous, my dear?"

"A little." She wished he'd come over to her and do the rest, but he showed no signs of wanting to move from his chair.

Slowly she pulled her slip over her head. As she did so, she remembered that he was still married. She had seen *Rocky Mountain* at the Palace. That was the movie where he'd met Patrice Wymore, his current wife. Belinda thought she was awfully pretty and certainly lucky to be married to a man like Errol Flynn. Of course, since he was here with her instead of with Patrice, the rumors of their breakup must be true. She had read enough movie magazines to know how hard it was to make a marriage work in Hollywood.

She took her panties off before her bra. She wasn't sure why. Maybe because she knew her titties were her best feature and she was saving them for last. When she was naked, she saw by the direction of Flynn's gaze that he liked them, too.

"Come here, my dear."

Embarrassed, but excited, she walked toward him. He stood and reached out to touch her chin. The feel of his hand was like an electrical charge, and she nearly gasped with the excitement

35

it brought her. She waited for him to kiss her, but he didn't. Instead, his hands slipped down to her shoulders. At first she felt a flash of disappointment. She had wanted his kiss, the same one he had given Olivia De Havilland and Maureen O'Hara and all the rest of the glittering women he had loved on the screen. Then he opened his robe, and she saw that he was naked beneath it. Her eyes denied the looseness of his suntanned skin, mercifully tightened the flaccid muscles of his chest.

"I'm afraid you'll have to give me a bit of help, my dear," he said. "Vodka and lovemaking aren't always the best of companions."

She looked up into his eyes. "Of course." It would be her privilege to help him, except she wasn't exactly sure what he wanted her to do.

Not being a stranger to the ways of young girls, he seemed to understand her hesitation, and he offered her a specific suggestion. She was shocked, but at the same time fascinated. So this was the way famous men made love. It was strange, but somehow it seemed appropriate.

Slowly she lowered herself to her knees.

It took a long time, and she got tired, but eventually he pulled her up and laid her on the bed. The mattress sagged as he rolled over on top of her. She waited for him to kiss her, but to her disappointment, he didn't. The failure was hers, she knew, not his, and she didn't judge him for it.

There was a nudge at her legs, and she quickly parted them for him. She noticed that his eyes were closed, but she kept hers open so she could treasure every moment. Errol Flynn was going to do it to her. Errol Flynn. It was like a star-spangled chorus singing in her heart. She felt a probing. A push. It was really Errol Flynn!

Her body exploded.

Later that night he asked her what her name was, and then he offered her a cigarette. Even though she didn't smoke, she accepted. It was exciting, leaning against the headboard next to him and smoking. She made sure she took short drags so she wouldn't choke. For the first time in hours she remembered about Jimmy. Poor Jimmy, to have died so young. As long as she lived, she would never forget him. Life could be so cruel. How lucky she was to be here alive and so very happy. She wondered what Billy had done when she disappeared so suddenly and then realized she didn't care. It would serve him right if he'd spent the whole evening looking for her.

Flynn told her about his yacht, the *Zaca,* and a little about his recent travels. Belinda didn't want to pry, but she was curious about his wife. "Patrice," she said hesitantly. "She's very beautiful."

Flynn nodded. "A wonderful woman. I've treated her badly." He drained the glass he was drinking from and then reached across her body to the nightstand to refill it, digging his shoulder into her breast as he poured. "It's a habit I have with women. I don't mean to, but I can't seem to help it. I just wasn't made for either marriage or fidelity."

"Will you get a divorce?" She self-consciously tapped off the dead ash of her cigarette.

"Who knows? Probably. Although, God knows, I can't afford it. The IRS wants me for almost a million, and I'm so far behind on alimony that I've lost track.

Belinda's eyes filled with sympathetic tears. "It doesn't seem fair that a man like you should have to worry about such things. Not with all the pleasure you've given people over the years."

Flynn patted her knee. "You're a sweet girl, Belinda. And a beautiful one, too. There's something in your eyes that makes me forget how old I'm getting."

She took the liberty of resting her cheek against his shoulder. "You mustn't talk that way. You're not old."

He smiled and kissed the top of her head. "Sweet girl."

By the end of the week Belinda had moved into Flynn's bungalow at the Garden of Allah. He said it made him feel young again to have her around. At the end of October he gave her a gold charm to celebrate their first month together. It was a small disk suspended from a wishbone frame, with LUV engraved in the center of one side, and I at the top and U at the bottom of the other side. When she flicked the charm with the tip of her finger, it spun around and the message I LUV U came together. She knew he didn't mean it, but she treasured the charm nonetheless and wore it with pride as a symbol to the world that she belonged to Errol Flynn.

In his presence her old feelings of invisibility vanished, and she could feel herself flourishing in the reflected glow of his fame. Never in her life had she felt so pretty, so smart, so important. They slept late, spent their days on the *Zaca* or alongside the pool, their nights in clubs and restaurants. She learned to smoke and drink, she learned not to stare when she met famous people, no matter how excited she felt inside, and she also learned that a lot of famous people seemed to like her. An actor who was a friend of Flynn's told her that it was because she offered no judgment, only adoration. The remark puzzled her. How could she judge? It wasn't up to ordinary people to pass judgment on celebrities.

Sometimes at night she and Flynn made love, but more often they just talked, and it hurt her to see how sad and troubled he was beneath his devil-may-care facade. She devoted herself to making him happy.

She saw *Rebel Without a Cause,* and it made her think of Jimmy again. Maybe her dream didn't have to die too. Her whole life was still ahead of her, and it suddenly seemed as if anything were possible. She was meeting studio executives now, not lowly assistant casting directors. She would take advantage of those contacts, prepare herself for the inevitable time when Flynn would move on to another woman. She had no delusions about that. She wasn't important enough to hold him for very long.

Flynn bought her a daring lipstick-red French bikini and sat by the side of the pool in his swim trunks, sipping his vodka while he watched her play in the water. Although no one else at the Garden was quite adventurous enough to wear one of the new bikinis, Belinda didn't feel at all embarrassed. She loved watching Flynn watch her; she loved coming out of the water to be wrapped in the towel he held for her. She felt sheltered, protected, and adored.

Late one morning while Flynn was still sleeping, Belinda donned the red bikini and dove into the pool. With the exception of some children playing near the steps at the shallow end, the pool was deserted, and she swam several easy laps across the width; then she swam the length, opening her eyes underwater to look at the initials of Alla Nazimova that had been carved into the concrete just below the water line. When she came to the surface, she found herself staring at a pair of highly polished leather shoes.

"*Tiens!* It seems a mermaid has taken over the pool at the Garden of Allah. A mermaid with eyes bluer than the sky."

Treading water, Belinda squinted against the morning sun to see the man standing over her. He was distinctly European. His oyster-white suit had the sheen of silk and the immaculate press of a man who kept a valet. He was of medium height, slim and aristocratic, with dark hair that had been skillfully cut to disguise the fact that it was beginning to thin, eyes that were small and slanted, and a rather broad nose with a slight hook at the end. He was not handsome, but he was imposing, and the smell of money and power clung to him as tenaciously as his expensive cologne. She judged him to be in his late thirties or early forties, French by his accent, although there was something about the arrangement of his features that did not fit her conception of a Frenchman. It occurred to her that he might be a European filmmaker, and she gave him a saucy grin.

"No mermaid, *monsieur*. Just a very ordinary girl."

"*Ordinaire?* I would hardly say so. *Très extraordinaire*, in fact."

She accepted his compliment graciously, and in her best accented high school French replied, "*Merci beaucoup, monsieur. Vous êtes trop gentil.*"

"Tell me, *ma petite* mermaid. Is there a tail beneath that *charmant* red bikini?"

Amusement glinted in his eyes, but Belinda sensed that there was something calculated in his audaciousness. This was obviously a man who did nothing, who said nothing, by accident. "*Mais non, monsieur,*" she replied evenly. "Only two ordinary legs."

He raised an eyebrow. "Perhaps, *mademoiselle*, you will let me be the judge . . ."

She stared at him for a moment, taking her time, and then she dove underwater and swam in long, clean strokes for the ladder at the opposite end of the pool. When she climbed out, he had disappeared. Somehow she was not surprised to walk into the bungalow half an hour later and find him talking with Flynn over Bloody Marys.

Mornings were not Flynn's best time, and next to the immaculately groomed stranger he looked rumpled and old, although Belinda guessed there was less than ten years difference in age between them. Still, despite Flynn's disheveled condition, Belinda found him much the handsomer of the two men. She walked over, sat on the arm of his chair, and placed her hand on his shoulder. He looped his arm around her waist. "Good morning, my dear. I understand the two of you have already met."

She nodded, wishing she had the courage to plant a casual good-morning kiss on his cheek, but the sporadic nighttime intimacies that passed between them did not make her feel entitled to that kind of informality. "We met by the pool."

The stranger's eyes slid down over the long suntanned legs that were revealed beneath the terry wrap she had tossed on over her bikini. "Not a tail after all," he sighed, and then he rose gracefully to his feet. "Alexi Savagar, *mademoiselle.*"

"How do you do."

"He's being modest, my dear. Our visitor is actually Count Alexi Nikolai Vasily Savagarin. Did I get it right, old sport?"

"My family left the title behind in St. Petersburg, *mon ami,* as you very well know." Alexi's voice was faintly reproachful, but still Belinda sensed that he was pleased by Flynn's use of his title. "We're now hopelessly French."

"And bloody rich. Your family didn't leave their rubles behind in Mother Russia, did they, old sport? Not by a long shot." Flynn turned toward Belinda. "Alexi is in California buying a few old cars to ship back to Paris for his collection."

"What a peasant you are, *mon ami.* A 1927 Alfa Romeo is hardly just an 'old car.' Besides, I'm here on business."

"Alexi is adding to the family fortune by meddling in electronics. What was that gadget you were telling me about? Has something to do with vacuum tubes?"

"The transistor. It's going to replace the vacuum tube."

"Transistor. That's it. And if it will make money, you can bet he's sitting on a pile of the little buggers. You'd think he'd be willing to lend me some of his profits to produce a picture." Although he was looking at her, Belinda had the feeling he was really talking to Alexi.

Alexi was obviously amused. "I haven't made my fortune by throwing good money after bad. Now if you're finally willing to part with the *Zaca,* my dear Baron, that's quite another story."

"You'll get the *Zaca* over my dead body," Flynn replied, a slight edge to his voice.

"From the looks of things, *mon ami,* I may not have long to wait."

"Spare me your lectures. Belinda, would you fix us two more Bloodys?"

"Of course." She took their glasses and went into the small kitchenette that opened off the living room. Neither man made any effort to lower his voice, and she could hear their conversation plainly as she rinsed out their glasses and then refilled them from a fresh can of tomato juice. At first they talked about the transistors and Alexi's business, but then the conversation became more personal.

"Belinda is a definite improvement over the last one, *mon ami,*" she could hear Alexi saying. "Those eyes are quite *extraordinaire.* A little old, though, isn't she? Past sixteen."

"Casting stones, Alexi?" Flynn laughed. "I'd advise you not to get any ideas of your own about her; you'd only be wasting your time. Belinda is my joy, you know. Rather like a faithful dog, but beautiful and housebroken. She gives only adoration, sport. She never nags, never lectures me about my drinking, puts up with my moods, and she's surprisingly intelligent. If more women were like Belinda, there'd be more happy men."

"*Mon Dieu!* You sound as if you're getting ready for another trip to the altar. Are you sure you can afford it?"

"She's merely a diversion," Flynn replied with a trace of belligerence. "And a damned pleasant one at that."

Belinda's cheeks were flushed as she brought their drinks in to them. She hadn't much liked the remark about the dog, but she reminded herself that he had intended it as a compliment. Besides, he had said other things about her that were very nice.

"There you are, darling. I was just telling Alexi about you."

When she had first entered the bungalow, she had sensed a subtle tension between the two men, and now, although neither had visibly changed his posture, the tension seemed to have grown. There was an alertness in the way each was sitting that she hadn't noticed before.

"You're a paragon, *mademoiselle,* if I am to believe the Baron here," Alexi said. "Intelligent, adoring, beautiful—although my views of your beauty have been somewhat limited, so he may be lying to me."

Flynn took his drink from her and sipped from it carefully. "I thought you met her at the pool."

"She was underwater. And now, as you see . . ." He shrugged dismissively toward the terry cloth wrap.

A long look passed between the two men. Was it some sort of challenge she saw in Alexi's eyes? Belinda got the feeling that she was witnessing an old, familiar game between them, a game that she didn't understand at all.

"Belinda, darling, take that off, would you?" Flynn asked as he crumpled an empty cigarette pack.

"What?"

"Your wrap, my dear. Take it off, there's a good girl."

She looked from one man to the other. Flynn was concentrating on putting a fresh cigarette in the amber holder, while Alexi watched her, a trace of something that might have been sympathy underlying his amusement.

"You've embarrassed her, *mon ami.*"

"Nonsense. Belinda doesn't mind." He rose from his chair and walked over to her, then he tilted up her chin just as she had seen him do so often to Olivia De Havilland. "She'll do anything I ask her. Won't you, darling?" He brushed a kiss over her lips.

She nodded and, after a short hesitation, dropped her fingers to the tie of her wrap. Flynn touched her cheek with the back of his hand. Slowly she loosened the knot and the tie fell away. Turning her body toward Flynn, she allowed the wrap to drop to the floor.

"Let Alexi see you if you don't mind, my dear. I want him to have a good view of what his money can't buy."

She looked at Flynn unhappily, but he was not watching her. Instead, he was watching Alexi, and his expression was vaguely triumphant. As she slowly pivoted toward the Frenchman, she was conscious of the chill of the air on her bare skin and the clamminess of the small bikini halter against her breasts. She told herself it was childish to feel so embarrassed. This was no different, after all, from standing at the edge of the pool. But no matter what she told herself, she knew that it *was* different, and she couldn't bring herself to meet the slanted, Russian eyes of Alexi Savagar.

"Her body is lovely, *mon ami,*" he said. "I congratulate you. Actually, I believe you are wasted on this faded matinee idol, *mademoiselle,* and I think I shall steal you away." His voice was light, but when she finally looked at him, she had the unsettling impression that his words had not been spoken casually.

"I think not." She tried to sound cool and sophisticated, like

42

Grace Kelly in *To Catch a Thief*, but it didn't quite work. Something about him frightened her. Perhaps it was his air of power, the sense of authority that he wore every bit as well as the oyster-white suit. She bent over to retrieve her wrap, but as she straightened, she felt Flynn's hand cup her bare shoulder, effectively preventing her from covering herself.

"Take no notice of Alexi, Belinda. Our rivalry is an old one, going back to our younger years." His hand moved down the length of her arm and then splayed possessively across her bare midriff, his little finger resting in the hollow of her navel. "He can't abide seeing me with a woman he can't have, not since the days I used to steal them all away from him. My friend is a very bad loser."

"You didn't steal all of them away. I seem to remember a few who were more attracted to my money than to your pretty face."

Flynn's hand, warm and possessive, settled over the lipstick-red crotch of her tiny bikini. "But they were old. Not our type at all."

Belinda sucked in her breath. Against her will she looked up and saw Alexi leaning back in his chair, one immaculately trousered leg crossed over the other, a portrait of aristocratic indolence. Then he lifted his eyes to hers, and for a fraction of a second, she forgot Flynn was in the room.

CHAPTER 4

They saw Alexi frequently during the next month. He cruised with them on the *Zaca*, took them out to dinner at the best restaurants in Southern California, and became a general presence in Belinda's life. Sometimes he bought her gifts of jewelry, dainty and expensive. She kept them all in their boxes and wore only Flynn's small spinning charm on a chain around her neck.

Alexi berated Flynn for the charm. "What a vulgar bauble. Surely Belinda deserves better."

"Oh, much better," Flynn replied. "But I couldn't afford it, old chap. Not all of us were born with your silver spoon."

The two men had met on the private yacht of the shah of Iran nearly a decade ago. Flynn was immediately impressed by Alexi Savagar's intelligence and aristocracy and had courted the younger man's friendship, but over the years Flynn's admiration had developed an edge. In many ways the Frenchman was everything Flynn wanted to be, so that when they were together, he found himself too aware of his own past mistakes and lost opportunities. Still, he admired Alexi, and never stopped hoping that some of his friend's wealth could be diverted in his own direction. In the end, it was Alexi who felt the rivalry more keenly.

Beneath his charm Alexi Savagar was a man who took life seriously. He was a dangerous combination of aristocrat and businessman, both of them ruthless and both of them possessing good reasons for disliking Errol Flynn. The aristocrat looked down on Flynn's inferior breeding and lack of formal education, while the businessman was scornful of his playboy lifestyle and contempt for self-discipline. Still, the two men continued to see each other. For a time Alexi told himself that each visit would be his last, until he finally admitted that he had no desire to end their relationship. At thirty-eight—his fortune secure and his power unquestioned—he had discovered that amusement was the most difficult commodity to come by. Besides, Flynn had never posed a serious threat to him. Not until the moment Alexi had gazed down into the pool at the Garden of Allah.

It wasn't the first time that the men's rivalry had extended to the bedroom. Their tastes were similar—young girls with the bloom of innocence still on their flushed cheeks. At first glance Flynn's extraordinary good looks and sexual magnetism would have seemed to give him a distinct advantage, but Alexi's wealth was a formidable aphrodisiac, and his charm could make more handsome men seem dull. More frequently than Flynn liked to admit, a woman he coveted ended up with his rival. Now he saw Belinda as a new pawn in the game. He had no way of knowing that Alexi saw her quite differently.

It was laughable, Alexi Savagar told himself, at the end of the first week. His intense, visceral reaction to Belinda Britton had taken him by surprise. She was a silly child, who was absurdly obsessed with movie stars. Except for her youth, which he enjoyed perhaps even more than Flynn, she had little to recommend her. Although she was intelligent, she had been badly educated and lacked any breadth of knowledge or culture. She was undeniably beautiful, but so were other women he had known. Still, his more sophisticated female companions suddenly seemed old and weary by comparison.

At first he had tried to tell himself that his attraction to her was merely an extension of his rivalry with Flynn, but as the days passed and his feelings grew stronger, he knew it wasn't so. He found her air of tainted innocence irresistible. She was the perfect combination of whore and child, her body lush and experienced, but her mind untouched. Still, he realized his attraction to her went deeper than sexual desire. She was like a bright-eyed child, eager for life to begin and full of trust that it would be good. He found that he wanted to be the one to introduce her to the world; he wanted to be the one to shelter and protect her, to mold her into the ideal woman she could become. When he looked at her, the accumulated years of his cynicism seemed to peel away. She made him feel like a boy again, with his life stretching before him, fresh and full of promise.

Flynn announced he was going to Mexico for a week. Secure in Belinda's blind adoration of him, he asked Alexi to watch after her. "Of course," Alexi replied, giving Belinda a slow smile. "Although if I were you, I might think twice before deserting the field."

Flynn laughed. "Belinda won't even wear the little trinkets you've given her, will you, my dear? I don't think I have much to worry about."

Belinda laughed as if it were all a wonderful joke, but secretly she felt uneasy. No one had ever treated her with as much courtesy and deference as Alexi Savagar, and she was uncomfortably aware of him whenever he was around. It confused her. Although he was undeniably an important man, he wasn't a movie star, and he wasn't Errol Flynn, so why should she be so disturbed by him?

For the next week, Alexi was her attentive companion. They drove everywhere at breakneck speed in a fire engine red Ferrari that began to seem as if it was an extension of Alexi's own well-tuned body. She found herself watching his hands as they moved over the controls, observing the sureness of his touch, the steady grip of his fingers. What was it like to be so self-confident? As they blazed through the streets of Beverly Hills and she felt the surge of the car's engine through her thighs, she could almost hear people wondering who she was—this blond-haired woman who had managed to capture the interest of two such important men.

In the evening they went to Ciro's or Chasen's. Alexi seemed to know everyone, and he entertained her with gossip about the stars and anecdotes calculated to amuse her. Sometimes they spoke in French, with Alexi keeping his vocabulary simple so she could follow it. He described his collection of classic cars, he detailed the beauties of Paris, and one night, with the Ferrari parked high on a hill so the city lights were spread at her feet, he told her about his family.

His father had met his mother, Solange, in Paris in 1911, quickly married her, and then transported her back to his family estate near St. Petersburg. It had taken Solange exactly eighteen months to convince her husband that Russia's troubles could only get worse. The two of them, along with the bulk of the Savagarin fortune, were resettled in Paris just in time for World War I to break out. As a reward for her foresight, Nikolai Savagarin let himself be persuaded to shorten his surname to Savagar so they would blend more easily into French society.

Alexi was born in 1917, a year before the war was over, and a week before his father was killed. Even so, Nikolai's heritage had been passed on to the son he did not live to see. Although Alexi had grown into a man of great culture and impeccable taste, he was, beneath it all, relentlessly Russian. Belinda sensed the ruthlessness beneath his charm, and it both fascinated and frightened her. She had no way of knowing that nearly every woman who met him felt the same way.

It surprised her when she discovered that she was talking about herself to him, describing her parents and the loneliness of her early life. While he listened with flattering intensity, she shared her dreams of stardom and told him things she had never told anyone else. It was Alexi, however, who brought up the subject of Flynn.

"He will leave you, *ma chère.* You must understand that."

"I know," she replied. "I've never allowed myself to believe I could hold him." She tried to explain it to him. "I'm just grateful I've had a chance to be part of the life of such a famous man, even if it's only a small part. Probably it won't last much longer. I suspect he's sending me off with you so he can be with other women, maybe even his wife." She looked imploringly at him. "Please don't tell me if you know. I don't want to hear it. He can't help himself, you see. I understand that."

"Such adoration." Alexi's mouth gave a slight twist. "As always, my friend is a lucky man. It's a pity he doesn't appreciate it. Perhaps you will be luckier in your choice of companions the next time."

"You make me sound like I'm some sort of tramp, passing myself from man to man," Belinda snapped. "I don't like it."

Alexi's strange, slanted eyes seemed to pierce through her clothing, through her skin, into a place so secret that only he knew of its existence. "A woman like you, *ma chère,* will always need a man." He picked up her hand and played with her fingertips, sending a little shiver through her. "You are not one of those fierce, modern women. You are a woman who needs to be sheltered and protected, molded into something precious and fine." For a moment she thought she saw pain in his eyes, and then the impression faded as his voice grew harsh. "You sell yourself too cheaply."

She snatched her hand away. How could he say such a thing?

He didn't understand at all. How could he think that there was anything cheap about giving herself to Flynn?

Alexi left for San Francisco the same day Flynn returned from Mexico, and she was surprised by how much she missed him. Now she sometimes felt lonely, which was silly, really, because she had Flynn. Still, when Alexi reappeared ten days later, she was unreasonably glad to see him. Sitting between the two men in the city's best restaurants, she felt as if she were the most important woman in the world.

Everything came to a crashing end shortly after Christmas when Flynn tired of the game they were playing. They were all sitting at a banquette in Romanoff's when he slipped a cigarette into his amber holder and said that he would be leaving them to spend a few months in Europe. From the way he avoided looking at her, Belinda understood she was not invited to go along.

She felt a great, suffocating mass growing in her chest. This was what she had been expecting, so why wasn't she better prepared? But the hurt was more than she could bear, and the surrounding tables began to waver as her eyes flooded with tears. Just as she felt the last vestige of control slip from her, a sudden sharp pain gripped her thigh. It took her only a moment to realize it was Alexi's hand squeezing her under the table, forbidding her to humiliate herself. His strength seemed to flow into her, and somehow she managed to endure the rest of the evening. When Flynn left three days later, Alexi took her in his arms and finally let her cry. Later, she read in the newspaper that Flynn's new traveling companion was only fifteen.

Although she realized Alexi must have finished his business in California long ago, he made no move to return to Paris, and she was grateful. The rental on the bungalow had been paid through the end of January—not, she suspected, by Flynn, although she didn't ask—and they spent nearly every evening together, frequently sipping champagne on the patio before he left her for the night. One evening, unexpectedly, he leaned over and kissed her lightly on the lips.

"Don't! Don't touch me!" She jumped up, furious with him for the intimacy. Alexi wasn't Flynn, and she wasn't a tramp. She rushed through the patio doors into the living room and snatched a cigarette from the china holder that sat on the coffee table.

Years of iron control and self-discipline shattered inside Alexi

Savagar. He jumped up and stormed into the room. "You stupid little bitch!"

She spun around, stunned by the venom in his tone, and then, as she saw his expression, she took a step backwards. The well-polished Gallic mask was gone, baring a face that was atavistic in its nakedness, the product of countless generations of noble Russian breeding.

"How dare you think you can refuse me!" he snarled. "Do you know what you are? A whore. Nothing more. But instead of fucking a man for his money, you fuck him for his fame."

She let out a muffled, terrified scream as he advanced upon her, catching her by the shoulders and jamming her up against the wall behind her. His hand grabbed her jaw and forced it upward, but before she could scream again, he had covered her mouth with his own, biting at her lips and forcing them open. She tried to clamp down on the tongue that he thrust into her, but his fingers closed tightly around her throat, making his meaning clear. She must subjugate herself to him. He was Count Alexi Nikolai Vasily Savagarin, omnipotent overlord of serfs, entitled by right of birth to take possession of whatever he desired.

When his rape of her mouth was complete, he pulled his head back. Through the veil of her fear, she saw a smear of blood beneath his bottom lip and vaguely wondered if it was his or her own.

"I am worthy of respect," he hissed. "Flynn is a fool, a court jester. He lives on charm and then whines when things go badly for him. But you are too stupid to see that, so I must teach you."

She gave a strangled sob as she felt his hand on the skirt of her dress, pushing it up, roughly pulling at her panties, ripping them. "Don't!" she screamed.

"Shut up!" He separated her legs by shoving his knee between them, and then, ignoring her sobs, ruthlessly violated her with his aristocratic fingers, claiming each place he imagined Flynn had claimed. Through her horror she felt his arousal hard against her thigh, so she didn't understand that his assault had more than one clear dimension. She didn't understand that she had pushed him too far, that his passion was an act of possession, a living out of the divine right of kings and czars, an

49

indelible reaffirmation of the proper social order of the classes, in which the nobility outranked movie stars.

She was crying when his hands opened her blouse, barely noticing that he was gentler now, with no barbaric ripping of fabric or tearing of buttons. Her tears fell on his hands as he pushed her bra aside and caressed her breasts, kissing them with surprising tenderness, murmuring to her in French, perhaps even Russian, words she did not understand. Slowly he soothed her.

"I am sorry, *mon amour*. I am so sorry to have frightened you." And then he turned off the lights, picked her up, and cradled her in his lap. "I have done a terrible thing to you," he whispered, "and you must forgive me—for your own sake as well as for mine." His lips touched her hair. "I am your only hope, *chérie*. Without me, your promise as a woman will never be realized. Without me, you will drift through your days trying to see your reflection in the eyes of men who are unworthy of you." He stroked her hair until her body relaxed and she fell asleep in his arms.

As he stared into the quiet darkness, he wondered how he could have let himself fall so foolishly in love with a woman half his age. Belinda, with the hyacinth-blue eyes that worshiped a man, eyes that sang anthems of adoration. She stirred feelings in him that he had not known were possible, strong emotions that frightened him because he had long ago learned the dangers of vulnerability. He was not a coward, but his childhood had taught him to live his life from a position of strength, and for the first time in years he was uncertain what to do. He didn't doubt his ability to win her love—such a task was trivial, especially since she already cared far more for him than she was willing to admit. No, winning her love did not frighten him. It was the power she had gained over him that was so terrifying.

He examined his earlier loss of control. How could he have permitted such a thing to happen? He, who had been taught self-discipline before he was old enough to do his sums. An image flashed into his mind, one he had thought long forgotten. He had been a small boy, ill with some childhood disease that left him burning with fever. His mother had come into his bedroom, a composition book dangling from her ringed fingers, her eyes hard and accusing. Was it true, she asked, that he had not finished his Latin translation? He was sick, he explained. His body was hot and his head hurt so. You are not my son, his mother had replied. Only a peasant would find excuses to shirk his responsibilities. She pulled him from his bed and set him at his desk. Eyes bright with fever, hand shaking, he worked until the translation was done. She stood at the window, ruby bracelets glittering in the sunlight, and smoked one cigarette after another, gazing at him with scorn whenever his head sagged down on the desk top.

Not long afterwards he had been sent to a spartan boarding school where punishments were severe and rewards few. Here the heirs to France's greatest fortunes were shaped into men worthy of their family names, and here the last remnants of childhood had been stripped from him before his twelfth birthday. The lessons of self-discipline were hard learned, but they stood him in good stead as he had wrestled control of the Savagar fortune—first, from the group of aging trustees who had grown fat and lazy on his money, and finally from his mother. Now no one could dispute his position as one of the most powerful men in France. He had homes on two continents, a priceless collection of European masterpieces, and a string of mistresses who catered to his every whim. Until he met Belinda Britton, with her untainted optimism and bright child's view of the world, he had not realized there was anything missing from his life.

Belinda awakened in her bed the next morning, still dressed in her clothes from the night before, the thin chenille spread thrown over her. She turned her head, half expecting to see— Flynn? Alexi?—she wasn't sure which one, but instead, her eyes fell on a piece of hotel stationery propped on the pillow. Quickly she read the few lines of spidery handwriting:

> *Ma chère,*
> I am flying to New York today. I have already neglected business far too long. Perhaps I will return, perhaps not.
>
> Alexi

She crumpled the note into a ball and angrily pitched it to the floor. Damn him! After what he had done to her last night, she was glad he was gone. She hoped she'd never see him again. He was evil, wicked, a horrible monster who had done a terrible thing to her. She swung her feet over the edge of the bed only to feel her stomach pitch violently. As she fell back on the pillow, she closed her eyes and admitted to herself that she was afraid. For a long time now, Alexi had taken care of her, and without quite realizing how it had happened, she had grown used to it.

Throwing her forearm across her eyes, she tried to reason away her fears. She'd managed for herself before Alexi, before Flynn, and she'd do it again. Carefully she forced herself to reconstruct James Dean's face in her mind—the disobedient hair, the sulky eyes and rebellious mouth. Think about Jimmy, she told herself, and gradually she grew calmer. A man is his own man, a woman her own woman. She had let her ambitions drift while she was with Flynn. It was time to take charge of her life again.

She spent the rest of the month reestablishing her contacts. She placed some telephone calls, wrote notes to the studio executives she had met through Flynn, and began making the rounds again. Nothing happened.

The rent came due on the bungalow at the Garden of Allah, and she was forced to return to her old apartment. It was her final separation from Flynn, and it made her feel as if her life had slipped backwards. Every minute she spent in the apartment was torture. She fought with her roommates until they told her they wanted her to move out, and then she ignored them. They were stupid cows, content with so little.

Disaster arrived in a pale blue envelope. It was a letter from her mother telling her they had decided it was not in her best interests to continue to support her foolishness. Enclosed was her final check. She made a halfhearted attempt to get a job, despite the fact that she had been feeling sick, plagued by mysterious headaches and a perpetual upset stomach, like a case of the flu that wouldn't quite take hold. But she had no real job skills, so she abandoned the effort after three humiliating interviews.

She began hoarding the money she had left, going without meals she didn't want to eat anyway, eliminating her trips to Schwab's, wondering all the time how such horrible things could be happening to her. She was the woman Errol Flynn had loved. Didn't anyone understand that?

In a desperate effort to change her luck, she spent twenty precious dollars to enroll in an acting class taught by a rotund little man who advertised himself as having "known Mr. Belasco." He talked to them about rhythm and spine, about emotional memory and controlled energy, none of which meant anything to her. She attended two classes, and then she never went back.

The knowledge that she was pregnant with Flynn's child didn't come to her in a great, blinding flash of revelation. Instead, it occurred to her gradually, seeping into her mind until the day came when she couldn't force herself to get dressed to make the rounds of agents' offices. For two days she lay in her cheap Hollywood bed, staring up at the stained ceiling overhead, trying to comprehend what had happened to her.

She remembered horrified whispers about Indianapolis girls who had gone too far, rumors of shotgun weddings or, even worse, no weddings at all. But those were girls from the wrong side of the tracks, not Dr. Britton's daughter Edna Cornelia. Things like this didn't happen to nice girls. They got married first, and then they had babies. To do it the other way around was unimaginably shameful.

The possibility of an abortion didn't occur to her for the simple reason that she barely knew such a thing existed. Back-alley operations were part of a world that had never touched her. She did think about trying to contact Flynn, but then she dismissed the idea. Not only did she have no idea where to locate him, but he was still married, so she didn't see how he could help her. Instead, she found herself more and more preoccupied with thoughts of Alexi Savagar.

Once she made up her mind, it took her two days to locate him. She waited until her roommates had left the apartment and then made a series of long-distance telephone calls that she couldn't pay for, contacting every New York City hotel she could remember reading about in Earl Wilson's newspaper column. On the second day she learned that he had checked out of the Pierre the week before, leaving the Beverly Hills Hotel as a forwarding address. She called the Beverly Hills and left a message: Miss Britton would be waiting for Mr. Savagar in the Polo Lounge that evening at five o'clock.

The day was cool, and she dressed carefully in a butterscotch velvet suit and a white nylon blouse so thin that it revealed the lacy detail of her slip beneath. She wore the small string of cultured pearls bought for the high school graduation she had never attended and the companion pearl button earrings. Her hat was a butterscotch tam, and she perched it on the side of her head in as jaunty and carefree a fashion as she could manage. With the addition of proper white cotton gloves and slightly improper needle-pointed heels, she was ready for the drive to Schwab's, where she left her battered Studebaker and called a taxi to deliver her to the elegant porte-cochere that marked the front entrance of the Beverly Hills Hotel.

Although Flynn had taken her to the Polo Lounge several times, she still felt a thrill as she stepped inside. She gave the maître d' Alexi's name, and he led her to one of the curved banquettes that faced the door, priority seating in what was, perhaps, the most famous hotel cocktail lounge in the world.

Even though she didn't like martinis, she ordered one since it was sophisticated and she wanted Alexi to see her with it. While she waited for him to arrive, she tried to distract herself from her nervousness by studying the other patrons. George Jessel was sitting with a tiny blonde who looked even younger than herself. She spotted Greer Garson and Ethel Merman at separate tables, and, across the room, one of the studio executives she had met when she was with Flynn. He looked past her.

A page dressed in a brass-buttoned jacket came through. "Call for Mis-tuh Jessel. Call for Mis-tuh Jessel." George Jessel lifted his hand, and the tiny blonde giggled as the page delivered a pink telephone to his table.

She toyed with the long, cool stem of her glass, refusing to notice that her hands were trembling. Alexi wouldn't arrive at five o'clock, she was certain of that. She had damaged his pride too much the last time they were together, and he wouldn't forget it easily. The question was, Would he come at all, and what would she do if he didn't?

Gregory Peck and his new French wife, Veronique, arrived and were led to a banquette. Veronique was a former newspaper woman, dark-haired and beautiful, and Belinda could feel envy coiling inside her like a snake. When they were seated, her famous husband gave her a small, private smile and said something that only she could hear. Veronique laughed and then placed her hand over his, the gesture tender, casual, thoughtlessly proprietary. In that instant Belinda hated Veronique Peck as she had never hated another human being.

At six o'clock Alexi walked into the Polo Lounge and Belinda's heart turned over. For a moment he paused in the doorway, exchanging a few words with the maître d' before he moved toward her banquette. He was dressed in a pearl gray silk suit, immaculate as always, and several people greeted him as he passed their tables. She had forgotten how much attention Alexi attracted. Flynn had said it was because he was one of a small handful of men with the gift for turning old money into new.

He slid wordlessly into the banquette, bringing with him the expensive scent of his cologne and the whisper of raw silk. Turning his head to study her, his expression was unfathomable as always. Was he pleased to see her or not? A small shiver passed through her. Why did she never know what he was thinking?

"Château Haut-Brion, 1929," he said to the waiter who appeared to take his order. And then he gestured toward her half-finished martini. "Take that away. Mademoiselle will have wine with me."

As the waiter disappeared, Alexi slowly lifted her hand to his lips and kissed it. She tried to smile, but she found herself remembering the last time they were together, when his kiss had not been gentle at all.

"You seem nervous, *ma chère*."

The time for doubts was long past, driven away by the small collection of cells relentlessly multiplying inside her, and she forced herself to lift her shoulders in a casual shrug. "A little maybe. It's been a long time. I—I missed you." Her feelings of injustice suddenly sprang to the surface. "Really, Alexi. How could you go off like that? Without calling me or anything."

He looked faintly amused. "You needed time to think, *chérie*. To see how you liked being alone."

"I didn't like it at all," she snapped.

"I didn't think you would." He studied her in that concentrated way of his that made her feel as if she had been mounted between glass slides and pushed under a microscope. "Tell me what you learned during your time of introspection."

She replied carefully. "I learned that I had come to depend on you. Everything fell apart for me so fast after you left, and you weren't there to help me. I guess I'm not as independent as I thought I was."

The waiter appeared with the wine, which he uncorked and poured for sampling. Alexi took a sip, gave a distracted nod, and then waited until they were alone before he turned his attention back to her. Carefully she told him what had taken place in the past two months—the humiliation of her acting class, her failure to capture the interest of a single producer, the fact that her parents would no longer support her—all her miseries except the most important one.

"I see," he said. "So much to have happened in such a short time. Is there anything else you haven't told me? Any other disasters you wish to lay at my feet?"

She swallowed hard. "No, nothing else. But I'm out of money, Alexi, and I have to make some decisions. I need your help with that."

"My help?" For the first time since he had sat down with her, his expression hardened. "Why don't you go to your former lover, Belinda? Surely he'll help you. Rush to your side on his white charger, sword flashing, slaying your villains for you. Why don't you go to Flynn, Belinda?"

She bit down hard on the inside of her cheek to keep herself from saying everything she shouldn't. Somehow she knew she had to ease Alexi's bitterness, or he would never help her. He didn't understand Flynn. He never had. "Those days at the Garden," she began slowly. "They were like nothing that had ever happened to me before. But in my mind, in some funny way, I guess I mixed the two of you together. I made myself believe all the good feelings came from Flynn, but after you left, I knew that they came from you, too." She had rehearsed what she would say, but now her words made her uncomfortable because she realized there was more truth to them than she liked. "I need help," she said abruptly. "And I don't know where else to turn."

"I see."

But he didn't see—not at all. She dipped her head and began pleating her napkin to avoid looking at him. "I—I'm out of money, and I can't go back to Indianapolis. I—I'd like you to give me a loan—just for a year or so until I can get the studios to notice me." She took a sip from the wine she didn't want. She had to have the money. Then she could go away someplace where no one knew her and have her baby. Money would give her time to think about what to do afterward.

He didn't say anything, and her nervousness grew. "I don't know where else to turn. I'll die if I have to go back to Indianapolis. I know I will."

"Death before Indianapolis." His voice carried a note of amusement, which gave her a small stirring of hope. "How childishly poetic," he said, "and how like you, my sweet Belinda. Tell me, what do I receive in return for my *largesse?*"

The page brushed by their table, brass buttons glinting in the carefully controlled light of the Beverly Hills Hotel. "Call for Mis-tuh Peck. Call for Mis-tuh Peck."

"Whatever you want," Belinda said.

He stiffened next to her, and she realized, too late, that she had made a terrible, horrible mistake. "I see," he hissed. "You are selling yourself again! Tell me, Belinda, what sets you apart from those overdressed young women the maître d' is turning away at the door? What sets you apart from the whores?"

Her eyes clouded at the injustice of his attack. It was no use. He wasn't going to help her. What had ever made her think that he would, and why did she feel so betrayed? She stood and snatched her purse from the table so she could make a blind dash to the door before she humiliated herself by committing the unpardonable sin of crying in the public glare of the Polo Lounge, but before she could move away, Alexi had caught her arm and pulled her gently back into her seat. "I'm sorry, *chérie* —once again I have hurt you. But you keep throwing these knives at me, and sooner or later you must expect me to bleed."

She bent her head so no one could see the tears spilling down her cheeks, making little dark smears on the skirt of her butterscotch velvet suit. "Maybe you can take from people without giving something in return, but I can't," she said, while she fumbled at the clasp of her purse, trying to open it to get a handkerchief. "If that makes me a whore in your eyes, there isn't anything I can do about it, except wish that I'd never come to you for help."

"Please don't cry, *chérie.* You make me feel like a monster." A handkerchief, folded into a precise rectangle, dropped into her lap. She closed her hand around it so that only one corner was visible and lifted it to her eyes, trying to be as inconspicuous as possible as she dabbed at her tears, certain that George

Jessel was watching her, and the tiny blonde with him, and Veronique Peck. When she finally raised her head, she saw that no one had noticed her at all.

Alexi leaned back into the banquette and regarded her so intently that she once again stared down into her lap. "Everything is simple for you, isn't it?" he said. "Perhaps it was the same with me when I was a child, although I don't believe so." His voice was suddenly husky. "Will you put away your fantasies, *chérie?* Will you give me your adoration?"

He made it seem so simple, but he must know it wasn't simple at all. She was fascinated by him. He protected her and, she admitted, even excited her. And people always looked at them when they were together. But his face was the same size as hers. It had never been magnified on a screen until it was big enough for all the world to see.

He pulled a cigarette from a silver case and lit it. For a moment she thought she saw his fingers trembling on the lighter, but then the flame held steady, and she decided she was mistaken. "I will help you, *chérie,*" he said, "even though some part of me knows I shouldn't. When I have finished my business here, we will go to Washington and be married there in the French embassy."

"Married!" She couldn't believe she had heard him right. "No, I—I don't believe you. What kind of a game are you playing with me?" She finally let herself look at him and was startled by what she saw. The serious lines around his mouth had softened, and his eyes were full of emotion. For the first time since they had met, he seemed vulnerable.

"No game, *chérie.* I want you—not as my mistress, but as my wife. Foolish of me, *non?*"

"But why marriage? I've already told you—"

"*Ça suffit!* Do not make your offer again!" Frightened by his intensity and the sudden realization of how deeply he cared, she drew back from him.

"As a businessman, I never gamble foolishly, and there are no guarantees with you, are there, *chérie?*" He traced the stem of his wineglass with his finger. "*Hélas,* I am also a Russian. . . . A film career is not what you really want, although you don't understand that yet. In Paris you will take your place as my wife. It will be a new life for you. Unfamiliar, I know, but I will guide you, and you will become the talk of the city—Alexi

58

Savagar's child bride." He smiled. "You will love the attention."

Her mind raced. The baby. She had to tell him about the baby; it wouldn't be right not to. She couldn't imagine herself as Alexi's wife, always under the scrutiny of those strange, slanted eyes. The talk of Paris, he had said. Alexi was rich and important, famous in his world. But she couldn't give up her dreams. She was going to be a star!

"I don't know, Alexi. I haven't thought—" She could feel him withdraw, see the planes of his face grow harsh again. If she were to refuse him now, if she were to hesitate for even a moment longer, his pride would never let him forgive her. She would have only this one chance.

"Yes!" Her laughter was high-pitched and strained. "Yes. Yes, of course, Alexi. I'll marry you. I want to marry you."

For a moment he didn't move, and then he lifted her hand to his mouth. With a smile, he opened his lips and covered the pulse beating on the inside of her wrist. She returned his smile, ignoring the pounding of her heart, the fearful rushing of blood that asked her what she had done.

He ordered a bottle of Dom Perignon. "To the end of fantasy," he said, lifting his glass to hers.

"To us, Alexi," she replied nervously.

At the next banquette, Veronique Peck's soft laughter chimed like a string of silver bells.

CHAPTER 5

Somewhat to Belinda's surprise, her wedding night didn't occur until the night of her wedding, two weeks after her meeting with Alexi in the Polo Lounge. They were married in the French embassy in Washington and left immediately after the ceremony for the ambassador's home, which had been offered to them for the weekend as a wedding present.

Belinda's nervousness grew as she stepped from the tub in the ambassador's bathroom and dried herself with a thick, nutmeg-brown towel. She had never quite gotten around to telling Alexi about the baby. She had decided that if she was lucky, and the baby small, he might believe the child was his, born prematurely. If he didn't believe it, then he would almost certainly divorce her, but the baby would still have his name and she would not have to live with the stigma of being an unwed mother. Then she could go back to California and start all over again, but this time with Alexi's money.

Despite her uneasiness, the past few weeks had been wonderful. Alexi treated her like a queen, and every day she saw astonishing new evidence of the depth of his caring, not only in the gifts he lavished upon her, but in his unending patience with the silly little mistakes she made as she entered his world. There was nothing she could do, it seemed, to make him angry. The thought brought her comfort.

She looked over at a dress box wrapped in silver paper sitting on the basin. It was something he wanted her to put on for him that night. She hoped it was a peignoir set, black and lacy like a gown Kim Novak would wear, but whatever it was, she knew it would be expensive. Alexi only bought the best.

When she unwrapped the dress box and saw what was inside, she almost cried with disappointment. The long white cotton garment that lay beneath the cloud of tissue paper looked more like a child's nightgown than the peignoir of her fantasies. Although the fabric was sheer and fine, the neck was cut high with only a small edging of lace and a row of pink bows stretching down the front to hold the bodice modestly closed. As she pulled the garment from its box, something fell at her feet. Leaning over, she picked up a pair of matching white cotton underpants with tiny little ruffs of lace at the leg openings. Was Alexi trying to make a fool of her? But then she remembered his pride, and the fact that she wasn't coming to him as a virgin. . . .

It was past midnight, and the drapes in the bedroom had been drawn for the night. Decorated in pale green brocade with thick jade plush carpeting and polished wood that glowed in the light filtering through the cream silk lampshades, the room was elegant but somehow lifeless. Or perhaps it was just that Belinda could not help but make an unconscious comparison between the tastefully decorated room and the wonderfully tawdry Spanish interior of the bungalow at the Garden of Allah.

Alexi was wearing a pale gold dressing gown and standing near the windows. As she studied him, she realized it was the first time she had seen him in anything other than a suit. Alexi, with his small eyes and dark, thinning hair. On screen, he could only play a villain, never a hero. But a powerful villain—the kind who controlled empires and, with a flick of his hand, changed a person's destiny. He turned and gazed at her. She began to feel nervous as the silence in the room grew thickly oppressive.

"This gown isn't quite what I expected, Alexi," she said to ease her tension.

His expression was closed, unreadable as always. "You're wearing lipstick, *chérie?*"

"Yes. Is something wrong?"

He stood and pulled a handkerchief from the pocket of his dressing gown. "Come over here near the light." She did as he said, padding across the carpet on bare feet, while she thought, illogically, of a lacy peignoir and a pair of black satin mules with high heels and rosettes at the toes.

He took her chin in his hand and gently wiped at her mouth with his white linen handkerchief. "No lipstick in the bedroom, *mon amour*. You are beautiful enough without it." Stepping back, he slowly raked his eyes down over her body, stopping at her scarlet painted toenails. "Sit down on the bed."

She did as he asked. He walked over to her cosmetic case and dumped the contents on top of the bureau. Then he picked out a bottle of nail polish remover and came back to her. Kneeling in front of her, he put her right foot up on his knee, and began to remove the polish from each of her toes with his handkerchief. When he was done, he picked up her left foot, lightly bit the instep, then touched it with his tongue. "Are you wearing the panties, Belinda?"

Embarrassed, she dropped her eyes to the collar of his dressing gown and nodded.

"Bon. You are my sweet bride, then, come to please me. You are shy, inexperienced, a little frightened perhaps. That is as it should be."

She nodded her head because she *was* frightened. Alexi was treating her as if she were an innocent—his soft words, the virginal nightgown, the lack of cosmetics. Didn't he understand that he couldn't change what had happened? He couldn't erase her time with Flynn. The memory of the night he had assaulted her wormed its way into her thoughts, even though she tried to tell herself she was being silly. He had been jealous that night because of Flynn, but now that she was his wife, he would never hurt her. She wondered if he suspected that Flynn hadn't been the first.

He had walked over to the bed, and now he held out his hand. "Come to me, *chérie.* I have been waiting so long to make love to you." She moved toward him slowly, telling herself that she would pretend he was Flynn, or maybe she would close her eyes and imagine he was Jimmy. He touched her arm, and then gently eased her onto the bed. When she was lying down, he leaned forward and brushed his mouth over her lips. "Put your arms around me, *chérie,"* he murmured. "I am your husband."

She did as he asked, closing her eyes as his face drew near, trying to pretend that he was Flynn. But the pretense was difficult because she was frightened and because Flynn had so seldom kissed her, and never with Alexi's intensity.

"You kiss like a child," he said, his lips moving against hers. "Open your mouth for me. Be gracious with your tongue."

Cautiously she parted her lips. It was Flynn kissing her, she told herself. Flynn's mouth covering hers, pulling at hers. But she knew it wasn't Flynn, and despite her fear, she could feel her body becoming warm. Her arms involuntarily pulled him closer, and her tongue suddenly grew bold in his mouth. She moaned softly when he moved away from her.

"Open your eyes, Belinda. You must watch me make love to you." She could feel cool air on her skin as he tugged open the bows that held the nightgown together and then separated the bodice. "Watch my hands on your breasts, *chérie.*"

Slowly she opened her eyes to the burning intensity of Alexi's gaze, the searing eyes that seemed able to pierce through flesh and bone to uncover even the smallest seed of deception. Panic mixed with her excitement, and she tried to pull the fabric back together.

He chuckled, the sound deep and low in his throat, and she realized he had mistaken her fear for shyness. Before she knew what had happened, he had peeled the nightgown down over her hips until she was lying on the bed, clad only in the lace-trimmed cotton underpants. He grasped her arms and placed them at her sides. "Let me look." His hands moved to her breasts, handling them gently, tracing light, feathery circles around them until her nipples hardened into tiny bells. He touched each tip. "I'm going to suckle you," he whispered.

Waves of heat shot through her as his head dipped forward. She saw where his hair had thinned at the crown, and then her eyes slipped shut as he drew her nipple deep into his mouth, sculpting it with his tongue and then sucking at her as if she were giving him his life's nourishment. Excitement spread through her body like a betrayal, burning hotter and fiercer as he began stroking the insides of her thighs. His fingers moved beneath the lacy leg band of the panties just as Billy Greenway's had once done so many lifetimes ago and then slid deep inside her with a practiced touch that was far different from the awkward fumbles of her past.

"You're tight," he whispered, withdrawing from her. He pulled the underpants down over her hips, separated her legs, and began doing something to her with his mouth that was so forbidden, so horrifyingly exciting, she could barely believe it was happening. At first she fought against it, but her resistance was no match for Alexi's skill, and in a humiliatingly short span of time, he had taken control of her body. She surrendered to him, crying out as he brought her to an orgasm so exquisite she felt as if she were shattering into disconnected pieces. After it was over, he lay down beside her, but she couldn't bear to look at him. What he had done was dirty, nothing a respectable person would do, certainly nothing a movie star—

"That has never happened to you before, has it?"

She heard the satisfaction in his voice and turned her back to him.

"What a sweet little prude you are," he laughed, "ashamed of yourself for having enjoyed something so natural." He leaned over to kiss her, but she turned her head away. Nothing in the world was going to make her kiss a mouth that had been where his had been.

He laughed and imprisoned her head between the palms of his hands. Then he brought her tongue to his lips. "See how sweet you are," he whispered. He covered her mouth with his, sucking her tongue deep inside and holding it there. Finally satisfied, he deserted her for a moment to open his dressing gown and let it fall to the floor. His body was lean and swarthy, covered in dark hair, and fully aroused. "Now I will explore you for my pleasure," he said.

He touched every part of her body, leaving no spot she could call hers alone, putting the mark of Alexi Savagar everywhere, and once again setting her afire with desire. When he finally entered her, she wrapped her legs around him and dug her fingers into his buttocks, begging him to go faster. Just before his orgasm, he muttered thickly in her ear, "You are mine, Belinda. I am going to give you the world."

In the morning there was a smear of blood on the sheet from a long, thin scratch he had made on her hip.

Paris was everything Belinda had ever imagined it would be, and Alexi was a loving and attentive bridegroom. He stole hours away from his imposing offices on the Boulevard St.-Germain to take her to all the places tourists adore. At the top of the Eiffel Tower exactly an hour before sunset, he kissed her until she thought her body would float out above the lacy steel-work and lose itself in the skies. They sailed a small boat in the *bassin* at the Luxembourg Gardens and wandered through Versailles in a thunderstorm. In the Louvre he found a deserted corner where he felt her breasts to see if they were as plump as the Renaissance Madonnas'. And then he showed her the Paris he knew: twisting alleys with names like *Rue du Chat-Qui-Pêche,* Street of the Fishing Cat; the Seine at dawn near the

Pont St.-Michel when the newborn sun struck the windows of the ancient buildings and, for one brief moment, set the city on fire. He showed her Montmartre at night, and the wicked, smoky cafés of Pigalle, where he titillated her with whispered sex talk that left her hot and breathless. They dined on trout and truffles in the Bois de Boulogne beneath glass chandeliers that hung from the chestnut trees and sipped Château Lafite '29 in an out-of-the-way café where sunflowers grew in the window. As each day passed, Alexi's step grew lighter and his laugh grew readier until he almost seemed like a boy again.

At night, he sealed them both away in the great bedroom of his gray stone mansion on the Rue de la Bienfaisance and took her again and again until her body no longer seemed to have an existence separate from his. She found herself resenting the demands of the job that stole him away from her each morning. Alone, she felt exhausted, confused, and deeply troubled.

He took her to the catacombs cut beneath the hills of the city, the repository of millions of skeletons from the ancient cemeteries and the home of the Resistance during the fateful August of 1944. As they walked through the narrow underground passages, he told her a little of his work as a *passeur* with the Resistance, secretly transporting the enemies of the Third Reich out of France during the occupation. When they finally emerged from the catacombs into the afternoon sunlight, he led her to an iron bench.

"No one who was here could ever forget what it was like to be in Paris on the day it was liberated." He pulled a cigarette from a silver case and lit it. "The GI's rode in jeeps covered with flowers through the streets, and their faces were smeared with lipstick from all the women who had kissed them. Everywhere you went, the *Marseillaise* was being sung over and over until the music seemed to become part of the air. It was a day of new beginnings, when all things seemed possible. Like the day I met you."

In the mornings after he had left for his offices, she lay in bed and thought about the child she was carrying. As one day slid into another, the child gradually stopped being an abstraction and became a piece of living flesh, something to love and care for. Flynn's baby was growing inside her, a child of her blood and his. Her imagination caught fire. Dreams could still come true. She and her baby would go back to California where life

65

would be new again. She could see herself walking along an endless stretch of beach with a little boy, as handsome as his father, or a little girl, more beautiful than any little girl had ever been. Sometimes her imagination played tricks on her, and Alexi walked with them. . . .

It did not take her long to discover that life on the Rue de la Bienfaisance without him was nearly unbearable, and she found herself pacing the thick, carpeted floor of their bedroom, waiting for the hour when he would come home. She had not been prepared for the grandeur of the gray stone mansion with its salons and apartments and dining room that could seat fifty guests. It had been built in the eighteenth century by one of the architects of the house of Bourbon, and at first she had been nearly giddy with excitement at the idea of living in so much splendor, but it was not long before the huge house began to oppress her. The oval foyer was paved with funereal red and green veined marble and gruesome tapestries depicting martyrdom and crucifixion hung on its walls. The ceiling in the main salon was painted with allegorical figures clad in capes and armor who battled giant serpents. Friezes stretched above the heavily draped windows, pilasters flanked them. Everything towered above her, making her feel small and defenseless. Adding to her feeling of helplessness was the fact that it was all ruled over by Solange Savagar.

Although Belinda had known about Alexi's mother, she had not been prepared for her actual presence. Solange was a tall, thin woman with carefully dyed black hair cut close to her head, a large nose, and papery wrinkles so transparent that the tracery of blue veins beneath them was visible. Each morning at ten o'clock she dressed in rubies and one of an endless number of white wool suits designed for her by Norell before the war, and then she took her place on a Louis Quinze chair at the center of the main salon, where she began her daily rule over the house and its inhabitants.

The possibility that Belinda, as Alexi's wife, would take Solange's place was never discussed. The mansion on the Rue de la Bienfaisance was her domain, and nothing but death would make her give it up, certainly not the arrival of an unforgivably young American who had somehow managed to bewitch her beloved son.

Alexi had made it clear that his mother was to be respected, so Belinda tried to be pleasant, but Solange made it impossible. She refused to speak English, except to criticize, and she took delight in laying out each *gaucherie* Belinda committed for Alexi's later inspection. Every evening at seven o'clock they gathered in the main salon, where Solange would sip from a glass of white vermouth and smoke one lipstick-tipped Gauloise after another while she chattered at her son in staccato French and ignored her daughter-in-law.

Alexi kissed away Belinda's complaints. "My mother is a bitter old woman who has lost much," he murmured into her neck. "This house is all the kingdom she has left." His kisses strayed to her breasts. "Humor her, *chérie*. For my sake."

And then, abruptly, it all changed.

She decided to surprise Alexi one night by modeling a transparent black negligee she had bought that afternoon. As she pirouetted next to the bed, his face grew stark and pale. Without warning, he stalked out of the room. She waited in the dark, furious with herself for not having realized how much he would hate seeing her in anything but the simple white gowns he had selected for her. The hours dragged by and there was no sign of him. When morning came and he had still not returned, she wept until her pillow was soaked with tears.

The next night she went to her mother-in-law. "Alexi has disappeared. I want to know where he is."

The ancient rubies on Solange's wrists winked like evil eyes. "My son tells me only what he wishes me to know."

He returned two weeks later at the beginning of April. Belinda stood on the marble staircase in a Balmain dress that was too tight at the waist and watched him hand over his briefcase to the butler who tended the front door. He seemed to have aged ten years. She took a step forward, and he glanced up and spotted her. His mouth curled in the cynical twist she had not seen since she had first met him. "My dear wife," he said. "You look beautiful as always."

The next few days confused her. In public, everything was just as it had been before. He treated her with deference and courtesy, even presenting her with an antique jade jewelry box emblazoned with the imperial eagle of Russia. But in private everything was different. He tormented her with his lovemaking, abandoned tenderness for conquest, and kept her poised on the brink of fulfillment for so long that her pleasure crossed the boundary into pain. At the end of the week he announced that they were going on a trip, but he would not tell her where.

Abandoning the chauffeured Daimler for a 1933 Hispano-Suiza from his collection, he drove with utter concentration. She was glad to be spared the effort of making conversation and watched out the window as the long rows of poplars that lined the Seine near Paris gradually gave way to the bare, chalky hillsides of Champagne. Despite the charm of the scenery, she couldn't make herself relax. By her calculations she was nearly four months pregnant, and the effort of deceiving him was sapping all her strength. She pretended to have menstrual periods that never came, secretly adjusted the buttons on the waists of her new skirts, and plotted to keep her body away from the light when she was naked. She did everything she could to postpone the time when she would be forced to tell him about the baby.

They reached Burgundy in the late afternoon, just in time to watch the vineyards that were set into the hilly slopes turning lavender in the evening shadows. The inn where they would spend the night was charming, with a red-tiled roof and pots of geraniums set in the windows, but she found she was too tired to enjoy even the simple, well-cooked meal that was set before them.

The next day Alexi drove her past women doing their laundry in the Seine and then out into the Burgundian countryside. They ate a silent picnic lunch on a hilltop covered with wildflowers, dining on a *potée* Alexi had purchased in the neighboring village. It was filled with lettuce and fresh chervil, tarragon and chives, all of it accompanied by chunks of freshly baked bread crusted in poppy seeds, a runny Saint Nectaire cheese, and a raw young wine that was the only thing Belinda could bring herself to touch, even though it made her shiver as she drank it. After the meal was done, she tied the cardigan she had been wearing around her shoulders and walked along the hilltop to escape his oppressive silence.

"Enjoying the view, *mon amour?*" She jumped as he came up behind her and put his hands on her shoulders.

"Yes, it's very pretty."

"And are you enjoying being with your husband?"

"Of course, Alexi. I always enjoy being with you."

"Especially in bed, *n'est-ce pas?*"

She didn't say anything, and apparently he didn't expect a response, for he began pointing out several of the vineyards to her. Gradually, he seemed like the Alexi who had shown her the sights of Paris, and she began to relax.

"Over there, *chérie*. Do you see that collection of gray stone buildings? That is the Couvent de l'Annonciation. The nuns there run one of the best schools in France."

"Oh?" Belinda was more interested in the vineyards. Although she had taken instruction in the Catholic faith in order to remarry Alexi in the Church as he had insisted, she did not really consider herself a Catholic. In Indianapolis, Catholic children had been different from the rest of them, inferior somehow. Their houses always smelled of cooking, and they had crucifixes hanging on their walls, with palm fronds, bleached and brittle from age, stuck behind them.

"Some of the best families in Europe send their children to the nuns to be educated," Alexi went on. "The sisters even take babies, although the male children are sent to the brothers near Langres when they are five."

Belinda was shocked. "Why would a rich family send away its babies?"

"It is necessary if the daughter is unmarried and a proper husband can not be found. The sisters keep the babies until a discreet adoption can take place."

The talk of babies was making her nervous, and she tried to change the subject, but Alexi was not ready to be distracted. "The sisters take good care of them," he said. "They have the best food. They're not abandoned to spend their days in cribs as happens in some institutions."

"I can't imagine a mother turning over her baby to the care of someone else if she didn't have to." The afternoon seemed to have grown chill. She untied her sweater and slipped into it. "Let's go, Alexi. I'm getting cold."

He didn't move. "You can't imagine it because you still think like the *bourgeoisie*. You will have to think differently now that you are my wife, now that you are a Savagar."

Her hands closed involuntarily over her abdomen, and she turned slowly. "What are you saying, Alexi?"

"I'm saying that as soon as your bastard child is born, it will go to the sisters at the Couvent de l'Annonciation to be raised."

"You know," she whispered.

"Of course."

The sun drained out of the day, and all her nightmares came home. "Your belly is swollen," he said, his voice laden with contempt, "and the veins of your breasts show through your skin. That night when I looked at you standing in our bedroom in that transparent black nightgown, it was as if blinders had been ripped off my eyes. How long did you think you could deceive me?"

"No!" Suddenly it was all more than she could bear, and she did what she had sworn she would never do. "The baby's not a bastard!" she cried. "It's your baby! It's your—"

He slapped her hard across the face, holding her tightly by the arm so she would bear the full force of his blow. "Do not humiliate yourself with lies that you know I will never believe!" She tried to pull away from him, but he held her tight. "How you must have laughed at me that day at the Polo Lounge as you poured out all your silly troubles to me, never once mentioning the only one that was of any importance! You trapped me into marriage just as if I were some silly schoolboy! You made a fool of me!"

"I'm sorry, Alexi," she sobbed through her tears. "I know I should have told you, but then you wouldn't have helped me, and I didn't know what else to do. I'll go away. After our divorce, I'll never see you again."

"Our divorce? Oh, no, *ma petite*. There will be no divorce. Did you not understand what I was telling you about the Couvent de l'Annonciation? Did you not understand that now you are the one who has been trapped?"

His earlier words suddenly rushed back to her, enveloping her in a cloud of fear. "I'll never let you take away my baby!" she sobbed.

The expression on his face turned fierce and hard, ripping through months of tenderly nurtured illusions and destroying the foolish dream castles she had allowed herself to build. "There will be no divorce, and if you run away, you will never have a *sou* from me. You are not good at surviving without other people's money, are you, Belinda?"

"You can't take my baby away! That baby's mine!"

His voice grew deadly quiet. "You are mistaken. Legally your bastard will be mine. French law gives the father complete authority over his children. And, Belinda, I warn you now, if you

70

ever tell anyone of your foolishness, I will ruin you. Do you understand me? You will be left with nothing."

"Alexi, don't do this to me," she whimpered.

But he was already walking away from her.

They drove straight back to Paris, neither of them speaking on the way. As Alexi pulled the Hispano-Suiza through the gate and into the drive, Belinda looked up at the house she had grown to hate. It loomed over her, like a great, gray tombstone, a monument commemorating things of the past that had no meaning for her. She fumbled blindly for the door handle and jumped from the car.

Alexi was at her side almost immediately. "Enter the house with dignity, Belinda, for your own sake."

Her eyes filled with tears. "Why did you marry me, Alexi?"

He gazed at her, letting the seconds pass one after the other, time ticking away lost promises. His mouth drew tight with bitterness. "Because I loved you," he said.

She stared at him, and a lock of hair whipped across her cheek. "I hate you for this! I'll hate you forever!" Pulling away from him, she ran blindly down the drive toward the Rue de la Bienfaisance, her misery stark against the sunny beauty of the spring afternoon.

Alexi turned and stared after her, trying to remember why he had ever loved her. But any remaining tenderness that had been lurking in the corners of his heart had dissolved on the hillside overlooking the Couvent de l'Annonciation.

She fled into the leafy shadows near the gate where the old chestnut trees were laden with heavy white blossoms. Petals dripped down onto the pavement and lay in great snowy drifts at the curb. As she turned out onto the street, a gust of wind from a passing car swept up the fallen petals from the sidewalk and enveloped her in a cloud of white. He stood unmoving and watched her—Belinda captured for one heartbreaking beat of time in a swirling cloud of chestnut blossoms that came from the earth instead of the sky.

It was a moment he would remember for the rest of his life. Belinda in blossoms—silly and shallow, agonizingly young. Heartbroken.

Belinda's Baby

"Whatever the others must do,
I must fight."

Errol Flynn:
My Wicked, Wicked Ways

CHAPTER 6

He was ferociously ugly, with a filthy, matted beard and a long robe stained with dirt. For once the dining room at the Couvent de l'Annonciation was free of its customary morning chatter, delivered in as many as five different languages. The girls pressed themselves more closely together, and delicious quivers of fear shot through their stomachs, making them wish they hadn't eaten such big bowls of *bouillie d'avoine* for breakfast.

One of the younger girls let out a shrill little squeal as the old man lifted his arm and cracked the ugly black whip he held over his head. Even the older girls, who had just last night agreed that they were much too sophisticated to be frightened by the *fouettard*, felt their throats go dry.

Please, Blessed Mother, don't let it be me. I'd be so mortified. Please don't let it be me.

They knew it wouldn't be, of course. It never was any of them. Every December 4, the *fouettard* singled out only the very worst girl at the Couvent de l'Annonciation to receive his bundle of birch twigs, and everybody knew who that was going to be. Several of them looked in her direction, some sympathetically, others with condescension.

She stood slightly apart from them, near one of the plastic Christmas wreaths that were fastened to the dining room wall along with a construction paper chain and a poster of Mick Jagger that the sisters had not yet spotted. Even though she was dressed the same as her classmates in a blue plaid uniform with a white blouse and dark knee socks, she managed to look different. Part of it was her height. Although she was just thirteen, she towered over all of them. She also had huge hands and paddleboat feet and a face that was much too big for her head. Her streaky blond hair was pulled back in an unruly ponytail that fell well past her shoulders. The pale color contrasted with a set of thick, dark eyebrows that almost met in the middle and looked as if they had been painted on with a blunt-tipped marking pen. Her mouth spread across her face and held a full set of silver braces; her arms and legs were long and ungainly, all pointy elbows and knobby knees, one of which bore a scab and the dirty outline of a Band-Aid. While the other girls wore slim Swiss wristwatches, she wore a man's chronometer, the black leather strap fitting her so loosely that the face of the watch hung to the side of her bony adolescent wrist.

But it was not just her size that set her apart from the other girls. It was the way she stood, with her chin thrust forward, her funny green eyes glaring defiantly at anything she didn't like—in this case the *fouettard*. There was something about her expression that dared him to touch her with the whip, but at the same time her attitude seemed to suggest that, even if he did touch her, she wouldn't be bothered one bit. No one but Fleur Savagar could have quite managed that look.

By that winter of 1969 the more progressive areas of France had outlawed the *fouettard*, the wicked "whipper" who threatened to give French schoolchildren birch sticks instead of presents for Christmas if they weren't good. But at the Couvent de l'Annonciation changes were never made lightly, even though, on the day of his appearance, the nuns who supervised the infirmary were overrun with little girls complaining of headaches and upset stomachs. The tradition lingered on, and over the years had been expanded to include the bestowing of a handful of birch sticks on the worst-behaved girl at the *couvent*. Such shameful notoriety, it was thought, would breed reform. Unfortunately, it hadn't quite worked out that way.

For the second time the *fouettard* cracked his whip above his head, and for the second time Fleur Savagar didn't move, even though everyone at the *couvent* knew she had good reason to be worried. In January she had stolen the keys to the mother superior's old Citroën, bragging that she could drive it and then promptly running it into the side of the garage. In March she had broken her arm doing bareback acrobatics on the convent's bedraggled pony and then stubbornly refused to tell anyone she had hurt herself. If her arm had not swollen up so badly that she couldn't put her uniform on, they might never have found out. After that came the incident with the fireworks, then the destruction of the toolshed, and finally the half-day disappearance of the six-year-olds.

The *fouettard* pulled the hated handful of birch twigs from an old gunnysack on his back and let his eyes slide over the girls before they finally came to rest on Fleur. Walking over to her, he placed the twigs at the toes of her scuffed brown oxfords. Soeur Marguerite, who found the custom barbaric, looked away, but the other nuns clucked their tongues and shook their heads. They tried so hard with Fleur, but they never seemed to make any headway. She was like quicksilver running through their disciplined lives: changeable, impulsive, aching for life to begin. They loved her dearly because she had been with them the longest and because it was impossible not to love her. But they also worried about her incessantly. What would happen to her when she was away from their firm control?

They watched for some sign of remorse as she leaned over and picked up the pile of twigs. She was thirteen now, no longer a baby, certainly too big to be swinging from the maple tree with her skirts over her head and her underpants showing just as poor Père Étienne was climbing from his car. She had to understand that, as much as they loved her, they couldn't allow her to behave so recklessly.

She looked down at the twigs and, for a moment, seemed to be ruminating over past misdeeds. Suddenly she thrust up her head, flashed them all a mischievous grin, and clamped the twigs into the crook of her arm, like roses bestowed on a beauty queen. She blew kisses and made mock bows until all the girls were giggling. Fleur Savagar was impossible, but really, you couldn't help liking her.

As soon as Fleur was certain that everybody understood she didn't care anything at all about the stupid *fouettard* and his stupid twigs, she slipped out the side door of the dining room and grabbed her old wool coat from the row of hooks in the hallway. Stupid bitches! She hated all of them. Punching at the bar on the back door with the heel of her hand, she ran outside.

The morning was cold and her breath formed frosty clouds as she raced across the hard-packed earth, leaving the gray stone buildings behind her. Without altering her pace, she reached into the pocket of her coat for her battered blue Cubs hat and shoved it on. It pulled at the rubber band on her ponytail and hurt her head, but she didn't care. She liked wearing the hat. Belinda had bought it for her last summer.

Fleur was only permitted to see her mother twice a year, for a month in August and during the Christmas holiday. In exactly fourteen days they would be together again at the pink stucco hotel near Antibes where they spent every Christmas. Fleur had been marking the time off on her calendar with an orange crayon since the last day of August, when Belinda had delivered her back to the *couvent*. She loved their time together more than anything in the world; Belinda never scolded her for talking too loud, or upsetting a glass of milk, or even for swearing. Belinda loved her more than anybody in the whole world.

Fleur had never seen her father. He had delivered her to the *couvent* when she was only a few weeks old and had not come back. She had never been to the house on the Rue de la Bienfaisance where all of them lived without her—her grandmother, her father, her mother, and her brother Michel. It wasn't her fault, her mother said.

She slowed down and gave a shrill whistle as she reached the fence that marked the edge of the *couvent* property. She used to whistle better before she got her braces. When she was a little girl, she thought that nothing could make her uglier than she already was, but that was before she knew about braces.

The chestnut whickered as he came up to the edge of the fence and stuck his head over the post to nuzzle her shoulder with his muzzle. He was a *Selle Français*, a French saddle horse owned by the neighboring vintner, and Fleur thought he was the most beautiful animal in the world. She ran her hand over his forehead and then pressed her cheek to his neck. She would give anything to ride him, but the nuns wouldn't let her, even though the vintner had given permission. She wanted to disobey them and ride him anyway, but she was afraid if she did they would find a way to keep her from coming here and she couldn't stand the idea of that happening.

Someday she was going to be a great horsewoman. She would ride in shows and win ribbons, and all the people in the stands would clap when they saw her. She was already the best athlete at the school. She could run faster than anybody else, swim farther, and she was the best field hockey player they had ever had. She was as good as a boy, anybody could see that. Being as good as a boy was important to her. Fathers liked boys, and maybe if she was the bravest and the fastest and the strongest, just like a boy, her father would let her come home. . . .

For Fleur, the time before the Christmas holiday dragged on

endlessly. When the day finally arrived for her mother to come for her, she was packed hours in advance and waiting. One by one, the nuns passed through the chilly front hallway. "Do not forget, Fleur, to keep a sweater with you. Even in the South, it can be cool in December."

"Yes, Sister Dominique."

"Remember that you're not in Châtillon-sur-Seine where you know everyone. You mustn't talk to strangers."

"Yes, Sister Marguerite."

"Promise me you'll go to Mass every day."

She crossed her fingers in the folds of her skirt. "I promise, Sister Thérèse."

An inordinately large number of nuns managed to be in the hallway when Belinda arrived. Fleur's heart nearly burst with pride as her beautiful mother swept into their midst, looking like a bird of paradise who had descended into a flock of chimney swifts. Beneath a snow-white mink coat, Belinda wore a yellow silk top over indigo trousers that were gathered at the waist with a belt of braided orange vinyl. Platinum and lucite bangles clicked at her wrists and matching disks swung from her ears. Everything about her was colorfully mod, stylish, and expensive.

At thirty-two Belinda's features had lost their soft edges. She was a costly gem, cut to perfection by Alexi Savagar and polished by the luxuries of the Faubourg St.-Honoré. She was thinner, more nervous, prone to small, quick gestures, but the eyes that drank in her daughter's face had not changed at all. They were the same innocent shade of hyacinth blue they had been the day Errol Flynn first gazed into them.

Fleur bounded across the hallway rather like an overgrown Saint Bernard pup and threw herself in her mother's arms. Belinda took a small step backward and then steadied herself. "Let's hurry," she whispered into Fleur's ear.

Fleur waved a hasty good-bye and grabbed her mother's hand, pulling her toward the door before the sisters could waylay her. Belinda hated it when they bombarded her with an account of Fleur's latest misdeeds. "Do you know what I want to say to them?" she would tell Fleur afterwards. "I want to say, 'Listen to me, you old crows, my daughter has a wild, free spirit and I don't want any of you to change one thing about her.'"

She loved it when her mother talked like that. Belinda said wildness was in Fleur's blood.

A silver Lamborghini stood at the bottom of the front steps. As Fleur slid into the passenger seat and shut the door, she gulped in the sweet, familiar scent of her mother's Shalimar.

"Hello, baby."

She slid into Belinda's arms with a small sob, cuddling into the mink and the Shalimar and everything that was her mother. She knew she was too grown up to cry, but she couldn't seem to help herself. Just for now it felt good to be Belinda's baby again.

Belinda and Fleur loved the *Côte d'Azur,* mainly because it had little in common with the rest of France. It was the world's most expensive carnival, gilded with aging movie stars, imported date palms, and neon-lit casinos, all held together by suntan oil and money. They had driven from their pink stucco hotel near Antibes into Monaco along the famous Corniche du Littoral, the serpentine road that twisted around the cliffs of the coastline and always made Fleur carsick. Belinda told her she would feel better if she looked straight ahead instead of staring out the side, but the view was so beautiful that Fleur always forgot.

As soon as they arrived in Monte Carlo, they went to the market at the foot of the palace hill, where Fleur, her stomach fully recovered, bounded from one food stall to another pointing out everything that caught her eye for their lunch. The weather was warm, and she wore khaki camp shorts, her favorite T-shirt, which said, "Draft beer, not students," and a new pair of Jesus sandals Belinda had bought her the day before. Belinda wasn't like the nuns about clothes. It was one of the things Fleur loved about her. "You wear what makes you happy, baby," she said. "Develop your own style. There's plenty of time for high fashion later."

Belinda was wearing Pucci.

After Fleur made her selections at the market, she dragged her mother up the steep path that led to the palace. Whenever Belinda lagged, she danced around her, chattering between mouthfuls of ham and poppyseed roll. She spoke four languages, but she was proudest of her English. It was flawlessly American. Someday she and Belinda were going to live in California, and she wanted to be ready when it happened. There were always one or two American students at the *couvent—*

80

daughters of government officials, bankers, or the bureau chiefs of the American newspapers—and she made sure they were her best friends, even those she didn't like very much. She adopted their slang and their attitudes and stopped thinking of herself as French. When the time came, she was going to fit right in. She wished she and Belinda could go to California now, but Belinda wouldn't have any money if she divorced Alexi. Besides that, Alexi wouldn't let her get a divorce. Fleur wanted to go to America just about more than anything in the world.

"I wish I had an American name," she said, tearing off another bite of sandwich with her teeth and, at the same time, scratching a bug bite on her thigh. "I hate my name. I really do. I wish you'd named me Frankie, especially since I read *Member of the Wedding,* by Carson McCullers. The girl's name is Frankie and she is so much like me it gave me the shivers. Fleur is such an absolutely ridiculous name for somebody so big. I like Holden, too, for Holden Caulfield, but that's a boy's name."

"Stop!" Belinda collapsed on a bench and tried to catch her breath. "Frankie is a perfectly hideous name and so is Holden. Fleur was the closest I could get to a female version of somebody I cared about." She delved into her purse for a cigarette. "Fleur Deanna. It's a beautiful name for a beautiful girl."

Fleur grinned. Belinda thought she was beautiful. It was another thing she loved about her mother. She said things like that, even though they weren't true. Abruptly, her thoughts flew in another direction. "I hate having my period. It's disgusting."

"It's part of being a woman, baby."

Fleur made a face to show Belinda exactly what she thought of that, and her mother laughed. Fleur pointed up the path toward the palace. "I wonder if she's happy?"

Belinda didn't have to ask who she meant. That was the way it was with them. "Of course she's happy. She's a princess. One of the most famous women in the world." She lit her cigarette and pushed her sunglasses on top of her head. "You should have seen her in *The Swan,* with Alec Guinness and Louis Jourdan. God, she was beautiful. Her most beautiful picture."

Fleur sprawled down on the bench and stretched out her legs. They were covered with fine, pale hair, and pink with sunburn. "He's kind of old, don't you think?"

"Not at all. Men like Rainier are ageless. He's quite distinguished, you know. Very charming."

"You've met him?"

"Last fall. He came for dinner." Belinda suddenly pulled her sunglasses back over her eyes, and Fleur knew that she was wishing they hadn't started this particular conversation.

She tapped the heel of her sandal into the dirt. "Was *he* there?"

"Hand me some of those olives, darling." Belinda gestured toward one of the paper cartons. Her fingernails were shaped like perfect almonds and painted the color of ripe raspberries. Fleur handed her the carton. "Was he?"

"Alexi owns property in Monaco. Of course he was there."

"Not him." Fleur's sandwich had lost its taste and she began pulling off little pieces and tossing them across the path to the ducks. "I didn't mean Alexi. I meant Michel." She used the French pronunciation of the name.

"Michel was there. He had a school recess."

"I hate him. I really do."

Belinda set aside the carton of olives without opening it and dragged deeply on her cigarette.

"I don't care if it's a sin," Fleur went on. "I think I hate him even more than Alexi. Michel has everything. It's not fair."

"He doesn't have *me,* honey. Just remember that."

"And I don't have a father. But it's still not even. At least Michel gets to go home. He gets to be with you."

"Come on, baby. We're here to have a good time. Let's not be so serious."

Fleur refused to be sidetracked. "I just can't understand Alexi. I can't understand anybody hating a little kid so much. Maybe now that I'm grown up, it makes sense, but not when I was a baby."

Belinda sighed. "We've been through this so many times. It's not you; it's just the way he is. God, I wish I had a drink."

Belinda had explained it to her dozens of times, but Fleur still didn't understand. How could a father want sons so much that he would send his only daughter away and never see her again? She was a reminder of his failure, Belinda said, and Alexi couldn't stand to fail. But even after Michel was born, he hadn't changed. Belinda said it was because she couldn't have any more children.

Fleur had pictures of her father that she'd cut out of the newspapers. She kept them in a manila envelope in the back of her closet, and sometimes at night when she was lying in bed she pretended that the nuns called her down to the office and that Alexi was there. He would tell her he'd made a terrible mistake and had come to take her home; then he'd hug her and call her "baby" the way her mother did. "I hate him," she said. "I hate them both." And then, for good measure, "I hate my braces, too. None of the girls like me because I'm ugly."

"That's not true, darling; you're just feeling sorry for yourself. Remember what I keep telling you. In another few years all the girls are going to want to look like you. You just need to grow up a little more."

Fleur's bad mood slipped away. She loved her mother. She really did.

The palace of the Grimaldi family was a sprawling stone and stucco edifice sprouting an unfortunate number of square turrets which, in Belinda's opinion, made the whole thing look something like a penitentiary. Fleur, however, had seen too little of the world to be cynical, and she quickly forgot her bad mood as she exclaimed over the candy cane guard boxes and uniformed guards with their pith helmets and red and white striped *fourragères* curving around their shoulders.

As Belinda watched her daughter darting through the crowd of tourists to climb on top of one of the cannons that overlooked the yacht basin, she could feel a lump forming in her throat. She was Flynn's child. She had his wildness, his restless zest for living, but all of it was softened somehow, made sweeter.

Belinda had wanted to blurt out the truth to her so many times. She wanted to tell her that she could never have been fathered by someone like Alexi Savagar, that she was Errol Flynn's daughter. But fear had kept her silent. She had learned long ago on that hilltop overlooking the Couvent de l'Annonciation not to cross Alexi. There had only been one time she had truly beaten him—one time when he had been the helpless one instead of her—and that had been when Michel was born.

They drove back to the hotel, where Belinda had a double Scotch and then took a shower while Fleur washed her feet. After a leisurely dinner and another Scotch, Belinda bought a paper to see what movies were playing. It was Fleur's turn to choose, and she selected an American western with French subtitles. Belinda loved Paul Newman, so the choice was fine with her.

The film was nearly half over when Belinda saw him for the first time. She thought afterwards that she must have made some sort of sound because Fleur looked over at her.

"What's wrong?"

"Nothing," she managed. "It's just . . . That man . . ." Fleur turned back to the screen and then looked at her quizzically.

Belinda studied the man who had just entered the saloon where Paul Newman was playing poker. It didn't seem possible. She knew it couldn't be. And yet . . .

All the lost years seemed to disappear. It was James Dean.

The man was tall and lean, with legs that didn't stop and a long, narrow face that looked as if it had been chipped from flint by a rebellious hand. The features were sharp planes, irregularly arranged, a face that had passed beyond arrogance to a kind of confidence that becomes a statement all its own. The camera went in for a close-up. He was young, not more than twenty-two or twenty-three, and certainly not movie star handsome. He had straight brown hair, a long nose that was narrow and bumpy at the bridge, and a sulky mouth. His front tooth was slightly crooked and chipped at the corner, his eyes restless and bitter blue.

It was only gradually that she realized he didn't really look like Jimmy. There was a resemblance, but he was taller and not as handsome. Still, the quality he projected was the same, and that was what had caught her so unexpectedly. Here was another rebel, a man who lived life on his own terms. She shivered.

After the film had ended, she stayed in her seat, clutching Fleur's impatient hand while she watched the credits roll. His name flashed on the screen and she felt excitement welling inside her. Jake Koranda . . .

It was as if Jimmy had sent a sign to her to tell her that she mustn't lose hope. Just the existence of someone like Jake Koranda proved that the dream was still alive. *A man is his own man; a woman her own woman.* Jake Koranda. Somehow she could still make the dream come true.

CHAPTER 7

Fleur was sixteen the summer the boys of Châtillon-sur-Seine discovered her.

She had just come out of the *boulangerie* carrying an éclair and was dabbing with her tongue at the chocolate frosting that was melting in the July heat when a drop of it fell on the front of her white cotton shift. "Damn," she whispered under her breath. It was ridiculous of the nuns to make the girls wear dresses every time they came into town, especially when it was so hot. Even this dress, which was lightweight and had a hemline that ended well above her knees, was too much. And the back of her neck was hot. She had stopped wearing her ponytail, preferring to pull her hair away from her face with a set of brown plastic barrettes and let it hang free down her back, but when it was this hot, she decided she would have to return to her ponytail.

"Salut, poupée!"

She looked up, a smear of chocolate dotting her chin. Three boys were lounging in the doorway of the *pharmacie* next door, where they were smoking cigarettes and listening to a portable radio that was blaring out Elton John singing "Crocodile Rock." One of them stubbed out his cigarette with the toe of his shoe. *"Hé poupée, irons voir par ici!"* He made a small, beckoning gesture with his head.

Fleur glanced over her shoulder to see which of her classmates was standing behind her.

The boys laughed, and one of them nudged his friend, pointing at her legs. *"Regardez-moi ces jambes!"*

Fleur looked down to see what was wrong. A dab of chocolate dripped onto the blue leather strap of her Dr. Scholl's. She looked back up and the taller of the boys winked. They were admiring her legs, she realized. *Her* legs.

"Qu'est-ce que tu dirais d'un rendez-vous?" he asked.

A date. Oh, God. She dropped the éclair and ran up the street to the bridge where all the girls were to meet. Her streaky blond hair flew behind her like a horse's mane, and the boys laughed and whistled.

When she got back to the *couvent,* she dashed to her room and stared at herself in the mirror. Those were the same boys who used to call her *l'épouvantail,* the scarecrow. What had happened? Her face looked the same to her—thick, marking-pen eyebrows, green eyes set too far apart, mouth spread all over. At least she had finally stopped growing, but not until she had reached five feet eleven and a half inches. The braces were gone now. Maybe that was it.

Not knowing what else to think, she shrugged the incident aside, but the next time she went into Châtillon-sur-Seine, the same thing happened. It was not long before the other girls began to notice and look at her with new respect. Fleur finally stopped running when the boys called out to her, but she wouldn't look at them either.

She and Belinda spent the month of August on Mykonos, their favorite of the Greek islands. The first morning as they walked along the beach, enjoying the dazzling white sunlight that never seemed so white anyplace else, Fleur told her mother what had happened. "It's creepy, Belinda, having them call out to me like that. I always think they're making fun of me, but when I look at their faces . . ."

She searched for the words to explain what she meant, but it was hard to describe. Absentmindedly, she tugged down on the leg opening of the apple-green bikini Belinda had brought for her. It was ridiculously small, and she had covered up the rest of her body as much as she could with an old orange T-shirt. Belinda was wearing an oatmeal striped tunic and a chrome Galanos slave bracelet. Both of them had bare feet, but Belinda's toenails were painted burnt umber to match her fingernails. Fleur's were unpainted and decorated only with a circular bandage on her little toe where her new pair of riding boots had rubbed a blister.

Belinda took a sip from the Bloody Mary she had brought with her. "When you look at their faces, you realize the boys aren't making fun of you, is that it?"

"I guess."

"Poor baby, it's tough not being the ugly duckling anymore,

isn't it? Especially for someone who's been so dedicated to the idea." She slipped her arm around Fleur's waist, her hipbone brushing the very top of her daughter's thigh. "For years I've told you the only problem with your face was that you weren't grown-up enough to fill it, but you wouldn't listen to me. You're stubborn, baby. You believe what you want to believe, and you won't listen to anyone else. Not that you can help it, of course. It's in your blood."

The way Belinda said it made Fleur feel her stubbornness was something to be proud of. She flopped down on the sand and leaned back against one of the outcrops of rock. Belinda settled neatly beside her. Fleur asked, "Did you ever read a book called *Love Without Fear?* One of the girls at the *couvent* has it. There's a chapter called 'The Kiss of Love.' It's disgusting." She shuddered. "I can't see how anybody could do anything like that."

Belinda said nothing.

Fleur dug her feet into the sand. "I don't think I could ever enjoy sex. I mean it, Belinda. I am *never* going to get married. I don't even like men."

"You don't *know* any men, darling," Belinda said dryly. "Believe me, you'll feel differently once you've gotten away from that godforsaken convent."

"I don't think so. Can I have a cigarette?"

"No. And men are wonderful, baby. The right men, of course. Powerful ones. Men who are important. When you walk into a restaurant on the arm of an important man, everyone looks at you. You can see the admiration in people's eyes. You can tell that they're thinking you must be someone very special to attract a man like that."

Fleur felt a prickle of uneasiness in the pit of her stomach. It almost sounded like . . . She reached over and picked at the bandage on her toe. "Is that what it's like when you're with Alexi? Is that why you won't get a divorce from him?"

Belinda sighed and then tilted her face up into the sun. "It's money, darling. Just like I've always told you. I'm afraid I'm not a very talented woman. I don't have the skills to support us."

Fleur stood up. She was thinking a lot of things, but she didn't say any of them. "We'd better get back. I want to ride before it gets any hotter."

"You and your horses." Belinda looked at her with tolerant amusement. "The nuns really got you on that one, didn't they?"

Fleur made a face. Several years ago the nuns had blackmailed her with her love of horses. They told her that if her classwork for the week was completed satisfactorily, she would be permitted to spend Saturday afternoons on horseback. In the space of three months she had moved from the bottom of her class to second from the top, and that same December, the birch twigs had gone to someone else.

It did not take Fleur long to discover that the young men who roamed the beaches of Mykonos were no different from the boys of Châtillon-sur-Seine. She told Belinda she wasn't going to the beach anymore unless it was deserted, because they made her so nervous that she couldn't enjoy her new snorkling mask. Why were they acting so stupid?

Belinda said she was immature for someone who was nearly seventeen because of the way she'd been raised, and that most girls would love the attention.

Fleur said she couldn't do anything about the way she was raised, and that, as far as she was concerned, the boys were the ones who were immature.

Belinda said to ignore them because they weren't important anyway.

They spent several days with an acquaintance of Belinda's from Paris who appeared unexpectedly. She was Madame Phillipe Jacques Duverge, but Belinda said she had been Bunny Gruben from White Plains, New York, before she was married. She had also been a famous Casimir model during the early sixties and was still quite beautiful. Bunny kept looking at Fleur in a way that made Fleur uncomfortable.

Their weeks on Mykonos passed much too quickly, and before Fleur knew it, they were standing in front of the Couvent de l'Annonciation holding each other and crying. As Fleur watched her mother drive away, she felt as if a little piece of herself had died. It should get easier after so many years, but it never did. She tried to cheer herself up by remembering that this was her last year at the *couvent*. This was the year she would take her *bac,* the all-important examination that would determine her placement in the French universities. Except she wasn't going to a French university. She had made Belinda promise to talk to Alexi about sending her to school in the

United States. "He should be happy to let me go," she pointed out. "He'll be getting rid of me forever. Tell him, Belinda."

Belinda had seemed doubtful, but Fleur felt more optimistic. She couldn't imagine her father wanting anything more than to put an ocean between them. She tried not to let herself think about her father very much anymore, and she certainly didn't indulge in those childish fantasies she used to have. He wasn't ever going to come and take her home, and the fact that Alexi Savagar would never be the loving daddy of her fantasies was something she could accept now. He hated her, and that was that. Still, she was unprepared for the letter from Belinda that arrived several weeks later.

> Baby,
>   I'm afraid I couldn't pull it off. Alexi won't hear of your attending an American university and has already had you registered at a private women's college in Switzerland. More nuns, I'm afraid.
>   I'm so sorry, baby. I know how much your heart was set on this, but I don't think it will be so bad. The vacation schedule will be more flexible, so we can be together more often.
>   Please, baby, don't be sad. Someday it's all going to come true for us. You'll see.
>   All my love,
>   Belinda

Fleur crumpled the letter in her fist. She had no patience left in her for Belinda's "somedays." Bastard.

She ran away that same night. It was a stupid thing to do, impulsive and unplanned, and the police found her before morning. As she stepped out into the hallway of the police station in Dijon, a strobe went off in her face.

Alexi Savagar was too intelligent to try to keep Fleur's exisence a secret over the years. Instead he had made it a practice to look somewhat pensive whenever her name was mentioned. As a result it was generally assumed that his daughter was handicapped, perhaps even retarded—such tragedies happened in the best of families, but the four-column photograph that ran on the front page of *Le Monde* put a permanent end to that kind of speculation. The astonishingly beautiful young woman with the wide mouth and startled eyes could never be mistaken for anybody's closet skeleton.

Alexi was furious. He tossed the morning newspaper down on the bed where Belinda was drinking a cup of coffee and threatened never to let her see her bastard daughter again. But it was too late; people were already asking questions. Perhaps it would have all been forgotten if Solange Savagar had not picked that particular time to die. Under normal circumstances Alexi would have been relieved. She had been in pain for nearly a year and had grown increasingly difficult to manage. But the timing was unfortunate. He would have to submit himself to vulgar speculation if the daughter about whom everyone in Paris now knew was absent from her grandmother's funeral. He ordered Belinda to send for her bastard.

As the limousine turned through the great iron gates that opened off the Rue de la Bienfaisance, Fleur was thinking about what she was wearing. It was ridiculous; her whole life was about to change, but all she could do was worry about her clothes. Still, it was better than throwing up, which was what she really wanted to do.

She had settled on black. For one thing, there had been a death and she wasn't going to let anyone think she was insensitive; for another, the nuns would never have let her out the door in anything else. But she had decided against the dresses and skirts and blouses that she had pulled from her closet. She had to make certain he understood that she wasn't trying to impress him. Even the thought of it made her sick.

She had chosen a pair of tailored wool slacks, a cashmere sweater with a cowl neck, and her old tweed blazer with the black velvet collar. Then she'd added her silver horseshoe stickpin for confidence. Two of her friends had tried to talk her into putting her hair up, but she refused. The barrettes that were holding it back from her face weren't an exact match, but they were close. She'd been too nervous to remember what she'd done with her best pair.

The limousine pulled up to the front door and the chauffeur got out. Fleur swallowed hard and wished that she still believed so she could say a prayer. She knew she was going to be sick. The house was huge and forbidding, just as Belinda had described it. A maid led her down an endless hall to a small salon where Belinda was waiting, elegant in a black Dior suit with a discreet diamond spray on the lapel and low black pumps that had pear-shaped openings cut into the toes. Fleur wished that she'd worn a dress.

"Baby!" Belinda splashed some of the liquor from her glass onto the tabletop in her hurry to set it down. They hugged each other in the center of the room, and as Fleur inhaled Belinda's Shalimar she found herself feeling better. Belinda cupped her cheek. "I'm so glad you're here. But it's not going to be easy, baby; Alexi is still furious about the photograph. Just stay out of his way, and we'll hope for the best."

Fleur saw the shadows under her mother's eyes and felt the faint tremor in her hand. "I'm sorry about the photo. Really I am. I didn't want to make trouble for you."

"I know you didn't. It's just that he's been impossible ever since Solange got sick. The truth is, I'm glad the old bitch is dead. She was getting to be a trial, even for him. Michel is the only one who's really sorry to see her go."

Michel. Fleur had known he would be here. Of course she had known. She just hadn't let herself think about it. Belinda squeezed her hand. "Alexi called him home from school two weeks ago when it became obvious she was going to die. Michel was the one with her at the end."

There was a soft click as the door opened behind them.

"Belinda, did you telephone the Baron de Chambray as I asked? He was especially fond of mother." The voice was low and full of authority. The kind of voice that never has to be raised because there is never a need.

He can't do anything else to me, Fleur thought. Nothing else. Belinda had stiffened beside her, and she found herself feeling strangely protective toward her mother. She looked so fragile today, and she didn't want her frightened. Slowly she turned to face her father.

The newspaper and magazine photographs had not shown how well his fifty-six years hung on him. He was surgically well groomed, his hands and fingernails immaculate, his thin, steel gray hair impeccably neat. He was wearing a necktie the color of old sherry and a dark vested suit that spoke of expensive fabric and matchless tailoring. Next to Pompidou, he was said to be the most powerful man in France, and that was exactly what he looked like, a man of wealth and position, the ruler of an industrial empire, the bearer of ancient Russian blood.

"So, Belinda, this is your daughter." He gave a small, elegant snort. "She dresses like a peasant."

That son of a bitch. Fleur thrust up her chin. "At least I don't have the manners of one!" She spoke English deliberately. Indiana English. Strong, clear, and contemptuous.

There was a quick intake of breath from Belinda, but Alexi showed no reaction at all to Fleur's impertinence other than to let his eyes slowly drift down over her, taking his time, searching for flaws, telltale signs of weakness. She had never felt bigger, uglier, more awkward, but she held her ground, matching him stare for stare.

From her position at Fleur's side, Belinda watched the duel that was taking place before her, and experienced a sudden rush of pride. This was her daughter: strong, full of spirit, achingly beautiful. Let Alexi compare her with his son.

Belinda waited for him to see the resemblance, and then knew the exact moment when it happened. Her hands fell still at her sides, and for the first time in longer than she could remember, she felt calm in his presence. When he finally looked her way, she gave him a small, triumphant smile.

It was Flynn's face Alexi confronted in Fleur, the young, unblemished Flynn, with his features softened and transformed, made beautiful for his daughter. Her face had the same strong nose and wide, elegant mouth, the same high forehead. Even her eyes bore his mark in their shape and generous spacing. Only the green-gold color was Fleur's own. Without speaking a word, he turned on his heel and left the salon.

Fleur stood at the window of her mother's bedroom and watched Alexi pull away from the house in a chauffeured Rolls. The silver car glided down the drive and through the great iron gates out onto the Rue de la Bienfaisance. The Street of Charity. What a stupid name! There wasn't any charity here, just an awful man who hated his own flesh and blood. Maybe if she had been tiny and pretty—But that was ridiculous. Fathers were supposed to love their daughters no matter what they looked like. She gazed over at Belinda napping on the bed and thought about making a noise to wake her up so she wouldn't have to be alone any longer with this heavy weight in her chest that seemed to be growing bigger by the minute. But Belinda looked so frail curled on the bed, and there was still dinner to get through.

She had to stop thinking about how awful her father had been or she would start crying again, and she was seventeen now, too old for baby tears. Slipping into a pair of comfortable loafers, she crept out of the bedroom and crossed her mother's sitting room into the hallway. A few minutes' exploration revealed a back staircase that led down into the garden. As her eyes grew accustomed to the sunlight, she forced herself to concentrate on the geometrically laid out beds of shrubbery and flowers. She was lucky to have been sent away. Think what it would have been like to be raised by someone who kept such neat gardens. The gardens at the *couvent* were better. At the *couvent* a cat could sleep in the flower beds. Lots of cats. And there were weeds, and toads, and . . .

Dammit, dammit, dammit. She swiped at her eyes with the sleeve of her sweater. She was seventeen years old and crying like a little kid. How could she have been so stupid to let even a tiny part of her believe that it would be different? What did she think was going to happen? Did she think he was going to be like the boys of Châtillon-sur-Seine? Did she think he was going to take one look at her and fall down on his knees and beg forgiveness?

She took a deep breath and tried to distract herself with her surroundings. A long, T-shaped building sat at the back of the grounds, gray stone like the house, but only one story and without windows. It looked like some kind of vast garage, and yet it was landscaped with manicured shrubbery and a row of stone urns. With one last swipe at her eyes, she walked down the path that led to it. When she found the door at the side unlocked, she let herself in.

It was as if she had wandered into a great jewel box. The inside was like nothing she had ever seen, and she stood unmoving as she gazed around her. The floor was of gleaming black marble, the walls and ceiling covered with black watered silk. From the ceiling, small, recessed spotlights shone down in starry clusters like a Van Gogh night sky, each cluster lighting one of several dozen of the most beautiful automobiles she had ever seen.

Their highly polished finishes reminded her of old gemstones

—rubies, emeralds, amethysts, and sapphires. Some of the automobiles rested on the marble floor, but most of them sat on platforms of varying heights, so they seemed to be suspended in the air like a handful of jewels flung into the night and frozen in time before they could fall to the floor.

She walked further into the room, noticing as she moved closer that each car was labeled with an engraved silver plaque set into a slim column of Lucite. She walked among them, the heel plates of her loafers clicking on the black marble floor. Isotta-Fraschini Type 8, 1932 . . . Stutz Bearcat, 1917 . . . Rolls-Royce Phantom I, 1925 . . . Mercedes-Benz SSK, 1928 . . . Hispano-Suiza Type 68, 1931 . . . Bugatti Brescia, 1921 . . . Bugatti Type 13, 1912 . . . Bugatti Type 59, 1935 . . . Bugatti Type 35 . . .

She realized that all of the automobiles grouped in the center wing of the T-shaped room bore the distinctive red oval of the Bugatti. Then she noticed a brightly illuminated platform somewhat larger than the rest, positioned in the exact center of the room. It was starkly empty. Curious, she walked over to read the label at the corner of the platform.

BUGATTI TYPE 41 ROYALE. . . .

"Does he know you're here?"

She spun around and found herself gazing at the most beautiful young man she had ever seen. He was not much more than a boy really, with hair that looked like fine yellow silk and small, delicately formed features. Dressed in a faded green pullover and a pair of rumpled chinos fastened at the waist with an oversized cowboy belt, he was short—the top of his head looked as though it would barely reach her chin—and small-boned as a woman, with long, tapered fingers whose nails had been bitten to the quick. Even from where she was standing she could see dark shadows smudged in the hollows beneath his eyes, eyes that were exactly the same brilliant shade of blue as the first spring hyacinths.

"Who are you?" she demanded. But she knew the answer. She would have known him anywhere. It was as if someone had stamped Belinda's face on a young man. Her old bitterness rose up like bile in her throat.

He nibbled on the remnants of a thumbnail. "I'm Michel. I didn't mean to spy." He gave her a sad, sweet smile. "You're mad at me, aren't you?"

94

"I don't like sneaks."

"I wasn't really sneaking, but I guess that doesn't matter. Neither of us is supposed to be in here. He'd be pissed if he found out."

His English was as American as hers. "I couldn't care less," she said belligerently. "He doesn't scare me at all."

"That's because you don't know him."

"I guess some of us are luckier than others." She made the words as nasty as she could.

"I guess." He walked over to the door and began flicking off the ceiling lights from the panel of switches. "You'd better go now. I have to lock up before he finds out we've been in here."

She took her time to show him that he couldn't order her around, and when she finally reached the door, she glared down at him. "I'll bet you do everything he tells you to do, don't you? You look like that kind of person to me. A scared little rabbit."

He didn't say anything. She turned her back and walked outside, hating him for being so tiny and pretty, for looking as if a puff of air would blow him away. She thought about all those years she had worked so hard to be the bravest and the fastest and the strongest. The joke certainly was on her, except it didn't seem very funny.

With Fleur gone, Michel stood motionlessly. He shouldn't have let himself hope that he and his sister would be friends, but he had wanted it so much, wanted something that would help fill one small part of the aching chasm left inside him by his grandmother's death.

His grandmother had raised him. She said he was her chance to make up for past mistakes. She was the one who had tried to explain to him how it was with his parents. One night she had overheard Belinda screaming the news of her pregnancy at Alexi, telling him she hated him for it and would give no more love to the child she was carrying than he was giving to the tiny baby abandoned at the Couvent de l'Annonciation. His grandmother told him how his father had laughed at Belinda's threats, saying he didn't believe for a moment that she would be able to resist her own flesh and blood. This baby, he told her, would make her forget the other one.

But his father had been wrong. Solange had been there the first time Michel had been brought to his mother after his birth. Belinda had turned away from him, and she had been turning

95

away ever since. It was his grandmother who had held him, his grandmother who had finally negotiated the uneasy truce between his parents. To spare the Savagar family embarrassment, Belinda agreed to be seen in public with her son; in return, she was permitted to visit her daughter twice a year. But the truce did not affect the relationship between Belinda and Michel. She told him he was his father's child, and then looked past him as if he were invisible.

Even as a small boy, Michel had understood that all the trouble in his family had somehow happened because of his sister, the mysterious Fleur. For years he had tried to learn about Fleur, but if his grandmother knew why she had been sent away, she had never told him, and now she had carried the secret to her grave.

He knew he should be glad his grandmother was finally free from the pain that had consumed her final days, but selfishly he wanted her back. He wanted her puffing away on her lipstick-stained Gauloise and stroking his hair as he knelt in front of her, telling him how much he meant to her, how special he was, bestowing on him all the love that the others in the house on the Rue de la Bienfaisance denied him.

He looked around distastefully at the classic automobiles that were his father's passion. Sometimes he came here to try to find a bond with his father, but the cars were lifeless pieces of the past, cold like Alexi. Michel's own passions were far different.

Leaving the garage, he walked across the garden to the kitchen stairs that led to his own rooms in the back attic of the house. They were rooms he had selected for himself, gradually transporting his belongings up the stairs over a period of months until no one remembered how it was that the heir to the Savagar fortune came to be living in the attic. When he reached the top, he dug into his pocket for the key. As always, he felt a sense of homecoming as he unlocked the door.

As soon as he was inside, he stripped off his clothes. The room was even more orderly than usual because, in the back of his mind, he had thought that he might bring his sister here to see it. Clad only in his briefs, he pulled on a collarless 1940s Van Heusen shirt that he had found in a used clothing store in Boston not far from the expensive prep school he attended. Without bothering to secure any but the last two buttons, he lay down on his bed and, locking his hands behind his head, gazed

96

up at the enormous white parachute he had hung on the ceiling to serve as a canopy to his small iron bed. The parachute always made him feel better. He liked the way it rippled in the moving air currents of the room, the way it sheltered him like a great, silken womb. In this room he could be himself, safe from his father's scorn and his mother's neglect.

Hidden from his eyes by the parachute was the sloping ceiling he had painted himself, soft blue with billowing white clouds, their edges blurred so it was not clear exactly where sky ended and cloud began. He had whitewashed the brick walls, turning them into an unobtrusive background for dozens of framed photographs.

Michel never tired of looking at the photographs, and now as he propped himself up on a gaudy assortment of cheap sateen carnival pillows, he let his eyes roam over his collection. Gradually he could feel some of his tension easing. Directly in front of him was Lauren Bacall wearing Helen Rose's classic red sheath from *Designing Woman*. It was a perfect red, not orangey, not muddied by purple, but the sharp, color-drenched red of a thirties lipstick. Next to her Carroll Baker swung from a chandelier in *The Carpetbaggers* clad in Edith Head's wonderfully gaudy sprinkle of beads and ostrich plumes. Above his desk was Rita Hayworth wearing Jean Louis's famous Gilda gown, and by her side Shirley Jones in the deliciously tawdry pink slip from *Elmer Gantry*. From Greta Garbo to Sandra Dee, the women and their wonderful costumes enchanted Michel, making him feel clean and good.

He picked up the sketch pad he kept next to his bed and flipped it open to an empty page. With a few deft strokes of his pencil, he could transform people into whatever he wished them to be. When he was little, he used to create soft, pretty dresses for his mother. He always drew her standing in a park or next to a whirling carousel with her arm outstretched and her hand holding the hand of a very small boy. Now his pen sketched a different female figure, tall and thin, with bold slashes for eyebrows and a wide, generous mouth curved into a smile. Just as he had begun to drape the figure in a swath of filmy fabric, the telephone rang. He reached for the receiver, the unbuttoned Van Heusen shirt gaping open to reveal the bony ridges of his sixteen-year-old chest. *"Allô."*

"Allô, chéri."

At the sound of the voice on the other end of the line, Michel could feel his fingers begin to tremble around the receiver.

"I just heard the wretched news about your grandmother. I'm so sorry. This must be very difficult for you."

Michel's throat constricted at the warm sympathy he heard in the caller's voice. "Thank you, André."

There was a pause on the other end of the line. "Is it possible for you to slip out this evening? I—I want to see you. I want to comfort you, *chéri.*"

Michel settled back into the pillows, closing his eyes for a moment at the thought of André's skillful hands and light, healing caresses. Before André had come into his life, he had been a prisoner of furtive experiments conducted with boys his own age, sordid couplings that had left him feeling dirty and freakish. André had taught him the beauty of two men loving together and freed him from shame.

"I'd like that," he said softly. "I've missed you."

"And I've missed you. England was beastly. Danielle insisted on staying through the weekend even though I wanted to return. Poor Edouard came down with a cold and was impossible the whole time."

Michel winced. He didn't like to be reminded of André's family—Danielle, his wife, and their son Edouard, who had been Michel's best friend until Michel's delicacy and Edouard's passion for football had separated them. He wanted André to be his alone. And soon he would be. Soon André was going to leave his family and quit the position he had held with Alexi Savagar for the past twenty-five years, the job that sapped his strength and made it difficult for him to sleep. Then everything would be perfect.

He and Michel were going to live together in a small fishing cottage in the south of Spain. Michel had dreamed about it for months. In the mornings he would keep house for them, sweeping the terra-cotta floors of the cottage and plumping up the cushions on the chairs and sofas. They would have wicker baskets everywhere and earthenware pitchers filled with flowers. In the afternoons while André read poetry to him, he would create beautiful clothes, sewing them on the machine he had taught himself to use, and at night they would hold each other, making love to the music of the Gulf of Cadiz lapping at the sandy shore just outside their window. "I could meet you in an hour," he said softly.

"*Bon.* An hour it is." André's voice dropped in pitch. "*Je t'adore, Michel.*"

Michel choked back his tears. "*Je t'adore, André.*"

CHAPTER 8

Belinda insisted she dress for dinner. Although Fleur put up a token protest, she was secretly glad that her mother refused to budge and felt even gladder when she saw the dress that was waiting for her. It was the most sophisticated dress she had ever owned, a long-sleeved black sheath, with a design of small, overlapping leaves picked out at the shoulders in tiny black beads. Belinda put her hair up in a loose chignon and then fastened chunks of onyx to her ears.

"There," she muttered, stepping back to observe her handi-work. "Let him call you a peasant now."

Even Fleur had to admit that she looked good, but as they seated themselves at the table, she couldn't tell if Alexi noticed.

They dined on *potage parmentier,* out-of-season white aspara-gus, and *coquilles Saint-Jacques.* It was a silent, oppressive meal, and the only thing that made it easier for Fleur was Mi-chel's absence. She glanced uneasily toward her mother. Be-linda was tense and edgy, drinking a lot of wine but only toying with her food.

Fleur halved a scallop with her fork and then halved it again so it wouldn't stick in her throat. Belinda ground out a cigarette on her dinner plate, and as a servant whisked it away, Fleur fought to control her nausea. If only everything weren't so *white,* she thought. The table was set in white linen and lit at each end by matching candelabra supporting tapered ivory can-dles. Heavy alabaster vases held dozens of full-blown white roses. Their fragrance was cloying as it mixed with the aromas of the food. Even the meal was white—the cream soup, the asparagus, the scallops. Fleur set down her fork. The three of them, all dressed in black, looked like ravens perched around a funeral bier, with Belinda's bloodred fingernails the only spot of color. She reached clumsily for her water glass.

"Since you do not seem to be hungry, Fleur, I will take you

100

to view your grandmother now." Alexi's voice was so unexpected that she jumped.

Belinda's fork clattered against her plate. "For God's sake, Alexi. There's no need . . ."

"It has been a difficult day for you, Belinda. I suggest you go upstairs and rest."

"No, I—I'm not tired. I—"

Fleur couldn't stand the twisted, scared expression on her mother's face, and she stood abruptly. "I'll go with you, Alexi." He nodded slowly. A servant pulled back her chair while Belinda sat frozen, her skin as pale as the white roses in front of her.

The hallway of the great house looked as if it were part of a museum instead of a private residence. As they walked toward the front of the house, their footsteps seemed unnaturally loud, traveling up to the vaulted ceiling where the echoes bounced among the frescoed myths and allegories until the sounds seemed to have lost all human association. Fleur could feel her palms growing moist. There was something really awful about this house.

"While you are here, you will address me as *papa*," Alexi said suddenly. "Do you understand me?"

She stopped walking and turned to him. Even though the heels on her black pumps were low, she was still several inches taller than him. "I understand you very well . . . Alexi." She glared at him to make sure he did understand.

His mouth curled unpleasantly. "Do you really think you can defy me? Do you actually believe I would permit such a thing?"

"You don't seem to have much choice. You need a daughter at your side for the funeral, don't you?" She was trembling now and he could probably see it, but at the moment she didn't care.

"Are you actually threatening me?"

"I've been facing bullies all my life. It's something I had to learn at a young age."

"And is that what you think I am? A bully?"

"No, Alexi," she said quietly, "I think you're a monster."

For a moment neither of them moved. Then he nodded his head slowly, as if they had reached an understanding, and led the rest of the way in silence. Fleur tried to feel some satisfaction—after all, she had stood her ground—but she suspected it wasn't over.

A pair of gilded doors marked the entrance to the main salon. He opened one of them and then gestured for her to precede him. The room was empty of furniture except for a shining black casket banked in white roses that was positioned in the exact center of the polished floor, and a small ebony chair set next to it. Fleur had seen a corpse before, when Sister Madeleine had died, but even so she was struck by the stillness of the figure in the satin-lined casket. Solange Savagar's wrinkled face looked as if it had been molded from old candle wax.

"I want you to kiss your grandmother's lips as a sign of respect."

Her first reaction was an urge to laugh. He couldn't be serious! She turned to tell him that he could go straight to hell and then stopped cold when she saw the expression on his face. She had seen that expression before on the faces of the girls at the school, a smugness that the powerful permit themselves to show only to the weak. She understood then that what he was asking of her had nothing to do with respect. He was testing her courage. He was offering her a dare, *un défi*. And she knew by his expression that he didn't imagine for one moment she could meet it.

Tears stung the backs of her eyelids. The bastard. How she hated him. She hated him more than she had ever believed she could hate anyone. She moved toward the casket slowly, fighting the weakness, fighting the part of her that wanted to run from the silent house, away from the Street of Charity, away from Alexi Savagar, back to the safe, suffocating comfort of the nuns. She wouldn't think. No, she'd think about something else. Mykonos. The boys. God, she was crying. Don't stop walking. If she stopped she wouldn't be able to start again. She was going to show him. She was going to throw his hatred back in his face and watch him choke on it. Let him see what he'd tossed away. Bending over, she touched her lips to the cold, still ones of her grandmother. . . .

There was a sudden, sharp hiss behind her, and then she felt his hands grab her shoulders, jerking her upward. "No!" He uttered a vicious curse and shook her so hard that her head snapped back. *"Salle garce!* You're just like him. You'll do anything to save your pride!" He shook her again and her hair came loose, tumbling down her back.

She cried—not knowing what she was saying—not caring.

102

He shoved her down in the chair next to the casket and rubbed at her mouth with his bare hand, smearing her lipstick over her cheek and his own fingers, wiping away the kiss.

"Let me go, you bastard," she sobbed, struggling to get up. "Don't touch me. I hate you. I can't stand to have you touch me."

His hand on her mouth became less rough, and his grip loosened on her arm. He said something so softly she could barely hear it, but the whispered words sounded like *pur sang*. All of her strength seemed to leave her, and she stopped struggling. Just for a moment. Just until she felt better. He began stroking her mouth with his fingers, and his touch felt gentle. He traced the line where her lips came together. And then, unexpectedly, his finger slid inside her mouth and moved gently along the barrier of her teeth.

"Enfant. Pauvre enfant." He crooned to her as if he were singing a lullaby. "You have been caught up in something you don't understand."

She couldn't move, even though she wanted to pull away from him, away from the finger between her lips. She had to let him understand how much she hated him, but she couldn't find any words. His touch was so gentle. Was this the way fathers touched their daughters? Fathers who loved their daughters?

"You are extraordinarily beautiful," he murmured. "Even the picture in the newspaper didn't prepare me . . ." He gently tangled his fingers in the tendrils of hair that were sticking to her wet cheeks. Only a touch. Not hurtful. "I've always loved beautiful things," he said softly. "Fine clothing. Beautiful women. And cars, especially cars. The older I grow, the more important they become to me."

She felt his hand running along the line of her jaw. What was he talking about? Why couldn't she move? She smelled his cologne, faintly spicy, and he began to speak again.

"As with women, at first I loved them all indiscriminatel but during the past ten years I've become obsessed with onl one—the Bugatti. Do you know the Bugatti?"

What was he asking her? She couldn't concentrate on his words while his fingers stroked her face, casting a spell from which she could not break free. He waited, his eyes staring through her. She shook her head . . . nodded . . . she did not know which.

"The Bugatti is the car of genius," he said softly, "built like no other. The greatest car in the world." The tips of his fingers brushed over the chunks of onyx in her earlobes and pulled gently. Her eyes drifted shut. "Ettore Bugatti called his cars *pur sang,* pure blood, like a thoroughbred horse. I have the finest collection of *pur sang* Bugattis in the world, but I'm lacking the crown jewel—the Bugatti Royale." His voice was soft and loving. It was hypnotizing her. "Ettore Bugatti built the Royale in the thirties, only six of them. During the war a Royale was left in Paris. I was one of three men who hid it from the Germans in the sewers beneath the city. That car has become a legend, and I'm determined to own it. I must own it because it is the very best. *Pur sang,* do you understand me, *enfant?* Not to possess the best is a sign of weakness." He stroked her cheek.

She nodded her head, although she didn't understand at all. Didn't care. The old fantasies were back, catching her and holding her and making her feel soft and warm inside. . . . He had seen her and he wanted her. After all these years, he wanted his baby back. . . .

"You remind me of that car," he whispered. "Except you are not *pur sang,* are you?"

At first she thought it was his finger on her mouth, and then she realized it was his lips she felt. Her father had leaned over and was kissing her. Her father . . .

"Alexi!" It was a shriek, shrill and horrible, the kind of sound that comes from an injured animal. Fleur jumped up from the chair. Belinda stood at the door, her face twisted with anguish. "You bastard!" she hissed. "Get your hands off her! I'll kill you if you touch her again! Get away from him, Fleur. He's a monster. You mustn't ever let him touch you!"

It was the only time in her life Fleur could remember resenting her mother. "He's my father!" she cried. "You have no right!"

Belinda looked as if she had been slapped, and Fleur felt sick inside. What was she saying? What was wrong with her? He *was* a monster. She jerked away and ran to her mother. "I'm sorry! I didn't mean it."

"How could you?" Belinda's voice was almost a whisper. "Does one meeting with him make you forget everything?" Fleur shook her head miserably, but the truth was, just for an instant, she had let herself forget. "Come upstairs with me. Now," Belinda said stonily.

Fleur hesitated, not because she wanted to disobey, but because she had to make her understand what had happened.

"Go with your mother, *chérie.*" His voice slid between them like silk. "We will have time to talk after the funeral tomorrow. We must make some plans for your future."

Belinda's fingernails dug into her arm, making Fleur feel sick and guilty for the sweet, fluttery sensations her father's words had produced inside her.

That same night a silent maid admitted Alexi into a small brick house on the outskirts of the Faubourg St.-Germain. He passed by her without speaking and went into a sitting room where he poured a measure of brandy from a decanter on a silver tray that also held one perfect pear and a small wedge of Roquefort. Settling himself into an armchair, he rubbed his eyes wearily. The day had been far more difficult than he had anticipated.

He swirled the pool of brandy at the bottom of his glass and finally permitted himself to think about Fleur. He should have been better prepared for her. The newspaper photograph had given more than a hint of her beauty, but how could he have prepared himself for the rest? She was a study of contradictions, a child poised on the threshold of womanhood, disciplined and yet unpredictable, completely unaware of her sensuality. The injustice of it was nearly more than he could bear. And the triumph on Belinda's face had been intolerable. How could she have produced such a child for Flynn when the son she had given him. . . .

But thoughts of Michel led him to a path he had no wish to follow. Finishing his brandy, he frowned and rose from his chair. He would deal with Fleur just as he had dealt with her mother in the past. It would take time to do the job properly, but he was no longer an impatient young man.

Upstairs, the bedroom door had not been shut all the way, and a wedge of light lay across the carpet. Alexi pushed on the knob and stepped inside.

She was curled on the bed reading a magazine, the bodice of her plain white cotton slip hanging open where her small breasts did not quite fill the cups. For one fraction of a moment he forgot her name.

"Alexi! I had almost given up on you. Oh, darling, I'm so happy you came to see me."

There was just a hint of desperation in her greeting, which told him that she suspected he was tiring of her. Setting the magazine aside, she jumped up from the bed and ran to him, her pink dust mop slippers padding noislessly on the carpet. She had pale hair, cut straight just below her ears and long, baby-fine bangs. Her seventeen-year-old face was scrubbed free of makeup, and as she lifted her arms to throw them around his neck, she smelled of soap rather than perfume. Everything about her appearance was carefully calculated to please him. He disengaged himself from her grasp. "I'm tired, Anne-Marie."

He could see that his brusqueness had made her uneasy. She backed away slightly, but the smile was still fixed firmly to her face. "Poor Alexi. Let me help you undress and then I'll rub your back with lotion."

"No."

Her smile faded. He could almost see her mind working as she made her way back to the bed, trying to decide how best to regain his attention. When she reached the bed, she sat cross-legged in the exact center, her slip hiked high on her pale thighs so that the crotch of her cotton schoolgirl underpants was exposed for his viewing. He regarded her with distaste. Beneath the innocent garment there were no mysteries left for him, only a flat, almost concave stomach, and the tiny puff of ginger-colored pubic hair that had once fascinated him.

He poured himself a second brandy, something he seldom permitted, and slumped down into an overstuffed chair. She began to toy nervously with the stitching on the comforter, but when she looked up at him, her expression was cunning. "I've been very naughty today, Alexi. I stuffed myself with choco-lates, even though I know they make my skin break out. It was bad of me, but I don't seem to have any discipline." She stretched out on the bed, positioning herself on her stomach with her knees bent, slippers dangling in the air. She wiggled slightly, and the movement hitched up her slip to the base of her flat buttocks. "When a little girl is naughty, she needs to be spanked."

He looked at her with disgust. How stupid she was. This

wasn't the first time she had hinted at such a pastime, and it infuriated him that she thought that kind of perversion would hold his interest, as if his special needs had something in common with the unnatural desires of those sick men who beat women for pleasure. It was his own fault for looking for innocence in the arms of a whore.

Once again he found his thoughts turning to Fleur. As he closed his eyes, he could see her face printed against the backs of his eyelids, so impossibly beautiful, so incredibly innocent. And then, for some unaccountable reason, the image shifted and he saw Belinda—not as she was now, jangled and as brittle as a piece of spun glass—but as she had been during those first months of their marriage when the world had been theirs alone, and life had been full of promise.

Several miles away, Belinda stood in her bedroom looking through the trees at the headlights flickering past on the Rue de la Bienfaisance. There was the soft click of a record dropping down on the stereo across the room and then Barbra Streisand began to sing the theme from *The Way We Were,* emitting the first two crystal-pure notes and extending them. Belinda started to cry.

It seemed that all she had left were memories. She was only thirty-six years old, but already she was living in the past like an old woman. Those sun-drenched, chlorine-scented days at the Garden of Allah, when she had been the woman Errol Flynn loved had somehow become sharper and more real to her than the events of her daily life.

Flynn. He had been dead for nearly fourteen years. How could that be? He had died without ever knowing about Fleur. Tears, muddy from her mascara, trickled down her cheeks and dripped onto the collar of her ice-blue robe. She had never been able to forget those first days in Paris, the days of her honeymoon with Alexi, and the nights in the great bedroom when he had loved her so tenderly. Sometimes she lay in bed and shut her eyes and remembered what it had been like when Alexi Savagar had loved her.

Now he planned to steal Fleur away from her. Her baby. Her beautiful baby sleeping in the next room with her hair tangled in her fingers. Why couldn't he have loved her enough to have forgiven her for Fleur? But tonight she had taken care of Fleur.

Tonight she had protected her baby from Alexi's venom. With one phone call she had changed everything.

Tripping on the hem of her robe, she stumbled over to the stereo and jerked at the arm. The record scratched to a stop. She heard herself whimper, a sound as soft as the mewing of a cat, and she wiped at her nose with the edge of her sleeve. She was so frightened. What had she done with her drink? She needed her drink. After tonight there could be no more drinks.

The glass was on the floor next to the pile of record albums she had pulled out. She sat down in the midst of them and picked up the album that lay on top. It was the sound track from *Devil Slaughter,* the second Caliber picture. She stared down at the picture on the cover.

Jake Koranda. Actor. Playwright—the critics said he was the best of a new breed. Jake, who had showed them all that he wasn't just another pretty face. She loved the Bird Dog Caliber movies, even if the critics didn't. They said Jake was prostituting his talent by appearing in such junk, but she didn't feel that way. Bird Dog Caliber was everything a real man should be— strong, ruthless, able to handle any woman who came his way. She stroked her fingernail along the line of his jaw. He wasn't as handsome as Jimmy, but still, there was something. . . .

The cover photo had been taken from the opening scene of *Devil Slaughter.* It showed Jake as Bird Dog Caliber, staring into the camera, his face weary and creased with dirt, the soft, sulky mouth slack, almost ugly, the pearl-handled Colts holstered at his side. She leaned back and shut her eyes, reaching for the fantasies that made her feel better, letting the bedroom and the sounds of distant cars slip away, until there was only breathing—heavy, moist, hot on her ear. *"It's the end of the trail, Belinda. Time to settle old scores."*

She closed her eyes and felt his hands on her breasts, kneading them, relishing their fullness. *"No,"* she pleaded. *"It's not right. I can't. I . . ."*

Bird Dog Caliber's face grew hard, his hands rough as he shook her. *"You don't have any choice, little lady. We're all alone here and nothing's gonna stop me from having my way with you."*

"No . . . please . . ." She struggled, but Bird Dog was too strong for her. And then he had her on the ground, tying her wrists to a post with velvet cords, ripping off her clothes, strok-

ing her and loving her. His hands were on her and in her and the cords melted away.

"Yes, Jake. Oh, yes. Oh, yes, my darling Jimmy. . . ."

The record album dropped from her fingers and fell to the floor, jarring her from her fantasy. She sank down on the edge of the bed and reached for the crumpled pack of cigarettes. It was empty, and she tossed it down, trying to think where she had another pack. She had meant to send someone out after dinner, but she couldn't remember if she'd done it or not. Everything seemed to be slipping away from her.

She looked down at Jake Koranda's picture again. She wanted forceful love from him. It wasn't fashionable anymore for a woman to have erotic thoughts about rape, but she still thought about it all the time. Rape by the man of her choice, of course. She remembered seeing Robert Redford and Faye Dunaway in *Three Days of the Condor*. At the beginning of the movie, Redford had tossed Faye down on the bed to keep her quiet. While he was holding her down, Faye had gazed up at him and whispered, "Please don't rape me." Belinda had been the only person in the movie theater who had laughed. Robert Redford, for God's sake.

She heard the sound she had been waiting for, Alexi's footsteps on the stairs, but she didn't go to the door at once. First she half filled her glass from the decanter of Scotch on her dresser and then dipped her hand into the puddle of cold water at the bottom of the bucket for the remaining ice cube. When she finally opened her bedroom door, he was already far down the hallway.

"Alexi." He turned, and she saw that his face had a drawn look to it. "I'm out of cigarettes. Do you have one? I need a cigarette." As she walked toward him, her robe slipped loosely down over one naked shoulder.

"You're drunk."

"Only a little." The ice cube clinked dully against the side of her glass. "Only enough so I can talk to you."

"Go to bed, Belinda. I'm too tired to satisfy you tonight."

"I just want a cigarette."

Watching her carefully, he drew out his silver case and opened it. She took her time choosing the cigarette she wanted, as if there were some difference between them, and then, having made her choice, pulled it from the case and stepped past him into his bedroom.

Alexi followed her inside. "I don't remember inviting you in." His voice was hard.

"Pardon me," she said sarcastically. "I forget this has turned into no-man's-land. Or should I say, no woman's land." As she pulled a lighter from the pocket of her robe, she looked toward the bed. "No, that's not quite right either, is it? What should we call your bedroom, Alexi? Kiddie land?"

"Go away, Belinda," he said flatly. "You look old and ugly tonight. Like a desperate woman who knows she doesn't have anything fresh to bargain with."

She shut her eyes. She couldn't let his words hurt her; she had to be strong. She had to concentrate on the awful obscenity of Alexi's mouth covering her daughter's lips.

He took off his jacket and tossed it over a chair. "Don't bore me with one of your scenes, Belinda. I've heard them all. Outraged mother, outraged wife. What will it be tonight? Outraged whore? It has been a long time for you, *non?*"

She mustn't listen to his words. She mustn't think about what he was saying. He was wearing suspenders under his jacket; that's what she would think about. How long had he been wearing suspenders? "I won't let you have my daughter," she said.

"Your daughter? Don't you mean *our* daughter?"

"I'll kill you if you touch her, Alexi."

"Bon Dieu, chérie. I believe your drinking has made you irrational." His cuff links hit the top of his bureau. "For years you have begged me to include her in our family. Isn't that true?"

She thought of his series of teenage mistresses and felt herself losing control.

A smile, thin and cruel, formed on his mouth, and she knew that once again he had read her thoughts. "What a filthy mind you have, Belinda. A gutter mind. Did Flynn teach you to think that way, or is it merely a result of your bourgeois upbringing?"

She fought to keep her voice calm, to remember that he didn't know about the phone call. "Don't be too confident, Alexi. You don't have many holds on me anymore. Or on Fleur. In fact, now that she's older it seems to me things are beginning to reverse themselves."

His fingers paused for a fraction of a moment on his shirt studs. "How do you mean?"

Belinda braced herself. "I mean that I have plans for her, and before you try to interfere with them, you should know that I don't care anymore if the whole world learns that Alexi Savagar has been raising another man's daughter." It wasn't true. She did care. As much as she wanted to shout it to the world, she knew Fleur would never understand why she had stayed with Alexi if she knew he wasn't her father. And she couldn't bear for her daughter's love to turn to hatred.

Alexi laughed. "Is this blackmail, *chérie?* I might be worried except I know how much you like your luxuries. I've told you before that if anyone learns the truth about Fleur, I'll cut you off. You can't survive without my money, Belinda. You couldn't keep yourself in stockings, much less Scotch."

Belinda walked slowly toward him. "We'll see, Alexi. You may find out that after all these years you don't know me as well as you think you do."

"Oh, I know you, *chérie.*" His fingers trailed a path down her arm. "I know you better than you know yourself."

She gazed up into his face, searching for some softness there. But all she could see was his mouth crushed against her daughter's lips. The anger came flooding back to her, the anger, the fear, and that other emotion . . . the one she did not want to name . . . that shameful, burning jealousy.

CHAPTER 9

The day after Solange's funeral, Belinda woke Fleur before dawn and whispered to her that they were leaving for Bunny Duverge's home in Fontainebleau. As they drove through the quiet outskirts of Paris, she quickly told Fleur of her contacts with Bunny since they had met in Mykonos and what had happened as a result.

"I don't believe it," Fleur said for the fifth time. "I really don't. This is crazy." She kicked off her loafers and pushed her feet against the dashboard. The pressure seemed to ease the butterflies in her stomach. "Tell me again, and don't go so fast this time."

Belinda dug into her purse for a cigarette, her eyes darting nervously to the rearview mirror. "Bunny called me the day I got back from Paris," she said. "All she could talk about was you—how extraordinary your features were, how beautiful your hair was—she went on and on. Naturally I was flattered, but her husband is away a lot and I've always had the feeling that Bunny doesn't have enough to keep her busy, so I didn't take her too seriously. Then she told me she'd sent the snapshots she took of you on the beach to Gretchen Casimir. Well, I was excited, but I could just imagine what Alexi would say if he found out. Even though Casimir is one of the most famous agencies in New York, modeling isn't exactly an occupation he'd consider suitable for a Savagar. Anyway, I made Bunny promise to keep her mouth shut so I could have time to think."

"But it's ridiculous!" Fleur exclaimed. "Who ever heard of a model six feet tall?"

"You're five eleven and a half, baby; don't exaggerate. According to Bunny, you have the kind of face and body that ad agencies are crazy about. She should know."

"I think Bunny's the one who's crazy," Fleur said unhappily. "Look, Belinda, I don't understand why we had to sneak away, especially after Alexi said he'd talk to me. I—I think he liked me a little bit. Maybe he would have changed his mind about letting me go to school in the States."

It was the wrong thing to say. Fleur watched Belinda's hands tighten on the steering wheel, and she felt awful. She had tried to explain to Belinda that she'd been tired that night and upset. She told her she hated Alexi just as much now as she ever had —she wasn't so stupid that she was going to let a few minutes of sympathy from him make her forget all those years he'd ignored her—but what was the harm in talking to him?

Belinda wouldn't listen. She said Alexi was going to try to separate them.

"Listen to me." Once again Belinda glanced in the rearview mirror. "For years you've been begging me to leave Alexi so it could be just the two of us. Now I've finally done it."

"You mean you're going to get a divorce?"

"Not exactly a divorce. That would be too difficult right now. It'll be more like a separation. But, baby, it's not going to work if we can't support ourselves. Gretchen Casimir has been persistent, baby. On the strength of the snapshots Bunny sent her, she wants to do some proper test shots of you. I told her it was impossible, that my husband would never agree. She kept calling me. Fleur, she is talking about an astronomical amount of money if those test shots are good."

Fleur didn't say anything. It was all hard to take in. The possibility of not having to go back to the *couvent* was irresistible, but Belinda's schemes seemed impossible to her. Fashion models were beautiful, sophisticated women, not clumsy, tootall seventeen-year-olds.

The Duverge estate lay just south of Fontainebleau. It consisted of a two-hundred-year-old château, a carp pond, and a gallery full of old masters—Bunny Gruben had gotten lucky the day she walked into Bergdorf's for a box of Prestat chocolates and walked out with Phillipe Jacques Duverge instead.

She welcomed Belinda and Fleur and swept them into the house, explaining that her husband was in Saudi Arabia until November so they could be just girls, wouldn't that be fun? Fleur suspected that it might not be, but she didn't mention that to Bunny.

By the end of her first week, Fleur knew that she heartily disliked her hostess. Bunny subjected her to endless lectures on makeup, how to walk, who was who in New York fashion, and went on forever about her years as a model. The longer Fleur spent with her, the bigger and more awkward she felt. Bunny clucked over Fleur's lack of interest in clothes and her uncanny ability to bump into small pieces of furniture. Fleur told her she couldn't help it; she was an outdoors person. Bunny rolled her eyes.

She also disliked Fleur's American accent. "She could have been born in Nebraska, Belinda," she complained more than once. "A French accent is so appealing to Americans." Still, she swore to Belinda that Fleur had *it*. When Fleur asked what *it* was, Bunny waved her hands dismissively and said *it* was elusive, impossible to explain.

The second week she brought in the most famous *coiffeur* in Paris and swore him to secrecy. He circled Fleur, one finger tapping his cheek, and then snipped her hair delicately, a quarter of an inch here, a half-inch there. When he was done, Fleur thought her hair looked the same as when he had started, but Bunny had tears in her eyes and called him Maestro.

To Fleur's surprise, Belinda seemed to be taking everything Bunny said seriously, and she sometimes snapped if Fleur made a joke. Not that Fleur's jokes were all that funny, but she felt nervous a lot of the time, and she thought laughing might make everything easier. She was worried about the future, and she was worried about Belinda, too. Her mother was nervous and jumpy, looking over her shoulder all the time as if she expected Alexi to jump out at her from behind doors. Fleur tried to calm her. "Belinda, the worst thing that can happen is that Alexi will find us and send me back to school. Try not to worry so much."

"You don't understand, baby. If he finds out about Casimir, he'll stop it. He'll try to take you away from me. You don't know him; his ego is incredible. We have to get ourselves established in New York before he finds out. Baby, this is the only chance we're ever going to have."

Fleur got uncomfortable when Belinda talked like that. It was still hard for her to believe that everybody was so serious about this, and she hated the idea that Belinda was pinning their hopes for the future on her. The only good thing was that they were together and that Belinda hadn't had a drink since they'd arrived. Fleur was glad about that. She had started to think Belinda was drinking a little bit too much.

It took the arrival of Gretchen Casimir's favorite photographer from New York to convince Fleur that maybe she should start paying attention to the things Bunny Duverge was telling her. . . .

Gretchen Casimir stared at the photos scattered across the top of her desk. Even though she had looked at them dozens of times in the past week, she still felt the same excitement that had taken hold of her when she had first pulled them from the envelope, that queasiness in the pit of her stomach, a sure sign that she had stumbled upon something important. She owed Bunny for this one. God, did she ever.

Glancing down at the gold Patek-Phillipe watch strapped to her wrist, she realized that she was going to have to hurry if she expected to be ready on time. Her date for the evening was a United States senator better known for his liberal politics in the bedroom than for his unsuccessful presidential campaigns, and she had been looking forward to trying him out for some time. But other than unfastening the top four buttons of her green and turquoise Diane Von Furstenburg shirtwaist, she made no move toward the shower in the private bathroom that opened off her office. Instead, she picked up one of the photographs.

The girl was breathtaking. Hers was the kind of face that appeared maybe once every ten years. Like Suzy Parker's, Jean Shrimpton's, and Twiggy's, Fleur's face would shape the look of a decade. There was a quality about her that reminded Gretchen of Shrimpton and of the great Verushka, although Fleur's look was more innocent, more expectant somehow.

She was staring into the camera, her bold, almost masculine features surrounded by a great mane of streaky blond hair billowing out in every direction. It was a magical picture. There wasn't a woman in the world who wouldn't give anything to look like that. Gretchen set down the close-up and picked up her favorite of the full-body shots. Kentucky Mountain Girl, she called it. Fleur was barefoot, her hair in a single braid, her big hands hanging slack at her sides. She was wearing a plain cotton shift that had been soaked with water so that the hem hung heavy and uneven around her knees. Her nipples were erect, and the wet material defined the endless line of hip and leg more clearly than if she had been nude. The people at *Vogue* were going to be in raptures.

115

Gretchen Casimir was an ambitious, self-made woman who had attended Mount Holyoke on a hard-earned scholarship, worked her way from copyeditor to assistant fashion editor at *Vogue* in less than two years, and then, to the relief of several people at Condé Nast, who knew a rival when they saw one, resigned to start her own business. She had built Casimir Models from a tiny one-room office into an organization that was nearly as prestigious as the powerful Ford agency. But "nearly" wasn't good enough for Gretchen Casimir, and as she openly admitted to anyone who asked, she wouldn't be satisfied until Eileen Ford was eating her dust.

Fleur Savagar was going to do it for her.

As the cab jockeyed for position in the midafternoon traffic, Fleur couldn't sit still. She went from window to window, leaning over Belinda, turning around to look out the back, shoving her face against the scratched plastic panel that separated them from the driver. Everything was dirty and beautiful and wonderful. New York City felt just right to her.

"I can't believe it, baby," Belinda was saying as she stubbed out her fourth cigarette. "I can't believe we got away. God, Alexi will be so furious when he finds out. His daughter, a model. I'd give anything to see his face; he thinks actors are vulgar. But we're not going to need his money, so what can he do. Ouch! Be careful, baby."

"Sorry." Fleur pulled her elbow in. "Look, Belinda, you can see the East River. What a beautiful street!"

The cab pulled up to the curb in front of a luxury highrise. Fleur looked at the numbers cut into the glass above the door and her forehead puckered. She knew Belinda had asked Gretchen to rent something modest for them for the first few months, and this building hardly matched that description. She didn't feel any better as the concierge wheeled their suitcases past the fresh-cut flowers and into the elevator. The last occupant had been wearing Joy.

Her stomach gave a little jump as the elevator shot upward. What if she couldn't do it? What if the test shots had been a fluke? The elevator stopped and she stepped out, her feet sinking into thick celery-green carpeting as she followed Belinda and the concierge down a short hallway.

He stopped in front of a paneled door, unlocked it, and set

their suitcases inside. Belinda went into the apartment first. As Fleur followed her, she noticed a funny smell. It was familiar, and yet . . . She looked past Belinda's shoulder and saw that every surface of the apartment was banked in full-blown white roses.

"No." Belinda's exclamation was soft and muffled, and Fleur had the strangest feeling she had heard it before, that this had all happened in some previous life. The apartment . . . the roses . . . and Alexi Savagar stepping toward them from the center of the room, a brandy glass in his hand.

"Welcome to New York, my darlings."

The Glitter Baby

"All my life I have tried to find my mother, and I have never found her."

Errol Flynn:
My Wicked, Wicked Ways

CHAPTER 10

Alexi pressed his lips against Fleur's cheek. She tried to think how terrible it was that he had appeared just when everything was going so well, but the feeling of his jaw, the slight roughness where it brushed her skin, distracted her. His kiss felt different from Belinda's.

"I trust you had a pleasant flight, Fleur." His gaze swept from the jeans she had tucked into a pair of high leather boots to her old tweed blazer. He arched a disapproving eyebrow, but made no comment.

"What are you doing here?" Belinda's voice was little more than a whisper.

"Quelle question. My wife and daughter strike out for the New World. Should I not at least be here to greet them?" He gave Fleur a disarming smile, inviting her to share the joke.

Fleur actually started to smile, but then she saw how pale Belinda was and once again experienced that funny surge of protectiveness. She slipped her hand into her mother's. "I'm not going back, Alexi," she said. "And you can't make me."

He seemed amused. "Whatever makes you think I would want you to?"

Fleur could feel Belinda stiffen, and she squeezed her hand reassuringly. "I'm going to model for Gretchen Casimir. She's given me a contract."

"It's a very generous one, too," he said. "My attorneys have examined it, and it seems quite fair."

Fleur began to feel a little foolish. "You know about Casimir?"

"Chérie, I do not mean to sound immodest, but there is very little that escapes my notice. And certainly not something as important as the future welfare of my only daughter."

"Don't believe him, Fleur!" Belinda exclaimed. "He doesn't care about your welfare at all!"

Alexi sighed. "Please, Belinda, do not inflict your paranoia on our daughter." He walked over to a small bombé chest where he set his brandy glass down next to one of the rose-filled vases. "Enough of this. Let me show you the apartment. I hope you like it, but if not, I will find you something else."

Fleur couldn't quite manage to hide her surprise. "You found this apartment for us?"

"A father's gift to his daughter"—he gave her a smile that made her feel soft inside—"as a small token of my best wishes for her future career. It is past time, I think, for me to begin to make amends."

Belinda made a small, inarticulate sound, and her hand tightened convulsively around Fleur's.

Alexi stayed in New York for a month, occupying one of the Carlyle's tower suites. Since Gretchen Casimir had managed to stir up a great deal of interest with the test shots of her mysterious new discovery, Fleur began working almost immediately. But when she was free, she spent her time with Alexi. He would show up unexpectedly at the apartment with theater or ballet tickets, or reservations at a restaurant where the food was simply too wonderful for her to miss. Once they took a trip to Connecticut to track down the rumor that a 1939 Bugatti was hidden away on a Fairfield estate.

Belinda asked her to promise never to see Alexi alone. Fleur wanted to refuse, but there was something about Belinda's expression that made it impossible, so she agreed. Although he never specifically included Belinda in the invitations, she went everywhere with them, smoking an endless chain of cigarettes and saying very little. Every once in a while Fleur found herself wishing Belinda would stay home, and then she felt guilty. Belinda thought she had forgotten about all those years Alexi had kept them apart, but she hadn't, not even while she was laughing at one of Alexi's jokes or sampling some tidbit he held out to her on his fork. It's just that she'd finally realized Belinda wasn't completely reliable where Alexi was concerned. Look at how certain she had been that he would object to her career.

One afternoon, Belinda lost a filling in a tooth and made an emergency appointment with her dentist. While she was there, Alexi called to say he was returning to Paris that night and wanted to tell her good-bye. Fleur knew it wasn't a very honorable thing to do after she'd promised her mother she wouldn't see him alone, but she said she'd meet him in the park.

She had dropped hints before, hoping Alexi would explain why he had abandoned her, but he always managed to slide away from the topic. This time she asked him directly.

"It was childish jealousy," he said, stroking the palm of her hand. "The pathetic insecurity of a middle-aged husband deeply in love with a bride twenty years his junior. *Amusant,* is it not? I was afraid you would take my place in her affections, and so after you were born, I simply made you disappear. The power of money, *chérie.* Do not ever underestimate it."

"But I was just a baby, Alexi." She kept her eyes on her lap because she wasn't absolutely positive she could hold back her tears. "How could you do something like that to a baby?"

"It was unconscionable; I suppose I knew that at the time. Also ironic, *non?* It drove your mother away from me far more than one small child could ever have done. By the time Michel arrived, it made no difference." He kissed the palm of her hand, pressing his lips into her flesh as if he were her lover. "I don't ask you to forgive me, *chérie.* Some things are not possible. I merely ask that you give me some small place in your life before it is too late for both of us."

He reached into his pocket and drew out his handkerchief. Then he held it to her nose and told her to blow, just as if she were a baby. His story was different from the one Belinda had told her, but she wanted her father so badly that she didn't care. "I do forgive you, *papa,*" she said, even though it wasn't quite true.

When Alexi returned to Paris, Belinda seemed to come alive. She began to laugh again and to accept invitations, and she stopped smoking so much. Fleur's first cover appeared on the newsstands, and Belinda bought two dozen copies, propping them up all over the apartment. The magazine sold more copies than any issue in its history, and Fleur's career took off like a comet. Belinda began to talk about Hollywood.

People magazine did a story on Fleur, and during the course of the interview Belinda said, "My baby doesn't just shine; she glitters." That was all *People* needed. The cover read, "Glitter Baby Fleur Savagar—Six Feet of Solid Gold." When Fleur saw the nickname, she told Belinda that she was never going to go out in public again. Belinda laughed and said it was too late; Gretchen had hired a press agent to make certain it stuck.

They traveled to San Francisco and the Bahamas. Fleur shot caftans in Istanbul and resort wear in Abu Dhabi. She did her first television commercials and endorsed a perfume that she told Belinda smelled like Solange's funeral. Gretchen's press agent began referring to her as the Face of the Decade, and no one objected except Fleur. Everyone told her how grateful she should be because success had come so easily to her, but each morning while she was brushing her teeth, she found herself looking in the mirror and wondering what all the fuss was about.

The first movie offers rolled in, but Gretchen thought they were unimpressive and advised Belinda to turn them down. Belinda did, but each time, she was depressed for days afterwards. "You'll never know how tempted I was, baby. I've dreamed about us going to Hollywood for so long. But Gretchen's right; your first movie has to be special." Fleur began to think it was all happening a little too quickly, but she took a deep breath and held on tight.

Time put her on its cover, headlining its story, "The Glitter Baby is Big, Beautiful, and Rich." This time, Fleur told Belinda, she really meant it—she was never going out in public again!

The *Time* headline dramatized another change that neither Fleur nor Belinda was prepared to deal with—the responsibility for managing the huge sums of money Fleur earned. At first they were merely grateful that their worries over money had come to nothing, but gradually they learned that managing money required skills neither of them possessed.

"What should we do?" Belinda wailed, her hands fluttering helplessly over a stack of papers. "I'm not good with figures, and everybody gives us different advice. Tax shelters, real estate, stocks and bonds—it's all so complicated. Long term. Short term. Adjust for inflation. Honestly, baby, the one good thing I'll say about Alexi is that he never made me bother with any of this."

Fleur tried to help, but she was too busy with her job to spend the time required to understand the complexities of her own finances. Belinda began giving her a long list of questions to ask Alexi when they talked on the telephone, and his answers were so succinct and so helpful that they gradually began to rely more and more on his advice until they finally dumped the entire matter into his capable hands and left themselves with the pleasant task of spending the money rather than worrying about how to invest it.

Although Fleur didn't talk too much about it, especially not to Belinda, she found the actual work of modeling dull. Still, she decided it was a small price to pay for the joy of being part of New York. The whole city was a whirling kaleidoscope of colors and sensations that seemed to have been created just for her. She sank her teeth into the Big Apple and gobbled it up in great big bites. Tucking the streaky blond hair that had become her trademark beneath a Yankees cap, she tromped with the tourists to the top of the Statue of Liberty, devoured Nathan's hot dogs by the dozen, and made every new piece of slang she heard her own. New York, New York, really was a hell of a town! She sang every song to a rock beat, and then threw in a tap dance for good measure. She was in love, and the whole city seemed to love her right back.

"A little farther to the right, sweetheart."

She tipped her head and smiled into the camera. Her neck hurt, and she had cramps from starting her period that morning, but Cinderella hadn't whined at the ball just because her glass slippers pinched a little, and neither did she.

"Beautiful. That's beautiful, honey."

She was sitting on a stool in front of a small table with a mirrored top, which was elevated like an easel. Her champagne silk blouse was open at the throat, revealing a magnificent string of square-cut emeralds. Below the waist and out of camera range she wore cut-off jeans, patched at the front, and a pair of pink rubber shower thongs.

The photographer leaned back from his camera. "Her eyebrows need to be fixed."

The makeup man jumped up from his stool and handed her a tiny comb, then he dabbed at her nose with a small, clean sponge. She leaned forward over her reflection and combed her thick brows back into place. She used to find things like eyebrow combs funny, but she didn't think about them much anymore.

"Nancy, has the dress arrived yet?" Out of the corner of her

125

eye, Fleur saw the art director hang up the telephone and call over to the stylist.

The girl shook her head. "Not yet."

Fleur gave her a sympathetic smile. The mix-up with the dress had been bothering Nancy all morning. As a stylist, it was her responsibility to locate clothes and accessories, to have them ready, and to keep them looking neat throughout the shooting. If a hem was too long, she fastened it up with double-sided tape. If a pair of slacks were too baggy at the hip, she gathered up the excess material in the back and secured it with T-pins, metal clamps, or even clothespins. The beautiful clothes of the magazine pages, Fleur had often thought, were like false-fronted buildings on a movie set.

Nancy put her hand inside the collar of the champagne blouse and checked the piece of Scotch Tape she had stuck to Fleur's neck to raise the height of the emerald necklace. "I'm really sorry about the mix-up," Nancy said. "They promised the messenger service would pick it up by ten."

The art director slammed down the Styrofoam coffee cup he had just picked up. "Shit. They've had an hour. Call those fucks back and tell them to get their asses in gear."

Fleur glanced over at the folding wooden chair where Belinda was reading a magazine. Sure enough, she was frowning. Belinda hated it when anyone swore around Fleur.

"I've already got two rolls on the emeralds," the photographer announced. "As long as we've stopped anyway, do you want to take a break now?"

The art director nodded. "We'll take ten and then do the sapphires in the Galanos. Nancy, after you finish with Fleur, show me what you brought with you in case the dress doesn't make it."

Unfastening the bottom buttons of the blouse, Fleur got up and padded across the bare parquet floor of the studio, stepping around Nancy's ironing board and into a tiny, curtained cubicle, where she changed into her own open-necked gauze shirt. With the blouse and the emeralds once again in Nancy's safekeeping, she poured herself a cup of coffee and wandered over to Belinda, who was studying a magazine ad.

Fleur still felt something warm inside her whenever she thought about how much Belinda had changed. The quiet, nervous gestures had disappeared, and unless the subject of Alexi

126

was mentioned, she was more confident than Fleur could ever remember. Prettier, too—tan from weekends at their Fire Island beachhouse and healthy-looking. She was dressed today in a Gatsby white tank top and skirt with mulberry kid sandles. Her only jewelry was her wedding band and a slim gold ankle bracelet.

"Look at her skin, Fleur." Belinda tapped her fingernail against the page. "She doesn't have any pores. God, it makes me feel ancient. When I look at photos like that I can feel forty breathing hard down my neck." She sighed. "I think I'll schedule two weeks at the Golden Door next month."

Fleur leaned over and looked at the photograph more closely. It was an ad for one of the more expensive cosmetics lines, showing a close-up of an exotic big-eyed brunette dressed in red satin. "Belinda, don't you know who that is?"

"No. Should I?"

"It's Annie Holman."

"The name doesn't mean anything to me."

"Don't you remember? A couple of months ago. The Bill Blass layout we did together." Belinda continued to look blank. "Mother, Annie Holman is thirteen years old!"

Belinda gave a weak laugh. "It's no wonder every woman over thirty in this country is depressed. We're competing with children."

Fleur smiled, but then she wondered if that was the way women felt when they looked at her photographs. Was she earning eight hundred dollars an hour to make people feel bad?

"Telephone, Fleur. Paris," Nancy called out.

Fleur forgot about the magazine ad as she dashed for the phone. *"Allô, papa!"* She turned her back to Belinda.

"How is my glitter baby?"

She wrinkled her nose. "Fine, and don't tease me. You know I hate that name."

"I'm sorry," Alexi said. "I couldn't resist. You are so infinitely teasable."

"How did you find me?"

"Gretchen gave me your number. I wanted to tell you that you will find a surprise waiting for you when you get home today. An early birthday present. It is a small engraving I found. The girl reminds me of you."

Fleur frowned. "You said you were going to give me my present when you came to New York."

"I know I said that but . . . I'm afraid I have bad news."

She knew what he was going to say. Why had she been so sure this time that it wouldn't happen? "You're not coming."

"I'm sorry, *chérie*. Something unanticipated . . . Perhaps next month. If you could come to Paris, it would be different. But as it is . . ."

She twisted the telephone cord around her fingers and tried to sound casual. "Maybe I could. I don't have to work on Monday. Maybe I could fly over for the weekend."

"You know that is impossible, *chérie*. I will not go against your mother's wishes, and she has made it painfully clear that you are not to come to Paris."

"I'll be nineteen next month. I'm not exactly a child."

"I forbid it, *chérie*. Unless your mother gives her approval, I can not allow you to visit me here. We must wait until I am able to get to New York."

"But that could be months. It's really not fair. I don't want . . ." She stopped and then began again, more calmly. "This is the third time you've canceled, Alexi." She knew he didn't like it when she called him by his first name, but she didn't care.

"I realize that," he said, a trace of chill in his voice. "And you must believe that it pains me even more than it pains you. If your mother would be reasonable, then perhaps we would not be put in this situation."

"I'll talk to her again."

"You can try, *chérie,* but I think you know it will be useless. Your mother is a bitter woman. She is using you to hurt me."

Fleur said nothing. She hated it when Alexi criticized Belinda, even though she and Belinda had argued about this very issue several times already.

"Tell me, Fleur," he went on. "How is she? How is her drinking?"

Fleur flattened the worn pink rubber toe of her shower thong against the leg of the telephone table. "I've told you before—she doesn't drink anymore."

"Not that you know about anyway. Watch her, *chérie*. Watch her for me."

Across the room Belinda tossed down her magazine and walked over to the bathroom. Once inside, she locked the door and closed her eyes, then leaned her cheek against the cool, white-painted wall. Even though she hadn't been able to hear the conversation, she could guess what was being said. She wasn't surprised; in fact she had been expecting it.

It had taken her a while to realize that Alexi was deliberately planning trips to New York to be with Fleur and then canceling them, that it was all part of his plan. Tonight Fleur would beg her for permission to go to Paris, and Belinda would refuse. Although Fleur probably wouldn't say it, she would think Belinda was being neurotic and unreasonable, a jealous mother keeping her daughter separated from a sweet, loving daddy. Damn.

She opened her eyes and saw that next to the bathroom mirror someone had written in neat block letters, "Elizabeth Cady Stanton lives." Beneath it, in a different handwriting, was the addition, "And she's screwing Sigmund Freud." Belinda smiled grimly to herself. Freud would have a field day with this one.

To give Fleur credit, she had held out longer than Belinda had expected, and even now she maintained a small trace of reserve with him. Belinda knew that he sensed it and didn't like it, but there wasn't much he would do about it. He called Fleur several times a week, sent her gifts calculated to make her feel his presence, and kept himself geographically distanced from her. Belinda knew she had to keep Fleur away from Paris, where Alexi would be in control. Here she was in a better position to protect her. But how could she explain her reasons? Your father—who, by the way, doesn't happen to be your father—is seducing you? Fleur would never believe it.

Fleur tried to hide her disappointment as she hung up the phone. She had really thought it was going to work out this time. She wanted to see Alexi. She needed to. Hearing a small sound behind her, she turned to see a young man in jeans and an NYU T-shirt holding out her coffee. He was the photographer's assistant, a boy named Chris Malino, and he was the reason she had been looking forward to the shoot today.

"Thanks." She took the cup from him and gave him what she hoped was her friendliest, most encouraging smile. He was still shy with her, like so many of the young men who were near her own age. It was so frustrating. She was the same person she had always been, but only the older ones, or the ones who were celebrities themselves, didn't seem to be intimidated. They intimidated her, however, and she only went out with them when Gretchen and Belinda forced her, which was a lot more often than she liked.

What she really wanted was a chance to go on a regular date where she could wear jeans instead of designer gowns and talk about things other than agents and contracts and who was in town, and where there were no photographers from *Women's Wear Daily.* But the kind of men who went on dates like that weren't making a habit of asking her out; they probably thought she wouldn't accept if they did. With Chris Malino, she had made up her mind to change all that. No guts, no glory. It was her favorite new expression.

She had liked him from the first time they had worked together shooting a swim suit ad at Montauk in March. During their breaks he brought her blankets and hot cups of tea. She asked him about himself, and he finally loosened up enough to tell her about the classes he was taking in filmmaking. She liked watching him while he talked. With his shaggy sandy hair and irregular features, he wasn't as handsome as the male models she worked with, but he appealed to her while they didn't. Something about his open, friendly face made her feel good inside.

"How's school going?" she asked. It was a less than imaginative opening, but the best she could come up with on the spur of the moment.

He shrugged, and she could tell he was trying to act casual, as if she were just another one of the girls in his classes. She liked that. "Same old stuff."

"Like what?"

"You know. Reading Kracauer and studying the Russians. *Potemkin* frame by frame. That kind of thing. You know."

She didn't know, but she nodded her head anyway. "I brought back the Bazin essays that you loaned me."

His face brightened with enthusiasm and he gave up any pretense of acting casual. "What did you think?"

"They're sort of difficult when you don't know much about film aesthetics, but it was good for me to read something challenging. Since I finished working with my tutor, I've been letting my brain turn to oatmeal."

He stuck his thumb into the pocket of his jeans and then pulled it back out again. "You like the Jets?"

For a moment she didn't know what he was talking about. "Oh, the football team!" *Way to go, Fleur. Now you really sound like an idiot.* "I don't know too much about football. In France, everything is soccer. But I'd like to learn," she added quickly, "if somebody had the patience to explain it to me." *Smile, stupid, smile. And don't be so big.* She eased herself down into one of the folding chairs. It creaked as she sat.

"That's right, you're French. I forgot because you don't have an accent." He looked down at the light meter he was holding in his hand. "Listen, Fleur, I have tickets for a Jets game two weeks from Sunday. I mean, I'll understand if you have other things going on; I know you've got a lot of guys asking you out but . . ."

"I don't," she said quickly, hopping back up from the chair. "I know everybody thinks I do—that everybody's asking me out. But it's not true."

"Well, I mean, I see your picture in the paper all the time with movie stars and Kennedys and everybody."

"Those aren't really dates. Gretchen and my mother arrange most of that for publicity."

"Does that mean you'd like to go with me?"

Fleur grinned. "I'd love to."

They were smiling at each other when Belinda appeared beside her. "Darling, Nancy wants you. You have to get ready."

"Okay." Fleur nodded at Chris. "I'll read up on football before the game."

"What game is that, baby?" Belinda's manner was politely inquisitive.

"The Jets game, Mrs. Savagar," Chris replied. "They're playing the Steelers two weeks from Sunday, and Fleur said she'd go with me."

"Did you, baby?" Belinda's forehead puckered with concern. "I wish you'd checked with me first. I'm afraid you're going to have to disappoint Chris. We already have plans for that weekend. It's your birthday, remember?"

Fleur had forgotten. Gretchen Casimir was throwing a party for her at P. J. Clarke's, and her escort for the evening was already arranged—Shawn Howell, a twenty-two-year-old film star with an IQ that matched his age. On their first date he had spent the evening complaining that everybody was "out to screw him," telling her in excruciating detail how he had

131

dropped out of high school because all the teachers were creeps and faggots. Afterwards, she had begged Gretchen not to arrange any more dates with him, but Gretchen had been adamant. Business was business, and Shawn Howell was hot.

When she tried to discuss her feelings with her mother, Belinda had been as mystified as if she had suddenly begun speaking Arabic. "But, baby, he's a star. Just being seen with him makes you twice as important. My goodness, there's not a girl in America who wouldn't do anything to be in your shoes."

When she complained that he kept trying to put his hand under her skirt, Belinda had smiled. "He's a famous man, baby. Celebrities are different from ordinary people. They don't have to follow the same rules. I'm sure you can handle him."

Fleur could see disappointment written all over Chris's face, and she knew it was exactly the way her face looked, too. "But, Belinda," she protested, "the party is Saturday night, and the game isn't until Sunday. We can still go."

Belinda squeezed her hand. "I don't think that would be a very good idea. You'll be out late, and you need your rest. I'm sorry, Chris. Maybe some other time."

"Sure, Mrs. Savagar." He nodded at Fleur. "Some other time."

Fleur nodded back. "Sure." But there wasn't going to be another time, and she knew it. It had taken all of Chris's courage to ask her out once, and he'd never do it again.

It was evening before Fleur had an opportunity to talk to her mother about what had happened. Belinda had gotten rid of the antiques and brocade that had originally been in the apartment and decorated it in a starkly contemporary style, as different from the house on the Rue de la Bienfaisance as she could manage. The living room walls were covered with buff suede. Ficus trees grew in pots in the corners, casting shadows over black lacquered screens and pieces of bronze sculpture set in great chunks of polished wood. Much of the room was taken up with a pit sofa covered with an assortment of pillows printed with brown and black graphics. Nearby were chrome and glass Mies van der Rohe tables and Wassily chairs with canvas slings in shades of buff and black.

Fleur thought the room was cold and had liked the antiques better. Still, the furniture didn't bother her nearly as much as the long wall that Belinda had covered with window-sized enlargements of Fleur's face. A creepy feeling came over her whenever she looked at them. They were photographs of herself, but then again, they weren't. It was as if the makeup and the clothes had formed a shell that fit over her own body, and that was what the photographers had captured. The photographs didn't seem to have anything to do with her except for making her feel uncomfortably schizophrenic whenever she looked at them.

She heard the front door open as Belinda came back from her dinner party. Fleur had begged off, and for once Belinda had let her get away with it.

"Not in bed yet?" She tossed her beaded purse on the glass coffee table top and sank down on the sofa next to Fleur. She was wearing a lacy white blouse to accompany the summer's current symbol of New York chic, a floor-length patchwork skirt made by Sharon Rockefeller's West Virginia mountain people. Fleur had teased her about the skirt the day she brought it home from Bergdorf's. "Now you can show everyone you have a social conscience while you're eating their beluga." Belinda hadn't found the comment very funny.

"Have a good time?" she asked, leaning over a pillow to peck her mother on the cheek.

"Lovely. Everybody asked about you. Liza Minelli was there. She sang for an hour and a half even though she was a guest. God, does she have gorgeous boobs."

"So do you," Fleur grinned, looking down at her own less than spectacular breasts flattened even further by the too small striped pajama top she was wearing over her cut-offs. "I don't know why I couldn't have inherited your chest instead of Alexi's!"

Belinda reached for her purse and her cigarettes, fumbling at the clasp with sudden awkwardness, and Fleur wished she had kept her mouth shut. "You have an early shooting tomorrow, darling. Did you forget? You'd better get to bed."

"I wanted to talk to you first."

"Is anything wrong?"

"Not really wrong. I just . . ." Fleur tugged on one of the loose threads on the bottom of her cut-offs. She hated arguing with Belinda. It didn't happen very often, but when it did, she always felt guilty. "Belinda, I want to talk to you about what happened today."

133

Belinda sighed and her shoulders sagged ever so slightly. She tossed the unopened pack of cigarettes back down on the table. "Darling, we talked about it in the cab. I know you think it's horrible of me not to let you go to Paris, but I can't help it." She reached over and cupped Fleur's thigh. "I'm sorry. I know what being with Alexi means to you, but I just can't let you go. He's not good for you. I don't even expect you to understand."

"It's not Paris, Belinda. I'm not happy about that, but I can't stand to see you so miserable whenever the subject comes up. I'm willing to let it rest for awhile, even though you're being totally unreasonable about it."

Belinda gazed at Fleur and some of the wariness left her face. "I love you, baby. There's not another daughter in the world who would be as understanding. Sometimes it's hard for me to believe you're only eighteen. I'll make it up to you somehow."

"I'm not understanding," Fleur said crossly. "I just said I'd let it rest." She tucked her legs under her and then she smiled apologetically at her mother. "Matter of fact, I have the perfect way for you to make it up to me. It has to do with Chris."

Belinda looked blank. "The photographer's assistant?"

Fleur nodded. "I really wanted to go out with him, and I wasn't too crazy about the way you told him I couldn't go."

"Chris is a nobody, Fleur. Why on earth would you want to go out with him?"

"I like him," she said. "I like to talk to him. You shouldn't have refused him like that. It made me feel like I was twelve."

"I see." Belinda's voice was chilly. "You're telling me that I embarrassed you."

Fleur felt a little flutter of panic deep inside her. "Of course not," she said. "Of course you didn't embarrass me."

Belinda didn't move, but even so she seemed to have withdrawn from her in some indefinable way. Fleur reached out until her fingers brushed against Belinda's skirt. "Forget I mentioned it. It's really not important." Except it was important. Why was she giving up so easily?"

"But of course it's important," Belinda replied. "I know it's sometimes hard for you to accept the fact that you can't lead the same kind of life that other eighteen-year-olds lead, but you must always remember that you're not like the others, you're special."

The chill, the air of withdrawal seemed to have disappeared.

Belinda reached out to settle a hand over Fleur's wrist, and Fleur felt a rush of relief, as if she had been dangling far out over the edge of a cliff only to be snatched back to safety at the last minute.

"You have to trust me, baby. Let me guide you. I know what's best for you."

Some incautious devil made her whisper, "I know that you *think* you do."

"No, baby, I *do.*" She reached up and brushed aside a tendril of hair that had fallen over Fleur's forehead. "Don't you feel the bond between us, like we're one person instead of two?"

Fleur nodded her head. That was the way she felt. She and Belinda always together. No more separations. No more nightmares in which she was standing in front of the Couvent de l'Annonciation, watching Belinda's car disappear down the drive.

"You have to trust me more, baby. Trust me to do what's right. I have a clear vision for you. You're going to be famous, more famous than you've ever dreamed. You'll never know what it's like to be passed over, to feel invisible."

Fleur gave a shaky laugh. "I'm too big to feel invisible."

Belinda didn't even smile. "I don't ever want you to be unhappy, baby. I don't want you to think I'm interfering in your life. If it's that important to you, call Chris in the morning and tell him you'll go out with him."

It was exactly what she wanted to do, but now it didn't seem right. "I—I don't think . . ."

She felt her mother's lips pressing to her cheek. "I love you, baby. You're my most wonderful baby in the whole world."

She gave her mother a quick, tight hug. She would make it up to her. She would be nice to Shawn Howell at the party. And she wouldn't call Chris in the morning.

After Fleur had gone to bed, Belinda remained on the sofa smoking a cigarette. As she stared at the photographs on the wall, her throat tightened with determination. She was going to protect Fleur from all of them—from Alexi, from nobodies like Chris, from anyone who stood in their way. It wasn't going to be easy, but she would do it.

Feeling the blanket of depression beginning to settle over her, she reached for the telephone at her elbow and quickly dialed a number. A sleepy male voice answered. "Yeah."

"It's me. Did I wake you?"

"Yeah. What do you want?"

"I'd like to see you tonight."

There was the sound of a yawn. "When you coming?"

"I'm leaving now. I'll be there in half an hour." As she began to pull the phone away from her ear, she heard his voice on the other end.

"Hey, Belinda?"

"Yes?"

"How 'bout you leave your panties at home."

She smiled and hung up the phone.

It took her forever to find a cab, so nearly an hour had passed before he opened the door and let her in. He was naked except for a pair of white briefs. As he turned his back to fasten the bolt, she saw the seat was worn so thin that the pale flesh of his rear was visible through the material.

"Hey, babe."

"Hello, darling." She moved into his arms, running her hands up over the hard, young muscles of his back. His kiss tasted stale, like flat beer, as she slid her tongue into his mouth. She felt a tug at her patchwork skirt, and then his hand moving up beneath it. He thrust between her thighs like a kid diving into a grab bag. No finesse, but she had known that from the beginning. Very nice all the same.

"You've got some great body, Belinda," he muttered.

"For such an old broad, you mean."

"You said it, not me." Grinding his crotch against the bunched skirt, he fumbled impatiently with the fastenings on her blouse.

She moved slightly back from him. "Let me do it before you tear the material."

He looked at her through his heavy-lidded eyes. "You mean you wouldn't like that, babe? Gettin' your clothes ripped off by a movie star?"

"Uhmm . . ." Slowly she slid back into his arms. "Maybe we should try it your way, Shawn."

CHAPTER 11

Hollywood didn't know what to do with Jake Koranda. They knew what they wanted to do, but wanting and doing had proved to be two different things. They wanted Koranda staring at a piece of street scum over the barrel of a .44 Magnum. They wanted him using pearl-handled Colts on a band of desperados and then slapping around a big-tit broad before he walked out the saloon doors. They wanted Jake Koranda smart-assed and mean. Two Eastwoods were better than one, anyway you counted it.

Even though Jake was younger than Clint Eastwood and not as good-looking, he had that same rough outlaw image that male audiences liked as much as female audiences. Jake was a real man, not one of those limp-wrists who carried a hair dryer around in his hip pocket. He had hit it big as an actor in the early seventies, playing a drifter named Bird Dog Caliber in a low-budget western that grossed thirty million before the year was over. It was followed by two more Caliber pictures, each one bloodier and more violent than the last, and a host of action-adventure movies that were pretty much cut from the same mold, except they used fast cars instead of horses. Then Koranda got stubborn. He said he needed more time to write his plays.

The moguls tapped their manicured fingernails and stared grimly at the calendar while they dreamed about more Caliber pictures. They could almost taste the bottom line, feel that black ink under their fingertips—a bigger office, a new Rolls. And then they would shake their heads glumly and ask themselves what they were supposed to do when the best action actor to come along since Eastwood wrote plays that ended up in college anthologies? Actors were supposed to be stupid, for chrissake! And Koranda had the same problem Eastwood did— fuckin' actor who wouldn't stay in front of a camera where he

137

belonged. At least Eastwood was practical, but Koranda . . . The fuckin' Pulitzer Prize had ruined him.

When Koranda started to peddle his first screenplay, the moguls turned their backs. "That highbrow stuff is all right for New York City," they told him, "but the American public wants tits and guns." Koranda gave them the finger and went to the Spano brothers, who agreed to produce his screenplay, *Sunday Morning Eclipse,* in exchange for a big-budget cops-and-robbers. The moguls prayed that the picture would go down the toilet. If it didn't, they could kiss their new Rolls good-bye.

The projection room was full of smoke from Dick Spano's cigar and a particularly pungent cigarillo that the assistant sitting beside him was smoking. "Run Savagar again," Spano called out. The assistant looked nervously toward the man slouched in the seat in front of him, and waited for another explosion. For three days they had been running tests, and as of yesterday, Jake Koranda was the only one still holding out.

Johnny Guy Kelly, the film's legendary silver-haired director, popped the lid on a can of Orange Crush and pointed it toward the screen. "Jako, boy, we don't want you unhappy, but I think you left those genius brains of yours in bed with your latest lady friend."

"She's wrong for Lizzie," Koranda said. "I can feel it in my gut."

Johnny Guy took a swallow from the can. "You take a long, hard look at the cupcake up there and then you tell me you don't feel something someplace other than in your gut. The camera loves her, Jako. And she reads her lines real pretty."

"She's a model, for chrissake," Koranda exclaimed, "not an actress! Just another glamour girl who thinks she can hit it big in Hollywood." He swung around in his seat toward Dick Spano. "Did you check on Amy Irving again?"

Dick Spano shook his head. "Irving is tied up; and even if she wasn't, Jake, I got to tell you I'd go with Savagar right now. She's hot. You can't pick up a magazine without seeing her on the cover. She's got her own line of clothes, her own shampoo, her own perfume. Producers have been after her for a couple of years now, and everybody's been waiting to see what she chooses for her first film. It's built-in publicity."

Koranda pulled his leg down from the seat in front of him.

"Screw the publicity. Doesn't it bother her ego that we're not even paying that much?"

"Low budget, high prestige, Jako," Johnny Guy replied. "She's got some smart people behind her, and they've been waiting a long time to find the right picture. They also need a leading man tall enough to play with their girl."

Koranda didn't say anything. Dick Spano exchanged a long look with Johnny Guy Kelly. They both knew from experience that the rough edges of Jake's background had never quite worn off. It was one of the qualities that made him a hit at the box office—audiences sensed that there was a lot of Bird Dog Caliber in Jake Koranda—but it could also make him a real prick if he thought one of his projects was being threatened.

The essential elements of Jake's story were familiar to tabloid readers everywhere, despite the fact that he was fanatical about his privacy and refused to give interviews. Born John Joseph Koranda, he had been raised in the worst part of Cleveland by a mother who wore herself out cleaning houses during the day and offices at night. He had a juvenile police record—petty theft, shoplifting, hot-wiring a car when he was thirteen—but he was evasive when asked how he managed to turn himself around. "Just a punk who got lucky with a basketball," he shrugged. He also refused to talk about his short-lived marriage or his time in Vietnam. He said his life was his own and he didn't owe anyone explanations.

"Sorry, Jake," Spano finally said, "but I'm afraid we've got you outnumbered. We're making her an offer this afternoon."

Koranda uncoiled from his seat and walked slowly toward the door. "You do what you want," he said, "but don't expect me to be happy about it. And don't expect any red carpet welcomes, either."

Johnny Guy shook his head as Jake disappeared, and then he looked back at the screen. "I just hope our cupcake up there knows how to take some heat."

Fleur signed the contract for *Sunday Morning Eclipse* with her emotions swinging back and forth between excitement and a gut-wrenching fear. She was getting more and more bored with modeling, but she wasn't sure she was ready to do a movie. Even though she had been taking acting classes for almost six months, it was pretty evident that Glenda Jackson didn't have much to worry about. Still, she wasn't embarrassingly awful either.

Belinda had no such worries. Her baby was finally going to Hollywood to be a star. *Sunday Morning Eclipse* was Jake Koranda's first screenplay, the most talked-about film of the year, and her baby was going to be the star. She repeated it again and again until Fleur told her she'd throw up if she heard it one more time. Belinda laughed and patted her cheek. Her baby was going to be doing love scenes with Jake Koranda, lucky, lucky baby.

That was the other thing. Fleur didn't exactly share Belinda's fascination with Jake Koranda. In point of fact, he scared her to death, although she neglected to mention that to anybody. There was something so rough about him. She tried to tell herself it was just his movie image; over the years Belinda had dragged her to every picture he'd made, and she had hated them all. He was always slapping women around or drilling somebody in the belly with his gun, and there was something about the way he did it that made her think he might enjoy it. On top of all that, Parker Dayton, her agent in the negotiations with Spano Productions, told her Koranda had been outspoken in his opposition to her casting. As her plane circled L.A. airport, it occurred to Fleur that maybe Jake Koranda was smarter than he looked.

He had written the male lead in *Sunday Morning Eclipse* for himself, a role different from the sort he usually played, although the violent edge was still there. He was playing the part of Matt, an ex-infantryman who returns home to Iowa from Vietnam, tortured by memories of a My Lai type massacre he has witnessed. On his return he finds his wife pregnant with a child that isn't his and his brother caught in a scandal involving faulty building materials and a new school. He is drawn to Lizzie, his wife's kid sister, who has grown up in his absence. Lizzie was the part Fleur was to play. Untouched by either the smell of napalm or the corruption of his own family, she makes Matt feel innocent again. When they get into a playful argument over the best place for a hamburger, he takes her on what becomes a week-long odyssey crisscrossing Iowa in search of an old-fashioned root beer stand. The root beer stand becomes a tragicomic symbol of a country's lost innocence, and a personal symbol to Matt as he discovers that Lizzie is neither as guileless

140

nor as virginal as he thinks she is. Fleur found the screenplay both tragic and funny, but as much as she liked it, she still had the feeling she was being pushed into something before she was ready.

There had been only one battle in the *Sunday Morning Eclipse* negotiations that she had won. She told Belinda that she didn't care what they did about the movie's nude love scene—whether they used a body double or cut it—but *she* wasn't going to do it. Even the thought of it made her feel sick. Belinda spent three days trying to make her change her mind. She told her she was being a prude, that it was hypocritical after appearing in all the swimsuit ads, but Fleur wouldn't budge. Swimsuits were swimsuits, and naked was naked. Belinda finally gave in.

It was actually an old battle between them. She had been asked to do nude artwork by any number of highly respected photographers, but she had always refused, no matter how much pressure Belinda and Gretchen put on her. Belinda said it was because she was still a virgin, but the fact was, Fleur couldn't stand the idea of a nude picture of her going up on their living room wall with all the rest, and the thought of having her naked body blown up to movie screen proportions was even more horrifying.

The limousine dropped her at the front door of the Spanish style Beverly Hills house Belinda had rented for them. She already knew that it had six bedrooms, four decks, two Jacuzzis, and much more space than they needed, but Belinda told her it was important for them to maintain appearances. She also pointed out that they didn't need to cut corners, since Fleur had already earned nearly two million dollars, all of it carefully invested for her by Alexi. When Fleur had mentioned the size of the house to her father during one of their phone conversations, he told her, "Remember that in Southern California lack of ostentation is vulgar. Follow your mother's lead, and you will be a wonderful success."

It was a snotty remark, but Fleur let it pass. She was finally resigned to the fact that the problems between her parents were too complex for her to solve.

A housekeeper met her at the front door and showed her around the two-story house with its terra-cotta floors and sweeping expanses of window looking out over the pool at the back. Not for the first time that day, Fleur found herself missing Belinda, even though she understood why she had booked herself into the Golden Door for two weeks. Although Fleur never said it out loud, she knew that, in a lot of ways, the movie was more important to Belinda than it was to her.

"I have to look my best, baby," she told Fleur over the phone. "Let them see what they passed up in 1955."

Still, Fleur wished her mother was there to help her settle in and distract her from her butterflies.

The doorbell rang, and the housekeeper appeared to announce that there was something waiting outside for her. Fleur looked out the front door. In the center of the driveway sat a buttercream Porsche topped with a giant silver bow.

She raced to the phone, catching Alexi just as he was leaving for a dinner engagement. "It's beautiful!" she cried. "What a wonderful surprise! I'm going to be scared to death to drive it."

"Remember that it is you who control the car, *chérie,* not the other way around."

She laughed. "This coming from the man who's spent a fortune trying to buy the Bugatti Royale that spent the war in the sewers of Paris."

"That, my dear, is different."

"Hypocrite."

The filming had already been under way for several weeks by the time Fleur arrived in California. Although she wasn't needed for another five days, she had arrived early so she could spend some time on the set as an observer before she had to go in front of the cameras. Pulling through the studio gates, she followed the directions the guard gave her to the soundstage where they were filming that day. Even the pleasure of driving the Porsche hadn't calmed her. Whenever she wasn't concentrating on changing gears, she was talking to herself. She had to remember she was just going to watch today. She didn't have to do anything. And even when she finally went in front of the cameras, it wouldn't be anything new. She'd made dozens of television commercials, and she was familiar with the technical aspects of filmmaking. She downshifted into second and ticked off her accomplishments: she knew how to find her marks and stick to them, she didn't argue with directors, she was reliable.

Still she was nervous.

She had dressed that morning in a peony-colored Sonia Rykiel body sweater and, perversely, a pair of pinky-beige lizard strap sandals with three-inch heels. Jake Koranda was tall, but her three-inch heels would just about even them out. Her hair was nearly waist-length now, and she had pulled it away from her face with a set of enameled combs so that it fell long and straight down her back. She was even wearing makeup. It had been obvious to her as she dressed that morning that Fleur Savagar wasn't up to the job, so she had let the Glitter Baby take over.

"Fleur, sweetheart! It's good to see you." Dick Spano welcomed her at the door with a kiss and an admiring look at the long leggy expanse that the knee-length body sweater put on display. Fleur had talked with Spano several times in New York and decided she liked him, despite his rather oily middle-aged looks. He had seemed straightforward to her, and besides that, he liked horses. He slipped his arm around her shoulders and led her toward a pair of heavy doors. "They're just getting ready to shoot a scene. Let me take you in."

Fleur recognized the brightly lit set at the front of the soundstage as the kitchen of Matt's house in Iowa. Standing in the middle of it, she saw Johnny Guy Kelly deep in conversation with Lynn Davids, the tiny auburn-haired actress who was playing Matt's wife, DeeDee. Dick Spano gestured her into a canvas director's chair just behind the cameras and off to one side. As she sat down, she had to resist the urge to sneak a peek behind her to see if her name was stenciled on the back.

"You ready, Jako?"

Fleur watched as Jake Koranda stepped out of the shadows. The first thing she noticed was his impossible mouth, soft and sulky as a baby's. But his mouth was the only thing babylike about him. His walk was loose-jointed with a rolling, slouch-shouldered gait that made him look more like a range-weary cowboy than a playwright–movie star. His straight brown hair had been cut shorter than he wore it in the Caliber pictures, making him look both taller and thinner than his screen image. His features were also rougher, and not quite as handsome in real life as in the movies, or maybe it was just her prejudice. Offscreen, she decided, he didn't look any friendlier than he did onscreen.

Johnny Guy called out for quiet, and the noises on the set

143

stopped abruptly. Lynn stood with her head down, not looking at Jake. He leaned one shoulder against the door frame and glared, all sulky mouth and hard blue eyes. Johnny Guy called for action.

"You can't help being a tramp, can you?"

As soon as she heard the line, Fleur wanted to climb back into the Porsche and drive home. They were filming one of the more violent scenes in the movie, the scene that immediately followed Matt's finding out about DeeDee's infidelity. In the editing room, it would be interspersed with quick cuts of the village massacre Matt had witnessed in Vietnam, shadow images that prod him on until he loses control and lashes out at DeeDee in a macabre duplication of the violence that he'd witnessed. It was Fleur's least favorite scene in the film, unnecessarily violent as far as she was concerned. But what could you expect from a man who had made his reputation with a pair of pearl-handled Colts?

Jake began walking across the kitchen floor, his body radiating menace.

"It wasn't like that, Matt." With a small, helpless gesture, DeeDee touched the necklace he had given her earlier. She was so tiny next to him, a fragile little Kewpie doll about to be broken.

His hand slashed out and caught her by the arm, and then he ripped off the necklace. She screamed and tried to get away from him, but he was too big and too strong. He shook her, and she started to cry. Fleur could feel her mouth going dry, as if she had just swallowed cotton.

"Cut!" Johnny Guy called out. "We've got a shadow by the window."

Fleur eased her grip on the wooden chair arm, but just as she began to relax, she heard Jake's angry voice. It was not all that much different from Matt's, she noticed.

"I thought we were going to try to do this in one take, Johnny Guy. What the hell's going on?"

There was a short discussion, only part of which Fleur could hear. She found herself wishing she hadn't picked today to arrive on the set, and then she began wishing she hadn't picked any day at all. She wasn't ready to do a movie. She especially wasn't ready to do a movie with Jake Koranda. Why couldn't it have been with Robert Redford or Burt Reynolds? Somebody nice. She tried to make herself look on the bright side. At least she didn't have any scenes where he beat her up.

Somehow it wasn't much consolation, especially when she thought about the scenes she did have with him . . .

Johnny Guy called for quiet and she once again found herself squeezing her fingers around the arms of her chair.

"You can't help being a tramp, can you?"

She listened to the same harsh words and watched Matt bearing down on DeeDee, yanking off the necklace. DeeDee screamed and struggled with him. He shook her harder, his expression so vicious that Fleur had to remind herself he was acting. God, she hoped he was acting. He pushed DeeDee against the wall and hit her. Fleur couldn't watch anymore. She closed her eyes and tried to think of something else, but all she could think about was how much she didn't want to be where she was right at that moment.

"Cut!"

Lynn Davids's crying hadn't stopped with the end of the scene. Fleur considered making a dash for the ladies' room, but she didn't know where it was and asking someone would make her too conspicuous. She opened her eyes and saw that Jake was holding Lynn in his arms with the top of her head tucked under his chin. At least that was nice, she thought. Maybe he wasn't as bad as he seemed.

Johnny Guy rushed forward. "You okay, Lynnie?"

Jake rounded on him. "Just leave us the fuck alone for a minute, will you!"

So much for nice guys, Fleur thought.

Johnny Guy nodded and moved away. A moment later he spotted Fleur and she found herself enveloped in a rather comic bear hug, since she stood nearly a head taller than he did. "Now, aren't you just what the doctor ordered for these tired eyes. Pretty as a Texas sunset after a spring rain."

Fleur wasn't fooled by Johnny Guy's good ole boy routine. He had the reputation of being one of the best directors in the business, and she had liked him since she had first met him in New York when he had gone over the part with her. He had seemed sensitive to her inexperience without being patronizing. "Who are you kidding, Johnny Guy?" she smiled. "I heard you were born in Queens."

"That's just a piece of malicious gossip that Herb Ross

spread around. Don't you believe a word of it. Now come on over here with me. I want you to meet everybody."

He began introducing her to the crew, telling her something personal about each one. She tried to concentrate, but the names and faces flew past her too quickly for her to remember them. "Where's that pretty mother of yours?" he asked, pointing out a cable before she tripped over it. "I thought she'd come with you today."

"She'll be here next week."

"I remember her from the fifties," he said. "I was working as a grip then. I saw her once at the Garden of Allah when she was with Errol Flynn."

Fleur looked at him curiously. Belinda had chronicled every movie star she had ever met, but she had never mentioned Errol Flynn. He must be mistaken.

Johnny Guy suddenly looked uncomfortable. "Come on, darlin'. Let me take you over to meet Jake and Lynnie."

That was just about the last thing Fleur wanted to do, short of slitting her wrists, but Johnny Guy was steering her toward them in a single-minded fashion that didn't give her much room for debate. She grew even more uncomfortable when she saw that Lynn Davids still seemed teary-eyed. Fleur touched Johnny Guy's arm. "Why don't we wait—"

"Jako, Lynnie. I've got somebody here I want you to meet." He propelled her forward and introduced her.

Lynn managed a weak smile of acknowledgment, but Jake just looked at her with Bird Dog Caliber's eyes, first studying her face, and then sweeping contemptuously down over the Sonia Rykiel body sweater. Fleur's only satisfaction lay in the fact that her three-inch lizard strap sandals let her eyeball him dead on, and she refused to flinch. An awkward silence followed, broken finally by a young man with several days worth of stubble on his chin. "We're going to have to do it again, Johnny Guy," he said. "I'm sorry, but there was a problem. We've got it fixed now."

Koranda pushed past Fleur as if he'd been shot from a cannon and stalked toward the front of the set. "What the hell is wrong with all of you?" he shouted. "Are you guys going to get your act together or what? We were going to get this one without any problems, remember? How many is it going to take?

146

How many times are we going to have to go through it for you?"

The busy set fell quiet, and then an anonymous voice filled the stillness. "Sorry, Jake, but it couldn't be helped."

"The hell it couldn't!" He punched the air in the direction of the voice, and Fleur waited for him to pull out the Colts. "Everybody get their shit together this time! We're only going to do it once more."

"Easy, boy," Johnny Guy said. "Last time I checked, I was the director around here."

Koranda's voice was cold. "Then how about doing your job."

Johnny Guy was quiet for a moment. "I'm gonna pretend I didn't hear that, Jako, and chalk this up to a full moon. Now let's everybody get back to work."

Fleur slid away as inconspicuously as possible. Temper tantrums weren't new to her—she'd seen some doozies in the last few years—but they still embarrassed her. She looked down at the fat runner's watch with the black plastic strap that she was wearing on her wrist, and then she yawned. It was a technique she'd developed when something happened that made her uncomfortable. She'd look at her watch and yawn. It let people know they couldn't get to her, even when they could.

As she slipped back to her chair, she wondered what Belinda would have thought if she'd seen her idol in action, but then she knew that was a foolish question. *Celebrities are different from ordinary people, baby. They don't have to follow the same rules.*

There was a short delay and then the scene began again. This time she didn't watch, but even so, the sounds of DeeDee's screams were enough. She couldn't relax until it was finally over and Jake and Lynn had disappeared.

After a short break, they began shooting close-ups. A messenger arrived asking Fleur if she'd go see the wardrobe mistress. When she returned to the set, the crew was taking a lunch break, and Lynn and Jake were sitting by themselves off to the side, eating sandwiches. They were both wearing jeans, and Fleur felt like an overdressed outsider.

"Have a seat," Lynn said. "Sorry we didn't get a chance to talk earlier."

She walked over to them. "That's okay. You were a little busy." Lynn frowned, and Fleur wished she hadn't made even an inadvertent reference to the scene she had witnessed.

Jake stood up, balling his sandwich in the wrapper, and Fleur had to force herself not to take a step back. He was the most intimidating man she had ever met. It was probably just his height, she told herself; she wasn't used to being around men who were that tall. She suddenly realized she was staring at that impossible mouth of his again. His front tooth was crooked, with a tiny chip at the corner. "See you later, Lynn," he said. "I'm going out to shoot some baskets."

He walked off without even acknowledging Fleur's presence. There was an awkward pause, and then Lynn held out half her sandwich. "Eat this so I don't gain any more weight. It's salmon with low-cal mayonnaise."

"Thanks." Fleur took the friendship offering and settled into the chair Jake had vacated. According to Belinda, Lynn Davids had come up from the soaps to a small part in *The Godfather*, and then gone on to do a series of second female leads, receiving some critical acclaim for her performances. Fleur judged her to be about twenty-five, with the kind of round-faced, dewy-eyed femininity that always made her feel self-conscious about her own looks.

Lynn was returning the inspection. "You don't look like you have to worry about your weight."

"I do," Fleur said, swallowing a bite of sandwich. "My body wants to be a hundred and forty-five, but with the cameras I can't go above one thirty-five. That's pretty hard with my height. I love bread and ice cream, so it's a problem."

"Good, then we can be friends." Lynn grinned, showing a row of small, straight teeth. "I can't stand being around women who can eat anything they want." They talked for a while about the vagaries of weight, height, and bone structure before Fleur introduced the subject of the film. She found Lynn enthusiastic about the challenge of playing DeeDee.

"Critics say Jake's women aren't as well written as his men," Lynn observed, "but I think DeeDee's an exception. She's foolish, but she's vulnerable, too. Everybody has a little of DeeDee in them."

Fleur nodded her head in agreement. "It's a good part. More straightforward than Lizzie. I'm a little nervous about playing her. I guess I'm not too sure of myself." She let her words trail off. This was hardly the way to inspire confidence in someone she was going to be working with so closely.

Lynn, however, didn't seem to think it was strange. "A lot of actors feel that way at the beginning. Once you get into it, you'll be more confident. Talk to Jake about Lizzie. He's good about that kind of thing."

Fleur grimaced. "From what I've heard, I don't think Jake's going to be too interested in talking to me about anything. I guess it's not much of a secret that he wasn't thrilled about my casting."

Lynn popped the last bite of sandwich into her mouth. "When he sees you're committed, he'll come around. Give him time."

"Oh, I will," Fleur said with just a little more cynicism than she had intended. "Time and a wide berth."

Lynn looked at her sharply. "Jake's the last of the good guys, Fleur."

"You could have fooled me."

"What do you mean?"

"I mean that I wasn't too impressed with the way he handled himself today." And that, she thought, was an understatement.

Lynn was thoughtful for a moment, and then she seemed to make up her mind about something. "Listen, Fleur, Jake and I were an item a couple of years ago. Nothing very serious on his part, but we got to know each other pretty well. Once we stopped sleeping together, we became good friends, and I confide in him a lot. Jake drew on something that happened to me when he wrote that scene. He knew it was going to bring back bad memories for me, and he wanted to get it over with as soon as possible for my sake."

"I'm sorry," Fleur said, hoping she didn't sound as unconvinced as she felt. "I'm not too comfortable with men like Jake."

Lynn's smile was mischievous. "That's what makes men like Jake irresistible."

It wasn't quite the word Fleur would have used, but she let it pass.

For the next few days, she kept out of Jake Koranda's way as much as possible, but even though she tried not to, she found herself watching him when he wasn't looking. He and Johnny Guy sparred constantly, frequently going out of their way to disagree. At first their arguments made her uncomfortable, but then she noticed that the two men seemed to thrive on conflict.

After Jake's outburst the first day, she was surprised to see how popular he was with the crew. In fact, he seemed easy with everybody except her, and other than giving her a brief nod in the morning, he acted as though she didn't exist. She was glad her first scene was going to be with Lynn.

The night before, she studied her lines until she was letter-perfect and then had the housekeeper cue her. Since she had a seven o'clock makeup call, she showered, called Belinda, and was ready for bed by ten. The assistant director phoned her just as she was turning out the light to tell her there had been a schedule change. They would be shooting the opening scene between Matt and Lizzie the next morning.

It was midnight before she was confident enough of her lines to go back to bed, but by then she was too nervous to sleep. She thought about taking one of Belinda's Nembutals, but visions of *Valley of the Dolls* kept dancing in her head, and she decided against it. The last time she looked at her digital clock, it read 3:18.

They were working on the back lot, where the exterior of the Iowa farm house had been built, and Johnny Guy came to see her the next morning while she was in makeup to discuss the opening scene. He explained that she was to look up from the porch swing where she would be sitting, spot Matt standing at the end of the drive and call out his name, then hurl herself off the porch, across the yard, and into his arms. The more difficult part of the scene would be shot that afternoon when they had their first exchange of dialogue.

Fleur listened carefully, but it was hard for her to concentrate. She was groggy from lack of sleep, and she knew she was going to be terrible. It wouldn't be so bad, she thought, if she didn't have to work with Jake on her first day of shooting. She'd seen what a perfectionist he was. No wonder he didn't want her in his film. And she hated her first costume. Although it was actually early May, in the movie it was August and they'd put her in a skimpy white bikini with little red hearts on it and a man's blue workshirt tied in a knot at the waist. Her stomach was bare, and the high cut of the suit made her look like she was all legs.

To show the contrast in Lizzie's nature, they'd put her hair in a loose braid down her back. The hair stylist had wanted to tie a red bow on the end, but she told him to forget it. She wasn't

going to wear bows in her hair, and neither was Lizzie. He
didn't challenge her, but if he had she would have shown him
that Jake Koranda wasn't the only one who could throw a
temper tantrum. That's exactly how nervous she was. Just as
she made her fourth trip to the bathroom, the assistant director
called for her.

Fleur took her place on the porch swing, trying to concentrate on what she had to do. Lizzie hadn't seen Matt yet, but
she knew he was home. She was expecting him, but she couldn't
show it. Lizzie couldn't show a lot of things—how much she
hated her sister, how much she lusted after her sister's husband . . .

Even though she didn't want to, she found herself looking
over at Jake, who was standing near one of the trailers wearing
the soldier's uniform that was his costume at the beginning of
the film. Could she lust after him? It was a stupid question—she
didn't even like him, for Pete's sake. From a magazine article
she knew he was nine years older than she—twenty-eight to her
nineteen—but even if he were nine years younger, he'd still be
too old for her. She yawned and looked at her watch only to
realize that she wasn't wearing one.

He stuffed one hand in his pocket and leaned back against the
trailer, planting the sole of his shoe up against the tire in a sexy,
slouchy kind of posture that looked like his publicity photographs. All he needed was a cigarette in his mouth and a squint
to make Bird Dog come to life. She started to think about lust
again. Lust and Jake Koranda.

It sounded like a headline in the *National Enquirer*.

"Show time, boys and girls," Johnny Guy called out over his
bullhorn. "You ready, Fleur honey? Let's walk it through."

She followed his directions, carefully noting the path he
wanted her to run. Then she returned to the swing and waited
nervously while the crew made the final adjustments. Excitement . . . she had to think excitement. But not too soon.
Don't anticipate. Wait until you see him before you let it show
on your face. Don't worry about anybody watching. Don't
think about them. Just concentrate on Matt. Matt, not Jake.

Johnny Guy called for action. She lifted her head. Spotted
Matt. Matt! He was back! Jumping up, she ran across the
porch, taking the wooden steps in one leap, her braid slapping
between her shoulders. She had to get to him. Touch him. He

151

was hers, not DeeDee's. She ran across the yard, excitement surging through her. This was right. This felt right. She wasn't going to be so bad after all. There he was, just ahead of her. "Matt!" She called out his name again, reached out for him, touched the uniform, catapulted herself into his arms.

He stumbled backwards, and they both crashed to the ground.

There was an explosion of laughter from the crew. Fleur lay sprawled on top of Jake Koranda, pinning him down with her half-naked body, more humiliated than she had ever been in her life. She wanted to die, to crawl away in a corner and die. She was an elephant. A big, clumsy, giant of an elephant, and she'd make herself look like a jackass.

"Anybody hurt here?" Johnny Guy chuckled as he came over and helped her up.

"No, I—I'm all right." She kept her head down, concentrating on brushing the dirt from her legs to give herself a chance to recover. One of the makeup people ran over with a wet cloth, and she wiped herself off without looking up at Jake. If this hadn't convinced him that he was right about her, nothing would. Damn it, what did she care about what he thought, and why wasn't Belinda here? She needed her mother.

"How 'bout you, Jako?"

"I'm okay."

Johnny Guy patted her arm. "That was real nice, honey," he grinned. "Too bad this boy's so puny he can't stand up to a real woman."

She knew he was trying to make her feel better, but it wasn't working. She felt big and clumsy and awful, and she knew everybody was staring at her. "I—I'm sorry," she said stiffly. "I think I've ruined this suit. The dirt doesn't want to come out."

"That's why we have spares. Go on and get changed."

In all too short a time, she was back in the porch swing and they were ready to go again. She tried to concentrate, to re-create the feeling of excitement. She saw Matt, jumped up, ran down the steps and across the yard. *Please God, don't let me knock him over again.* She checked herself ever so slightly and slid into his arms.

Johnny Guy hated it.

They did it again, and she stumbled going down the steps. The fourth time the porch swing bumped against the back of her legs. The fifth time she made it all the way to Jake, but again, she checked herself at the last moment. Her misery was growing by the minute, and she was perspiring through the workshirt.

"You're not relating to him, honey," Johnny Guy said as Jake released her. "You're not connecting. Don't worry so much about where you're putting your feet. Do it the way you did it the first time."

"I'll try." She had to endure more humiliation as wardrobe brought her a shirt that didn't have half-moons under the arms. She turned her back on the two men and headed for the porch swing knowing there was no power on earth that was going to make her throw her body full force at Jake Koranda again. Her chest felt tight, as if she was going to cry, and she swallowed hard.

"Hey, wait up."

Slowly she turned and watched Jake walk up to her. "I was off balance the first time," he said curtly. "It was my fault, not yours. I'll catch you the next time."

Sure he would. She nodded and started to walk away.

"You don't believe me, do you?"

She stopped walking and turned back to him. "Look, I know I'm not exactly a lightweight."

His mouth curved in a cocky, absolutely infuriating grin that looked strange on Bird Dog Caliber's face. "Hey, Johnny Guy!" he called out over his shoulder. "Give us a few minutes, will you? Flower Power here thinks she's got me beat."

"Flower Power!" It was too much! She wanted to slap his silly face. "That's pretty rotten, even coming from you, Mr. Koranda!" Shoving her chin up in the air, she turned to walk away.

"Yeah?" He grabbed her arm before she could go anywhere and began to propel her none too gently around the side of the house away from the crew. "You're the one who issued the challenge, Flower Power. Put your money where your mouth is. I've got ten bucks says you can't knock me over again."

They were behind the house, ankle deep in weeds, before he let her go. How had she gotten herself into this? She shoved a hand on her bare hip, trying to look formidable. "This is ridiculous. I'm not going to get into a wrestling match with you."

"What's the matter? Is the Glitter Baby worried about messing up her hair? Or is she just afraid she's going to win?"

Her temper snapped. "You son of a bitch! You're obnoxious, do you know that? Even more obnoxious than those cretins you play on screen. You really are unbelievable, and I don't have to take this from you!"

He didn't blink an eye. "Ten bucks, Flower. Put up or shut up."

He was baiting her on purpose. She knew it, but all of a sudden she didn't care. In one way or another he had been bothering her for weeks, and now she was going to wipe that stupid smirk off his stupid mouth. "Okay, Koranda. You asked for it." She stepped backwards, keeping her eyes pinned to his.

"I'm scared, Flower. Real scared." He stepped back himself, putting more distance between them, and she could see that he was bracing his weight. A lot of good it would do him.

"I'm trembling with fear, kiddo," he taunted. "The glamour girl might mess up her mascara."

God, she hated him! And she hated his smart-ass mouth! "I'm warning you, Koranda . . ."

"Come on, little girl. Just you try it."

She charged him then, coming at him full force. She dug her feet into the sandy ground, pumped her arms, and ran as fast as she could. It was like hitting a wall.

If he hadn't caught her, the impact would have sent her to the ground, and this time she would have gone by herself. She realized he was holding her tightly against him, and she jerked away, trying to catch her breath. Her chin hurt where she'd bumped it against his shoulder, and her chest was aching above her left breast. She started to lift her hand to rub it, but then she knew she'd die before she gave him the satisfaction of knowing she'd hurt herself. She began to stomp away.

"Hey, Flower." He ambled forward with his worn-out cowboy gait and reined in next to her. "That the best you can do? What's the matter? Afraid you gonna get that skimpy white bikini dirty again?"

She looked up at him incredulously. Her whole body was aching, her chin was killing her, and she couldn't seem to catch her breath. "You are a certifiable crazy person," she gasped. "Do you know that!"

"Double or nothing. And this time get farther back."

She couldn't help it. She rubbed her chest. "I think I'll pass."

He laughed. It was a nice sound, and it surprised her. "Okay, Flower. I'll let you off, but you owe me ten bucks."

He looked so smug that she actually opened her mouth to take him up on his challenge. And then her common sense returned and she realized, whether he had intended to or not, he'd done a nice thing for her. They began walking back around the house in something that bore a resemblance to a companionable silence. "You think you're pretty smart, don't you," she said.

"Haven't you read the critics, kiddo? I'm a boy genius. It's true; read any of them. They'll tell you."

She gave him her sweetest smile. "Glamour girls don't read. We just look at the pictures."

He laughed and walked away.

They did the scene in the next take, and Johnny Guy said it was just what he wanted, but Fleur's few brief moments of satisfaction disappeared as he rehearsed them for the next scene. Still in Matt's arms, Lizzie was to greet him and give him a sisterly kiss. There was an exchange of dialogue, then Lizzie would kiss him again, but this time it wasn't to be sisterly. Matt would pull away, and the camera would show him trying to take in the changes in her since he had last seen her.

She handled the sisterly kiss without any problem. The exchange of dialogue required more takes than she would have liked because her delivery was a little stiff, but she didn't think it was too bad considering the fact that Lizzie couldn't have been all that comfortable either. They broke for lunch and then finished shooting close-ups. By the time they were done, she had perspired through her third shirt, and the wardrobe people had started sewing dress shields in her other costumes.

She was going to have trouble with the next kiss. She knew it, and she didn't have the foggiest idea what to do about it. She'd kissed men on camera, and off camera for that matter, but she didn't want to kiss Jake Koranda.

The assistant director called for her. Jake was already in place talking to Johnny Guy. While Johnny Guy explained the shot, she found herself staring at Jake's mouth, that soft, sulky, baby's pout. The minute she realized what she was doing, she yawned and asked the prop girl what time it was.

"I hope we're not holding you up," Jake said sarcastically.

She gave him a look that was supposed to be withering, and turned her attention back to Johnny Guy.

"What we've got to have here, honey lamb, is a real open-mouth tonsil bouncer. You know what I'm talkin' 'bout? Lizzie's got to wake Matt up."

Fleur gave Johnny Guy a grin and a thumbs up. "Gotcha." Inside the butterflies started a war dance. She wasn't the greatest kisser in the world. One of her dates had told her he thought she was frigid.

Jake put his arms around her, his hands flat against the bare skin just above her bikini bottom, and pulled her close. At that moment, she realized she'd spent almost the entire day crawling over his body in one way or another.

"Your feet, honey," Johnny Guy said.

She looked down at them. They were as big as ever.

"A little closer, baby lamb."

Although her chest was pressed against Jake's, she saw that she had pulled her bottom half as far away as she could. She quickly adjusted herself. With his shoes and her bare feet, he was at least four inches taller than she was.

It's Matt, she told herself as Johnny Guy moved out of camera range. You've been with other men, but Matt is the one you want. Johnny Guy called for action and she ran her fingers over the front of his uniform, then she looked up at him. God. She quickly closed her eyes and touched her lips to his soft, warm ones. She held them there, trying to think about Matt and Lizzie.

Johnny Guy was less than impressed. "You didn't put too much into that one, honey. Suppose we try it again."

During the next take she tried to fake it by moving her hands up and down the sleeves of Jake's uniform. Johnny Guy took her aside. "You got to relax, honey. Forget about the people watching you. All they're thinking about is getting home for dinner. Lean into him a little more."

The people who were watching weren't the problem, but Fleur wasn't going to tell Johnny Guy that.

She talked to herself all the way back to her mark. This was a technical piece of business, just like opening a door. She had to relax. Just relax, dammit! She thought the next kiss was a lot better, but Johnny Guy didn't seem to agree. "Do you think you could open your mouth a little, honey lamb?"

Muttering to herself, she stepped back into Jake's arms and then quickly glanced up to see if he had heard. "Don't look at me for help, kiddo," he said. "I'm the passive party here."

"I'm not looking for help!"

Johnny Guy called for action. She did her best, but when the kiss was over, Jake sighed. "You're putting me to sleep, Flower. Want me to ask Johnny Guy for a break so we can go behind the house and you can practice on me?"

"I think I'll pass," she snapped. "I'm still aching from the last practice session I had with you."

He grinned and then, unexpectedly, leaned down and whispered in her ear. "I got a twenty-dollar bill says you can't wake me up, Flower."

It was the sexiest, most devastating, bedroomiest whisper she had ever heard in her life.

The next take was better, and Johnny Guy said to print it, but Jake told her she owed him twenty bucks.

CHAPTER 12

Fleur arrived home to a house filled with the scent of Shalimar and found Belinda on her way out to the patio, carrying a Chinese bowl brimming with floating blossoms. "I couldn't stay away any longer," Belinda confessed, after she had set the bowl in the center of the patio table and hugged Fleur. "I missed you too much, baby. Besides, I feel wonderful. I'm ready to face them all now. I think I just needed a rest."

"You look wonderful, too," Fleur replied. It was true. She felt grubby in comparison to Belinda, who looked fresh and pretty in a pair of belted linen trousers with a sleeveless red and yellow batik print top.

"Do I look good enough to make them wish they'd noticed me when I was eighteen?"

"You're going to break their hearts. Let me take a quick swim, and then we can talk."

She changed into a suit and swam a few laps, enjoying the sight of Belinda rearranging the place settings the housekeeper had laid out on the deckside table. After a quick shower, she slipped into a T-shirt and shorts, then pulled her wet hair back with a set of lavender plastic combs and padded barefoot outside, where Belinda was setting out pottery plates generously heaped with Fleur's favorite salad, a tangy mixture of baby shrimp, chunks of pineapple, and fresh watercress.

"Give me plenty. I'm starved," she said.

"You're always starved." Belinda's gaze swept down over her daughter's figure. "It's a sin how good you manage to look even without makeup. If I didn't love you, I'd hate you. Now sit down and tell me everything."

Fleur filled in the events of the last week, including some of what had happened with Jake Koranda that day, although she didn't tell Belinda about the kiss. She usually told Belinda everything, and she wasn't quite sure why she was holding back, but she did tell her about the fall and the episode behind the house.

"I knew it!" Belinda exclaimed. "He's one of the biggest names in film, but he understood how embarrassed you were. I knew he'd be like that! You should listen to me more often, Fleur. I'm a good judge of character." Belinda shook her head, smiling. "He's just like Jimmy. Jimmy would have behaved like that, all rough on the outside, but sweet and sensitive inside."

It wasn't exactly how Fleur would have described Jake Koranda, but by now she was familiar with Belinda's conviction that Jake embodied all the qualities of her beloved James Dean. For the first time the comparison irritated her. "He's a lot taller, Belinda. And they don't look anything alike."

"Hmmm. A lot you know. The quality is the same, baby. Jake Koranda is a rebel, too."

"You haven't even *met* him, for God's sake. He's not like anybody else. At least he's not like anybody I've ever known." Belinda gave her a funny, fishy look, and she shut up.

Rosa, the housekeeper, stepped out on the patio. "Mr. Savagar is on the phone." She plugged in the telephone she was holding and set it on the table. As Fleur reached over, Rosa shook her head. "For Mrs. Savagar."

Belinda gave Fleur a puzzled shrug and then, tugging off her earring, picked up the receiver. "What is it, Alexi?" She tapped her fingernails on the glass tabletop. "Well, what do you expect me to do about it? . . . Surely you're not surprised. . . . No, of course I haven't. . . . Don't be ridiculous. . . . Yes, I'll call you if I hear anything."

As she hung up, Fleur asked what was wrong.

"Michel disappeared from the clinic, and Alexi wanted to know if he'd contacted me."

"You don't seem too concerned."

Belinda clipped her earring back on and pushed aside a stalk of watercress with her fork as she looked for another shrimp. "You know how I feel about Michel. I know I shouldn't admit it, but I can't help feeling a certain satisfaction when I see what a disappointment he's been to Alexi. It must be obvious, even to your father, that he gave away the wrong child. My daughter is beautiful and successful. His son is a homosexual weakling."

Fleur wasn't hungry anymore, and she set down her fork. Several months ago, Michel had been discovered in a homosexual affair with one of Alexi's oldest friends and most trusted employees. The affair had been exposed by the man's son, and afterwards, when the man had suffered a fatal heart attack, Michel had attempted suicide. Accustomed to the open homosexuality in the fashion world, Fleur had thought the whole thing ridiculous at the time, but Alexi had been furious. He had refused to let Michel return to school in Massachusetts and had locked him away in a private clinic in Switzerland. When it had happened, Fleur told herself that she should feel sorry for Michel. Part of her did, but there was another part of her that saw a certain awful justice in making Michel the outcast for a change.

The projection room in Culver City was filled with the stench of Dick Spano's cigar and a lingering oniony odor from the rubble of fast-food containers. Jake sat slumped in his favorite seat at the end of the row, his legs propped on the back of the chair in front of him, a bottle of Mexican beer in his hand, and watched the rushes. As an actor it was something he didn't generally do, but as a fledgling screenwriter he wanted to see how his dialogue was working and study the pacing of the scenes to decide what might need to be rewritten.

"You nailed it there, Jako," Johnny Guy called out from across the room in response to the first exchange of dialogue between Matt and Lizzie. "When you set your mind to it, you write like a sonvabitch. Don't know why you waste your time with those New York faggots."

"They feed my ego, Johnny Guy." Jake kept his eyes on the screen as Lizzie began to kiss Matt. "Damn."

The men watched silently, one cut after another, of the kiss.

"It's not bad," Dick Spano offered at the end.

"She's on the right track," Johnny Guy said.

"It sucks." Jake swallowed the rest of his beer and set the bottle on the floor. "She's okay up to the kiss, but I'm telling you now, she's never going to be able to handle the heavier stuff."

"Jako, why do you insist on giving that little girl such a hard time? It's not going to do you any good. She's got an ironclad contract."

"I got this bad feeling, Johnny Guy. I just don't think it's in her to handle Lizzie. She's feisty and she puts up a good front,

160

but that kid doesn't have any *miles* on her, and she's not an experienced enough actress to hide it."

"You're being a pessimist, Jako." Johnny Guy peeled the wrapper from a Milky Way. "She's a hard worker, and the camera loves her. She'll come through."

Jake slumped farther down in his seat and watched as they ran the rushes again. Johnny Guy was right about one thing. The camera did love her. Her features didn't get lost, and her skin had a funny way of reshaping the light. He liked those knockout chorus-girl legs, too, and the way she moved on them. She wasn't conventionally graceful, but there was something appealing about her big, strong stride.

Still, he knew she was wrong for Lizzie. The innocence was there, even the sensuality, but it was unconscious and a far cry from Lizzie's manipulative sexuality. He didn't see how she would ever pull off the final love scene. In that scene Lizzie had to dominate Matt. She had to be experienced and worldly, ripping apart his last illusions about her innocence. Fleur Savagar went through the motions, but he had seen women going through the motions all his life, and this little girl didn't ring true.

Even to himself, he hated to admit how important the success of this film had become to him. Over the past few years he'd written a lot of screenplays, but all of them had ended up in the wastebasket. It had been hard for him to transfer his words into the visual images demanded by the screen, but with *Sunday Morning Eclipse* he was finally satisfied. He wanted to prove to a lot of people in this town that there was a whole audience over the age of twenty-five just waiting to go to the movies. He had also wanted to write himself a part where he could use more than two facial expressions, even though he was the first to admit he was never going to win any awards for his acting.

Jake had written his first play in Vietnam, working on it in secret and finishing it not long before he was shipped home. He rewrote it after he was released from a military hospital in San Diego and mailed it to New York the day he was discharged. A casting agent saw him before he made it back east, asked him to read for a small part in a Paul Newman western, and signed him the next day. Shooting on the picture had just begun when he got word that an Off-Broadway producer was interested in talking with him about his play. He managed to hold the guy off long enough to finish the film, and then he caught the red-eye east.

It marked the beginning of his double life. The producer liked his play and wanted to stage it. No money, but a lot of glory. The California men liked what they saw on the screen, and an offer came his way for a bigger part. The money was too good to turn down, especially for a kid from the wrong side of Cleveland. He learned to juggle—West Coast for money, East Coast for love.

Before long, supporting roles gave way to leads. He signed for the first Caliber picture and began a new play. Bird Dog buried the studio under an avalanche of fan mail; the play won the Pulitzer. He thought about quitting Hollywood then, but the play that had won the Pulitzer had also brought him less than half of what he could get for his next picture, so he made the picture, and he'd been making them ever since. No regrets, or at least not very many—as long as everybody understood that he stayed away from the press.

He turned his concentration back to the screen. Despite the way he'd teased Flower Power today, he had the feeling she didn't have the slightest idea how goddamned beautiful she really was. He'd noticed that she never touched her hair or looked into a mirror unless one was shoved in front of her face, and even then she didn't spend an extra second admiring herself. She'd surprised him today. Fleur Savagar was more intelligent than he'd expected, more vulnerable, too.

Maybe he wasn't being fair to her. Maybe the problem was that she didn't look at all like the real Liz. Amy Irving did, and that might be his hangup about the casting. Too damned many old memories, all of them leading to Vietnam—the sounds of Otis Redding, Creedence Clearwater—the nightmare he couldn't escape.

He distracted himself with emptier memories—the lazy mornings he and Liz had spent making love instead of going to class . . . walking back from the library in the evening with her taking two steps to every one of his . . . seeing her sitting in the stands while he was playing ball, her black hair caught back with the silver clip he had bought her. All the American pie bullshit. He stood up abruptly and stalked out of the projection room, kicking a wastebasket out of his way before he reached the door.

Johnny Guy picked up another can of Orange Crush and looked over at Dick Spano. "I don't want you to start thinking I'm a fruit or anything, Dicky boy, but I been havin' real sweet daydreams about Eastwood lately."

The next morning Belinda gave Fleur a kiss before she went into makeup and then waited at the back of the soundstage until she heard his footsteps. As he came closer, the years seemed to slip away. She felt eighteen again, standing at the counter of Schwab's drugstore. She half expected him to pull a crumpled pack of Chesterfields from the pocket of his uniform jacket. Her heart began to pound. The slouch to his shoulders, the dip of his head—a man is his own man. Bad Boy James Dean.

"I love your movies." She stepped forward, neatly blocking his path. "Especially the Caliber pictures."

"Thank you, that's nice to hear."

"I'm Belinda Savagar, Fleur's mother." She extended her hand. As he took it, she felt dizzy, as if all the blood had suddenly rushed from her head.

"Mrs. Savagar. It's nice to meet you."

"Please. Call me Belinda. I want to thank you for being so nice to Fleur yesterday. She told me how you'd helped her."

"It's hard the first day."

"But not everyone is kind enough to realize that."

He shrugged off her compliment, and she could see he was getting ready to move away. "Forgive me if I'm being presumptuous," she said, "but Fleur and I would like to thank you properly. We were going to toss a few steaks on the grill Sunday afternoon and put out some deviled eggs. Nothing fancy, Mr. Koranda. Strictly Indiana backyard cookout."

His eyes skimmed Indiana down over her navy Yves St. Laurent tunic and white gabardine trousers, and she could see his spark of interest. "You don't look like you're from Indiana, Belinda."

"Hoosier born and bred, and proud of it." She favored him with a mischievous look through her lashes. "We're going to light the charcoal around three."

She could see his moment of hesitation. "I'm afraid I'm tied up this Sunday," he said. "Do you think you could hold that charcoal off a week?"

"I think I just might be able to do that."

As he smiled and walked away, she knew she had done it

right, just like she would have done it for Jimmy—plenty of cold beer, potato chips served in the bag, and hide the Perrier. God, how much she had missed real men.

Fleur glared down at her mother. Belinda lay on a lounge at the side of the pool, her white bikini and gold ankle bracelet glimmering against her oiled body, her eyes closed beneath oversized tortoiseshell sunglasses. It was five minutes past three on Sunday afternoon, and she was still upset. "I can't believe you did this, Belinda. I really can't! I haven't been able to look him in the eye since you told me. I mean, you put him in a ridiculous position, not to mention me. I'm sure the last thing he wants to do on his only day off is come here. God."

Belinda didn't move other than to open her fingers a little so the sun could tan between them. "Don't be silly, baby. He's going to have a wonderful time, we'll see to it."

Fleur grabbed the net and marched over to the edge of the pool. It was bad enough she had to be with Jake fourteen hours a day, but on Sunday, too. As she began skimming the surface of the pool for leaves, she told herself she wasn't going to act stupid today. She wasn't going to stare at him, or talk too much, or anything. In fact, she was going to leave him completely alone. Belinda had invited him, so she could entertain him. The idea didn't cheer her up.

Belinda tilted up her sunglasses and eyed the snagged seat of Fleur's oldest black tank. "I wish you'd go change into one of your bikinis. That suit is dreadful."

"Looks good to me." Jake came walking toward them from the house.

Fleur dropped the net and dived into the water. It was stupid and childish, but she couldn't help it; she absolutely could not face him. She felt breathless, panicky. Her hand touched the bottom, and she wished she *had* put on one of her bikinis, some minuscule speck of nylon that wouldn't leave anything to his imagination. She'd wanted to. She'd wanted to so badly that she'd put on her old black tank, determined that Jake wasn't going to put her in the same category as all those women who drooled over him with their eyes. Lynn called it the Koranda Sex Effect.

When she came to the surface she saw that he had taken the chair next to Belinda. He was wearing baggy navy swim trunks, a gray athletic T-shirt, and a pair of running shoes that had seen better days. She had already discovered that he was only neat when he was in costume. Out of costume, he was a terrible dresser, with more ragged jeans and faded T-shirts than she had ever imagined one man could own. And he looked great in every one of them.

As he tilted back his head and laughed at something Belinda was telling him, she felt a terrible flash of jealousy. Belinda always knew what to say. Men relaxed as soon as they started to talk to her. She wished she had her mother's talent.

She dived under again. Why didn't she just quit wiggling around it and admit that she had a terrible, horrible, Class A incredible case for Jake Koranda? Why didn't she just face it and take her lumps? Most girls seemed to go through it earlier, but she'd always been a late bloomer. It was puppy love. She would face it, try not to make a fool of herself, and ride the whole thing out. When *Eclipse* was over and she didn't see him anymore, it would all fade away, a bittersweet memory, like an old valentine. Everybody went through it at one time or another; it was part of growing up. Of course, everybody didn't go through it with a million-dollar playwright–movie star who had half the women in the world hanging all over him, but when had she ever made anything easy for herself?

She came to the surface again and saw Belinda swinging her legs over the side of the chaise. "Fleur, come entertain Jake while I get a cover-up. I'm starting to burn."

"Stay where you are, Flower." Jake stood and pulled his T-shirt over his head, then he kicked off his shoes and dove into the pool. He surfaced in front of her. "You got your hair wet, kiddo. I thought New York glamour girls only looked at the water."

He was irresistible with water streaming over his face and that crooked-tooth grin. Something ached inside her. Her retort was quick and sharp. "Shows how much you know about New York glamour girls."

She dived under the water, heading in the direction of the ladder, but before she could get away, a hand grabbed her ankle. "Don't you know I'm a hotshot movie star?" he said, pulling her to the surface. "Girls aren't supposed to swim away from me."

"Hotshot glamour girls can."

His grip eased on her ankle and she dived under again, this time making it to the ladder. "Not fair," he called out. "You're a better swimmer than I am."

"I noticed. Your form stinks."

"You're pushing me, kiddo." He climbed up on the deck next to her. "And you've got a nasty mouth."

"It sets off my sweet disposition." She wrapped a towel over her suit, tucking it at the front, and sat down in the chair he had vacated.

"Correct me if I'm wrong, Flower, but you seem less than delighted to see me today."

She should have known he would come straight to the point. At least he hadn't realized just how delighted she really was. "Sorry. Guess I'm just in a bad mood. I'm worried about the scene with you and Lynn tomorrow." That much was true anyway.

"Let's go take a run and work up our appetite for those steaks Belinda promised."

Fleur quickly agreed, anything to rechannel some of her nervous energy. She had been running nearly every day since she had come to California, and she liked the way it made her feel. Sometimes she ran alone, sometimes at the studio with Lynn when they had finished shooting.

Belinda came out onto the patio knotting the tie on a lacy cover-up, and Jake called out, "Mind if I steal your daughter for a while? I'm going to run off some of her blubber."

"Go ahead," Belinda replied with a gay wave. "And don't hurry back. I've got a new Jackie Collins I'm dying to cuddle up with."

Jake made a face, and Fleur laughed, then she hurried inside to slip into a pair of shorts and running shoes. As she sat on the bed to tie the laces, the book she had been reading dropped to the floor, opening to a paragraph she had marked that morning:

> Koranda writes with a special voice as he holds his personal mirror up to the faces of the American working class. His characters are the men and women who love beer and contact sports, who believe in an honest day's work for an honest day's wage, and sometimes even go to church. In language that is frequently raw and almost

always humorous, his plays, in sharp contrast to his film roles, show the best and the worst of the American spirit.

One of the other critics said it more plainly:

Ultimately Koranda's work is successful because he grabs the country by the balls and squeezes hard.

She had been reading a lot lately, including Jake's plays, which were wonderful, and some magazine articles that had been written about him, which weren't. Each one made references to the women he dated, and the names were hardly ever the same.

He was waiting for her near the street, where he was stretching out his legs. "Think you can keep up, Flower, or am I going to have to baby-sit you?"

"You're cocky, do you know that?"

"Old news, kiddo."

She smiled and leaned over to loosen the muscles in her own calves. "Lynn told me you played basketball in college. I've seen you shooting at the rim by the parking lot."

"I play a couple of times a week. If I don't, it's hard for me to write. Playing ball clears my mind."

They took off at an easy trot. Since it was Sunday, there was no sign of the army of Mexican gardeners hired to keep the unused front lawns of Beverly Hills immaculate, and the street looked even more deserted than usual. She felt a small moment of disappointment. Part of her wanted the whole world to see who was running with her. "I thought playwrights were supposed to be intellectuals, not jocks," she said. "You don't let yourself fit into any neat pigeonhole, do you?"

"Playwrights are poets, Flower, and that's what basketball is. Poetry."

"Basketball doesn't exactly fit my idea of poetry."

"You ever hear of a guy named Julius Erving?" She shook her head and picked up the pace. He wasn't going to have to hold back for her. He immediately altered his rhythm. "They call Erving 'The Doctor.' He's a young player with the New York Nets, and he's going to be the best. Not just good, you understand—not even great. He's going to be the best basketball player that ever lived."

Fleur mentally added Julius Erving to her reading list. Jake went on, "Everything about Doc is poetry. When he moves, laws of gravity disappear. He flies, Flower, do you know what I'm saying? Man can't fly, but Julius Erving does. That's poetry, kiddo, and that's what makes me write." He suddenly looked uncomfortable, as if he had revealed too much about himself, and she could almost see the shutters slamming down over his face.

"Will you pick up the pace, for chrissake," he growled. "We might as well be walking."

The sudden shift in his mood bothered her, but she didn't say anything. They cut over to a paved bike path that was one of her favorite parts of the route. "Tell me what your problem is with the scene tomorrow," he said.

They were both breathing heavily now—she more so than he—but the faster pace wasn't really bothering her. She tried to explain and control her breathing at the same time. "I don't know. It's just—I guess Lizzie seems so calculating to me."

"She is, Flower. One calculating little bitch."

She noticed patches of sweat breaking through his T-shirt. "But she loves DeeDee, and she knows how DeeDee feels about Matt. I can understand why she's attracted to him—why she wants to go to bed with him—but I just can't see her being so calculating about it."

"It's the history of womankind. Nothing like a man to break up the friendship of two women."

"Come on, Koranda, that's prehistoric male chauvinist crap." She thought of her earlier stab of jealousy as she'd watched Belinda make Jake laugh. "Women have better things to do," she declared firmly, "than fight over some guy who probably isn't worth all that much in the first place."

"Hey, I'm the one who's defining reality around here. You're just the mouthpiece."

She fortified herself with more air. "DeeDee seems a more complete character than Lizzie. She has strengths and weaknesses. You want to comfort her and shake her at the same time." She stopped herself just short of saying that DeeDee was better written, even though it was true.

"Very good. You read the script."

"Don't patronize me! I have to play Lizzie, and she bothers me."

Jake picked up the pace again. "She's supposed to bother you. Look, Flower, from what I understand you've led a pretty sheltered life, so maybe you've never met anyone like Lizzie, but women like that leave tooth marks on a man."

"Why?"

"Who cares? It's the end effect that counts."

"You don't say that about your other characters, good or bad, so why do you say it about Lizzie?"

"Lay off, kiddo. I've been around a little longer than you have." He pulled out ahead of her.

"And you've got a Pulitzer," she called out after him, "while all I've got are *Cosmo* covers!"

He slowed his stride. "I didn't say that." They ran side by side without talking, circling a small park that was as empty as the rest of the neighborhood. As they got ready to head out toward the street, Jake dropped back. "Let's walk for a while, Flower."

"You don't have to baby-sit me, Koranda."

"Hey, don't be a bitch, okay?"

She shrugged and slowed to a walk. "Let's have it out," he said. "Are you pissed about Lizzie or about the fact that you know I didn't want you to play the part?"

"You're the one defining reality. Take your pick."

He picked up the tail of his T-shirt and wiped his face. "Okay, let's start with your casting. You're beautiful on screen. Your face is magic; you've got knockout legs. Johnny Guy has been redoing the shooting script every night to add more close-ups of you from different angles. The man gets tears in his eyes watching the rushes." He smiled at her, and she could feel some of her anger dissolving. "You're also one of the world's great kids. You listen to other people's opinions, you're conscientious, and I swear to God, I don't think you have a malicious bone in your body. And that's why I had misgivings about your playing Lizzie. Even in your screen test I could feel that about you. Lizzie is a carnivore. The whole idea is foreign to your nature."

"I'm an actress, Jake. Part of acting is being able to play a role that is totally different from your own personality." Even while she was saying it, she felt like a hypocrite, but she wasn't going to let him know that.

He ran his fingers through his hair, making it stand up in little spikes along one side. "Look, Flower, Lizzie is a hard character for me to talk about. She's based on a girl I used to know. I was married to her a long time ago."

She could tell he was angry with her for forcing even that small amount of personal history out of him. Jake—the Greta Garbo of male actors. She told herself to leave it alone and not ask any more questions that were none of her business. "What was she like?"

"Christ!" He took a few steps and then stopped, splaying one hand angrily on his hips. "She was a man-eater. Ground me up between her pretty little teeth and then spit me out without ever getting her face dirty."

"There had to have been something about her that made you fall in love with her."

"Lay off, will you?"

"Tell me, Jake."

"I said lay off! She was a great fuck, okay?"

Fleur stuffed her fists into the pockets of her running shorts while he glared at her.

"You wanted to know, kiddo. She was top drawer. Coast to coast, she couldn't be beat. Thousands of satisfied customers found happiness between her legs, and the Slovak kid from Cleveland lapped her up like a puppy dog!"

She felt his pain then. It hit her in the face like a slap, and without knowing she was doing it, she reached out and touched his arm. "I'm sorry. Really. I'm sorry I pushed."

He jerked his arm away, and they ran back to the house in silence. Fleur lectured herself the whole way about being stupid and insensitive, and then she began to wonder how any woman could let herself lose Jake Koranda once she'd gotten hold of him. What kind of person was his former wife?

Jake's thoughts were following a similar path. He, too, was thinking about Liz. He'd met her at the beginning of his sophomore year in college on the way home from basketball practice when he'd wandered into a rehearsal at the university theater building and she'd been onstage. She was the most beautiful girl he'd ever seen, and he asked her out that same night. She refused him. It didn't happen very often, and it surprised him. He figured that she didn't know he was on the basketball team so he made sure she found out. It didn't change her mind.

He discovered her family was rich with Youngstown steel money and accused her of being a snob. She told him he had a reputation for being fast with girls, and she didn't like guys like that. Her resistance made her even more appealing. She was like a tiny dark-haired kitten, soft and sweet-smelling, and he fell asleep at nights thinking about stroking her.

He began hanging out at the theater building between practices. When he discovered she was going to take a playwriting class the following semester, he managed to fast-talk himself past the prerequisites and into the class with her. It changed his life. As he worked on his first assignment, the words seemed to come from nowhere, pouring out of him. He wrote about the men in the blue-collar bars of Cleveland where he had worked as a kid doing odd jobs. The Stashes and Petes and Vinnies who had gradually taken the place of the father he didn't have, the men who asked him about his schoolwork, and laid into him for cutting class, and one night, when they found out from his mother that he had been picked up by the police for trying to steal a car, took him into the alley behind the bar and beat the shit out of him.

The professor was impressed. So was Liz. They began to take long walks together talking about their past and their hopes for the future. Instead of being put off by his poverty, she was fascinated by it. Sometimes they'd drive to Columbus in her bright blue Mustang and picnic along the river. He felt protective of her. They read Gibran together and talked about "art" and "reality." He gradually let down all the walls he had built around himself on the back streets of Cleveland. She was sensitive, vulnerable. She hated sports, but she came to his games and watched him play, laughing afterwards about how silly and meaningless it all was. He laughed with her. They made love. Afterwards they went out for ice cream and talked about their lovemaking as a religious experience.

Despite their youth, it seemed natural to her that they should marry, especially when her father threatened to cut off her allowance. She told daddy she was pregnant, and he whisked them both to Youngstown for a fast ceremony, but when he found out the pregnancy was a sham, he stopped the checks. Jake lengthened his hours working at the town diner.

A new graduate student enrolled in the theater department, and when Jake came home at night, he often found him sitting with Liz at the gray Formica kitchen table talking about "art" and "reality." One night he found them in bed. The graduate

171

student hadn't had Jake's experience on the streets, so the fight didn't last long. Liz cried and begged Jake to forgive her. She'd been lonely, she said; it was hard getting used to being poor. He felt guilty for having changed her life so drastically and forgave her. Two weeks later he found her down on her knees working over one of his teammates with her tongue. So much for religious experiences. Her innocence, he soon discovered, had been shared with legions.

He took the keys to her Mustang, headed for Columbus, and enlisted. Afterwards, he drove the Mustang into the Olentangy River. The divorce papers reached him near Da Nang. Daddy had paid for it.

As he looked back from a perspective of almost ten years on what had happened, he knew he should laugh about what a naive kid he'd been, but he couldn't. Vietnam, coming so soon after Liz's betrayal, had ended any thoughts of laughter.

Liz's ghost had come back to haunt him when he'd written *Sunday Morning Eclipse.* While developing the themes of innocence and corruption he'd felt as if she were sitting on his shoulder whispering words into his ear. He'd written her into the screenplay as Lizzie—Lizzie with the open, innocent face and the heart of a harlot. Lizzie, who bore no resemblance at all to that beautiful giant of a kid who was running beside him.

He looked over and saw that she was watching him. A small alarm went off inside his head as he took in the tender expression in those green-gold eyes that were gazing at him. Don't do it, Flower, he thought. *Don't you dare!*

He reached out and gave her hair a quick tug. "You're a good kid, you know that. If I ever had a sister, I'd want her to be just like you. Except not so ugly."

CHAPTER 13

Film sets develop their own personalities, and *Sunday Morning Eclipse* was no different. Johnny Guy was a well-organized director, so the normal grumblings among the crew about inefficiency were almost nonexistent. Food on the set was decent, there weren't many attacks of temperament, and everything began to settle into a rhythm. The crew members developed that scruffy, rumpled look of people who have been sleeping in their clothes; the men stopped shaving, the women got lazy with their makeup. After a week of night shooting, everyone had a cold, and an oversized bottle of vitamin C stood on the food table alongside the coffee and danish. Still, the atmosphere remained positive. Everyone knew they were involved with a special film, one of those projects that would make all of them in years to come feel proud to say, "Yeah, I worked on *Eclipse* in seventy-six."

Belinda was one of the few sources of contention. She managed to antagonize a number of the women, especially those supervising Fleur's makeup and costuming, but the men loved her. She brought them coffee, teased them about their wives and girlfriends, and kept up with the Dodgers. In an age of bra burners, they saw Belinda Savagar as a precious relic, someone who still bowed to the differences between men and women.

Jake watched her weave her spell among the hard-bitten crew members and teased her about it, but when he was aggravated with Johnny Guy or having trouble with a rewrite, he sought her out himself. There was something comforting about being regarded with so much adoration. Besides, she never made any demands on him.

When an idea for a new play began burning away inside him, he found himself telling her about it. In the warm glow of her enthusiasm, his idea seemed to expand, to crackle with life and become even better than he had first imagined it. That evening

173

he invited her to meet him for dinner. She refused, telling him that she had to help Fleur with her lines for the next day, but that she'd be glad to meet him sometime when Fleur was away and didn't need her.

He got the message, and he didn't like it. Sneaking around wasn't his style.

Unlike Belinda, Fleur began to dread going to work each morning. She told herself it was the routine. When she made commercials, the whole business was over quickly, but this seemed to be dragging on forever—shoot twenty seconds of dialogue . . . wait thirty minutes for light and camera adjustments . . . shoot the twenty seconds again . . . wait another thirty minutes. She found herself watching the crew with envy. At least they were busy.

But she knew it was more than the routine that was bothering her. For one thing, she wasn't very good in the part. It wasn't that she was awful or anything; she just wasn't very good, especially in comparison to Lynn. Belinda told her she was too critical, that she was suffering from overachiever's syndrome, but for as long as Fleur could remember, it had been important to her to be the bravest and the fastest and the strongest, and old habits were hard to break.

It was also Jake. He mussed her hair, dragged her out to shoot baskets with him, yelled at her if she argued with him, and treated her exactly like a none-too-bright kid sister. She hated it. She hated it even more when he invited some junior petite with big boobs and a pug nose to the set and then disappeared with her at the end of the day. Watching them go off together was like dying inside; it was as simple as that. She did everything she could think of to improve her performance. Maybe if she were a better actress, he'd like her more.

She spent Sundays on horseback, riding until she was so exhausted she couldn't think anymore about the fact that she was tired of modeling and a mediocre actress and had a bad case of puppy love for a man who always seemed irritated with her. She decided it was because she was the only nineteen-year-old virgin left who wasn't cloistered. Hormones, she had read, could account for a lot of things, and hers were screaming for attention.

On the rare occasions when she didn't have an early call, she accepted invitations from a few of Hollywood's more eligible bachelors. Some of them were bores, but one of them wasn't, and after going out with him, she decided to transfer her crush. In addition to being terrifically smart and one of the most interesting people she had ever met, he was fun to be with. He was also better-looking than Jake and much more polite. His reputation as a ladykiller didn't bother her at all, since she was looking for an antidote, not a permanent commitment. On their third date, she asked him if he might like to go to bed with her. He didn't laugh, but he didn't take her to bed either. He said that he had a feeling she'd better think it over a little more carefully, and she was secretly relieved. Warren Beatty was definitely a nice guy. The only thing wrong with him was that he wasn't Jake Koranda.

One Friday night after they had finished shooting, the Spanos had a party catered to the set. She put on three-inch heels and a crepe de chine sarong that she tied at the bust, leaving her shoulders bare. Johnny Guy got drunk and tried to stick his tongue down her throat. Jake walked in on the struggle and went after Johnny Guy with his fists. Only Dick Spano's intervention put an end to the fracas.

Belinda passed the whole incident off under the guise of Boys Will Be Boys, but Fleur felt humiliated—angry with Johnny Guy for having put her in such a situation, even angrier with Jake for trying to protect what he had no interest in himself. When it came time for the company to leave for location, she was relieved. At least the scenery would be different.

Spano had taken over a motel not far from Iowa City to house the actors and crew as well as to serve as the production's command post. Its only advantages were the convenience of its location and the fact that it had a bar. Fleur's room was furnished in motel-modern, with ugly hanging lamps, plastic-lined wastebaskets, and a reproduction of Seurat's "Sunday Afternoon on the Grande Jatte" bolted to the wall, its cardboard center curled in like a potato chip. Belinda wrinkled her nose as she studied it. "Lucky you," she sniffed. "I got 'Sunflowers.'"

"Don't complain," Fleur said more sharply than she had intended. "You didn't have to come on location."

"Don't be cranky, darling. You know I would never have stayed behind. When I think now of all those miserable years in Paris with nothing to do but drink, I don't know how I ever survived. This has been the best year of my life."

Fleur gazed up from the stack of bras she had just put in the top drawer of the bureau. Belinda in her silk dress and gold chains looked totally out of place in the drab motel room, and yet she seemed completely happy. She wished she were that happy. Returning to her unpacking, she kept her eyes firmly fixed on the neat piles of underwear. "Belinda, I've been thinking about what I want to do after this is all over."

"Don't think too hard, darling; that's what Gretchen and Parker Dayton are for." Belinda rummaged through Fleur's cosmetic case and pulled out a brush. She ran it through her hair and then inspected the results in the mirror. "We *are* going to have to make a decision, though, about the Paramount thing. It really is tempting, and Parker is sure it's right for you, but Gretchen thinks we should close the deal with Estee Lauder first."

Fleur lifted a pair of running shoes from her suitcase. She'd been thinking about this for a long time, and even though she knew Belinda wouldn't like it, she'd decided that she could win her over if she went about it the right way. "Maybe we should just wait a while before we do anything," she said casually. "I wouldn't mind some time off, and you could travel a little, give some parties."

Belinda eyed her reflection in the mirror, tilting her head from one side to the other. "Don't be silly, baby." She fingered a lock of hair. "Maybe I should go lighter? I wish I could make up my mind."

Fleur abandoned all pretense of unpacking. She couldn't go into another movie right away, and the idea of returning to modeling was almost as depressing. "Belinda, I'd really like to have some time off. I've been working pretty steadily for two years, and I'd like a vacation."

Belinda laid down the hairbrush, and the atmosphere in the room was suddenly heavy with tension. "It's out of the question. It would be career suicide for you to drop out of sight at this point."

"Belinda, I need some time!" She had forgotten to be tactful, and now she tried to backtrack. "Everything has happened so quickly; I don't remember ever having made any choices. I mean, it's been wonderful and everything, but how do I know this is what I really want to do with my life?"

Belinda looked at her as if she had suddenly grown blue hair. "What more could you possibly want?"

176

Her disbelief was so total that Fleur could feel herself faltering. "I don't know," she admitted. "I'm not sure."

"You're not sure? Well, I must say I can understand your problem. It's a little difficult to find something else to do when you're already sitting on top of the world."

"Please, Belinda, try to understand. I'm not saying I want another career. I just want some time to see what my choices are and to make sure this is really what I want."

Belinda seemed like a stranger, cold and distant. "Do you have something else in mind? Some career more exciting than being the most famous model in the world? Something more glamorous than being a film star? What are you thinking about doing, Fleur? Teaching first grade?"

"No."

"How about becoming a nurse? You could take temperatures and scrub out bedpans. That would certainly be exciting. Is that good enough?"

"No, I—"

"Then what? What do you want?"

"I don't know!" She sank down on the edge of the bed, feeling miserable and confused.

Belinda punished her with silence. When she finally spoke, her voice was accusing. "You're spoiled, Fleur . . . very badly spoiled. You've had everything you could possibly want handed to you on a silver platter, and you've never had to work for anything. Do you realize how silly you sound? It might be different if you had some goal, but you don't even have that. When I was your age, I knew exactly what I wanted out of life, and I was willing to do anything to get it. You could use a little of that determination."

Fleur couldn't stand having Belinda look at her like that, so disapproving, almost contemptuous. "I'm sorry. Maybe you're right."

But Belinda wasn't going to let her off so easily. "I'm disappointed in you. For the first time since you were born, I have to tell you that I'm disappointed in you." She went to the door and rested her hand on the knob. "Think about what you're planning to throw away, Fleur, and when you're ready to talk sensibly, come find me." Without another word, she walked out.

Fleur had to remind herself that she wasn't a child any longer

—she wasn't back at the *Couvent de l'Annonciation* watching her mother disappear—but within minutes she found herself running down the hallway to Belinda's room. When there was no answer to her knock, she had to fight down her panic. Belinda had just gone to the lobby for a newspaper, she told herself. Just a newspaper, that was all. The lobby was deserted except for a few members of the crew, none of whom remembered having seen Belinda. Fleur retraced her steps, making casual inquiries of everyone she met, while her heart thudded painfully in her chest. Someone mentioned the bar.

Feeling sick inside, Fleur went back downstairs. It took a moment for her eyes to adjust to the dimness of the bar, another few seconds before she spotted Belinda sitting at a table by herself, twirling a swizzle stick in the glass that sat in front of her. After two years, her mother was off the wagon, and she was the one responsible. "Belinda, why did you come in here?" She reached down and put her hand over the top of the drink. It looked like Scotch. "Come on, let's go for a ride."

"I'd like to finish my drink, Fleur. I'm not feeling like the best of company at the moment."

Fleur slid into the chair opposite Belinda. "Please don't do this." She reached out and took her mother's hand. "Don't let the fact that you have a daughter who's a spoiled brat force you into taking a drink you don't really want. I need you too much."

"You don't need me, baby. It's pretty obvious that I'm pushing you into something you don't want."

"That's not true. It's like you said to me a long time ago. There's a bond between us, as if we're one person, not two." She was starting to cry. "Whatever makes you happy is going to make me happy. I've just been confused, that's all." She tried to smile, but didn't quite make it. "Let's go for that drive. We have to make up our mind about Paramount."

Belinda dipped her head. "Don't resent me, baby. I couldn't stand it if you resented me."

"That'll never happen. Come on. Let's get out of here."

They had already reached the rental car when Belinda remembered she had left her purse in the bar. Fleur went back to get it. As she leaned over to pick it up from the floor, she noticed that Belinda's drink was still sitting on the table. The glass was full. Belinda hadn't drunk from it at all.

Although Belinda was not officially part of the film company, she was always there if someone needed her. She ran lines with the actors, made phone calls for crew members, and rubbed away Johnny Guy's stiff neck. Once she was even seen in the town hardware store, standing at the counter in a Holly Harp jumpsuit, buying a bit for a power drill. Generally, however, she was with Fleur, although, her eyes frequently rested on Jake.

Toward the end of the first week, Jake had the day off while Johnny Guy shot a scene with Lynn and Fleur. He slept late and was just stepping out of the shower when he heard a knock. Tucking a towel around his hips, he opened the door.

Belinda was standing on the other side, a white paper sack dangling from her perfectly manicured fingertips. "Hi. Want some breakfast?"

"Is there coffee in there?"

"Of course."

"Come on in."

She set the sack on top of the television and pulled out two Styrofoam cups. Handing one to him, she took the other and walked over to the room's only chair, crossing her legs as she sat so that the slim skirt of her suit crept up above her knees. "I had a headache this morning, so I decided to stay behind."

He peeled off the lid of the cup and tossed it in the wastebasket. "Feeling better now?"

"How did you guess?"

"A flash of intuition." Tossing the pillows at the headboard, he sat down on the bed and leaned up against them.

"Do you consider yourself a rebel, Jake?"

"Not particularly. Why?"

"I do. A rebel without a cause. A man who follows his own drummer. That's one of the things that excites me about you."

"There's more?" He smiled, only to realize that she was perfectly serious.

"Oh, yes. Do you remember when you were on the run in *Devil Slaughter*? I loved it. I always love it when it's just you against them. That's the kind of picture Jimmy would have made if he hadn't died."

"Jimmy?"

"James Dean." She stood and walked over to the door, slip-

179

ping the Do Not Disturb sign off the knob. When she had hung it on the outside, she turned back to him. "You've always reminded me of him."

"Come here," he said.

She walked over to the bed, her breathing quick and shallow. When he took her hands to pull her down beside him, they were trembling. "Would you like me to get undressed for you?" she asked.

"Do you want to?"

"What do you want, Jake? Let me please you."

He leaned forward and, drawing her close, kissed her. At the first touch of his lips, she opened her mouth, and her hands went to his bare back, stroking the ridges. He kissed her more deeply and cupped her breast. She immediately pulled away and began to unfasten her blouse.

"Hey, slow down," he said gently.

She looked up at him, her eyes clouded with confusion. "Don't you want to see me?"

"Sure, but there's no fire. We've got all day."

"I just want to please you."

"That works two ways, Belinda." He pushed her down beneath him and released the front closure of her bra. She felt the warmth of his mouth covering her, and she remembered *Devil Slaughter* when Bird Dog had tangled with the beautiful Englishwoman who was getting too close. She remembered how he had jerked her off her horse and into his arms, running his hands over her body as he searched for the knife he knew she was carrying. When Jake took off her own clothing, she pretended he was searching her.

Her mouth fell open to his kisses . . . wonderful, deep kisses. The fire spread through her body. She opened her legs so she could make an offering of herself, and when he finally entered her, it was with a sharp, possessive thrust that was just right coming from that special kind of man. His beard was rough against her skin, scratching her, hurting her deliciously. She eased open her eyes and gazed at the face that was so close to her, real and not imagined. But it didn't look right so close, where she could only see segments and not the whole. She liked to see his whole face, so she shut her eyes again, visualizing the way he looked on the screen.

There. Better. So much better. Oh, yes. *Yes.*

The location shooting ran into its normal snags—a permit that hadn't been taken care of, a road that wasn't closed off in time for the day's filming, a week of rain when they needed good weather. They filmed the movie's final scene at a run-down root beer stand that had been constructed in the middle of nowhere, and then went back to shoot what they'd missed.

A few days before they were scheduled to return to California, Jake found himself sitting on the back of a tractor, stripped down to a pair of jeans, his chest covered with phony sweat. The thermometer had taken an unexpected dip into the low seventies, and he asked one of the women in wardrobe for a shirt while he waited for the next take. He saw Belinda sitting by one of the trailers reading a magazine, and he frowned. She seemed to be everywhere.

Although he had been with a lot of women, he'd never experienced anything quite like making love to Belinda Savagar. Being with her in bed, he had discovered, was a disconcerting experience—sometimes he wanted to wave his hands back and forth in front of her eyes to see if she was still with him. He had made up his mind to end the relationship. Although he'd enjoyed all that adoration in the beginning, now there was something about it that was beginning to make him uncomfortable. Besides, every time he looked at Flower Power, he felt guilty. He knew it was illogical, but he couldn't seem to help it.

"Here's your shirt."

He looked up in surprise to see Lynn Davids. "Since when are you working wardrobe?"

"It gave me a chance to talk to you. Have you been avoiding me, Jake?"

"Of course not."

"Then how come every time I try to get you alone, you disappear?"

"Overactive imagination, sweetheart." He slipped on the shirt and buttoned it.

"Sure." She folded her arms over the phony pregnancy padding beneath her maternity top. "What the hell is wrong with you? How long do you think it'll be before everybody figures out you and Belinda are screwing around?"

He decided he didn't owe her any explanations. "We're consenting adults. What's the big deal?"

He jumped down off the back of the tractor and began to move away, but Lynn planted herself in front of him. "Don't walk away from me, Jake. I don't like it any better now than I used to. You shouldn't be messing around with Belinda, and you know it. She's nothing but a well-dressed celebrity fucker."

"So what? You and I have been in this business long enough to know that women like her come with the territory."

Lynn shoved a piece of hair behind her ear. "What about Fleur?"

"What about her?"

"She's my friend, Jake. Despite the fact that she doesn't slobber all over you, I think she really cares about you. But you behave so strangely with her."

"What the hell are you talking about?"

"You know what. The big brother act. I've never seen you this way with a woman."

"Come on, Lynn. She's just a kid."

"I've heard you say that before. More than once, as a matter of fact, and I don't understand it now any better than I did the first time. You've dated women her age. Gone to bed with a few, too, if I remember right. Fleur has more class than all of them put together."

"What are you trying to say? You want me to go to bed with Fleur? I'm supposed to keep my hands off Belinda—who damned well knows what she's doing—but stick it to the kid with the big eyes. Get off it, Lynn."

"That's not what I mean, and you know it. Messing around with Belinda may not leave any scars on you, but Fleur loves that bitch, and you're setting her up for something pretty nasty when she finds out what Mommy's been up to. I don't want to see her hurt."

"Don't read more into this than there is, Lynn. Even if you're right, which is debatable, Fleur's nothing more than a kid with a schoolgirl crush."

"A *crush!* Aren't you even a little embarrassed by your choice of words? She's a beautiful, intelligent young woman and she's attracted to you."

"This is none of your business, Lynn. Leave it alone."

"All right. Subject closed. But I want you to promise me one thing."

"What's that?"

"I want you to promise me that you'll think about why it's so damned important for you to keep Fleur Savagar in pigtails."

Leaving the second unit to clean up, the company returned to California. Belinda knew without being told that it was over with Jake. She accepted it with the same kind of fatalistic resignation with which she had accepted Flynn's desertion. Jake Koranda was a star, immortal like Jimmy. It had been foolish of her to believe, even for a moment, that she was important enough to hold him.

Fleur grew increasingly miserable as they entered the final weeks of shooting. She couldn't wait for the whole thing to be over, except part of her couldn't stand the idea of never seeing Jake again.

The two of them had just finished shooting a scene when Johnny Guy pulled them aside. "We'll be shooting that last love scene in a couple of days, and I want both of you to start thinking about it. I don't want to rehearse it too much—it's got to be spontaneous. I don't want any damned choreographed ballet dance, either. I want sex, dirty and raw." He turned to Fleur. "The set will be cleared on the days we shoot to keep you as comfortable as we can, honey. Just me, the a.d., the boom, and camera. That's about as low as we can go. We'll put up a curtain; I'll have a woman on boom. If you want somebody from SAG standing by, we can do that, too."

Fleur felt the first trickle of alarm. "Johnny Guy, you'd better check the fine print. I'm not contracted to do anything that needs a curtain or a closed set. We're using a body double, remember?"

"Shit." Jake shoved his hands in his pockets and turned away.

Johnny Guy shook his head. "I don't know who told you that, honey, but you'd better check your information. A body double was discussed, but we wouldn't sign you under those conditions. It just wouldn't work. Your people knew that."

"There's a mistake, Johnny Guy," Fleur insisted. "I'm going to call my agent."

"You do that, honey. Go into Dick's office where you can have some privacy."

Fleur phoned Parker Dayton. When she hung up, she was white-faced and shaken, and she left the studio without a word.

She found Belinda at one of Beverly Hills' most fashionable watering holes, where she was lunching on salmon in sorrel cream sauce with the third wife of a popular television talk show host. Belinda took one look at her face and stood up. "Darling, whatever are you . . ."

"You lied to me," Fleur said.

Belinda's expression didn't change. She took Fleur's arm and smiled down at her luncheon partner. "Excuse us, will you, dear. I'll be back in a few minutes." Pulling Fleur with her into the rest room, she locked the door and said coldly, "What's this all about?"

Fleur felt a sharp pain in her right hand. She realized she was still clutching the Porsche keys and that they were cutting into her palm. The pain almost felt good. It was concrete, and she knew how to make it stop.

"I talked to Parker Dayton today," she said. "He told me there was never any provision in my contract for a body double. He said you'd told him I'd changed my mind."

Belinda shrugged. "They wouldn't agree to it, baby. I tried to talk to them; I explained how you felt. Parker tried, but they wouldn't agree. They said the scene couldn't be filmed that way."

"So you lied, even though you know how I feel about working nude. You told me it was taken care of!"

Belinda opened her purse with a quick, irritated jerk at the clasp and pulled out her cigarettes. "You wouldn't have signed if you'd known the truth. I had to do it to protect you. Surely you can see that by now."

"No, I don't see it. All I see is that if I don't do that scene on Friday morning, we face legal action."

"Of course you'll do the scene." For the first time Belinda looked faintly alarmed. "My God, a breach-of-contract suit would finish you in Hollywood. You're certainly not going to let some silly bourgeois prudery ruin your career."

There was silence between them for a moment, and then Fleur asked the question she'd been wanting to ask for a long time. "Is it my career, Belinda, or is it yours?"

"What a wicked, ungrateful thing to say. And how characteristic!" Belinda pitched the cigarette she had just lit to the floor and stubbed it out with the toe of her shoe. "You listen to me, Fleur, and pay attention to what I'm telling you—if you do

184

anything to jeopardize this film, it'll never be the same between us. You know it, and I know it, so we might as well face it."

Fleur stared at her mother, unable to believe what she was hearing. Belinda didn't mean it. She couldn't. But as she looked into her mother's face, she saw no sign of softening.

It took her several tries before the lock on the rest room door would give. She ran from the restaurant, paying no attention to Belinda's voice calling after her. There was a phone booth on Melrose—she remembered having seen it before—and she drove there to place her call. It took her almost an hour to locate Alexi in his suite at the Connaught. When she finally reached him, her dress was sticking to her skin, and she had gnawed a bloody spot in her bottom lip.

"Is something wrong, *enfant?*"

Quickly she told him what had happened. By the time she had finished, tears were dripping off her cheeks onto the receiver. "Belinda lied to me, Alexi."

"You are telling me that you signed a contract without reading it first?"

"Belinda always takes care of that."

The pause on the line was so lengthy that, at first, she thought the connection had been broken. "I am very much afraid, *enfant,*" he said quietly, "that you have just learned a most difficult lesson about your mother."

When she finally went home, the housekeeper said her mother had been there looking for her but had left again. She handed her a stack of phone messages. Fleur pitched them into the wastebasket without looking at them and then changed into a swimsuit and threw herself into the pool.

Jake found her as she was climbing out. He was dressed in a pair of shorts and a T-shirt so faded that only the darker outlines of Beethoven's face were still visible on the front. His wool sweat socks were stretched out at the calves, and one of them had fallen into accordion folds around his ankle. He was rumpled, mussed, a hard-fisted cowboy misplaced in Beverly Hills.

She was absurdly, insanely glad to see him. "Go away, Koranda. Nobody invited you."

"Get your shoes on. We're going for a run."

"Forget it."

"Don't piss me off, Flower. You've got a minute and a half to change your clothes."

"Or what?"

"I call in Bird Dog."

She picked up the towel she had thrown over the chaise and took her time drying herself off so he wouldn't think he could boss her around. Then she went into the house and changed. Why did she think that Jake would help her? All he'd done from the beginning was add to her misery. It was getting harder every day for her to pretend to herself that this was puppy love.

At night when she was falling asleep, she imagined that they were making love. She saw the scene through a vaselined lens. They were in a sun-drenched room filled with flowers and soft music, lying on a bed with pastel sheets that billowed over their bodies in the breeze from the open window. He pulled a flower from a vase by the bed and touched her body with it. He brushed the petals over her nipples and her stomach. She opened her legs and he touched her there, too. They were in love, and they were alone. No camera. No boom man. Just the two of them.

He was waiting for her in front. They began to run, but they had barely gone a block before she stopped and bent over to catch her breath. "I'm sorry, Jake. I can't today. You go on."

Normally he would have teased her, but today he didn't. He stopped running and took her by the arm. "Let's drive over to the park and shoot some baskets. It should be deserted now, so we won't have to sign any autographs."

She didn't really want to go, but she didn't have any energy left to protest. They walked back to the house and he pulled open the passenger door of the truck he drove. It was a '66 Chevy half-ton pickup that she knew from past conversations he had customized with a Corvette racing engine. He didn't say anything as he backed out of the driveway, and she found herself thinking that she might have been able to pull it off with another actor. She might have been able to approach that love scene like a professional and detach herself from it. But not with Jake. Not while she dreamed about a room filled with flowers and the strains of soft music.

"I don't want to do that scene, Jake."

"I know you don't." He parked the truck and reached behind the seat, pulling a basketball out from beneath his windbreaker and a spare pair of running shoes. Then he got out and came around to open the door for her. They walked across the grass to the basketball court. As they stepped onto the asphalt, he began to dribble the ball. "The scene isn't prurient, Flower. It's necessary." He made a quick dunk and then passed the ball to her.

She dribbled toward the basket, shot, and hit the rim. "I know that, but I don't want to do it. I don't work nude."

"Your people don't seem to understand that."

"They understand it."

"Then how did it happen?"

"Because I'm too stupid to read contracts before I sign them, that's how!"

He looked at her for a moment, and then made a quick jump from the side, sinking a clean shot. "We're not after the raincoat crowd, Flower. It'll be handled tastefully."

"Tastefully! Just what the hell does that mean?" She picked up the ball and then angrily batted it at him. "I'll tell you what it means, Koranda. It means it won't be your noodle everybody is seeing!" She stomped off the court.

"Flower." He sounded like he was laughing. She spun around and caught him grinning. Quickly he wiped the grin off his face and walked over to her, the ball tucked under his arm. "Sorry, it's not really funny; it was just your manner of expression."

He tapped her under the chin with his index finger. "Hey, kiddo, it won't be your noodle either. The most the audience will probably see is your backside. Mine, too, for that matter. They may not even see your breasts . . . depends on how Johnny Guy has it edited."

"You'll see them."

"Actually, Flower," he said, "it won't be a new experience. Not that I've seen yours in particular, but there are only so many variations. I mean, if you think about it, I should be the one complaining. How many noodles have you seen?"

She wanted to slap him. "You think all this is funny, don't you?"

"A little, I guess. Not the fact that you were misled—frankly, if I were you, I'd kick some tail—but the fact that you're making such a big deal out of all this. The scene is important. It's necessary to the picture."

His hand drifted down to cup the side of her neck, and he looked into her eyes. She had the horrible feeling she'd seen him do this before, that it was a scene he'd played in one of his pictures when he'd tried to get some stupid female to do what he wanted. But what if it wasn't? What if that tenderness she was seeing was real? She wanted to believe it. She wanted to believe it more than she'd ever wanted anything in her life.

"Flower, this is important to me," he said softly. "Will you do it? Will you do it for me?"

She jerked away from him. "Stop pretending I have a choice! You know I signed a contract; you know I have to do it!" She ran for the bike path. He didn't give a damn about her. All he cared about was his damned picture.

Jake watched her running away from him, and he could feel something tighten inside. God, she was beautiful. Her hair streamed out behind her like spilled gold paint. She turned onto the path, covering the ground with long, clean strides. She was the only woman he had ever been able to run with. From the very beginning, those knockout chorus girl legs had seemed to be a perfect match for his own. Lots of things about her had seemed to be a match—that smart aleck mouth, her quirky sense of humor, all that boundless energy. Everything except her fragile little-girl's heart.

CHAPTER 14

Johnny Guy called everyone together while Fleur was in makeup. "The first person who cracks a joke or does anything to make her uncomfortable today will be out on his butt, you all hear me? And as far as I'm concerned the union can go screw itself."

Dick Spano winced.

After the set had been cleared of all but the necessary few, Johnny Guy cornered Jake. "You watch those wisecracks today."

His remark made Koranda mean. "I'm not the one who's got his hands all over her whenever he gets a chance, Johnny Guy."

They were glaring at each other as Fleur came on the set. She didn't look at either of them. She was wearing a yellow cotton dress and a pair of white sandals. Her hair was down, held back from her face by an eyelet ribbon. It was the costume she had been wearing for several days as they shot the dialogue that led up to the love scene, but today was the day it came off, and it felt different to her.

"Let me show you what we're going to do here, honey lamb." Johnny Guy led her behind the curtained area of the set into the old farmhouse room with its faded wallpaper and iron bed. "You're going to stand here and look over at Matt. Keep looking at him while you unbutton the dress and step out of it. As soon as we get that, I'm going to shoot from behind while you take off your bra and panties. Real easy stuff. Take your time. Jako, when she's taking off her underwear, I'll start coming in on you. Questions?"

Jake shook his head.

Fleur cleared her throat. "I'd like a drink of water." The lack of noise bothered her. All the normal chatter was missing. No one was calling out insults; nobody was looking at her. She'd

189

become an invisible person. She took a sip from the glass that was held out to her and then handed it back.

"You okay, Flower?"

"Just peachy." She pushed a stray lock of hair back behind her ear.

Jake stepped off his mark and came over to her. "Hey, it's not the end of the world, kiddo. The tough stuff doesn't even start until this afternoon."

"Easy for you to talk," she said. "Your underpants don't have teddy bears on them." It was the smallest part of what was bothering her, but for now it was the easiest thing to worry about.

"You're kidding."

"They thought it would add to Lizzie's character."

"That's the stupidest thing I ever heard."

"That's what I told them."

Jake pushed past her. "Johnny Guy, some asshole put Flower in underpants with teddy bears on them."

"I'm the asshole, Jako. You got a problem?"

"Damn right I got a problem. Lizzie should be in the sexiest underwear you can find, for chrissake. Innocence on the outside with that little yellow dress, and corruption underneath. You're screwing with my metaphor."

"Fuck your metaphor."

The two men began to argue, and Fleur sank down on the straightbacked chair next to the bed. She tried all her tricks— yawning, pinching the side of her leg, biting the inside of her cheek—but she still felt like she was going to cry. It didn't take long for Jake and Johnny Guy to see what was happening, and they were immediately apologetic. Johnny Guy sent her off to have her makeup fixed and to change her underwear. She was given a beige lace set that didn't hide anything and made her wish she'd kept her mouth shut.

They were finally ready to shoot. Johnny Guy called for action, and she slowly began unbuttoning the top of the dress.

Cut. She was supposed to be looking at Matt.

She told herself she had to forget she was Fleur and think about Lizzie. Lizzie had undressed for men a dozen times. This was Matt. But as the cameras started to roll, she knew it wasn't Matt.

It took another hour, but the yellow dress finally slid to the floor, and she stood in front of him dressed in nothing but a few scraps of beige lace. It was only a lingerie ad. She'd done a zillion. Nothing special.

She slipped into a white terry-cloth robe while the crew moved the camera. They were going to shoot her from behind while she took off the bra and the panties. She was supposed to be slightly out of focus as the camera concentrated on Matt's reaction. But she wasn't going to be out of focus to Jake.

She fumbled with the clasp of the bra during the first take. Then Johnny Guy had to remind her to keep her head up. She wished everything weren't so quiet. The set was like a morgue. The crew kept studying the toes of their sneakers; Johnny Guy and the a.d. whispered. As she found her mark for the third time and shed the terry-cloth robe, she was suddenly certain she was going to cry. Desperately she looked over at Jake.

He had been spending a lot of time not looking at her, but now, instead of helping her, he let his eyes sweep down over her. Then he yawned. "Your body is nice, kiddo, but I'd like to get out of here early. The Doctor is playing ball on TV tonight."

Johnny Guy gave him a murderous glare, but Fleur felt a little better and even managed a weak smile. It was comforting to have someone finally acknowledge the fact that she was standing in front of them practically naked instead of acting as if nothing out of the ordinary was happening.

His remark seemed to break the tension and people started to talk. With the next take, she got the bra off. Jake looked at her breasts—except it wasn't Jake; he was Matt now. She leaned forward just as Johnny Guy wanted her to and slipped her thumbs into each side of the panties. She gave a little tug and pulled them down, thinking about the nuns and feeling like a whore as she did it. His eyes followed the direction of the panties and then returned to look at what they had been covering up. She hated it. She hated every minute of it, and she hated herself for selling out. This might be all right for other actresses, but she was a lousy actress and it wasn't right for her. More than anything in the world, she wanted to give herself to Jake with love. Instead it was a piece of business she was being paid to do.

The camera couldn't see the expression on her face, but Jake could. "Cut it," he said. "Just cut it. Shit." He stalked off the set, and the wardrobe mistress wrapped her up in her robe.

Belinda had friends on the set, and it didn't take her long to hear what was happening. She paced the tiled floor of the living room, kicking away a corner of the white rya rug when it got in her way. Fleur had barely spoken to her in four days; she had never imagined her daughter could stay angry for so long. And now this.

It was dark by the time she heard the motor of the Porsche. Fleur came into the house and walked past her without saying a word, and when Belinda tried to go after her, she discovered the door to her room was locked. She grabbed her purse and the keys to the Mercedes. Something terrible was happening, and she had to put a stop to it before everything she had worked so long for was blown away.

She parked in Fleur's space at the studio and nodded to the guard as she went inside. Nobody noticed her slipping into the back of the projection room; they were all too intent on the images on the screen.

"The whole fucking sympathy of the movie shifts to her." Johnny Guy popped a Maalox in his mouth. "Jake Koranda rapes Snow White. And I swear to God, Jako, if you say 'I told you so,' I'll beat the crap out of you."

"Cancel her call for tomorrow," Jake said wearily. "I'll go up to my place and do some rewrites this weekend. We'll have to cut a lot of her footage."

In the back of the room, Belinda dug her fingernails into her palms. Cut her footage! How could Fleur have let something like this happen?

"Maybe we shouldn't jump the gun," Dick Spano said. "Maybe she just had a bad day. We can give her another chance tomorrow."

Johnny Guy shook his head. "You weren't there, Dicky. There's no way in hell she's going to be able to do that scene the way it's written. Jake's right. We're going to have to do some fancy footwork. It's not the end of the world, but it's going to hurt us."

Belinda slipped out of the room and went back to the Mercedes. She moved it to the parking space next to Jake's pickup and waited. It was nearly one o'clock before she saw him coming across the lot, zipping up the front of his blue windbreaker. She slid out of the Mercedes and stood in the pool of light that was falling over the truck.

Jake frowned when he saw her. She told herself she wouldn't let that frown hurt her. It was over between them, just as she'd known it would be, but for a time he had given her a little piece of himself and a little piece of Jimmy. She had to be satisfied with that. "I need to talk to you, Jake."

"Can't it wait until Monday? I'm getting ready to leave as soon as I pick up a typewriter at my apartment and a change of clothes."

"Don't do any rewriting," she said. "It's unnecessary. Fleur can do that scene."

"Listening through keyholes?" He pulled a set of keys from his pocket.

"I saw the rushes, and I heard all of you talking. There's no need for a rewrite."

"If you saw the rushes, you know that Johnny Guy can't use much of anything we shot today. Believe me, I don't want to do this, but unless some magic happens with Fleur over the weekend, we'll need it." He flipped through his keys, searching for the one he wanted.

"Make the magic, Jake."

He looked up. "What are you talking about?"

She stepped closer to him, her mouth dry. "I think maybe Fleur is in love with you. She's sensitive, Jake, and very private. I think she's afraid to let herself go in that scene. She's afraid to let down the wall that she's built to keep her feelings safe."

"What are you suggesting, Belinda?"

"Break down that wall," she said quietly. "Take her away with you this weekend and break down that wall."

He didn't move. "Maybe you'd better explain what you mean by that."

She gave a small, nervous laugh. "Isn't it obvious? Fleur is nineteen. She's past the age of consent."

He shoved his hands into the pockets of his windbreaker. "I still don't understand what you mean. Say it, Belinda. Say it so I'm sure I understand."

"All right. I think you should make love to her."

He exploded. "Make love? Is that what you're talking about? Making love is something two people do for enjoyment. It's for

193

pleasure. It's not a business deal. You're pimping your own daughter, passing her on to an old lover!"

"Jake . . ."

"What you're talking about is fucking! Fuck my daughter, Koranda, so she won't blow her movie career. Fuck her so she won't blow *my* career."

"Stop it! It's not like that. You make it sound so ugly."

"Then make it pretty for me."

She had to think. She had to make him understand. "You're attracted to her, Jake. I know you are. I can feel it when the two of you are together. Is that so horrible? She won't fight you; she'll be better for it." She gazed at him, her eyes pools of innocence. "It's not like she's a virgin; she's had men before. The movie will be better, and this is important to me. I've worked hard. This is what I've wanted all my life. Don't you care about the movie, Jake?"

He pulled her away from the door of the truck. He could feel the bone beneath her flesh, and he tightened his grip; he wanted to hurt her. "Get away from me! Get the hell away from me." Jerking open the door, he climbed in and then slammed it behind him. As he drove away from her, he was breathing hard.

The house was dark when Belinda got home. Fleur's door was unlocked, so she slipped inside to look down at her sleeping daughter. A curl of hair was stuck to her cheek. Tenderly she pushed it away. Fleur stirred.

"Belinda?" she said groggily.

"It's all right, darling. Go back to sleep."

"Smelled your perfume," Fleur murmured, and then she was quiet.

Belinda sat awake the rest of the night. She had avoided letting herself think about Fleur and Jake because of her own jealousy, and she saw now how ridiculous that was. Jake needed a woman who was larger than life, someone like Fleur, who was a celebrity in her own right. They could become one of Hollywood's great, shining couples, like Gable and Lombard, or Liz Taylor and Mike Todd. And all that reflected starlight would fall on her.

The more she thought about it, the more certain she became that Fleur had frozen up because of her feelings for him. It would be typical of her silly convent prudery. The fact that she'd never confided in Belinda was part of the problem; she was too afraid someone would find out and she'd look ridiculous, even though it was perfectly natural for her to be attracted to him. What red-blooded female wouldn't be?

The more Belinda thought about it, the more certain she was that once Fleur had let down some of those defenses, she would be able to do the scene right. And what better place to let those defenses down than in Jake Koranda's bed. The question was, How could she bring it off? She smoked another cigarette and decided that, even though she couldn't force Jake to make love to Fleur, she could make it easy for him.

She wrote a script in her head, discarded it, and then wrote another that she discarded, too. But before long she came up with one that she thought might work. It was a little improbable, and so simple that it was nearly transparent, but that's what made it appealing. After all, this was Hollywood, where disbelief was suspended every day, and the impossible was commonplace.

She practiced on a pad of unlined stationery, using some handwritten notes Jake had made on Fleur's script as her guide. After several hours, she was satisfied. It certainly wouldn't bear close scrutiny, but the overall impression was right. She woke Dick Spano at six with a phone call and managed to get what she wanted without revealing her purpose. Then she went back to her notepad.

Fleur walked into the kitchen at nine and filled a mug from the Mr. Coffee on the counter, then looked over at Belinda sitting at the table in a seashell pink Fernando Sanchez silk robe. She looked tired, as if she hadn't slept very well.

"How much longer are you going to punish me, Fleur?"

"I'm not punishing you."

"Really? Do you call four days of silence normal?"

Fleur opened the refrigerator and pulled out a carton of milk. "What you did to me was wrong."

"I know that now."

Fleur turned to her, surprised that she was admitting it.

"I'm not perfect, baby. Sometimes my ambition for you gets the better of me. But you're special, and I won't ever let you forget that. The rules for celebrities aren't the same as those for ordinary people. Your destiny was carved out for you when you were conceived; it's in your blood. I love you with all my heart, and I want only the best for you. Forgive me, baby."

Belinda suddenly looked very fragile. Her eyes were glittering with tears and Fleur found herself wondering why she kept hurting the person she loved most in the world. A wave of panic shot through her. If she didn't have Belinda, who would she have? Without knowing quite how it happened, she found herself holding out her arms. "Of course I forgive you. I love you."

Belinda's smile quivered, and then she hugged Fleur to her. "Let's spend the day right here. We'll take the phone off the hook and sit by the pool and have a wonderful time, just like we always do. Rosa will fix us a special lunch, and we'll tell her to forget about calories."

Fleur had wanted to spend the day riding, but she nodded her head in agreement instead. "I'd like that."

Later that afternoon after artichoke soufflé and a game of five hundred rummy, Belinda tried to get her to talk about what had happened the day before, but Fleur wouldn't. She couldn't think about it, and she couldn't think about what was ahead of her on Monday morning when the undressing part was over and she had to make love to Jake.

They decided to get dressed and go to an early movie. As Fleur stepped out of the shower, Belinda came into the bathroom holding a stack of mail. "Darling, I found the strangest thing in the mailbox. It's a letter addressed to you, but there's no stamp on it. Someone must have put it in the box."

Fleur fastened the towel around her and reached for the envelope. She tore it open and pulled out two sheets of white stationery. The top sheet was covered with untidy handwriting.

Dear Flower,
It's after midnight and there are no lights on in the house, so I'm leaving this note. I have to talk to you, and it can't wait until Monday. Please, Flower, if you care about me, drive up to my place as soon as you can Saturday morning. You can be there in about three hours. I've enclosed a map. Don't disappoint me, kiddo. I need you.
Jake

"What is it?"
Fleur handed her the note.

196

"Goodness. What in the world could be wrong?"

"I don't know, but I wish I'd checked the mail earlier. There's no way I can get up there before dark."

"I'll pack an overnight case for you."

Neither of them mentioned the possibility that Fleur wouldn't go.

She pulled on the clothes Belinda handed her—a pair of lace panties, a flesh-colored slip, a little oatmeal string-knit cotton dress, and candy-striped sandals that tied at the ankle. Her hair was wet, and she left it down so it could dry. On her way out the door, Belinda clipped a pair of gold hoops to her ears and put a dab of perfume behind them. Fleur was on the freeway before she realized she wasn't wearing a bra.

As she stopped near Santa Barbara for gas, she wished she'd gotten Jake's phone number before she left and called him, but his note had seemed so urgent, and she'd been in such a hurry. Sliding back behind the wheel, she tried for the hundredth time to imagine what he wanted. The general drift of her thoughts had been the same since she'd first seen the note. Jake had finally realized he loved her and didn't want to wait any longer to tell her. She knew there could be any of a number of other explanations, but that was the one she liked best.

It was late by the time she passed through Morro Bay and found the turnoff marked on the map. The road was deserted, and she drove for some time before she saw the bend and the mailbox that was her next marker. She turned onto a steep gravel road that proved to be treacherously narrow. There were no signs of other houses tucked away in the stands of pine and chaparral that stretched on both sides of the road. She drove uphill for nearly a mile. Just as the engine began to labor, she saw the lights.

The house was a cantilevered saucer of concrete and glass that seemed to have grown out of the barren slope of the hillside. She pulled into the lighted drive that curved in front and turned off the ignition. As she stepped out of the car, the wind tossed her hair so that it slapped against her cheeks. The air smelled of salt and rain.

He must have heard the car, because the front door opened

just before she pushed the bell. The light shone from behind him, outlining his size but making his features indistinct.

"Flower?"

"Hello, Jake."

CHAPTER 15

Fleur waited for him to invite her in, but he just stood there scowling at her. He was wearing jeans and a black sweatshirt turned inside out with the sleeves chopped off at midarm. He looked exhausted. The bones of his face were sharper than ever and he hadn't shaved. But there was something else on his face besides exhaustion, something that reminded her of that first day on the set when she had watched him beat up Lynn. He looked jagged and mean.

"Can I use the bathroom?" she asked nervously.

For a moment she didn't think he was going to let her in. Finally, he shrugged and stepped aside. "I never argue with the Fates."

"What?"

"Help yourself."

The interior of the house was like nothing she had ever seen. It was an open space contained by outer walls of glass. Great concrete angles separated the areas of the house, and ramps took the place of stairs. Everything seemed to have been designed to confuse the boundaries between inside and outside. Couches covered with nubby upholstery grew out of the walls; woven carpets were scattered over the floors. Nothing had been done to soften the interior of the house, and even its colors were those of the outdoors: the pewter of the ocean, the whites and grays of rock and stone.

"It's beautiful, Jake."

"The bathroom's down that ramp."

She looked at him nervously. Something was obviously very wrong, but she needed a few moments alone to collect herself before she faced whatever it was. As she walked in the direction he had indicated, she spotted a study off to the side with a wall of books and an old library table holding a typewriter. Crumpled balls of paper littered the floor, one even resting high on a bookshelf, as if it had been thrown across the room in anger.

She shut the door and gazed around her at the biggest bathroom she'd ever seen, a cavern of black and bronze tile with a vast sunken tub and a wall of glass that hung out over the edge of the cliff. Everything in the room was oversized: the tub, the shower stall sculpted into the wall, the twin sinks that were at least six inches higher than normal.

She caught sight of herself in the mirror and suddenly forgot about the bathroom. She could hardly believe how she looked. The flesh-colored slip made it seem as if she were naked underneath the string knit dress, which wasn't far from the truth when she thought about it. Why hadn't she paid more attention when Belinda was handing her clothes? But then, as she studied herself more closely and thought about how forbidding Jake's expression had been when he saw her, she decided that maybe she was glad she hadn't. She definitely didn't look like anybody's kid sister tonight. It seemed as if the Glitter Baby had come to call on Bird Dog Caliber.

When she came out, Jake was sitting in the living room, a glass in his hand filled with something that looked suspiciously like straight whiskey.

"I thought you only drank beer," she said.

"That's right. Anything else turns me into a bad-tempered drunk."

"Then why—?"

"Do you mind telling me what the hell you're doing here?"

Her insides twisted. Stupid. How could she have been so stupid? If she'd only stopped to think before she'd run off so quickly. Her cheeks burned with embarrassment. Reaching inside her purse, she handed him the note.

As he read it the seconds ticked by, each one an eternity. Suddenly he crumpled the paper into a tight ball and shot it across the room toward the empty fireplace. What was wrong with her? She should have known he would never have written anything like that. It was some kind of joke. But who could have written it? She suddenly thought of Lynn with her well-meant but misguided attempts at matchmaking. She'd kill her. As Jake gazed in her direction, she felt like crawling into a hole.

"Frigging door-to-door delivery," he muttered.

"What?"

"You were set up. That's not my handwriting."

"I've already figured that out." She ran her fingers up and down the strap of her purse. "Look, I'm sorry. It must have been somebody's idea of a joke. Not a very good one."

Abruptly he drained his glass. Then his eyes flicked down over the little string dress, lingering on her breasts and her legs. Her embarrassment suddenly left her, and she felt more in control than she had felt since she arrived, as if some subtle balance between them had shifted in her direction.

"Tell me what went wrong on Friday," he said. "I've seen actresses who aren't crazy about taking off their clothes, but I've never seen anything like what happened to you."

"Pretty unprofessional, wasn't I?"

"Let's just say that you blew any chance of a career as a stripper." He walked behind a teak bar, pulled out a bottle of Wild Turkey, and filled his glass halfway to the top. "Why don't you tell me about it?"

She sat down on the couch and tucked one foot under her. The little string dress rode up on her thighs. Jake gazed at her legs, then took a deep swallow from his glass and stepped out from behind the bar.

"There's nothing much to tell," she said. "I hate it, that's all."

"Taking off your clothes, or life in general?"

"I don't like this business, Jake. I don't like acting and I don't like making films."

"Then why do it?" He leaned back against the bar, one arm resting on the top. All he needed was a dusty trail hat, she thought, and a polished brass rail to prop his foot on.

"It's not that simple."

"It's your life."

"Is it? Lives get all tangled up together."

"Belinda uses you."

"Belinda loves me. She just doesn't understand that people have different dreams. She only wants what's best for me."

"Do you honestly believe that? Do you really believe she's only thinking about your welfare?"

"Yes. Yes, that's what I believe." She glared at him, daring him to try to tell her differently, but he didn't say anything. "Look, I'm really going to try on Monday. I know how important the scene is. I think if I really try—"

"You weren't trying on Friday? Come off it, kiddo. This is Uncle Jake you're talking to."

"Don't do that!" she exclaimed. "I hate it when you do that! I'm not a child, and you're not my uncle."

Suddenly his eyes narrowed and his jaw set in a hard line. "We needed a woman to play Lizzie," he said. "Instead we hired a kid."

His words should have wiped her out. They should have broken her into a million pieces and sent her flying from the house in tears. Instead she stared into those narrowed eyes and studied that hard, set face, and felt strength flowing through her. No matter what he said, he wasn't looking at her as if she was a kid. Flickering beneath that shut-off expression she saw something she recognized because she had been feeling it for so long herself. Beneath his hostility, Jake wanted her. Suddenly she understood all the things that Lizzie understood, and she knew exactly what gave Lizzie her power.

"The only kid in the room," she said softly, "is you."

He didn't like that at all. "Don't play bitch games with me, kiddo," he hissed. "I've played them with the best, and believe me, you're not even in the running."

She knew then that she had him. She let her fingers trail through her hair and looked up at him through her lashes. "Is that so?"

"Careful, Flower. Don't do anything you're going to regret, especially when you're wearing that dress. It might be interpreted as a challenge."

"A challenge to do what?" She dropped her voice so that it was low and husky.

He hesitated. "I think maybe I'd better drive you into Morro Bay. There are a couple of nice inns there."

In another two weeks the picture would be over, and she might never see Jake again, and if she was going to prove to him that she was a woman, this was the time to do it, while she was wearing a sexy dress and while he kept looking at her legs. Despite his words, she could see the desire in his eyes. A man's desire for a woman. She stood and walked over to the window, her hair swishing across her back, the gold hoops swinging from her ears, and the little string dress playing peek-a-boo with her hips.

"What makes you think I'm challenging you?" Tugging seductively on one of the gold hoops, she turned to face him, her heart pounding in her chest.

His voice had a rough catch to it. "I mean that you're not looking as ugly as usual to me tonight, Flower, and I think you'd better go."

She leaned her shoulders back against the glass so that her hips were angled forward and her legs stretched out. "If you want me to go"—she bent one knee just until it tilted open, exposing the inside curve of her thigh—"you'll have to make me."

He slammed his glass down on the bar and wiped his mouth with the back of his hand, just like he'd done in a dozen films. "You want to play games? Okay, baby. Let's play."

He started coming toward her, and something in his face made her afraid she'd pushed him too far. This wasn't a film, and he wasn't Bird Dog. Jake was out of control.

Her hips bumped up against the window as she tried to move away, but he caught her before she could take a step, snagging her shoulders and pulling her against his chest. "Come on, kid. Let's see what you've got."

His head swooped down and he closed his mouth over hers. She felt like she was suffocating. His teeth ground into her bottom lip as he forced her mouth open. She tasted the whiskey on his tongue and tried to tell herself this was Jake and she didn't have to be afraid. His hands slipped under her dress, moving up along the sides of her hips and then sliding under her panties to cup her bare buttocks. As he pulled her hard against him, her newfound sense of power evaporated, and she decided maybe he was right. Maybe she was a kid, playing a woman's game, and maybe she'd just jumped in over her head. His hands pushed up higher, taking her dress with them. The front of his jeans scraped against the bare flesh of her stomach, and his tongue probed deeper into her mouth, while his thumb found her nipple.

This wasn't the way it was supposed to happen! He was too fierce, too scary. . . . She wanted music and flowers; she wanted tender bodies in soft focus. Pressing her hands against his chest, she started to struggle. "Jake . . ." She sobbed out his name.

"What's the matter?" The harsh sound of his breathing

rasped in her ear. "This is what you wanted, isn't it? You wanted me to treat you like a woman!"

"Like a woman, not a whore!" She jerked past him and ran toward the front door, numb with disappointment because he hadn't been the lover she'd dreamed he would be, crushed with a sense of her own inadequacy. What was wrong with her? How could she have been so wrong about him? Just as she reached for the knob, she remembered her purse lying on the couch with the keys to the Porsche inside. Slowly she turned back.

As soon as she saw him picking up the telephone, she realized that something wasn't right. He was too calm. Too sad. She made herself look at him with her heart instead of her head, and then he became as transparent as a wall of glass.

". . . have a suite available for tonight? Good. Yes, that'll be fine. No, just one ni—"

She walked over and pushed her hand down on the button, breaking the connection.

He jumped up from the arm of the couch. "What in the living hell do you think you're doing?" he shouted. "Haven't you had enough for tonight?"

She pushed her chin up and stared him straight in the eye. "No, Jake. I want a lot more."

"Dammit!" He slammed down the receiver.

"Why are you trying to scare me away?"

"What are you talking about?"

"Nobody's ever accused you of being the world's greatest actor, but even coming from you, that was a lousy performance."

He raked his hands through his hair. "This has gone far enough, Flower."

"You're a chicken. No guts."

"I'll drive you to the inn—"

"You want me," she said. "I know you do."

His jaw clenched, but he kept his voice even. "After you get a good night's sleep—"

"I want to sleep here."

"—I'll pick you up and take you to breakfast tomorrow. How about that?"

Her smile was tight with contempt. "Golly, Uncle Jake, it sounds super. Will you buy me a lollipop, too?"

His face darkened with fury. *"How much am I supposed to take?"* he shouted. *"What the hell do you want from me?"*

"Admit that I'm a woman! Admit that you want me!"

"You're a goddam kid. A kid, dammit! And I *don't* want you!"

She looked at him long and hard, certain he was lying to her. Almost certain. He had to be lying, didn't he? Suddenly she was no longer sure, and she hurt too much to go on. She wasn't going to beg him to love her; she had that much pride left. "I hate you!" she shouted, in a stupid, adolescent outburst, throwing away her last shred of dignity.

Grabbing her purse from the couch, she headed toward the door, but he caught her arm before she could touch the knob and spun her around, the fierceness in his eyes making her flinch. "Your exit line came too late, babe! You had your chance, and you just blew it."

He began pulling her through the house, and she had to go with him or fall. Down one ramp and then another . . . through an arch . . . up another ramp . . .

"Jake . . ."

"Shut up!"

"My arm is—"

"I don't care!"

He dragged her into a room that held the biggest bed she had ever seen. Covered with a gray and black satin spread, it stood on a platform directly beneath an enormous skylight. He scooped her up in his arms, climbed the two steps, and dropped her on the bed.

"Are you ready, Flower?" he growled. "Is everything taken care of?"

As far as she was concerned, nothing was taken care of, but his expression was so forbidding that she decided to keep her mouth shut and just nod.

"Okay, kiddo." He crossed his arms over his chest and pulled off his sweatshirt. "Time to play with the big boys."

A chill shot through her body, and her grip tightened on the coverlet. "Jake?"

"Yeah."

"You're scaring me."

His hands opened the snap of his jeans. "Tough."

Why wouldn't he look at her? She stared up at the stars

through the skylight, heard the harsh rasp of denim sliding against denim, and then turned her head to see him standing near the bottom of the bed, clad only in a pair of black briefs. She bit down on the inside of her lip. The briefs were all wrong. She wanted to see friendly white cotton. Or something baggy and faded like his swim trunks. She'd never seen that much of his stomach before, never imagined it so lean and flat. She concentrated on his stomach, traced the tendons with her eyes, did everything she could to keep her gaze from dropping lower to that forbidding vertical shaft that the briefs were much too small and much too tight to conceal. He did want her. She could see the evidence. So why was he being so mean to her?

She jumped as his hand shackled one of her ankles, jerking at the tie of her sandal and pulling it off her foot. Then he captured the other ankle and pitched the second shoe to the floor. He was no longer making any effort to conceal his desire. She could feel it like a wave of heat washing over her body as his eyes lingered on her skin. But why was he so grim? So rough?

She pushed herself up into the pillows, trying to move away from him. "I—I think I changed my mind. I don't want to do this anymore."

His eyes touched her breasts, her hips, swept down her legs. "Too late." He leaned forward and tugged open the tie at the top of her dress.

"I'd rather not—"

He caught her by the shoulder and pulled her up into a kneeling position, whipping the little string dress over her head. "I've busted my ass playing the good guy around you, and I'm sick of it! I tried to warn you away, but you wouldn't pay attention; you wanted to play games. So when all this is over, you'd damn well better remember who started it." She was crying now, but he ignored her tears as he reached for the hem of her slip.

"No!" She slapped hard at his arm. "No! I don't like this! This isn't what I want!"

A muscle ticked on the side of his neck. "It's my game now," he said tightly, "and we're playing by grown-ups' rules." With one hard jerk, he stripped off her slip, pulling it free from her hair and leaving her in nothing but her panties and the pair of swaying gold hoops. "That's more like it. Now I can see all those parts of you I had to pretend not to look at on Friday."

"No!" Tears were streaming down her cheeks. "I know what

206

you're trying to do, and I won't let you! Do you hear me, Jake Koranda? I won't let you make this *bad* for me."

His voice was tight and hard. "Bad? I don't know what you're talking about."

She shook her head frantically. "You're trying to ruin this. You want to keep this from being *important* to me!"

"It's not important!" he exclaimed harshly, pulling off her panties and covering her body with his own so she couldn't move. "This is copulation, kiddo. Animal copulation." His fingers found her, their touch clinical, almost impersonal. "Do you like the way this feels? Is this the way you like it?"

"No! No, I—" She tried to close her legs, but he wedged one of his knees between and held them apart.

"Tell me how you want it."

"Why are you doing this?" she sobbed. "You don't treat other women this way, so why are you doing it to me?"

"Fast? Slow? How do you want it, goddam it?"

"No!" The word was a scream. "I wanted flowers," she sobbed. "I wanted you to touch my body with flowers!"

A great shudder passed through his body. "God . . ." he muttered. "Shit."

He rolled away from her so that they were no longer touching and lay on his back staring up at the night sky. What was he thinking? she wondered. As the tears dried on her cheeks, she felt as if she were alone in the room. Why did he want to hurt her?

He reached out and touched her hand. Then he turned toward her and gently traced the curve of her shoulder with his fingers. "All right, baby," he whispered. "No more pretending. Let's do it right."

His mouth found hers in a soft, tender kiss that melted the great chill inside her. It wasn't anything like their kisses on camera. Their noses bumped. He opened his mouth and closed it over hers, the sound sweet and sloppy. His tongue slipped past the barrier of her teeth where she touched it with her own. It felt wonderful. Wet and rough and perfect. She wrapped her arms around his shoulders and pulled him so close she could feel his heartbeat on her breast.

Finally, he drew back, his fingers playing in her hair, his eyes gently gazing down at her. "I don't have any flowers," he murmured, "so I'll have to touch you with something else."

He dipped his head, and caught her nipple in his mouth. It swelled beneath his tongue, and she moaned as waves of pleasure washed through her. And then, like a lazy cowboy with all the time in the world, he roamed her body with his hands. His kisses trailed down over her stomach while he stroked her thighs, setting fires in all the empty spaces inside her. Then he drew up her knees and gently pushed them apart.

Moonlight washed in through the skylight, making patches of silver and shadow on his back, as his fingers played at the tight web of curls. Gently he opened her. "Flower petals," he whispered. "I found them." And then he dipped his head forward and covered her with his soft, sulky mouth.

The feeling was like nothing she had ever imagined. She called his name, but whether it was aloud or only in her mind, she didn't know. Spirals of pleasure whirled inside her, throwing off sparks like burning pinwheels, glowing brighter and hotter, ready to explode. . . . "No . . ."

He looked up at the sound of her strangled, panicked cry, but she didn't know how to tell him that she was afraid to go on a flight of her own. Smiling, he slid his body up beside her.

"Give up?" he murmured, his voice sexy and teasing and absolutely irresistible.

She felt the strong outline of him against her thigh and, unable to stop herself, slipped her hand beneath the waistband of his briefs. He was smooth and hard as a shaft of marble, and he let out a soft gasp as her fingers closed around him.

"What's the matter, cowboy?" she whispered. "Can't you take it?"

His breathing came in soft, sudden gasps. "Doesn't affect me one way or the other," he moaned.

She laughed and eased herself up to see him better, her hair brushing over his chest. "Is that so?" The briefs were in her way, so she peeled them off and experimented with the power of her touch. Here . . . there . . . here again . . . She stroked with the end of her finger, the pad of her thumb, a lock of her hair. Finally, she touched him with the tip of her tongue. . . .

His cry was hoarse and deep.

She licked him like a cat, feeling a deep, fierce joy swell inside her at the power she possessed. Then his hands settled around her shoulders, pulling her back up next to him.

"I give up," he said hoarsely, nibbling at her bottom lip.

"Quitter," she murmured.

His hand went to her breast, squeezing her nipple. "Looks like I'm going to have to remind you who's the boss."

"You and what army?" she said huskily, touching his crooked tooth with the tip of her tongue.

"The lady never learns." He covered her with the lean length of his body. "Open up, baby. You're about to meet your master." She opened for him gladly, burning to receive him and love him, laughing up into smoky-blue eyes that were bright with desire. . . .

He heard the sweet, soft woman's sound coming from deep in her throat, and it seared the edges of his soul. Gazing down into her eyes, he wordlessly begged her to hold something back, but she smiled all her love up at him, and the softness of her face sliced him in two. He stabbed himself deep within her. It was a harsh possession, much rougher than he intended. He had not expected her to be so tight. He had not expected . . . Christ.

She let out a small cry of pain, and he felt the bottom drop out of his stomach.

"Flower . . . My God . . ." He began to pull away, but she dug her fingers into his buttocks.

"No. If you do, I'll never forgive you."

He wanted to cry. He wanted to throw his head back and scream out his rage at Belinda's lies and his own stupidity. Why hadn't he scared Flower away like he wanted to? Why had he given in to his own lust? Lust. That's all it was. He'd wanted her from the first moment he saw her. He'd stood on that soundstage with Lynnie sobbing in his arms, and he'd looked over at that long, beautiful body and lusted after it.

He felt her chorus girl legs winding themselves around his own, felt her pulling him more deeply inside, even though it had to hurt her, and he couldn't find the strength to hurt her more by drawing away. It took all his will, but he held himself still, giving her time to grow accustomed to his size. "I'm sorry, Flower. I didn't know."

She moved her hips, trying to draw him tighter.

"Shhh." He stroked her hair, played at her lips. "Give it a minute," he whispered.

"I'm okay."

He wondered how he could stay hard inside her when he had just committed the world's greatest shitheel act. Jake Koranda,

King of the Shitheels. Still hard as a pike. Rutting like a mountain goat. Sticking it to the kid with the big eyes. He buried his head in her neck and tangled his fingers in her hair and began moving gently inside her. She shuddered and her hands dug into his shoulders.

He stopped at once. "Hurt?"

"No," she gasped. "Please—" He drew back so he could see her face. Her eyes were squeezed shut, her lips parted, not with pain, he suddenly realized, but with passion. He lifted his hips and stroked her, deep and long. Once . . . twice . . . And then he watched in delight as she shattered beneath him.

He calmed her through the aftershocks. Finally her eyes drifted open, unfocused for a moment, and then gradually cleared. She murmured something he couldn't quite hear, and then she smiled up at him. "That was wonderful," she whispered.

Amusement danced in his eyes. "Glad you were pleased."

"I didn't imagine it would be quite so—so—"

"Boring?"

She laughed.

"Tedious?" he suggested.

"Not exactly the words I'm looking for."

"How about—"

"Stupendous," she offered. "Colossal."

"Flower?"

"Yes?"

"I don't know if you've noticed, but we're not exactly done yet."

"We're not—" Her eyes suddenly widened. "Oh . . ."

He watched as her comprehension changed to embarrassment. "I—I'm sorry," she stuttered. "I didn't mean to be a pig or anything. I didn't know— I mean . . ." Her voice trailed miserably away.

He hid his smile by tugging on her earlobe with his teeth. "You can doze off now if you want to," he whispered. "Read a book or something. I'll try not to bother you." Once again he began to move inside her. He felt her body relax and then gradually grow tense again as her fingers dug into his sides. She was so soft and good, so sweet. . . .

"Oh . . ." she whispered. "It's going to happen again, isn't it?"

"You can bet on it," he said huskily.

Moments later, they fell off the end of the world together.

CHAPTER 16

"It was a stupid-ass thing to do."

"Stuff it, Koranda." She had awakened a little after two in the morning to find that she was alone in bed. Slipping on her panties and Jake's black sweatshirt, she'd found him in the kitchen devouring a serving bowl piled high with more ice cream than she had ever seen in a single helping. He had started to yell at her the minute he saw her, all the softness and the laughter of their lovemaking forgotten, and they had been arguing ever since.

Part of his anger, she supposed, was justifiable, but how was she supposed to have known he had been talking about birth control when he'd asked her if everything was taken care of? She told him her period was due in another three days, so she thought she was pretty safe, but he still yelled. It hadn't taken her long to figure out that he was really mad about the fact that he'd been the first.

"You should have told me before we did it." He set his dish in the sink and jerked on the faucet.

"Did it? You've got a real gift for self-expression. Ever think about becoming a writer when you grow up?"

"Don't be such a smart-ass. It wasn't right, Flower, not telling me first."

She smiled sweetly. "Afraid I wouldn't respect you in the morning?" She was getting good at it, matching him wisecrack for wisecrack. The world according to Koranda. How had she ever let herself love him so much when he didn't seem to want to give anything back? And why couldn't he just stop talking and kiss her?

"Damn, it, Flower! I wouldn't have been so rough!"

She couldn't stand it any longer, and she began opening drawers at random, looking for a rubber band. "Listen, I don't owe you any explanations," she declared. "Now just shut up, will you?" She found what she wanted and pulled her hair into a ponytail high on her head. Then she walked into the living room and scooped up a batch of chunky candles she had seen on the table.

"What do you think you're doing?"

"I'm going to take a bath," she replied.

"It's almost three in the morning."

"I can't help it. I'm stinky."

For the first time since she'd walked into the kitchen, he seemed to relax, almost managing that cocky grin that made her want to slap him and kiss him at the same time. "Yeah? Why is that?"

"You're the expert. You tell me." She knew his sweatshirt didn't completely cover her panties, and she twitched her rear just a little bit more than normal as she walked away from him.

She set the candles around the edge of the sunken tub and lit them before she turned on the faucet and poured in a generous amount of bubble bath from a bottle sitting on the side. Jake's bubble bath? Somehow she didn't think so. One of those junior petites probably. She hated every single one of them.

While the tub was filling, she twisted her hair on top of her head and secured it with some pins from the bottom of her purse. Despite Jake's abrupt mood swings, she didn't regret what had happened between them. When he had been inside her, she'd felt as if her heart would burst with the enormity of her love for him. She had chosen to give herself to him. Of all the choices in her life, that one had been hers alone. Pulling off her clothes, she slipped down into the water, remembering that sweet moment of pain when he'd entered her, remembering his tenderness afterward. The candle flames shone back at her from the wall of glass, and she felt like she was floating in space.

"Is this a private party, or can anybody join?"

She decided the question was rhetorical since he was already unzipping his jeans. "Depends."

"On what?"

"On whether you're done with your lecture or not."

"Lecture's over." He muttered something as he stepped into the tub and eased down beside her.

"What did you say?" she asked.

"Nothing."

"Dammit, Jake!"

"All right!" he yelled. "I said I was sorry."

"Sorry for what? Exactly what are you sorry for?" As she pushed herself up on her elbows, she could hear her voice shaking and she was afraid she was going to start crying again.

He must have heard it, too. He raised himself to his knees and pulled her into his arms. "Nothing, babe. I'm not sorry for a damn thing except being so rough on you."

And then he was kissing her and she was kissing him back, and her hair came undone and neither of them noticed. They wrapped their legs and arms together and fell back in the bubbles, and Fleur twisted her hair around them both. Jake pulled the plug so they could breathe; then he began covering her body with his mouth, loving her in that delicious way that made her cry out again and again until he stilled her with his kisses.

Afterwards he wrapped her in a towel. "Now that you've worn me out," he said, knotting another towel around his own hips, "how about feeding me? I haven't had anything but ice cream and potato chips since I got here, and I'm a lousy cook."

"Don't look at me. I'm a rich kid, remember."

"Are you trying to tell me you don't know how to cook?"

"Pancakes from a mix."

"God, even I can do better than that."

For the next hour, they made a mess of the kitchen, grilling steaks that didn't have the decency to thaw in the middle, incinerating a loaf of french bread under the broiler, and fixing a salad from a head of browning lettuce and some limp carrots. It was the best meal Fleur ever ate.

The next morning they started to go for a run, but went back to bed instead. In the afternoon they played cards and told terrible jokes and took another bath. Jake woke her up just before dawn on Monday morning for the drive back to Los Angeles. He had made arrangements to have the Porsche returned that afternoon so they could drive back together, but it wasn't long before Fleur began to wonder why he'd bothered, since he hardly talked the whole way to the studio.

By the time she'd finished with her makeup and walked on the set, she could see that Jake's mood had deteriorated even further. He was arguing with Johnny Guy about the revision he hadn't finished that weekend and being generally disagreeable to everyone in his path. He scowled when he saw her.

One little part of her was pleased by his bad temper. Even

though no words had been spoken, he couldn't have remained unaffected after everything that had happened between them. Besides, if he didn't care about her, he wouldn't be acting like this, would he?

Johnny Guy came over. "Now, honey, I know it was a little hard on you Friday, but we'll try to make things easier today. I've made some changes—"

"Forget the changes, Johnny Guy. Let's do it right."

He looked at her in surprise and she gave him a cocky thumbs-up—as if she were Amelia Earhart ready to take off over the Pacific. It was her life. If she wanted to do this scene, she could do it! She wasn't going to let Jake forget that she was a woman, not a kid.

Jake wasn't happy. "I thought we decided we were going to cut most of this. Hell, we already know she can't handle it. Why waste any more time?"

"The little lady says she wants to give it a try, so she gets her chance. Showtime, boys and girls. Let's go to work."

The cameras rolled. Jake glowered at her from across the tiny bedroom. She grinned at him, her hands going to her buttons. He was too cocky, and she was going to show him. She stepped out of the dress, never taking her eyes off him. They had secrets now, the two of them. It was just the two of them. He was funny and dear, and she loved him with all her heart. He had to love her, too—just a little—or he could never have made such sweet love to her. Please let him love her.

She unfastened her bra. Jake scowled and stepped off his mark. "Cut it, Johnny Guy!"

"God damn it, Jako, I'm the one who calls cut! She was doing great! What the hell is wrong with you!" Johnny Guy was furious. He slapped his hand against his leg, taking two jerky steps in an angry dance. "God damn it! Nobody calls 'cut'! Nobody! Not unless I say so!" The tirade went on for another few minutes as Jake grew more and more sullen. When he finally complained that a chair had been moved out of position, Johnny Guy nearly hit him.

"It's okay, Johnny Guy," she said, very much a woman in control. "I'm ready to go again."

The cameras rolled. Jake's face was a thundercloud. The bra came off. She did it slowly, tantalizing him, torturing him with her delicious, newfound power. Bending over, she pulled off the panties and walked over to him.

His body was rigid as she unbuttoned his shirt and slipped her hands inside. She touched the spot she had kissed just that morning when she had awakened. She pushed her hips against his, and then did something that hadn't been rehearsed. She leaned forward and flicked her tongue over one of his nipples.

"Cut and print!" Johnny Guy yelled, jumping around from the side of the camera like a jubilant jack-in-the-box.

Jake jerked the white terry cloth robe away from the wardrobe girl who had appeared around the curtain and thrust it at her. "What the hell's wrong with you?" he scowled.

The work proceeded well for the rest of the morning, and by lunchtime they had reshot all the material from Friday and were making steady progress toward finishing the scene. Unless the cameras were rolling, Jake barely talked to her, but she refused to let it bother her. He was acting like a jealous lover, she told herself. He didn't want anyone else to see her.

Johnny Guy captured everything—Jake's tension, his guilt, the anguish simmering just beneath the surface . . . and Fleur's relentless seduction. He captured it all and congratulated himself on a job well done.

Fleur hung on to her optimism as long as she could, but as the week dragged on and Jake kept his distance, she felt the first beginnings of despair. He had to love her; he just had to. . . . Instead of counting days, she began counting hours until the film was finished. She wanted to talk to him, to scream at him, to throw herself in his arms and beg him to love her as she loved him. On Thursday, when his work was done, he disappeared without a word.

"Didn't he say anything to you, darling?" Belinda asked. "Surely he's planning on being back for Johnny Guy's party this weekend."

"I really don't know. Jake doesn't report in to me."

Belinda smiled coquettishly. "Maybe you should do something about that, baby."

Fleur turned away. She didn't want her mother advising her about Jake. This was hers. Just hers.

The party to celebrate the end of the filming of *Sunday Morning Eclipse* had drawn Hollywood's A list, which was not surprising, since Marcella Kelly was one of the town's most successful hostesses. It was hardly her fault that Fleur was miserable. She had agreed to let Dick Spano escort her only at the last moment, when she had finally accepted the fact that Jake wasn't going to call, and even the snatches of conversation she overheard as they wove their way through the guests failed to distract her from her unhappiness.

"How can you say he's a snob?" a blond young man was asking his male companion. "I personally watched him cut the alligators off his shirts."

"Only after they were sunfaded, darling," the companion replied.

They moved closer to the bar and the smell of a Cuban cigar. ". . . high concept idea when you add the Dallas Cowboy Cheerleaders . . ."

She had dressed with more care than normal in an ecru silk gown with shimmering horizontal stripes of mocha, beige, and terra cotta. The dress was tubular and had a subtle Egyptian feeling that she had emphasized with matching gold cuff bracelets and a pair of flat sandals with a jeweled clasp at the instep. She had braided her hair wet the night before and brushed it out after it was dry so that it fell down her back in a cascade of tiny waves. Marcella Kelly told her she looked like a blond Cleopatra.

Marcella was as different from her husband as a wife could be. Thin and sophisticated, she considered herself a trendsetter, having been the first to fondue during the sixties, and later, knowing the exact moment to drop Huey Newton from her guest list. She kept pointing out hors d'oeuvres to her guests— salmon cured in tequila, canapés decorated with nopal cactus leaves, *beignets* made from hydroponically grown vegetables. And all the while, Johnny Guy was walking around with a can of Orange Crush. Fleur wished Jake were there to share the humor, but then she wished Jake were there for a lot of reasons.

She tried to look as if she were concentrating on Dick Spano's conversation, but in actuality she was watching the crowd over the top of his head. She saw that Belinda had wedged Kirk Douglas into a corner, and that the actor had a slightly bemused expression on his face. He was undoubtedly being bombarded with the history of every film he had made, some of which he would probably just as soon forget.

217

Fleur sipped at her drink, nodding at everything Dick was saying without listening to any of it. A new group joined them, and several of the men began preening themselves in front of her. The Glitter Baby. It seemed especially ridiculous to her tonight.

She had just about given up hope that Jake would appear when he walked in with Lynn Davids and the unemployed documentary director who was her latest lover. Her heart gave a jump, and she felt dizzy. Before he could spot her, Marcella Kelly had swooped down on him and begun leading him through the clusters of guests, her prize catch put on display. Fleur suddenly realized that she couldn't face him in the midst of so many people. Excusing herself, she made her way to the bathroom and sat on the edge of the tub. Didn't he understand that they might not see each other again?

When someone finally knocked on the door, she slipped outside to the pool. What was she going to say to him when she finally saw him? Why don't you love me like I love you? Stupid. She felt a sprinkle of rain and went back into the house with the other guests who had drifted outside. When she looked around for him, she saw that he'd disappeared. Then she realized he wasn't the only one who had slipped from sight.

It didn't mean anything, she told herself. It couldn't. And even if Belinda and Jake were together, what harm was in it? But her heart was pounding, and all she could hear was her mother's voice saying, *I only do what's best for you, baby.* She began her search in earnest, moving from room to room, weaving through the guests. She couldn't stand it if Belinda tried to interfere. She'd never forgive her. Never.

She moved upstairs, and other than an embarrassing intrusion on Lynn and her lover, she saw no sign of anyone else. Where were they? Just as she was getting ready to go back downstairs, she heard a muffled conversation coming from Marcella Kelly's bedroom. It was a room she had already peeked into, but she went back to double-check and saw that there was a dressing alcove off to the left that she had missed. Walking toward it, she stopped abruptly at the sound of Jake's voice.

". . . drag me up here, Belinda. There's nothing more to talk about. Let's go back to the party."

"Two more minutes for old times' sake." Belinda's voice

218

dropped until it was so soft Fleur could barely hear her. "We had fun together, Jake. Remember? Remember how it was in Iowa? That awful motel."

Fleur could feel the inside of her mouth go dry. There was such intimacy in Belinda's voice. Why was she talking to Jake like that? She took another step forward and their figures seemed to jump out of nowhere. She caught her breath, only to realize that one wall of the dressing alcove was mirrored and she was seeing their reflections—Belinda in shrimp pink Karl Lagerfeld evening pajamas and Jake wearing a jacket that looked almost respectable.

He leaned back against a ledge that ran the length of the wall, his arms crossed over his chest. Belinda reached out and touched his arm, a soft, terrible expression on her face. Why was she looking at him like that? "I think it must be your mission in life to break the hearts of the Savagar women," she said. "Of course it's not so hard for me because I understand your spirit. I understand about rebels, and I guess I knew from the beginning that I wasn't special enough for you. But Fleur is. Don't you see that? The two of you belong together and you're breaking her heart."

Jake pulled away from her. "For God's sake, Belinda . . ."

"I sent her to you, Jake!" she exclaimed. "I sent her to you and now you're violating my trust."

He turned on her in anger. "Trust! You sent her to me to save five minutes worth of film that you didn't want to see end up on the cutting room floor. Five minutes of your precious Glitter Baby's career! Fuck my daughter, Koranda, so she can save her career, that's what you told me. Admit it at least to yourself."

"Don't be so sanctimonious," Belinda hissed. "I certainly wasn't foolish enough to expect gratitude from you, but I didn't think you'd turn on me. I just might have saved your picture."

"Don't be ridiculous. The picture was never in any danger."

"That's not how it looked to me. I did what I had to do."

"Really? Dropping your daughter on my doorstep for mother's magic bedroom cure, was that what you had to do? Tell me something, Belinda. Is this going to be a lifelong pattern with you, trying out all of your daughter's lovers first? Are you going to audition them to make sure their performance is up to your standards before you let them into baby's bed? What the hell kind of woman are you?"

"I'm a woman who loves her daughter."

"Bullshit. The only person you love is yourself. You don't even know your daughter." He spun around and came face to face with Fleur's reflection in the mirror.

Fleur couldn't move. The pain inside her twisted like some terrible beast, stealing her breath and her life, turning the world black and ugly. "Christ." Jake was beside her in an instant. "I'm sorry, Flower. It's not what you think."

Belinda let out a soft, sharp gasp. "Oh, my God. My baby." She ran to Fleur and grabbed her arms. "Baby, it's all right. It's all right, baby."

Tears rolled down Fleur's cheeks and dripped off her chin, and she jerked away, taking awkward steps backward to put herself out of reach of the awful beast. "Don't touch me! Don't either of you touch me!"

Belinda's face twisted. "Don't look like that. . . . Let me explain. I had to help you. I had to. . . . Don't you see? You could have ruined it for us—your career, all our plans, our dreams. You're a celebrity now. The rules are different for you. Don't you see that?"

"Shut up!" Fleur cried. "You're filthy. Both of you."

Belinda took a step toward her. "Please, baby . . ."

Fleur drew back her hand and slapped her mother as hard as she could. Belinda let out a cry and stumbled backwards, falling against the bed.

"Fleur!" Jake came forward.

"Stay away!" She balled her hands into fists at her sides.

"Listen to me, Fleur." He reached out for her and she went wild, swinging at him, screaming at him, kicking him, killing him . . . oh, God, kill him. He tried to pinion her arms, but she broke away and ran from the room. Dozens of startled faces stared up at her as she raced down the front staircase and out the door.

The rain was a driving downpour beating at her and drenching her to the skin in seconds. She wished it were ice, hard slivers of ice pounding at her, cutting her up and slicing her body into tiny pieces of flesh and bone that could all be washed away in the rain. She raced down the driveway, jerking up her wet skirts so she could go faster. The straps of the sandals bit into her feet and the soles began to slip on the wet blacktop, but she didn't slow down. She cut across the grass and ran for the gates.

She heard him behind her, screaming her name over the rain, and she ran faster. There was the sound of a curse and a growl and then his hand caught her by the shoulder, throwing her off balance. She tripped on the wet silk, and they fell together like the first time.

"Stop it, Flower. Please, stop." He grabbed her in his arms, pressing the back of her shoulders against his chest. Holding her there on the rain-soaked ground, he was breathing hard into her ear, rasping. "You can't go off like this," he said. "Let me take you home. Let me explain."

She thought he'd wanted *her* that night. The little oatmeal string dress and the flesh-colored slip and the shining gold hoops that had swung back and forth from her ears. Belinda had sent her in costume, and all the time she'd thought he loved her. "Get your hands off me!"

He tightened his grip on her as he turned her around so that she was facing him. His jacket was soaked and streaked with mud. His hair was plastered over his forehead, rivulets running down the lines of his face. "Just listen to me for a minute. What you heard wasn't the whole story."

She barred her teeth like a small animal. "Were you my mother's lover?"

"Yes, but—"

"Did she write that note, send me to you so that you could make love to me?"

"Whatever Belinda's motives were, they never had anything to do with mine!"

She swung at him with her fist. *"You shit!* Don't tell me you took me to bed because you fell in love with me!"

He caught her wrists, squeezing hard on them, hurting them. "Flower, there are different kinds of love. Maybe what I feel for you isn't exactly what you feel for me, but—"

Fleur tried to punch at him again. "Shut up! I loved you! I loved you with every part of me! And I don't want to hear about brothers and sisters and uncles. I don't want to hear any of your shit! Just let me go!"

Slowly his grip on her eased, and he did what she wanted. She stumbled to her feet and the words came out in little gusts.

221

"If you really want to help me . . . get Lynn. And then keep Belinda . . . away from me."

"Flower . . ."

"Give me an hour, you bastard. I deserve that much."

They stood in the rain, both of them with their chests heaving, hair and clothing soaked, and then he nodded and turned back to the house.

Lynn drove without asking questions. She was clearly reluctant to leave when they reached the house, but Fleur told her she was going right to bed. As soon as Lynn drove away, she ran into her room and began throwing clothes into her largest suitcase and a shoulder bag. Then she tore off her ruined dress and exchanged it for a pair of jeans. Jake and Belinda. Plotting over her, using her. . . . She'd made it so easy for them. Had they talked about her in bed? But that thought was too awful and she pushed it away.

She closed the suitcase and called the airline. Space was still available on the next flight to Paris. There was only one thing she had to do before she left. . . .

By the time Jake finally let Belinda go, she was frantic—even more so when she reached the house and saw that the Porsche was gone. She ran to Fleur's room and found the bed littered with discarded clothing, and the wet Egyptian dress lying on the floor. She picked up a nightgown from the pillow and buried her face in the soft nylon. Fleur would be back soon. She just needed some time to think, that was all. Sometimes children needed time away from their parents. It didn't mean anything. She and Fleur were inseparable, everybody knew that. Two halves that fit together to form one person. She'd be back. They had plans to make.

Belinda noticed that the light was on in the bathroom and walked over to switch it off. She spotted the scissors first, gleaming against the white basin, and then she let out a soft, anguished cry. The tiled floor was littered with a great mound of wet blond hair.

Jake drove aimlessly, trying not to think, but the icy lump wouldn't dissolve in his chest. The rain changed to a soft mist and he put the windshield wipers on slow speed. Shit. When they'd passed out strength of character, he'd been at the goddamn end of the line. Why couldn't he have scared her away like he wanted to? It would have been so goddamn simple. He knew how she felt about him, but he still hadn't been able to send her out the door.

He realized that he had left the fashionable suburbs behind him and was driving through the heart of Los Angeles. The wet streets were deserted. He shrugged out of his ruined jacket and drove in his shirtsleeves. God, she'd been beautiful. Sensuous, exciting . . . He cringed as he remembered how he'd hurt her that first time, and how she'd still held on to him, how she'd kept right on trusting him. . . .

The playground was on a street littered with trash and end-of-the-line dreams. There was a jungle gym missing its horizontal bars and the skeletal frame of a swing set. A single floodlight shone over a backboard holding a rusted rim and the fragments of what once had been a net. He parked the truck and reached behind the seat for the basketball. Only a kid would be dumb enough to trust like she did. A spoiled rich kid who hadn't been knocked around enough by life to get smart.

He crossed the street to the empty playground, ignoring the puddles that lay in his path. She'd been knocked around now. She'd been so goddamn knocked around she'd never be dumb again. He stepped out on the cracked asphalt and began to dribble the ball. It pounded off the asphalt, off his hand, feeling good, feeling like something he understood. He wanted her out of his life, damn it! He didn't want to remember her beautiful and wet and dreamy-eyed, lying in his bathtub encircled by candles. He didn't want to think about how bleak his life was going to be without her.

He dribbled hard toward the basket, picking up his pace as he drew closer. Driving in, he slammed the ball home. The rim quivered and his hand stung, but he was barely aware of it as the crowd began to roar around him. He made up his mind to pull out the stops—show the crowd his stuff—get them screaming so loud he wouldn't be able to hear any of the other voices inside him.

He spun past an opponent and took the ball to center court. He was a loner. It was the style of life that suited him—the safest way. He faked to the right, to the left, then came off the dribble for a quick jump shot. The crowd went wild, screaming out for him.

Doc! Doc! Doc!

He grabbed the ball and spotted Kareem just ahead waiting for him, a cold killing machine. Kareem, barely human, the face of his nightmares. Fake him. He started to swing left, but Kareem wasn't human. Kareem was a machine who read minds. Quick, before he sees it in your eyes, before he feels it through his pores, before he knows all your darkest secrets. Now. He wheeled to the right, lightning fast, jumped, flying through the air . . . man can't fly, but I can . . . past Kareem . . . into the stratosphere. . . . SLAM!

Doc! They were on their feet. *Doc!* they screamed.

Kareem looked at him and they silently acknowledged each other with the perfect kind of respect that can only pass between legends. And then the moment was gone and they were enemies again.

The ball was alive beneath his fingertips. He thought only of the ball; he wouldn't let himself think of anything else. It was a perfect world. A world where a man could walk like a giant and never feel shame. A world with referees who clearly signaled right and wrong. A world that contained no tender babies with broken hearts.

Jake Koranda. Actor. Playwright. Winner of the Pulitzer prize. He wanted to give it all up and live his fantasy. He wanted to be Julius Erving, running down the court on feet with wings, leaping into the clouds, flying higher, farther, freer than any man. Slamming the ball to glory. *Yes.*

The screams of the crowd faded, and he stood alone in a pool of rusty light exactly at the end of nowhere.

Baby
on the Run

"I want no design for living, I want no one to tell me how to live. I will take it from day to day."

Errol Flynn:
My Wicked, Wicked Ways

CHAPTER 17

Fleur hoisted her shoulder bag higher on her arm and pulled her suitcase off the luggage carousel, staggering for a moment under the weight. It had been more than thirty-six hours since she'd slept, and the bag seemed to weigh a ton. She'd tried to sleep on the plane, but every time she shut her eyes, she kept hearing Jake's and Belinda's voices, over and over again. *Fuck my daughter, Koranda, so she can save her career.*

"Mademoiselle Savagar?" A liveried chauffeur was approaching her.

"Yes?"

He took her suitcase. "Your father is waiting for you."

She followed him through the crowded Orly terminal and out to a limousine parked at the curb. He held the door open for her, and she slipped inside, into Alexi's arms. *"Papa."*

He pulled her close. "So, *chérie*. You have finally decided to come home to me."

She buried her face in the expensive fabric of his suitcoat and began to cry. "It's been so awful . . . I've been so stupid."

"There, there, *enfant*. Rest now. Everything will be fine."

He began to stroke her, and it felt so good that she let her eyes close, just for a moment. . . .

When they reached the house, Alexi helped her to her room. She asked him to sit by her side until she fell asleep, and he did.

It was late when she got up the next morning. A maid served her coffee and a delicate Limoges plate piled with croissants and sweet rolls, which she pushed away. The thought of putting food into her mouth was unimaginable.

"Bon jour." Alexi came into the dining room, leaned over, and kissed her cheek. He frowned as he noticed the jeans and pullover she had slipped on after her shower. "Did you bring no other clothes with you, *chérie*? We will have to get you some today."

"No, I have other things. I just didn't have the energy to put them on." She could see that he was displeased, and she wished she'd made the effort to look better.

He surveyed her critically. "Your hair is terrible. How could you do such a thing? You look like a boy."

"It was a good-bye present for my mother."

"I see."

"I tried to straighten it up a little with the scissors this morning, but I guess I didn't do a very good job."

"Never mind. We will have it taken care of today."

He gestured for the maid to pour him coffee. As she left the room, he pulled a cigarette from the silver case he carried in his breast pocket. "Suppose you tell me what happened."

"Has Belinda called you?"

"Several times. She's quite frantic. This morning I told her you had finally contacted me and you were on your way to one of the Greek islands—you wouldn't tell me which. I also told her you wanted to be left alone."

"I'm sure she's already on her way to Greece."

"Naturellement."

They were silent for a few moments and then Alexi asked, "Does all this have anything to do with a certain matinee idol?"

"How did you know?"

"I make it my business to know everything that affects me. And those who belong to me as well."

She reached for her coffee and looked down into the cup, trying to hide the fact that her eyes were once again filling with tears. She was so tired of crying, so tired of the wrenching pain inside her. "I fell in love with him," she said thickly. "We went to bed together."

"Inevitable."

His offhandedness hurt her. "My mother had been there first," she said angrily.

Two narrow ribbons of smoke curled from Alexi's nostrils. "Also inevitable, I'm afraid. Your mother is a woman of little willpower where movie stars are concerned."

"They struck a deal."

"Suppose you tell me."

Alexi listened as Fleur outlined the conversation she had overheard between Jake and Belinda. "Your mother's motivations seem clear," he said when she was done, "but what about your lover's?"

She flinched at his choice of words. "I think his motivations were pretty clear, too. This was his first screenplay, and it was important to him. The love scene set up the climax of the movie. When I froze, he could see the whole thing going up in smoke."

In Alexi's experience, no film was destroyed by a single scene, but he didn't share that thought with his daughter. "Unfortunate, *chérie,* that you did not make a better choice for your first lover."

"I guess I'm not the world's best judge of character."

He leaned back in his chair and crossed his legs. On another man the gesture would have looked effeminate, but on Alexi it was elegant. "You are planning to stay with me for some time, I hope. I think it would be best for you."

"For a while anyway," she replied, "until I can get my bearings. That is, if you'll have me."

"It would be my pleasure, *chérie.* I have waited for this longer than you can imagine." He stood. "Before we have your hair taken care of, I have something I've been wanting to show you. I've been feeling a little like a child waiting for Christmas."

She followed him out through the back of the house and across the gardens toward the museum. He put the key in the lock and turned it. "Close your eyes."

She did as he asked, and he led her through the doorway into the cool, faintly musty interior of the museum. She found herself remembering the last time she had been here, the day she had met her brother. She should have asked Alexi about Michel —whether he had found him or not—but she hadn't. Michel was the one topic she wouldn't discuss with him.

"This has been a fortunate time for me," Alexi said. "I am seeing all of my dreams fulfilled." She heard the sound of a switch being flicked. "Now you may open your eyes."

The room was dark except for the group of spotlights in the center. They shined down on the platform that had been empty the last time she had been there. Now it held one of the largest, most magnificent automobiles she had ever seen, gleaming black, with an endlessly long hood that looked like a cartoon of a millionaire's car. Despite the hood, the automobile was exquisitely balanced, and even without its position on the center platform, she would have recognized it. She let out a soft exclamation and ran over to it. "It's the Royale, isn't it? Alexi, you found it! It's beautiful."

"I had not seen it since 1940." He walked over and stood beside her, telling her again the story she had heard so many times before. "There were three of us, *chérie.* We drove it far into the sewers of Paris and wrapped it in canvas and straw. All through the war, I didn't go near it for fear I would be followed, but when I went back after the Liberation, the car was gone. The other two men had been killed in North Africa, and I think now that the Germans found it, but at the time I wasn't certain. It has taken me more than thirty years to locate it."

"But how did you find it? What happened?"

"It doesn't matter—several decades of questions, money applied in proper and improper places." He flicked a handkerchief from his breast pocket and wiped at an invisible fleck of dust on the fender. "All that matters now is that I own the most important collection of *pur sang* Bugattis in the world, and the Royale is the jewel."

After enjoying the Royale and letting Alexi reacquaint her with the other cars in his collection, she went to her room, where a hairdresser was waiting. He had obviously been well paid to keep his mouth shut, because he asked no questions. He merely cut Fleur's hair close to her head and told her he could do no more until it had a chance to grow. After he left, she studied herself in the mirror. She looked horrible. There were dark smudges under her eyes, and her hair was nearly as bad as before, except shorter. She looked like a concentration camp victim—big eyes, oversized head, no hair. Her reflection gave her a perverse sense of pleasure. Now it matched how she felt.

Alexi frowned when he saw her and sent her back to her room to put on makeup, but it didn't help much. They went for a walk along the Rue de la Bienfaisance and talked about what they would do when she felt better. She took a nap in the afternoon, then they dined on breast of veal and listened to Sibelius in Alexi's study. He held her hand, and as the music washed over her, she could feel some of the knots of pain inside her gradually loosen. She had been so stupid to let Belinda keep her apart from her father these past few years. Typical. She had always let her mother manipulate her, afraid to rebel in even the smallest way for fear of losing Belinda's love.

She leaned her head against Alexi's shoulder and shut her eyes. Maybe God was punishing her because she had stopped going to Mass. It was a silly, juvenile idea, but it kept nagging at her. The Catholic conscience, Alexi called it. Damn it, if he hadn't wanted her to have a Catholic conscience, why had he kept her locked up with nuns for sixteen years? But she could no longer work up any real anger toward him, and she realized that in the middle of all her pain she had finally found herself able to forgive her father. He was the only one who had nothing to gain by loving her.

That night she couldn't sleep. She flicked on the bathroom light and reached into the medicine chest for a bottle of Belinda's sleeping pills that she'd packed into her luggage. She swallowed two capsules and slumped down on the lid of the toilet seat.

The worst part was losing her self-respect. She had let herself be led around by the nose, panting like a puppy dog, following her mother's every wish. Love me, Mommy. Don't leave me, Mommy. She felt sick thinking about it. And then there was Jake. Eating him up with her eyes, dreaming about him, loving him so much, and letting herself believe he loved her back. She concentrated on her pain, picked at it as if it were a scab.

"Are you ill, *chérie?*"

Alexi was standing in the doorway, knotting the sash of his robe. His thin steel-gray hair was as neat as if he had just come from his barber, and she wondered if it ever got mussed up. He was so different from Jake, who was always rumpled, whose hair in the morning looked as if it had been attacked by a panzer division. She shook her head.

He said, "You look like a young boy with that shirt on and your awful mangled hair. *Pauvre enfant.* Get in bed, now."

She did as he told her, and he tucked her in as if she were a child. *"Je t'aime, papa,"* she said softly, squeezing his hand where it lay on top of the covers.

He brushed his lips over hers. They were dry and unexpectedly rough. "Turn over. I will rub your back and help you fall asleep."

She did as she was told, and it felt good. His hands slid under her shirt, touching her skin, and she could feel some of her tension easing. The sleeping pill began to work, and she drifted into a dream of Jake making love to her, kissing her neck and touching her through the silky fabric of her underpants.

After the first few days in Paris, Fleur's life began to settle into a semblance of routine. She got up late and slipped on a pair of jeans; then she ate a small breakfast. Afterwards, she read or listened to music. In the afternoon she slept again, making sure one of the maids awakened her in time to shower and dress before Alexi came home. Sometimes they walked together, but walking made her tired, so they usually didn't go very far. Then they had dinner and listened to music afterwards. It was hard for her to sleep at night, so Alexi usually rubbed her back.

She knew she had to stop moping, and she tried to make plans, but the only thing she could decide was that she couldn't go back to the United States right away. Looking the way she did, it was doubtful anyone would recognize her, but if they did, she'd have to face reporters, and she couldn't do that. Besides, nothing in the world could make her go in front of another camera for a long time.

Belinda kept calling, and Alexi kept putting her off. Fleur must have changed her mind about Greece, he said; the detectives he had hired thought she might be in the Bahamas. And then he lectured Belinda on her failure as a mother and made her cry.

Fleur decided that the best thing might actually be to go to Greece now that Belinda had left. She had always loved the islands. She told Alexi that they needed to talk about the money he had invested for her because she was thinking about renting a house in Greece. She might buy a horse, too, or maybe she shouldn't buy one until she was settled somewhere.

But Alexi said it was impossible. The bulk of her money was tied up in long-term investments.

She told him to untie it.

He said she should understand it wasn't that simple. And then he told her not to worry about money; he would buy her anything she wanted.

She told him she wanted a house on the Aegean and a horse.

He said they'd talk about it when she felt better.

The conversation made her uneasy. It had been so simple to let Alexi take care of everything that she had stopped paying attention to his explanations about her investments long ago.

She'd signed the papers he'd sent her, and then returned them. The bills were always paid, she and Belinda had had as much money as they needed, and the complexity of her finances had been one less problem to worry about. Now she didn't know what to do, so she went to her room and took another nap.

They visited Alexi's offices on a Sunday when no one was there, and he displayed some of his treasures to her: a desk that had been bought at auction in London for two hundred thousand pounds, a Basrah Ghiordes prayer rug from Asia Minor, and a bone netsuke that had once held the smoking implements of an eighteenth-century samurai. There was also a T'ang horse that she especially liked, and he gave it to her. As they walked out onto the Boulevard St.-Germain to get into the limousine, a runner with a bright orange headband and a black chronometer on his wrist sped past them. She tried to remember what it had felt like to have that kind of energy.

That night, she hadn't been asleep for very long before she woke up, her nightgown soaked with perspiration. She'd dreamed about Jake again. She was back at the Couvent de l'Annonciation, and he was leaving her behind. Pulling off her nightgown, she slipped into the robe she had tossed over the footboard and went into the bathroom to get a sleeping pill. The container was empty, and she remembered that she had taken the last one the night before.

She went to find Alexi, but he wasn't in his room. Suddenly her heart was pounding in her chest and her pulse was racing with the thought that maybe Alexi had left her behind, too. And then she saw a dim light at the end of the corridor coming from the steps that led to the attic. She found herself climbing to the top, where the door was open.

It was the strangest room she had ever seen. The ceiling had been painted blue with fluffy white clouds racing across it. A bedraggled parachute, one side of which had collapsed, hung over the narrow iron bed. Alexi was sitting in a straight-backed wooden chair to the side, his shoulders slumped, an empty glass in his hand.

"Alexi?"

"Leave me alone," he snapped. "Get out of here."

She realized then that it was Michel's room, and that she had been so wrapped up in her own pain that she hadn't even noticed her father's.

She knelt down beside his chair. In all the time she had been with him, she had never known him to drink too much, but now he smelled of liquor. He was obviously having a bad night, something she understood much better now. "You miss him, don't you?" she asked softly.

"You know nothing about it."

"I know about missing people, Alexi. I know what it's like to miss someone you love."

He lifted his head, and she saw something cold and empty in his eyes that frightened her. "Your sentiment is touching, but unnecessary. Michel is a weakling, and I have cut him out of my life."

Like me, she thought. Like you once cut me out. "Then what are you doing in his room?"

"I've had too much to drink, and I'm indulging myself. It is as simple as that."

"What do you mean?"

"You should understand, Fleur. You of all people."

She was hurt. "You think I indulge myself?"

"Of course you do. The way you put Belinda on a pedestal . . . the way you've made me over in your mind to be the father you always wanted."

She felt a chill, and she stood up and rubbed her arms. "I haven't had to make you over. You've been wonderful to me these last few years."

"I have been exactly what I knew you wanted me to be."

She suddenly wanted to go back to her room. "Good night, Alexi. I'm going to bed now."

"Wait." He set the empty glass down on the table. "Pay no attention. I am having my own fantasy, so I shouldn't mock yours. I've been daydreaming about what would have been possible if Michel had been a son worthy of me instead of a perverted weakling who should never have been born."

"That's ridiculous," she snapped. "And medieval. Millions of men are homosexuals. It's not that big a deal."

He jumped up from the chair, and for a fraction of a moment she thought he was going to hit her. "You know nothing about it!" he snarled. "Nothing! Michel is a Savagar." He stalked across the room, his frenetic movements scaring her. "Such obscenity is unthinkable for a Savagar. It is your mother's blood; I should never have married her. She was the one mis-

234

take of my life, and I have never been able to recover from it. It was her neglect that perverted Michel. If you had not been born, she would have been a proper mother to him."

The liquor was talking. This wasn't her father. She knew she had to get away right then, before she heard anything else she didn't want to hear. She turned to go to the door, but he was already beside her.

"You do not know me very well at all, do you?" He ran his hand up her arm. "I think we must talk now. I've attempted to be patient and give you time to recover, but it's been long enough."

She tried to step away, but he didn't let her go. "Tomorrow, Alexi," she begged. "When you're sober."

"I am not drunk. Merely melancholy." He put his hands on her neck and ran his thumb gently over her ear. "You should have seen your mother when she was even younger than you are now. So full of optimism . . . so passionate. And as self-centered as a child. I have plans for you, *chérie*. Plans that I made the first day I saw you."

"What kind of plans?"

"You're frightened. Lie on Michel's bed and let me rub your back so we can talk."

She didn't want to lie on Michel's bed. She wanted to go to her room and lock the door and pull the covers over her head.

"Come, *chérie*. I can see I've upset you. Let me make it better." He smiled and steered her toward the bed.

She decided she was being irrational. Alexi missed Michel tonight, and she couldn't stand it, that was all. She was jealous as usual, still trying to pretend Michel didn't exist.

She lay down on the bare mattress and crossed her hands under her cheek. The bed sagged as he sat beside her and began rubbing her back through the thin material of her robe. "I have waited patiently for you, *chérie*," he said. "I've given you two years. I've let you fall in love. I've let you and your mother drag the Savagar name through the newspapers and smear it with your vulgar career."

She stiffened. "What do you—"

"Shhh. I'm talking now, *chérie*, and you must listen. The night I saw you gather your courage and lean over the coffin to kiss your grandmother's lips, I knew a great injustice had been done. I knew then that you were everything my son should have been, but I had to give you time with your mother so that you could understand what she is and not let false sentimentality stand between us. It's been a painful lesson for you, but a necessary one, because now you have seen your mother's weaknesses. You are finally ready to take your place beside me."

She turned over and looked up at him. "Alexi, you're frightening me. I don't know what you're talking about. What do you mean, take my place beside you?"

He put his hands on her shoulders and began to massage them. His eyelids were half closed, almost sleepy. She didn't want him rubbing her shoulders. She wanted to get up and leave before something terrible happened. She looked at the parachute. It hung limp and yellowed above her.

"You belong with me, *chérie.* At my side. You belong with me in a way your mother never did." He moved his hands forward, slipping his fingers just inside the open collar of her robe. "I am going to shape you into a magnificent woman. I have such wonderful plans for you." His hands dipped lower, pushing open the neck of the robe . . . moved lower again. . . .

"Alexi!" She reached up and caught his wrists.

He smiled so gently she was embarrassed at what she'd thought he was going to do. God.

"It is right, *chérie,* for us to be together. Do you not see it everytime you look at yourself? Can't you see your mother's faithlessness every time you look in the mirror?"

Faithlessness. For a moment she couldn't think what the word meant.

"It's time for you to know the truth. Give up the fantasy, *enfant.* Give it up. The truth will be much better."

"No. . . ."

"You're not my daughter, *chérie.* Your mother was pregnant when I married her."

The beast had come back. The great, ugly beast who wanted to chew pieces out of her. "I don't believe you. You're lying to me."

"You are the bastard of Errol Flynn, my oldest enemy."

It was a joke. She even tried to smile to show him she was a good sport. But the smile died and the painted clouds on the ceiling blurred as she remembered Johnny Guy talking about Belinda and Errol Flynn and the Garden of Allah.

Alexi leaned over and pressed his cheek to hers. "Do not cry, *enfant.* It's better this way. Don't you see?"

The clouds swam before her, and the beast nibbled at her toes, her fingers, taking tiny bites that weren't big enough to do the job right. She felt his hands touch her lightly through her robe.

"So beautiful. Small and delicate, not plump like your mother's."

"No! No! Damn you!" She shoved his hands away and tried to get up, but the beast seemed to have eaten up all her strength.

Alexi let her go at once. "I am sorry, *chérie.* I have been foolish, and I'm quite embarrassed. I must give you time to adjust, to see things as I do, to see that there is no harm in our being together. We share no blood. You are not *pur sang."*

"You're my father!" she whispered. *Please be my father.*

"Never!" he said harshly. "I've never thought of myself as your father. These past few years have been a courtship. Even your mother understood that."

She pulled herself up until she was crouching. The buttons on the mattress dug into her knees and her shins. The rough edge of one of them scraped her skin.

"Don't dwell on this now," he said. "I've been unforgivably clumsy. We'll just go on as we have until you're ready."

"Ready?" Her voice was thick. It sounded as if she were underwater. "Ready for what?"

"We'll talk of it later."

"Now! Tell me now!"

He seemed more annoyed than angry. "You're clearly distraught, Fleur."

"I want to hear everything."

"It will seem strange to you because you've had no time to adjust."

"What do you want from me, Alexi?"

He sighed. "I want you to stay with me, to let me spoil you. I want you to grow your hair again so you'll be as beautiful as you were."

There was more. She knew there was more. "Tell me, Alexi!"

"You've not had enough time."

"Tell me!" Her fingernails were digging into her palms.

237

Don't say what I know you're going to say, she prayed. Don't say you want me to be your lover.

He didn't.

He said he wanted her to have his child.

CHAPTER 18

She stood at the dirty attic window and looked out on the roof. Something pink lay on the tiles—the featherless body of a baby bird that had fallen from a nest in one of the chimneys. Alexi explained his plan. He walked around the attic room, his hands in the pockets of his robe, and neatly laid it out for her. As soon as she got pregnant, he would take her away somewhere for the duration, and then, when it was over, announce that he had adopted a child. The baby would have his blood, her blood, and Flynn's blood.

She stared out at the little featherless body. It had never had a chance at life, never even had a chance to grow feathers. She felt as lifeless as the baby bird. He assured her that his motives weren't those of a lecherous old man. *You said it, Daddy, not me.* After it was over, they could go right back to their old relationship and he'd be her loving father, just like she wanted.

"I'm going to hire a lawyer," she said, but her voice was so tight that the words came out as a broken whisper and she had to repeat herself. "I'm hiring a lawyer. I want my money, Alexi."

He laughed. "Hire an army of them, if you wish. You signed the papers yourself. I even explained it to you. It's all quite legal."

"I want my money."

"Don't worry about the money, *chérie*. Tomorrow I'll buy you sapphires or emeralds to match your eyes. I'll buy you anything you want."

"No."

"Your mother was alone once," he said, "penniless, with no prospects for the future . . . and pregnant, although of course I didn't know that at the time. You need me now just as much as your mother needed me then."

She had to ask him. Before she walked out of this room, she

had to ask him—except she was crying again, and she kept strangling on the words. Finally, she turned and gripped the dirty window ledge behind her. *"What do you know about me?"* she exclaimed.

Her question obviously puzzled him.

She felt as if she were choking. "What do you see in me that makes you think I would do something so horrible? What weakness do you see? You're not a stupid man. You wouldn't make this obscene proposal if you didn't think there was some chance I would accept it! What's *wrong* with me?"

He shrugged. It was an elegant gesture, and also a little pitying. "It's not really your fault, *chérie*. The circumstances forced it on you, but you must understand that by yourself you are nothing. You're a pretty decoration, certainly, a little bigger than life, but you don't have any value—you don't know how to *do* anything."

She wiped her nose with the back of her hand. "You're stupid, do you know that? I'm the most famous model in the world!"

"The Glitter Baby is Belinda's creation, *chérie*. You would fail without her. And if you didn't, it wouldn't be your own success, would it? I'm offering you a function, and the promise that I will never turn my back on you. We both know that's what is most important to you, isn't it?"

He really thought she was going to do it. She could see it in his eyes, that perfect arrogance. He had looked inside her, seen what was there, and decided that she was weak enough to do this obscene thing.

She ran from the attic room and down the stairs to her own room, where she locked the door and huddled under the covers. It was not long before she heard his footsteps in the hallway. They paused outside her door and then moved on to his own. She lay awake and listened to the pounding of her heart and waited until it was almost dawn. . . .

The key turned soundlessly in the lock as she let herself into the museum. Setting down her shoulder bag, she flicked on the panel of lights. Her palms were sweating, and she rubbed them on her jeans while she walked toward the small room at the back. Steady, she told herself. Hang on just a little bit longer.

Rows of evenly spaced shelves lined one wall of the toolroom, while the other was covered with pegboard. Everything was scrupulously neat, just like he was. Once again she felt his hands where they had touched her breasts, and she crossed her arms over herself. She made herself concentrate on the rows of tools, mentally discarding one after another until she found what she wanted. The hook pulled out of the pegboard as she lifted it off and tested its weight in her hands. Then she carried it out to the Royale.

Belinda was wrong. The rules were the same for everyone. If people didn't follow the rules, they lost their humanity. She let her eyes sweep down the length of the Royale. The ceiling lights were reflected like stars in the finish of the car, little white stars on a field of gleaming black. She thought of the car, so well cherished, carefully wrapped in canvas and straw so that no harm would come to it. And then she lifted the crowbar high above her head and brought it down on the shiny black finish. . . .

The jaws of the beast snapped shut.

CHAPTER 19

A rush of morning pedestrians hurried past the American Express office toward the Opéra station. She looked over her shoulder and then slipped into the crowd, her head down and her right arm hanging heavily at her side. It was sore from the vibrations of the crowbar. She had destroyed the Royale, systematically smashing the hood and the windshield, grill and lights, beating in the fenders and the sides, and then the heart of the car, Ettore Bugatti's peerless engine. The thick stone walls had held in the noise, and no one had rushed in to stop her as she'd destroyed Alexi's dream. Maybe someday she would regret what she'd done, but at the moment she just felt afraid.

Once again, she looked over her shoulder, half expecting to see Alexi coming after her, even though the destruction probably wouldn't be discovered for several more hours. No one seemed to be paying any attention to her, but still she rushed down the steps to the Métro. Her shoulder bag bumped into her thigh, and she clutched it more tightly to her side. She had almost nine thousand francs, two thousand dollars, tucked away in it. American Express had let her cash a check after she'd shown them her Gold Card.

The trip to the Gare de Lyon seemed to take forever. When she arrived at the station, she pushed through the crowd to the schedule board and studied the blur of numbers and cities, trying to make sense out of them. She finally understood that the next departure was scheduled for Nîmes, and she bought a ticket. Nîmes was four hundred miles from Paris—four hundred miles from Alexi Savagar's retribution.

The only other occupants of the second class compartment were an old couple who looked at her suspiciously. She turned her head to stare out the window and wished she had gone into the rest room to clean herself up so she wasn't so conspicuous. The cut on her cheek from the flying glass was stinging, and there was probably blood on her face. It was only a tiny cut, but she should clean it so it didn't get infected and leave a scar.

She shut her eyes and envisioned her face with a little scar on her cheek. And then she erased the image and started the scar at her hairline, letting it cut in a diagonal across her forehead and bisect one of her eyebrows. The scar would be thick enough to leave a white mark right in the middle and divide her eyebrow into two parts, and then it would pucker her lid and cut down over her cheek to the jaw. That would just about do it, she thought. A scar like that would keep her safe for the rest of her life.

Just before the train pulled out of the station, two young women came into the compartment, one holding a copy of *Europe on Fifteen Dollars a Day* and the other carrying a supply of American magazines. Fleur watched their reflections in the window as they settled into their seats and began studying the other occupants in typical tourist fashion, finally striking up a conversation with the older couple as Fleur closed her eyes. It seemed as if weeks had passed since she'd slept, and she was so exhausted she felt light-headed. She concentrated on the rhythm of the train, but all she could hear as she drifted into an uneasy sleep was the smashing of metal and the crunching of broken glass.

They were talking about her when she woke up. "It has to be her," one of the voices whispered. "Ignore the hair. Just look at those eyebrows."

Where was the scar? Where was that pretty white scar cutting her eybrow in half?

"Don't be silly," the other voice whispered back. "What would Fleur Savagar be doing traveling second class? Besides, I read that she's in California making a movie."

Panic began beating inside her, slamming at her ribs like the pounding of a crowbar. She told herself she'd been recognized a hundred times before and that this was no different, but just the thought of anybody connecting her with the Glitter Baby made her feel sick. She turned her face back to the window and slowly opened her eyes.

The women were looking at a magazine that was folded open in the taller one's lap. Fleur could just make out the page in the window's reflection, a sportswear ad she'd done for Armani.

She was wearing a big, floppy hat and a pouty face, and her hair was flying out in every direction from below the brim.

One of them finally picked up the magazine and leaned forward slightly. "Excuse me," she said. "Has anybody ever told you that you look exactly like Fleur Savagar, the model?"

She couldn't turn away from the window. She had known the question was coming, it had happened to her before, but now she couldn't turn to face them. The women looked at her curiously, waiting for some response.

"She doesn't speak English."

The taller one flipped the magazine closed. "I told you it wasn't her."

They reached Nîmes, and she found a room in an inexpensive hotel near the railroad station. As she lay in bed that night, the numbness inside her finally broke apart. She began to cry, deep racking sobs of loneliness and betrayal and awful, boundless despair. She had lost everything. Belinda's love had been a lie, her dream full of deceit, and Alexi had soiled her forever. How could she have been so blind—so obsessed with her own needs —that she couldn't see what he wanted from her? And then there was Jake. . . . She had thought he was the other part of herself, but Jake had raped her soul.

Their betrayals had ripped the blinders from her eyes, and she saw her own ugliness, her own weakness. People survive by their ability to make judgments, yet every judgment she had made was wrong. *You are nothing,* Alexi had said. As the night settled around her, she understood what hell really meant. Hell was being lost in the world, even from yourself.

"I am sorry, mademoiselle, but this account has been closed." Fleur's Gold Card disappeared, tucked like a magician's trick into the palm of the clerk's hand.

Panic gripped her. The only thing that had become clear after her sleepless night was that she needed more money. With money, she could hide someplace where she would be safe from Alexi, and no one would recognize her, someplace where Fleur Savagar could cease to exist. Now that was no longer possible. As she hurried through the streets of Nîmes, she couldn't shake the feeling that Alexi was watching her. She saw him in the doorways, in the reflections of the store windows, in the faces that passed her in the street. Clutching her shoulder bag close to her side, she fled to the train station.

When Alexi saw the wreckage of the Royale, he felt his own mortality for the first time. It took the form of a slight paralysis in his right side that lasted nearly two days. He closed himself in his room and saw no one.

Most of the time he lay still, holding a handkerchief in his left hand. Sometimes he stared at his reflection in the mirror across the room.

The right side of his face sagged.

It was almost imperceptible, except for the mouth. No matter how hard he tried, he couldn't control the trickle of saliva that seeped from the corner. Each time he lifted his handkerchief to wipe it away, he knew that the mouth was what he would never forgive.

The paralysis gradually faded, and when he could control his mouth, he called in the doctors. They said it was a small stroke. A warning. They ordered him to cut back on his schedule, stop smoking, watch his diet. They mentioned hypertension. Alexi listened patiently and then dismissed them.

He put his collection of automobiles up for auction at the beginning of December, and it attracted buyers from all over the world. He was advised to stay away, but he paid no attention. He wanted to watch as each car went on the block, study the faces of the buyers, print their expressions in his mind so he would always remember.

After the auction was over, he had the museum dismantled, stone by stone.

Fleur sat at a battered table at the back of a student café in Grenoble and finished her second pastry, which was as sticky and overly sweet as the first. Still, she ate every crumb, stuffed each cloying bite into her mouth until there was nothing left on her plate. For more than a year now, the food had brought her immediate comfort, a quick fix, and as her jeans had grown tight and she had been able to pinch that first, definitive fold of fat at the base of her ribs, she had felt a perverse sense of accomplishment. The Glitter Baby had disappeared. She imagined what Belinda's face would look like if she could see her precious daughter now—overweight, cropped hair, ugly clothes. And Alexi . . . She could hear his contempt secreted inside some honeyed endearment like a piece of candy with a tainted center.

She counted out her money carefully and left the café, pulling the collar of her man's parka tighter around her neck. It had snowed that morning, and the sidewalk was dark and icy. She tugged her wool hat further down over her head, more to protect herself from the cold than from fear that anyone would recognize her. That hadn't happened in months. A line had already begun to form at the cinema, and as she took her place at the end, a group of American girls fell in behind her. She gathered from their conversation that they were exchange students. The flat sounds of their accents grated on her ear. She couldn't remember the last time she'd spoken English.

Despite the cold, the palms of her hands were sweating and she shoved them more deeply into the pockets of her parka. A year was long enough to run. Tonight she was finally going to confront what had happened to her. She had that much courage left, didn't she? But just looking at the poster was making her sick, and she couldn't imagine how she was ever going to sit through the film.

At first she had told herself she wouldn't even read the reviews, but then she hadn't been able to stop herself from reading every one of them. The critics had been kinder to her than she'd expected. Several had even called her performance "a promising debut," and one had commented on the "sizzling chemistry between Koranda and Savagar." That comment had bothered her the most because only she knew how one-sided that "sizzling chemistry" had been.

As she waited in the corner of the lobby, a young French girl standing nearby began to tease her date. "Aren't you afraid I won't be interested in you tonight after I've spent two hours watching Jake Koranda?"

He glanced over at the poster and then back at the girl. "You're the one who should be worried. While you're watching Koranda, I'll be watching Fleur Savagar. Jean-Paul saw the film last week and he's still talking about her body."

Fleur cringed. Huddling more deeply into the collar of her parka, she pushed past them into the theater, where she took a seat in the last row. The lights began to dim. Every part of her wanted to run, but if she ran away now, she knew she would never be able to stop. This was something she had to do. An exorcism. She had to face the image on the screen, and then maybe she could face herself.

The opening credits rolled, the camera panned a long stretch of flat Iowa farmland, dusty boots walked down a gravel road. Suddenly Jake's face flooded the screen. Her hands tightened in her lap as she forced herself to look at him, to remember how he had betrayed her. But all she could remember was the tenderness and how happy she'd felt when she was with him. The first few scenes flickered by, one after another. And then Jake stood in front of an Iowa farmhouse and a young girl jumped up from a porch swing. . . .

The pastries formed a clump in her stomach as she watched herself running into his arms. She remembered the solid feel of his chest, the touch of his lips. She remembered his laughter, his jokes, the way he had held her so tight she'd thought he'd never let her go, and she knew then that she couldn't make it. Clutching her parka around her, she stumbled from her seat. She would rather run forever than spend one more painful moment with the screen image of the man she'd loved.

The last thing she heard as she fled from the theater was Jake's voice. "When did you get so pretty, Lizzie?"

The reports were delivered to Alexi's offices on the Boulevard St.-Germain at exactly three o'clock every Friday afternoon. He slipped them into his briefcase and adjusted the combination lock. Not until nighttime, when he was alone in his study, would he permit himself to look at the pages that had been prepared for him.

He had been so certain she would go back to New York and resume her career, but she had surprised him by staying in France. First it had been Lyon, then Aix-en-Provence, then Grenoble, Bordeaux, Montpellier—all towns with large universities. She foolishly believed she could hide from him in anonymous throngs of students. As if such a thing were possible.

After a year she had begun to take classes at some of the universities. At first he had been mystified by her choice of courses—lectures in calculus, contract law, anatomy, sociology. . . . It had taken him months to discern the pattern and realize that she chose only classes that were held in large lecture halls where there was little chance of anyone discovering that she was not a registered student. An official enrollment was out of the question, since she had no money. He had seen to that.

His eyes slid down the lists of ridiculously menial jobs she had held to support herself. Cleaning stables, caring for horses, waiting tables. Sometimes she worked for photographers, not as a model—such an idea was ludicrous now—but setting up lights and handling equipment. He read the report twice and then closed the folder and carried it over to his wall safe. For now, she had nothing of value that he could take away from her, but the time would come, and when it did, he would be ready for her. He was a patient man, and he would wait.

The bell that was attached to the front door jangled just as Fleur was setting the last box of film on the shelf, and she jumped at the suddenness of the sound. Unexpected noises always startled her, even though she should have gotten over that. Two years had passed. If Alexi had wanted her, he would have found her by now. She glanced at the wall clock. Her employer had been running a special on baby photographs that had kept them busy all week, but she had hoped the rush was over for the afternoon so she could get to her economics lecture. Dusting her hands on her jeans, she pushed aside the curtain that separated the small reception area from the studio.

Gretchen Casimir was waiting on the other side. "Good God!" she exclaimed.

Every muscle in Fleur's body tightened, and she felt as if someone had just clamped a vise around her chest.

"Good God!" Gretchen repeated.

Fleur tried to tell herself that it was inevitable someone would find her—she should be thankful it had taken this long—but she didn't feel thankful. She felt trapped and panicky. Why had she stayed in Strasbourg so long? Four months was way too long.

Gretchen pulled off her sunglasses. Her gaze swept over Fleur's figure. "You look like a blimp. I can't possibly use you like this."

Her hair was longer than Fleur remembered, and the auburn color was brighter. Her pumps looked like Mario of Florence, the beige linen suit was definitely Perry Ellis, and the scarf *de rigueur* Hermès. Fleur had almost forgotten what such clothes

248

looked like. She could live for six months on what Gretchen was wearing on her back.

"You must have gained thirty pounds! And that hair! I couldn't sell you to *Field and Stream.*"

Fleur tried to pull the old screw-you grin out of mothballs to show that she didn't give a damn what Gretchen thought, but it wouldn't fit on her face. "Nobody's asking you to," she said tightly. "Go away, Gretchen."

Gretchen ignored her. "This escapade has already cost you thousands. You've broken contracts. There are lawsuits. The litigation could take everything you have."

Fleur tried to slip one hand into the pocket of her jeans, but the fabric was stretched so tight that all she could manage was a thumb. Still, if she'd weighed her former one hundred and thirty pounds, she'd lose that nice safe feeling she'd been carrying around inside her. "Send the bill to Alexi," she said. "He has two million dollars of mine that should cover it pretty well. But I imagine you've already found that out." Of course it was Alexi, she thought. He knew where she was and, for some reason, he had sent Gretchen here. The room seemed to be closing in on her.

"I'm going to take you back to New York," Gretchen said, "and then get you into a fat farm. It'll be months before you'll be in shape to work, but I might be able to hold off some of the lawsuits if they know you're back in the country. That awful hair is going to hurt you, though, so don't think I can get your old price, and don't think that Parker can get you another film right away."

"I'm not going back," Fleur said.

"Don't be ridiculous. Look at this place. I can't believe you actually work here. My God, after *Sunday Morning Eclipse* came out, some of the top directors in Hollywood wanted you." She stabbed one stem of her sunglasses into the pocket of her suit jacket so that the lenses hung out. "This silly quarrel between you and Belinda has gone on long enough. Mothers and daughters have problems all the time; there's no reason to make such a big *thing* out of it."

"It's none of your business."

"Grow up, Fleur. This is the twentieth century, and no man is worth splitting up two women who care about each other."

So that was what everyone believed, that she and Belinda had quarreled over Jake. It was as good a reason as any.

Gretchen made no effort to conceal her scorn. "Look at yourself! Hiding away in the middle of nowhere, living like a pauper. Your face is all you have and you've done your best to ruin it! If you don't listen to me you're going to wake up one morning, old and alone, satisfied with whatever crumbs get thrown your way. Is that what you want? Are you that self-destructive?"

Fleur could feel her eyes stinging. Gretchen was trying to scare her, that was all. She'd get herself together soon. It was only a matter of time before she would feel better and everything would be fine again. "Leave me alone," she said. "I'm not going back to New York."

"I have no intention of leaving until—"

"Go away!"

"You can't keep on like—"

"Get out!" she screamed.

Gretchen stared at her for a moment, letting her eyes slide down over the ugly man's shirt, over the jeans, judging her, assessing her. . . . Fleur felt the exact moment when Gretchen Casimir decided she was no longer worth the effort.

"You're a loser," she said scornfully. "You're fat and pitiful, living a life that's hit dead end. Actually, I'm not surprised. Without Belinda behind you, you're nothing."

Fleur missed her economics lecture. She had already packed her shoulder bag and fled from Strasbourg.

As another year passed, Alexi had to counsel himself to remain patient. She had unwittingly discovered the only possible defense she could use against him. What could he take from a person who had nothing?

He seated himself in the leather chair in his study and lit a cigarette, the last of the five he permitted himself to smoke each day. The photographs before him looked much like the others that had been sent to him over the years. Ugly barbershop hair, threadbare jeans, scuffed leather boots. By ordinary standards, she could hardly be considered obese, perhaps forty pounds heavier than she had been, but for someone who should be at the apex of her beauty, the extra fat was obscene.

He heard footsteps and quickly slipped the photographs back

into the leather folder. Then he walked over to the door and unlocked it.

Belinda looked at him, her hair tousled from sleep, a smudge of mascara under her right eye. "I dreamed about Fleur again," she said. "Why do I keep dreaming about her, Alexi? Why doesn't it get better?"

"Because you keep holding on," he said. "You will not let her go."

Belinda reached out her hand and closed it over his arm, imploring him. "You know where she is. Tell me, please."

"I am protecting you, *chérie.*" His cold fingers trailed down her cheek. "I do not wish to expose you to your daughter's hatred."

CHAPTER 20

On Fleur's twenty-third birthday she looked at herself in a fly-specked mirror and hated what she saw—a fat, masculine face unsoftened by cosmetics, an ugly fringe of hair without sheen. She pulled on the spiky ends near her ears and remembered the streaky blond mane that had made her famous. She remembered how it had felt to be slim and strong, running two or three miles at a time. She remembered when she hadn't had to worry about her next meal or paying the rent on some shabby little room with a rust-stained sink and damp patches on the ceiling.

The worst of the pain was gone now. Sometimes an entire day would pass without her thinking about Jake. She could even look at a picture of Belinda and Alexi in the newspaper and feel a certain detachment. Of course Belinda had gone back to him. Alexi was one of the most important men in France, and her mother needed the limelight the way other people needed oxygen.

Occasionally she thought about going back to New York, but what would she do there? She was safe now. That fat kept her safe, and her academic gypsy life protected her. If she went back to that other world, she'd have to take risks that she wasn't ready for. It was easier to drift through the present than to rush into an uncertain future. Easier to forget about the young girl who had been so determined to have everybody love her. She didn't need other people's love anymore. She didn't need anybody except herself.

A week before Christmas, she threw everything she owned into a duffel bag, picked up her Eurail pass, and boarded the train to Vienna. She was stuck in France because it was the only place in Europe where she could work legally, but whenever she could afford it, she got away. She'd chosen Vienna on a whim after she'd read *The World According to Garp*. A place with bears on unicycles and a man who could only walk on his hands seemed just about right.

She found a cheap room in an old Viennese pension with a gilded birdcage elevator that the concierge told her had been broken by the Germans during the war. After lugging her duffel bag up six flights of stairs, she opened the door to a minuscule room with scarred furniture, and wondered which war he meant.

After a quick lunch she took a bus to the Spanish Riding School, only to discover that it was closed until March. When she returned to the pension, she peeled off her coat and her jeans and sat crosslegged on the bed in her underpants, pulling the coverlet around her for warmth in the cold, drafty room. The wind rattled the windows and the radiator clanked. She picked up an American magazine she had bought at the train station and thought about her favorite hotels: the Stanford Court in San Francisco, the Peninsula in Hong Kong, Kona Village Resort in Hawaii, L'Auberge de Sedona in Arizona with the little log cabins and the French country fabrics . . .

It was like pushing her tongue against a sore tooth, so she flipped through the magazine to distract herself. Her hands suddenly froze, and she stared down at the photograph. It showed Jake standing with a pretty, dark-haired woman.

Every time she saw his photograph, her stomach did a flip. It was like stumbling unexpectedly across a dead cat or bird— logic told you that the animal was harmless, but the corpse still made you jump. She turned the page. There was another photograph, this one of Jake and the same woman coming out of a theater. They looked comfortable together, despite the fact that he was scowling at the camera. Fleur couldn't help herself. She turned back to the beginning and started to read.

Since summer, actress Diana Brennan and actor/playwright Jake Koranda have been Hollywood's newest duo. Although both claim they're merely good friends, observers aren't convinced. "Jake and Diana have a lot in common," says actress Lynn Davids, a former Koranda live-in.

The past few years have been fallow ones for Koranda the playwright. Although his acting career is going

253

strong with such hits as *Blue Commando* and the new Caliber film, *Disturbance at Blood River*, he hasn't written anything since his 1977 Academy Award winning screenplay for *Sunday Morning Eclipse*. Friends are hoping his new companion will get him back to his typewriter. . . .

She couldn't read any more. She closed the magazine and pitched it into the wastebasket.

The next morning she walked through the Schönbrunn Palace and then had an inexpensive lunch at the Leupold near Rooseveltplatz. A waiter set a plate of tiny Austrian dumplings called *Nockerln* in front of her. They were delicious, but she had a hard time getting them down. The trip to Vienna wasn't working for her, she realized. There were no bears on unicycles, no men who walked on their hands, only the same old problems that no amount of running away could solve.

A Burberry trenchcoat and a Louis Vuitton briefcase brushed by her table and then backtracked. "Fleur? Fleur Savagar?"

It took her a moment to recognize the man standing in front of her as Parker Dayton, her former agent. He was in his midforties with one of those faces that looked as if it had been perfectly formed by some Divine Sculptor and then, just before the clay was dry, given a push inward, destroying the whole job. Even the neatly trimmed ginger-colored beard he had grown since she'd last seen him didn't quite conceal the less-than-impressive chin or balance out the squished-in nose.

Belinda had selected him to handle Fleur's movie career on the strength of Gretchen's recommendation. Parker Dayton, Gretchen had said, was a comer. Actually, he was Gretchen's lover at the time and not a member of the upper echelon of New York agents. Still, from the evidence offered by the Vuitton briefcase and the Gucci shoes, business seemed to have picked up.

"Fleur, I thought you'd fallen off the face of the earth! God, did I lose a bundle when you ran away. Wait till I tell Gretchen I've seen you."

"Maybe you'd better not. I probably owe her money." She gave him a weak smile and found herself wishing for a lipstick.

She'd never liked Parker very much, which was all the more reason she didn't want him seeing her looking like this.

He didn't smile back, but as she remembered, Parker had never had much of a sense of humor where money was concerned. Without waiting for an invitation, he took a seat across from her and settled his briefcase on the floor. "You were hot after *Eclipse,*" he said, "and some big directors were interested in you. You looked great onscreen—sexy as hell." Then he stared at her.

As the seconds ticked by, she wanted to scream at him. She didn't look *that* awful. She might not be a clothes hanger anymore, but she wasn't the circus fat lady, either.

"It must've cost Gretchen a bundle to settle on the modeling contracts you broke," he said. His hand moved down to the top of his briefcase, and she had the feeling he was itching to get to his calculator so he could punch out the numbers for her.

She leaned slightly forward. "It didn't cost Gretchen a penny, Parker. I'm sure Alexi paid the bills with my money, and *I* could afford it." Having made her point, she changed the subject. "So is the Dayton Agency still trying to steal away ICM's best talent?"

"I'm pretty much sticking to television and music now," he replied, lighting a cigarette. "Among other things, I'm managing Neon Lynx. That's why I'm in Vienna." He began fumbling in his pockets, finally pulling out a ticket. "Come to the concert tonight as my guest. We've been sold out for weeks."

She had seen the posters plastered all over the city advertising the opening concert of America's hottest rock group in their first European tour, and she took the ticket, even though she doubted she'd use it. Still, she wasn't beyond scalping it. "Somehow I can't see you as a rock manager, Parker. How did you get into it?"

"Greed, Fleur. If a rock band hits, it's like you've got a license to print money. Lynx was playing a third-rate club on the Jersey shore when I found them. I knew they had something, but they weren't packaging it right. They didn't have any style, you know what I mean? I could have turned them over to a manager, but business wasn't too great at the time, so I decided, what the hell, I'd give it a shot myself. I made some changes, and put them on the map. I'll tell you the truth, Fleur, I expected them to hit, but not this big. We had riots in two cities on our last tour. You wouldn't believe—"

He suddenly stood, waving to someone behind her, and in a moment a second man joined them. He was in his early thirties with bushy hair and a Fu Manchu moustache. Parker introduced him as Stu Kaplan, the road manager of the band. To her relief he didn't seem to recognize her. After the men had ordered coffee, Parker turned to Stu. "Did you take care of it?"

Stu slumped down in his chair. "I spent an hour at that employment agency, and then they told me they might have a girl for me in a week. Christ, we'll be in freakin' Deutschland next week!"

Parker frowned. "It's your problem, Stu, and I'm not getting involved in it. You're the one who's going to have to work without a road secretary."

They talked for a few minutes, and then Parker excused himself to go to the men's room. Stu turned on Fleur. "He a friend of yours?"

"Not really. We're just acquaintances."

"Well he's a freakin' dictator. 'It's your problem, Stu.' Hell, I'm not the one who knocked her up!"

"Your road secretary?"

"Yeah." He stared mournfully down into his coffee, his Fu Manchu drooping. "I told her we'd pay for the abortion and everything, but she said she was going back to the States to have it done right." Stu looked up and stared at Fleur accusingly. "For chrissake, this is Vienna. Freud's from here, isn't he? They gotta have good doctors in Vienna."

She thought of several things to say, and then discarded them all. He groaned, "I mean it wouldn't be so bad if this had happened in Pittsburgh or somewhere, but freakin' Vienna . . ."

"What exactly does a road secretary do?" The question came out of nowhere; she didn't even know why she had asked it. Curiosity, that was all. It was a polite, conversational sort of question—there was nothing more to it than that.

Stu Kaplan looked at her with the first spark of interest. "It's really a pretty cushy job—answering phones, double-checking arrangements, helping out with the band a little. Nothing too hard." He took a sip of coffee. "You—uh—speak any German?"

She sipped, too. "A little. Also some Italian and Spanish. Fluent French, of course." Her heart was pounding, but her voice sounded calm. It didn't make any sense, but she had the sudden feeling that a frail little lifeline had just been thrown in her direction.

Stu leaned back in his chair and looked at her. "The job pays two hundred a week, room and board provided. You interested?"

It was crazy. She had a job in Lille; she had her classes and her room, and she never did things impulsively anymore. But this was safe, something she could do for a month or so while she was figuring out what she was going to do with the rest of her life. "I'll take it."

Stu smiled and pulled out a business card. "Pack your suitcase and meet me at the Intercontinental in an hour and a half." He scrawled something on the card and then got up. "Here's the suite number. Tell Parker I'll see him there."

When Parker came back to the table and Fleur told him what had happened, he began to shake his head. "Sorry, Fleur, but you can't have that job."

Now that she had made her decision, she couldn't stand the idea of having the job taken away from her. "Why not?"

"You couldn't stick it. I don't know what Stu told you, but being road secretary to any band is a hard job, but with a band like Neon Lynx it's really tough."

There it was, the not-so-subtle implication that she wasn't worth very much. She answered quickly. "I've had tough jobs before, Parker. The last few years haven't exactly been peaches and cream for me."

He reached out and patted her hand patronizingly. "I'm sure they haven't, but let me explain something to you. One of the reasons why Neon Lynx has stayed on top is because they're all spoiled, arrogant bastards. It's part of their image, and to be absolutely truthful, I encourage it. Their arrogance is a big part of what makes them so good when they perform. But it also makes them terrible to work for, and it's not what you'd call a high-prestige job. Let's face it; you're used to giving orders, not taking them."

A lot Parker Dayton knew. "I can take care of myself," she said.

The man who didn't have any sense of humor laughed. "You

wouldn't last two hours as a road secretary. Look, Fleur, I don't know what happened with you, but it seems to me that you've managed to screw yourself up pretty good. Here's a little free advice. Take a pass on the bread and cookies for a while and then call Gretchen and get yourself back on track."

Fleur stood up. "Is it true that Stu Kaplan has the authority to hire his own road secretary?"

"Under normal circumstances . . ."

"Is it true or not?"

"Yes."

"Stu gave me this job, Parker, and I'm taking it."

She was out of the restaurant before he could say anything more, but halfway down the street she began to feel dizzy and had to lean against the side of a building. Her heart was pounding just like it did when she woke up in the middle of the night. This was safe, she told herself. A secretary's job. Nothing too complicated, nothing she couldn't handle. But her heart didn't slow down, and she knew she didn't really believe it.

An hour later when she walked into the suite at the Intercontinental, she felt as if she'd walked into Bedlam. Reporters were bunched together in the corner talking to Parker and two extravagantly dressed young men she assumed were band members, waiters were wheeling in trays of food, and three phones were ringing at the same time. Stu picked up two and gestured for her to pick up the third.

It was the manager of the hotel where the group was staying the next night in Munich. He told her he had heard rumors about the destruction of one of the hotel suites in London and regretted to inform her that Neon Lynx was no longer welcome at his establishment. She put her hand over the receiver and told Stu what had happened.

That was when she realized that the Stu Kaplan of the coffee shop was definitely not the same man she'd be working for. "Tell him it was Rod Stewart, for chrissake!" he screamed over at her. "Use your freakin' head, and don't bother me with the little shit." He tossed a clipboard at her. "Double-check the arrangements while you got him on the phone. Double-check everything, and then check it again."

She felt her stomach clench. She couldn't do this. She couldn't work at a job with someone screaming at her, expecting her to know things that hadn't been explained to her.

Parker Dayton looked over and gave her an I-told-you-so smile. Her palms went damp on the telephone receiver, and she half turned to get away from him. That was when she caught sight of her reflection in a window-sized mirror across the room. The mirror was the same size as those blown-up photographs Belinda had hung on the walls of their apartment, those oversized, beautiful faces that never seemed to belong to her. But as she stared at the pale, frightened face reflected across the room, all she could think was that it didn't belong to her, either.

She turned her attention to the telephone. "I'm sorry to keep you waiting, but you can hardly blame Neon Lynx for damage they didn't do." Her voice was pitched higher than normal, thin from lack of air. She took a quick breath, then began a systematic assassination of Rod Stewart's character. When she was done, she launched into a determined review of the room assignments from the instructions on the clipboard, then went on to detail arrangements for luggage carts and food. As the manager relayed the instructions back to her and she realized she had actually been able to convince him to change his mind, she felt a rush of satisfaction that was completely out of proportion to what she had done.

She hung up the phone, and it rang again. One of the "roadies" had been busted for drugs. This time she was prepared for Stu to yell and even made herself ask him what a "roadie" was when he finally stopped.

"For chrissake, don't you know anything? The roadies are the equipment men; they set up everything, for chrissake." He grabbed his jacket. "Hold on here while I get him out of jail, that is if any of those mothers know how to speak English."

He pitched another clipboard at her. "The schedule and the assignments are all there. Get those stage passes stamped for the VIP's and call Munich to make sure they've taken care of transportation from the airport—we were short on limos the last time. And check on the charter from Rome—make them give us a backup." He was still giving instructions as he walked out the door.

She fielded eight more phone calls and spent a half hour with the airlines before she noticed that she hadn't taken off her coat. As Parker Dayton left the suite, he gave her a smug smile and asked if she'd had enough yet. She smiled back and told him she was having a terrific time, but as soon as the door closed, she

259

sagged back into her chair. She had to last three days. Stu told her that Parker would be leaving the tour and going back to New York then, so she wouldn't have to listen to any I-told-you-so's when she quit. Three days wasn't anything. She could last that long.

Peter Zabel, lead guitarist for Neon Lynx, wandered in. Although she hadn't met him, she had taken a few minutes between phone calls to memorize everybody's name and face from the promotional kit. Zabel was in his early twenties with a small, compact body and curly shoulder-length black hair. She could see at least two earrings in his right lobe, one an enormous diamond and the other a long white feather. He asked her to put a call through to his broker in New York. He was worried about his Anaconda Copper.

After he got off the phone, he leaned back on the couch and propped his boots up on the coffee table. They had three-inch Lucite heels with goldfish embedded in them. "I'm the only one in the band who looks to the future," he said suddenly. "The other guys think this is going to last forever, but I know it doesn't happen that way, so I'm building a portfolio."

"Probably a good idea." She reached for the backstage passes and began to stamp them.

"Damn straight it's a good idea. What's your name anyway?"

"Fleur."

"You look familiar. You a dyke?"

"No." She slammed the stamp down on the pass a little harder than necessary. Who, did she think, was she kidding? Three days was forever.

Peter got up and headed for the door. Suddenly he stopped and turned back to her. "I know where I saw you. You used to be a model or something. My kid brother had your poster up in his room, and you were in that movie I saw about Vietnam. Fleur . . . whatsit?"

She hesitated. "Savagar. Fleur Savagar."

"Yeah. That's right." She noticed that he didn't seem very impressed.

He tugged on the white feather earring. "Listen, I hope you don't mind my saying this, but if you'd had a portfolio, you would of had something to fall back on after you were washed up."

"I'll remember that for the future," she replied solemnly.

The door shut and she realized that she was actually smiling for the first time in days. Around this crew anyway, the Glitter Baby was obviously yesterday's news. She leaned back in her chair and thought about that. It felt good, as if she suddenly had more air to breathe.

The tour was opening that night at a sports arena north of Vienna, and once Stu came back with the errant roadie, she didn't have a minute to think, which was just as well. First there was a ticket mix-up, and then the one-hour warning calls to the members of the band. She had to be down in the lobby early to double-check the transportation and take care of tips; then she had to make a second set of phone calls to all the band members telling them that the limos were ready. Stu yelled at her about everything, but he seemed to yell at everybody except the band members, so she tried to ignore it. As far as she could tell, there were only two cardinal rules: keep the band happy, and double-check everything twice.

As the members of the Neon Lynx wandered into the lobby, she identified each one. Peter Zabel, of course, she had met. Kyle Light, the bass player, wasn't hard to spot either; he had thin blond hair, dead eyes, and a wasted look. There was Frank LaPorte, the drummer, a belligerent redhead with a can of Budweiser in his hand, and Simon Kale, who played the keyboard. Simon Kale was the blackest, fiercest-looking man she had ever seen. His head was shaved and oiled. He wore silver chains across an overdeveloped chest, a slave collar around his throat, and something that looked suspiciously like a machete hanging from his belt.

"Where's that freakin' Barry?" Stu called out. "Fleur, go up and get that sonuvabitch down here. And don't do anything to upset him, for chrissake."

Fleur reluctantly headed for the elevator and the penthouse suite of lead singer Barry Noy. The promotional kit she'd studied billed him as the new Mick Jagger. He was twenty-four, and his photographs showed him with long sandy-colored hair that he wore either loose or in a ponytail and fleshy lips that seemed to be permanently set in a sneer. She'd already gathered from bits and pieces of conversations that Barry was "difficult," and she hadn't let herself think too hard about what that might mean.

261

She knocked at the door of his room, and when there was no answer, she tried the knob. It was unlocked. "Barry?"

He was stretched out on the couch, his forearm thrown over his eyes and the end of his ponytail trailing down over the edge of the couch and onto the carpet. He was dressed in the same satin trousers as the other members of the band, except his were Day-Glo orange with a red sequined star sewn strategically over the crotch.

"Barry? Stu sent me up to get you. We're ready to go."

"I can't play tonight."

"Any reason?"

"I'm depressed." He gave a protracted sigh. "I swear I have never been so depressed in my entire life. I can't sing when I'm depressed."

Fleur glanced down at her watch. It was a man's gold Rolex that Stu had loaned her that afternoon after synchronizing the time with his. She had five minutes. Five minutes and two and a half days.

"You want to tell me what you're depressed about?"

For the first time he looked at her. "Who are you?"

"Fleur. The new road secretary."

"Oh, yeah, Peter told me about you. You used to be a big movie star or something." He threw his arm back over his eyes. "I'm telling you, life is really shit. I mean I am *really* hot now; I can have any woman I want. But that little bitch Kissy has me wrapped right around her finger. I bet I called New York a hundred times today, but either I couldn't get through or she never answered the phone."

"Maybe she was out."

"Yeah. She was out all right. Out with some stud."

She had four minutes.

"Barry, do you really think any woman in her right mind would go out with another man when she could have you?" *You bet she would, Buster. Any woman in her right mind would go out with a kangaroo before she'd go out with you.* "I'll bet your timing was bad. The time zones are confusing. Why don't you try her after the concert? It'll be early morning in New York. You're sure to get her then."

For the first time he seemed interested. "You think so?"

"I'm sure of it." Three and a half minutes—if they had to

262

wait for the elevator, she was going to be in trouble. "I'll even put through the call for you."

"You'll come here after the concert and help me get the call through?"

"Sure."

He grinned. "Hey, that's great. Hey, I think I'm going to like you."

"Good. I'm sure I'm going to like you." *In a pig's eye, you degenerate.* Three minutes. "Why don't we go downstairs?"

She delivered Barry to the lobby with thirty seconds to spare. He propositioned her in the elevator between the ninth and tenth floors, and when she refused him, he turned sullen. That was when she told him she thought she might have a venereal disease. It seemed to make him happy.

CHAPTER 21

As soon as they arrived at the sports arena, Stu threw a clipboard at her and told her to double-check everything on it. She finished just as the opening act was nearing the end of its set and decided to go backstage to watch the show.

One end of the ice hockey rink had been closed off for the safety of the performers, and as she edged her way around from behind the towering set, she saw why. Ignoring the band that was performing, hundreds of fans were pushing against the phalanx of guards and wooden barricades in front of the stage. All of them were screaming for Barry Noy and his group.

The stage manager gestured for her to come over and then handed her a set of pink rubber earplugs. "Put these in," he told her. "Everybody wears them, even the musicians. You can still hear the music, but they'll keep you from popping an eardrum."

She put the plugs in just as the rink went dark. The screams turned into a solid wall of sound, and a voice bellowed out over the loud speaker, *"Meine Herren und Damen . . . Aus Amerika . . . in ihrem europäischen Auftritt . . . die Neon Lynx!!!!"*

The screams crested and four spotlights hit the stage like atomic blasts. There was a crash of sound, the beams of light collided, and Neon Lynx ran forward. The crowd exploded. Barry leaped into the air, hair flying, and then thrust his hips forward so that the red sequined star seemed to be on fire. Frank LaPorte twirled his drumsticks and Simon Kale slammed his hands down on the keyboard. Fleur watched as a young girl, not more than twelve or thirteen, fainted over the barricade. The crowd pressed up against her, and no one paid any attention.

The music was raucous and visceral, blatantly sexual, and Barry Noy played the crowd for all it was worth. As the song ended, there was another surge toward the barricades, and she could see that the guards were getting nervous. The spotlights flashed blue and then red in crisscrossing swords of light, and the band went into its next number.

She was afraid somebody was going to get killed. One of the roadies came up to stand beside her and she asked him if it was always like this.

"Naw," he replied. "Guess it's because we're used to the States. Crowd's dead tonight."

After the show she stood with Stu in the underground garage that had been roped off by the Viennese police and counted limos. The band came out the door, all five of them soaked with sweat. Barry reached out his hand and grabbed her by the arm. "Got to talk to you."

As he pulled her toward the lead limo, she started to protest, and then she saw Stu glaring at her and remembered rule number one about keeping the band happy. She already had a pretty good idea what that rule really meant—keep Barry Noy happy —which probably wouldn't be so bad if he weren't such a creep.

She piled into the limousine, and he pulled her down on the seat beside him. There was a shadow at the door and the clinking of chains as Simon Kale climbed in with them. Remembering how he'd twirled the machete on stage, she looked nervously in his direction. He lit a cigarillo and turned to stare out the window.

The limousine pulled out of the garage, where police were holding back a group of screaming fans. Suddenly a young girl broke through from the front and rushed toward the limousine, pulling up her shirt as she ran and exposing a pair of bare pubescent breasts. A policeman caught her before she could reach the car, but Barry paid no attention.

"So how did you think I was tonight?" he asked, taking a drink from a can of Bud he had brought with him.

"You were great, Barry," she replied, with all the sincerity she could muster. "Just great."

"You didn't think I was off tonight? Friggin' crowd was dead."

"I didn't think you were off at all."

"Yeah, I guess you're right." He drained the beer and then crumpled the can in his fist. "I wish Kissy could have been here. She wouldn't come to Europe with me, you know that? I mean, what does that tell you about the kind of dizzy broad she is?"

"It tells me a lot, Barry." She heard something that sounded like a snort coming from the other side of the limo and quickly asked, "What does Kissy do?"

"She says she's an actress, but I've never seen her on television or anything. Shit, I'm getting depressed again."

If there was anything she didn't need, it was a depressed Barry Noy. "Well then, that's probably it. Actresses who are trying to get work can't afford to leave town any time they want. They might miss their big break."

"Yeah, maybe you're right. Hey, I'm sorry about your VD and everything."

For the first time Simon Kale looked over at her, and she thought she saw a flicker of interest in his eyes.

Even after everything that had taken place that day, she still wasn't prepared for the pandemonium of the hotel lobby. Although the switchboard had orders not to give out any information, there were women everywhere, so word had apparently leaked. As the members of the band made their way toward the heavily guarded elevators, she saw Peter Zabel reach out and grab the arm of a buxom redhead. Frank LaPorte inspected a freckled blonde and then gestured toward both her and her bubble-gum-chewing companion. Only Simon Kale ignored the crowd of women.

"I don't believe this," she muttered under her breath.

Stu heard her. "Yeah, we're all hoping they don't speak English. That way we won't have to talk to them, too."

She glared at him. "That's the most disgusting thing I've ever heard!"

"It's the world of rock and roll, kid. Rockers are kings for as long as they can stay on top." He put his arm around one of the women and headed toward the elevators. Before the doors closed on him, he called out to her, "Stick close to Barry; he told me he likes you. And check the ID's on those girls who went with Frank. They looked young to me, and I don't want any more trouble with the police. Then get on the phone and see if you can get that freakin' Kissy to meet us in Munich tomorrow. Tell her we'll pay her two fifty a week."

"Hey, that's fifty more than I'm getting!"

"You're expendable, kid." The elevator doors slid shut.

She sagged against a pillar. The world of rock and roll. . . . It was one in the morning, she was exhausted, and if she didn't get to bed soon she would fall asleep on her feet. She was going to forget about Frank and his groupies—they probably deserved each other anyway—she was going to forget about Barry and his stupid Kissy and go to bed. In the morning she'd tell Parker that he'd been right about her. She couldn't handle the job.

But when the doors closed on the elevator, she found herself punching in the floor of Frank LaPorte's suite.

The two girls who were with him checked out, so she said as polite a good-night as she could manage and left them. Then she took the elevator up another floor to Barry's suite and dragged her body down the hallway thinking of the beautiful hotel room that was waiting for her. Clean sheets, heat, no knocking radiator, hot water. . . .

The guard let her in, and she was relieved to see that, in this suite at least, everybody still had clothes on. The three girls, none of whom looked particularly happy, were playing cards. Barry was stretched out on the couch watching television, and his face lit up when he saw her. "Hey, Fleur, I was just getting ready to call your room. I thought you forgot." He grabbed his wallet from the coffee table and riffled through it for a torn scrap of paper that he shoved toward her. "Here's Kissy's number. How 'bout calling her from your room; I gotta get some sleep. And take two of those bimbos with you when you leave."

She clenched her teeth. "Any two in particular?"

"I don't know. Whichever ones speak English, I guess."

Fifteen minutes later, as Fleur let herself into her own hotel room, she found herself wondering if anybody associated with this band of anthropoids had ever heard of Gloria Steinem. She undressed and stared wistfully toward the bed, and then she picked up the telephone. As she waited for the call to go through, she glanced down at the scrap of paper in her hand—Christie. Kissy Sue Christie. Lord.

The phone was picked up on the fifth ring, and the voice that answered it was distinctly southern and very angry. "Barry, I swear to God . . ."

"It's not Barry," Fleur said quickly. "Miss Christie?"

"Yes."

"This is Fleur, the new road secretary for Neon Lynx."

"Did Barry get you to call me?"

"Actually . . ."

"Never mind. Just deliver a message." In a soft, breathy voice that oozed generations of ladylike southern breeding, Kissy Sue Christie proceeded to reel off a list of instructions concerning Barry Noy and his anatomy. The contrast between the voice and the instructions was too much for Fleur, and before Kissy could get to the end, she started to laugh.

"Am I amusin' you?" the voice asked with a distinctive southern chill.

"Yes!" Fleur gasped. "Oh, I'm sorry. It's just that it's really late, and I'm so tired I can hardly keep my eyes open, and to tell you the truth, you're saying everything I've been thinking all day. The man is . . ."

". . . toad spit," Kissy Sue concluded.

This set Fleur off again, and before long Kissy joined in. When they had finally calmed down, Fleur apologized for having called her. "It's okay," Kissy said. "What's Stu offering this time to get me to come over? Last tour it was two hundred a week."

"It's up to two fifty now."

"No kidding. Shoot, I'd love to go to Europe, too, and I even have some vacation time coming up. The only places I've really seen outside South Carolina are New York and Atlantic City, but I'll tell you the truth, Fleur—I'd swear off men completely before I ever went to bed with Barry Noy again."

Fleur thought for a minute and then settled back on the bed. "You know, Kissy, there just might be a way." She explained the idea, they discussed it, and just before she hung up, she thought she saw Gloria Steinem's face smiling at her.

Her wake-up call came at six-thirty the next morning, and as she put the phone back on its cradle, she waited for the familiar heaviness to settle over her. It didn't come. She felt . . . How *did* she feel? She'd had less than five hours sleep, so she should be exhausted, but she wasn't. Her sleep had been deep and restful, with no pitching and tossing, no sudden heart-poundings, no dreams about the people she used to love. She felt . . ."

Competent.

Settling back into the pillows, she tried the idea on for size. She had a terrible job. The people were awful—spoiled, rude, totally insensitive as well as being blatantly immoral—but despite it all, she had survived her first day and done a good job under nearly impossible circumstances. Better than good. She'd done a *great* job. There wasn't anything they had thrown at her that she hadn't been able to handle, including Barry Noy. She was going to show Parker Dayton . . . She stopped herself. Damn it, she didn't care about Parker Dayton! She didn't care about Alexi's opinion of her, or Belinda's, or anybody's. The only person she had to prove anything to was herself.

The band's arrival in Munich was just as hectic as she had suspected it would be, and Stu coped with everything by yelling at her. This time she yelled back, which made him pout and say he didn't know what she was getting so mad about. The next two nights' concerts were a repeat of the concert in Vienna, with girls fainting over the barricades at the arena and a crowd of groupies waiting in the hotel lobby. Just before the last concert, Fleur sent a limousine to the airport to pick up the long-awaited Miss Christie, but to her dismay, it came back empty. She told Barry that the plane had been delayed and then spent the next two hours fruitlessly trying to track Kissy down. When Stu discovered what had happened, he yelled and said that she could personally explain the screw-up to Barry—after the concert.

Barry took it just about as she expected.

When she'd calmed him down with some half-baked promises she wasn't absolutely sure she could keep, she dragged herself to her room, passing Simon Kale in the hallway. He was wearing gray slacks and an open-collared black silk shirt with a single gold chain at the neck. It was the most conservative outfit she'd seen on anyone other than Parker since she'd joined up with the Neon Lynx circus, but she couldn't quite shake the feeling that he had a switchblade in one of his pockets.

She fell asleep within seconds of the time her head hit the pillow only to be abruptly awakened by a phone call from the hotel manager's office telling her that the guests were complaining about the noise coming from the fifteenth floor. He couldn't reach Herr Kaplan, he informed her, and so it was her responsibility to put a stop to it.

She had a fairly good idea of what was in store for her as soon as she stepped into the elevator and found Herr Kaplan passed out in the corner with an empty V.O. bottle in his hand and half of his Fu Manchu shaved off. It took her half an hour of begging and cajoling to get the party in the suite down to twenty-five, which was, she decided, about as much as she could do. She stepped over Frank LaPorte as she carried the telephone into a closet to call the lobby and tell them to put guards back on the elevators. When she came out, she saw that Barry had left with a few more of the women and decided it was safe to return to her room. And then she realized that she didn't really want to go. Tomorrow was a layover day, and she deserved a good time, too, or at least a drink before she headed back to bed.

After a short struggle with a cork, she poured several inches of champagne into a glass, and then Peter called her over to talk about OPEC, much to the disgust of the girls who were clamoring for his attention. Just as she began her second glass of champagne, she heard a furious pounding on the door. Groaning, she set down her glass and walked across the suite. "Party's over," she called through the door crack.

"Let me in!" The voice was female and vaguely desperate.

"I can't," Fleur told the crack. "Fire regulations."

"Fleur, is that you?"

"How did you—" Fleur suddenly realized that the voice on the other side had a strong southern accent. She quickly released the lock and pulled open the door.

Kissy Sue Christie tumbled into the room.

She looked, Fleur decided, like a rumpled sugarplum. She had short licorice curls, a candy apple mouth, and big gumdrop eyes. She was wearing black leather pants and an electric pink camisole with a broken strap. With the exception of a generous spill of breasts, everything about her was tiny. It was also vaguely lopsided, since she was missing one high-heeled shoe, but even lopsided, Fleur knew that Kissy Sue Christie looked exactly the way she had always wanted to look herself.

Kissy threw the bolt on the door and began her own inspection. "Fleur Savagar," she said. "I had the strangest feeling over the telephone that it was you, even though you didn't tell me your last name. I'm mildly psychic." She turned back to check the lock. "There's this Lufthansa pilot that I'm trying desperately to avoid. I would have been here earlier, but I was unexpectedly delayed." For the first time, she looked around at the other occupants of the room. "Tell me I'm a lucky girl and Barry's not here."

Fleur smiled. "You're a lucky girl."

"I suppose it's too much to hope that he was kidnapped or otherwise stricken?"

For a moment Fleur entertained the thought, and then she shook her head. "Neither of us could be that lucky." She suddenly remembered her duties, "Where's your luggage? I'll phone down and have somebody take you to your room."

"Actually," Kissy said, "my room is already occupied."

Fleur's curiosity must have shown on her face because Kissy gave a tug to the broken pink camisole strap and said, "Do you think there might be someplace where we could talk? And I wouldn't look unfavorably on the offer of a drink, either." Fleur scooped up her champagne bottle, two glasses, and Kissy. She had a funny urge to tuck her in her pocket.

The only unoccupied space they could find was the bathroom, so she locked them both in and took a seat on the floor. While she poured the champagne, Kissy kicked off her remaining shoe. "To tell you the absolute truth," Kissy said, "I think I made a mistake by letting him escort me to my room."

Fleur took a wild stab. "The Lufthansa pilot?"

Kissy nodded. "It started as a mild flirtation, as far as I was concerned, but I guess it got a little out of hand." She sipped delicately at her champagne and then licked her top lip with the tip of her tongue. "I know this is going to sound strange to you, Fleur, but like I said, I'm mildly psychic, and I have this strong feeling that we're going to be close. I might as well tell you from the beginning—I have a little bitty problem with promiscuity."

This had all the earmarks of an interesting conversation, so Fleur settled herself more comfortably against the side of the tub. "How little bitty?"

"Depends on your viewpoint." Kissy tucked her feet beneath her and leaned against the door. "You like hunks, Fleur?"

Fleur refilled her cup and thought about it. "I guess I'm sort of off men right now. Kind of neutral, you know what I mean?"

Kissy's gumdrop eyes widened. "Gosh, no. I'm sorry."

Fleur giggled. Whether it was the champagne or Kissy or the lateness of the hour, she didn't know, but she was suddenly fed up with all the high tragedy in her life, and it felt good to laugh again. She noticed that Kissy's cup was empty and refilled it.

"Sometimes I think hunks have just about ruined my life," Kissy said mournfully. "I tell myself I'm going to reform, but

271

the next thing I know, I look up and there's this piece of gorgeous male flesh standin' right in my path with big, broad shoulders and those little bitty hips, and I can't find it in my heart to pass him by."

"Like Lufthansa?"

Kissy almost smacked her lips. "He had this dimple—right here." She pointed to a spot just below the center of her cheek. "That dimple, it did something to me, even though the rest of him wasn't much. See, that's my problem, Fleur—I can always find something. It's cost me a lot."

"What do you mean?"

"The pageant, for one thing."

"Pageant?"

"Uhmm. Miss America. My mommy and daddy raised me from the cradle to go to Atlantic City."

"And you didn't make it."

"Oh, I made it all right. I won Miss South Carolina without any trouble. But the night before the Miss America pageant, I committed an indiscretion."

"Hunks?" Fleur suggested.

"Two of them. Both judges. Not at the same time, of course —well, not exactly. One was a United States senator and the other was a tight end for the Dallas Cowboys." Her eyelids drifted shut at the memory. "And oh, my, Fleur, did he ever have one."

"You were caught?"

"In the act. I tell you, Fleur, to this very day it annoys me. I got kicked out, but they both stayed on. Now does that seem proper to you? Men like that being judges in the greatest beauty pageant in the world?"

It seemed grossly unfair to Fleur and she said so.

"I suppose it all worked out, though. I was on my way back to Charleston when I met this truck driver who looked like John Travolta. He helped me get to New York and find a place to stay where I wouldn't have to worry about being mutilated on the doorstep. I got a job working at an art gallery so I could support myself while I waited for my big break, but I have to tell you, Fleur, it's been slow in coming."

"The competition's tough," Fleur commiserated.

"It's not the competition," Kissy said indignantly. "I'm really exceptionally talented. Among other things, I was born to do Tennessee Williams. Sometimes I think he wrote those crazy women just for me."

"Then what's the problem?"

"Trying to get the auditions in the first place, that's the problem! Directors take one look at me and won't even let me try out. They say I'm not the right physical type, which is another way of saying that I'm too short and my boobies are too big and I look altogether frivolous. That's the one that really annoys me. I'd have been Phi Beta Kappa if I'd stayed in college for my senior year. I'm tellin' you, Fleur, beautiful women like you with legs and cheekbones and all the other blessings of God can't even imagine what it's like."

Fleur nearly choked. "Kissy, you're the most gorgeous thing I've ever seen. All my life I've wanted to be little and pretty and look just like you."

After a few moments' rumination, this struck them both as being terrifically funny, and they dissolved in giggles. Then Fleur noticed their bottle was empty so she went on a scouting mission for more champagne. When she returned with a fresh bottle, the bathroom was empty.

"Kissy?"

"Is he gone?" The voice was coming from behind the shower curtain.

"Who?"

Kissy climbed out. "Somebody had to use the potty. I think it was Frank, who is a base pig, in my opinion."

They resettled themselves in their old spots. Kissy tucked several wayward licorice curls behind her ear and then looked at Fleur thoughtfully. "You ready to talk yet?" she asked.

"What do you mean?"

"I mean, I'm not exactly blind to the fact that I'm sharin' this bathroom with a woman who used to be one of the most famous models in the world—as well as a promising new actress—who disappeared off the face of God's earth after some interesting rumors about her association with one of our great country's truly outstanding hunks. I'm not obtuse, Fleur."

"I didn't think you were." She picked at the edge of the bathmat with her fingernail.

"Well?"

"Well, what?"

"Well, are we friends or not? I've told you some of the very

273

best parts of my entire life story, and it has to have occurred to you by now that you haven't told me one thing about yours."

"We just met each other, Kissy." As soon as she said it, Fleur knew that it was wrong and hurtful, even though she wasn't exactly sure why.

Kissy's eyes filled with tears, making them look all melty and soft, like blue gumdrops left too long in the sun. "Do you really think that makes any difference? This is a lifelong friendship that's being formed right now, don't you understand that yet? There's got to be some trust." Abruptly, she brushed her tears away, picked up the champagne, and took a swig directly from the bottle. Then she looked Fleur straight in the eye and held the bottle out to her.

Fleur thought about all the secrets that had been locked inside her for so long, and it suddenly seemed as if she were viewing the past three years of her life through a wide-angle lens. She looked at her own self-pity, her self-indulgence, the way she had run away from herself. She looked inside her own loneliness, too, and knew the fact that it was self-imposed didn't make it any less real. Kissy was offering her a way out if she wanted to take it, but there were risks involved, and it had been a long time since she'd let herself take a risk.

Slowly, she reached out for the bottle, and then she took a long swallow. "It's sort of a complicated story," she said finally. "I guess it really started before I was born. . . ."

It took Fleur nearly two hours to tell it all. Sometime between Bunny Gruben and her first meeting with Jake, they moved to Fleur's hotel room because people who wanted to use the bathroom kept pounding on the door. Kissy curled up on one of the double beds while Fleur propped herself against the headboard of the other, balancing on her chest the bottle of champagne that was helping her through the story. Kissy kept interrupting with pity, one-word character assessments of the people involved, but Fleur remained almost detached. Champagne definitely helped, she decided, when you were spilling your sordid secrets.

"That's a terrible story!" Kissy exclaimed, when Fleur finally finished. "I don't know how you can tell it without falling apart."

"I'm cried out, Kissy. If you live with it long enough, even high tragedy gets to be mundane."

"Like *Oedipus Rex,*" Kissy sniffed. "I was in the chorus when I was in college. We must have performed that play for every high school in the state."

Fleur nodded sympathetically. "Then you know what I mean."

Kissy flipped over on her back. "There's a master's thesis in here somewhere."

"How do you figure?"

"Give me the characteristics of a tragic hero."

Fleur thought for a minute, but with all the champagne, it was a little difficult to focus. "Uhm—person of high stature brought down by a tragic flaw, like *hubris,* the sin of pride. He loses everything. Then he achieves a catharsis, a cleansing through his suffering."

"Or *her* suffering," Kissy said pointedly.

"Me?"

"Why not? You had high stature, and you certainly have been brought down."

"What's my tragic flaw?"

Kissy thought a minute. "Bad parents."

Late the next morning, after showers, aspirin, and room-service coffee, there was a knock at the door. Kissy opened it and emitted a loud squeal. Fleur looked up just in time to see the Belle of the Confederacy hurl herself into Simon Kale's dark brown arms.

The three of them had breakfast in the revolving dining room on top of Munich's Olympia Tower, where they could gaze out over the Alps, sixty-five miles away. As they ate, Fleur heard the story of Kissy and Simon's long-standing friendship. They had been introduced shortly after Kissy had arrived in New York by a mutual friend, who had been one of Simon's classmates at Juilliard. Simon Kale, Fleur discovered, was just about as menacing as Santa Claus.

He laughed as he delicately wiped one corner of his mouth with his napkin. "You should have seen Fleur taming King Barry with her story of venereal disease," he told Kissy. "She was magnificent."

"And I suppose you didn't help her at all, did you?" Kissy gave him a none-too-gentle punch in the arm. "If I know you,

you were giving her that 'I-eat-white-girls-for-breakfast' look, just to amuse yourself."

Simon looked wounded. "I haven't eaten a white girl for breakfast in years, Kissy, and I'm hurt that you would even suggest such a thing."

"Simon's discreetly gay," Kissy informed Fleur. And then, in a loud whisper, "I don't know about you, Fleurinda, but I regard homosexuality as a personal insult."

By the time breakfast was over, Fleur decided she definitely liked Simon Kale. Beneath his cynical facade was a kind and gentle man. As she watched his small, delicate gestures and finicky mannerisms, she had the impression that he would have been more comfortable with the body of a ninety-pound weakling. Maybe that was why she liked him. They both lived in bodies that didn't feel like home.

When they got back to the hotel, Simon went off to make some phone calls, and Kissy and Fleur set out for Barry's suite. It had been restored to some semblance of order from the party the night before, and its occupant was once again in residence, nervously pacing back and forth across the carpet. He was so glad to see Kissy that he barely listened to her breathlessly convoluted lie about why she was late, and it was several minutes before he even noticed Fleur. Then he made it obvious with a number of less than subtle glances toward the bedroom door that her presence wasn't wanted. Fleur pretended not to notice.

Kissy leaned forward and began whispering something into his ear. As Barry listened, his expression grew more and more horrified. When Kissy had finished, she gazed down at the floor like a naughty child.

Barry looked at Fleur. Then he looked at Kissy. And then he looked at Fleur again. "What is this?" he cried. "A friggin' epidemic?"

Kissy's two weeks of vacation from the gallery where she worked ended, and she and Fleur said a tearful good-bye at Heathrow, with Fleur promising to telephone that evening at Parker Dayton's expense. She returned to the hotel, depressed for the first time since she had started her job, already missing Kissy's quirky sense of humor and Norman Vincent Peale view of life.

A few days later she missed her even more when Parker

called with a job offer to work with him in New York at nearly double her current salary. Panic-stricken, she hung up the telephone, and then called Kissy at the gallery.

"I don't know why you're so surprised, Fleurinda. You're on the phone with him two or three times a day, and he's obviously just as impressed with your work as everybody else. He may be slime mold, but he's not stupid."

"I—I'm not ready to go back to New York, Kissy. It's too soon."

The distinct sound of a snort traveled through three thousand miles of underwater ocean cable. "You're not going to start whining on me again, are you? Self-pity kills your sex drive."

"My sex drive is nonexistent."

"See! What did I tell you?"

Fleur twisted the phone cord in her hand. "It's not that simple, Kissy."

"Keep telling yourself that and you're going to be right back where you were a month ago. Ostrich time is over, Fleurinda. You've got to get back to the real world."

Kissy made it sound so easy, but Fleur knew it was more complicated. How long could she stay in New York before the press discovered her? And what if her job with Parker didn't work out? What would she do then? Her stomach rumbled, and she realized that she hadn't had anything to eat since the night before—another change that this job had made in her life. Her jeans were already too loose at the waist, her hair was growing down over her ears, everything was changing.

She hung up the telephone and walked over to the window of the hotel suite, pushing back the curtain to look down on the wet street. Below her, a jogger was dodging taxis in the rain. She remembered when she had been dedicated like that, running every day regardless of weather. The bravest, the fastest, the strongest . . . Now she probably couldn't run a city block without stopping to catch her breath.

"Hey, Fleur, you seen Kyle?" It was Frank, a can of Budweiser already in his hand at nine o'clock in the morning. Fleur grabbed her parka and brushed passed him without answering, running out into the hallway, into the elevator, through the well-dressed crowd of businessmen in the lobby.

The rain was an icy January drizzle, and by the time she reached the corner, it had dripped off the stubby ends of her hair and under the neck of her parka. As she crossed the street, her feet squished in her wet sneakers. They were cheap sneakers. The laces were frayed, and small holes poked above each of her big toes. There was no cushioning in them—no thick padding to support the arches and protect the balls of her feet.

On the other side of the street, she pulled her hands out of her pockets and gazed up at the steel-gray sky. Then she looked down the long block that stretched before her. One block.

She began to run.

CHAPTER 22

Fleur took a taxi from the airport to Kissy's apartment, which sat on top of an Italian restaurant in the Village. Her former roommate (Fleur didn't inquire too closely into the roommate's gender) had moved out several months before, and she had been looking for "someone whose presence she could abide" to share the rent. They both took it for granted that Fleur would be that "someone," at least for a while.

Kissy had taken over the lease on the apartment from an old boyfriend not long after she'd come to New York. The interior decorating looked just like her—lollipop colors, a collection of stuffed teddy bears, and a poster of Tom Selleck taped to the bathroom door. As Kissy was showing Fleur the way the make-shift shower worked, a bright pink lip print on the poster caught Fleur's eye. "Kissy Sue Christie, is that your lipstick on Tom Selleck?"

"So what?"

Fleur clucked her tongue. "You could have at least aimed for his mouth, Magnolia Blossom."

Parker had given her a week to get settled before she had to report to work, and she used the time to reacquaint herself with New York. It was early February, and the city was at its worst, but it looked beautiful to her. She finally felt as if she'd come home.

She ran every morning, only a few blocks before she had to walk to catch her breath, but each day she thought she could feel herself growing stronger. Sometimes she passed places she and Belinda had visited together, and she felt a pang so sharp and bittersweet that it forced her to realize how much she still missed her mother. Not once over the past three and a half years had Belinda ever tried to contact her. Of course, she was glad of that, but still, it showed what a hypocrite her mother was after all her phony, smothering love.

279

Her own weakness when she thought about Belinda made her angry. There wasn't any place for that kind of sentiment in her new life. She was going to carve out a career for herself, an independent future, and she wasn't taking any dirty laundry from the past with her. No more begging for love. No more tossing in bed at night thinking about Jake. From now on she would be just as single-minded and ruthless as she needed to be to get ahead.

She tested herself by sitting through a two-day Errol Flynn retrospective and trying to make herself feel something for the dashing swashbuckler on the screen. But Flynn didn't mean anything to her, and she refused to let herself indulge in any fantasies. In her mind, Alexi Savagar, bastard that he was, would always be her father.

The day before she had to start work, she returned to the apartment to discover that Kissy had thrown out all her clothes. "You're not going to wear those vile rags anymore, Fleur Savagar. You look like a bag lady."

"Dammit, Kissy, you had no right!" But she couldn't stay mad at her roommate for long, and she ended up trading in her old jeans for designer ones that fit her slimmer shape and bought a supply of funky tops to go with them—a Mexican peasant shirt, an old varsity letter sweater, some turtlenecks, and a pale blue belted tunic in case she had to impress anyone. Kissy didn't say anything about her new wardrobe, but she left a copy of *Dress for Success* conspicuously displayed next to the refrigerator. Fleur ignored it. The dress code for the entertainment world was casual, and there were only so many layers she was willing to peel away at one time.

It didn't take her long to find out that Parker wanted his pound of flesh for the generous salary she had forced him into paying her. From the beginning, her days blended into nights and, more frequently than not, spilled over into the weekends. She visited Barry Noy's purple-painted Tudor in the Somerset hills, where she consoled him on his loss of Kissy. She wrote press releases, studied contracts, and fielded calls from promoters. As she grew thinner, she also fended off Parker's repeated offers to contact his friends in Hollywood to see if anyone had a part for her. Gradually, her responsibilities grew until she was handling some of Parker's other clients. She learned who the record producers were and managed to keep track of the television executives as they played musical chairs at the networks. She was dependable, she honored her commitments, and before long, people began to ask for her. By summer, she knew that she had fallen deeply and permanently in love with the entire business of making stars.

"It's great to pull other people's strings for a change instead of having my own pulled," she confided to Kissy one Sunday afternoon as they sat on a bench in Washington Square Park eating ice cream cones that were dripping in the heat. It was one of their favorite spots for people watching. The park held its usual colorful complement of characters—tourists, leftover hippies, skinny black kids with ghetto blasters hoisted on their shoulders. The six months that had passed since Fleur had arrived in New York had produced changes in her appearance. Her hair swung in a blunt cut below her jaw, all the streaky, healthy color once again visible in the summer sun. She was tan and too slim for the navy blue shorts she was wearing.

Kissy looked up from her ice cream and frowned at her roommate's baggy, undistinguished outfit. Fleur still equated beautiful clothes with the Glitter Baby; she didn't even own a dress or a pair of pants that wasn't denim, and no amount of nagging could make her see differently. Kissy found herself waiting for the day Fleur would be forced to realize she was fighting a losing battle. Despite the unattractive clothes and the hair which still wasn't quite as long as it ought to be, in Kissy's judgment the old Glitter Baby couldn't hold a candle to the new Fleur Savagar. The years had given her face a maturity it hadn't had before, a strength that was the definition of classic beauty.

Not that Fleur would agree. Or even notice. For six months Kissy had watched the way she avoided spending any time in front of a mirror—a bare six seconds to slick on a light coat of lipstick, ten seconds tops to run a comb through her hair. She was a world-class champion at avoiding her own reflection, as if she were afraid acknowledging her beauty would bring the Glitter Baby back and destroy everything she was building for herself.

"You really love your job, don't you, Fleurinda?" Kissy circled the double-decker mound of raspberry ripple with her tongue and then pushed at one of the red plastic barrettes, shaped like a pair of lips, that was holding back her hair.

"It almost scares me how much I love it, even the bad parts, like dealing with Barry Noy's egomania. I love the wheeling and dealing and the fact that something is always happening. Every time I come out on top of one of our daily crises, I feel like one of the nuns just pasted a gold star next to my name."

"You're a hopeless overachiever—you know that, don't you?"

"Hopeless," Fleur agreed. She caught a dab of mint chocolate chip just before it fell on her shorts and pulled her legs back to save them from amputation by a skateboard. One of the drug dealers stopped talking in midsentence to appreciate them, but she didn't notice. "When I was a kid I thought if I could be the best at everything, I'd get to go home to my family. Overachieving got to be a habit. I think that's why I crashed so bad after everything fell apart for me—I'd done my best, and it still wasn't good enough. Believe me, working my tail off for Parker is a lot better than being holed up in France wallowing in self-pity."

"But don't you miss acting?"

"You saw *Eclipse.* You know that I was never going to win any Academy Awards."

"You were good in the part," Kissy insisted.

"Barely adequate. You read what the critics said: 'Fleur Savagar looks better than she acts.' "

"*One* critic said that. You got decent reviews for that film."

Fleur made a face. "I never felt comfortable acting. There was something too exposed about it." Out of respect for Kissy, she didn't mention that she also thought all the repetition involved in acting made it the most boring profession there was.

"You put your heart into modeling. You were the best, Fleurinda."

"Thanks to a lucky combination of chromosomes. It never had anything to do with *me,* Kissy, don't you see. The night Alexi and I played out our smutty little scene, he said I was nothing more than a pretty, oversized decoration, that I couldn't really *do* anything."

"Alexi Savagar is a whacko prick, if you want my honest opinion."

Fleur laughed. It was comforting, in a silly sort of way, to have Kissy dismiss Alexi so inelegantly. "He was also right. I spent three years running from the truth. Granted, I acquired an incredible university education on the way, but I'm not going to run anymore."

Kissy suddenly seemed to lose interest in her cone and got up to pitch it into the trash. "I wish I had your drive."

"That's a funny thing to say. Nobody could work harder than you do. You're always juggling your schedule at the gallery so you can get your hours in and still hit the auditions. You go to class in the evenings, you go to rehearsals. . . ."

"Rehearsals for walk-on's aren't exactly taxing, Fleurinda."

"The parts will come, Magnolia. You know I've talked to a lot of people about you."

"I know you have, and I appreciate it, but I think it's about time I face the fact that it's not going to happen for me. Directors won't let me read for anything other than comic sexpots, and I'm terrible in that kind of part. I'm a serious actress, Fleur."

"I know you are, honey." Fleur made all the proper commiserating sounds, but looking at Kissy with her pouty mouth and pillowy breasts and smudge of raspberry ripple on her chin made her think that she really was perfect for comic sexpot roles.

Kissy pushed her hands down into the pockets of her very short pink shorts. "I got a raise," she said, her expression as glum as if she had just announced a terminal disease. "I should never have taken my minor in art history. It's turned into a security blanket for me."

"You want to translate that?"

"It means, maybe if I had a more disagreeable job, I'd push myself harder." Her eyes slid over a good-looking young man who was walking past them. She surveyed him automatically, but Fleur had the feeling her heart wasn't in it. "I'm going to give up acting for a while. I can only take so much rejection, and I've just about had my fill. I do a good job at the gallery, and I get recognized for it. That's got to be enough for now. I don't know—maybe I just need some time to lick my wounds."

Fleur's forehead creased in a frown. "Hey, what happened to Norman Vincent Peale and The Power of Positive Thinking?"

"I think I'm thunked out."

Fleur said nothing. She hated the idea of Kissy giving up, but anything she said would sound hypocritical. She understood only too well what her roommate was feeling. "Come on," she said, "I'll buy you a hamburger. If we play our cards right, we can catch the beginning of *Butch Cassidy and the Sundance Kid* on television before we have to get dressed for our dates."

"Good idea. How many times will this make?"

"Five or six. I lost count."

"You haven't told anybody about this, have you, Fleurinda?"

"Are you nuts? Do you think I want the whole world to know?"

As they left the park walking side by side, a dozen pairs of male eyes watched them go.

Fleur's date for the evening was Max Shaw, a young actor currently appearing off-off-Broadway in a Tom Stoppard play. When she had begun to date again, she found herself most comfortable with unemployed actors. They were totally self-involved, and didn't ask her too much about herself. Max was good company, Hollywood handsome, and the man she had chosen to end her long period of celibacy. Not that she had ended it yet. But she was going to. Tonight.

The idea of sexual intimacy had been repugnant to her for so long that she was surprised when she found herself thinking about it again. But as exercise firmed her muscles and the extra pounds melted away, her sexuality came out of its long hibernation. The flow of water over her body in the shower, the slide of a soft sweater on her skin—everyday acts became fraught with unnerving sensuality. She found herself thinking about sex when she was in the middle of a business meeting or standing on a grimy subway platform. It was Kissy's influence, she told herself. But she finally admitted that her body was starved for male contact.

She wanted to be touched and stroked and cuddled. Was that so terrible? She wanted to be held by someone who shaved, someone with biceps and a hairy chest, someone who cussed and drank Mexican beer—no, not Mexican beer, because most of all, she wanted someone who would make her stop thinking about Jake, since the reemergence of her sex drive had brought with it a resurrection of longings that should have died long ago.

When Max Shaw picked her up that evening, she was wearing jeans and a black tank top she'd bought for $4.99 on the clearance table at Ohrbach's. They had planned to go to a party, but Fleur mentioned that she'd had a tough week and could use some peace and quiet. Max wasn't stupid. Within a short time, they found themselves in his apartment.

He was a rangy blond whose only drawbacks, as far as she was concerned, were a passion for old Mel Tormé records and a tendency to use phrases like "practicing my craft." She couldn't see that either would interfere with his abilities as a lover, unless, of course, he liked musical accompaniment, in which case she would ask for Rod Stewart or Burt Bacharach, depending on what was happening. As he poured her a glass of wine, she tried to recapture all those sexual stirrings that haunted her on subway platforms, but instead, she wondered whether she should mention the music now or later when she might break the mood, and then she wondered if her underwear was right. Maybe she should have chosen something less obvious than black. He settled next to her on the foam slab that served as both couch and bed in his one-room apartment, and she shifted nervously.

"You really turn me on, Fleur," he whispered, trailing the backs of his fingers along her arm and nuzzling her neck with his lips.

She wondered if she should say "thank you" and then decided his compliment was rhetorical. If only she weren't so nervous—what had happened to all the unbridled lust that had been driving her crazy for months?

"I've been wanting to sleep with you since I first saw you," he said, tracing the scooped neckline of her tank top. And then his hand closed over her breast, and she jumped.

"Is something wrong?"

"No! I—Kiss me, Max." She wrapped her arms around his shoulders, but she had trouble concentrating on the kiss. Instead, she found herself conscious of the position of their mouths, of a noise in the next apartment, of a crimp in her neck. And he smelled funny. Why did men wear cologne? She liked a man to smell like soap and a clean shirt. Like Jake. . . .

With that unwelcome thought, she rededicated herself to the kiss. Max groaned. He slipped his hands down over her hips and pulled her closer. She felt his arousal and understood that she would soon be opening herself to him, a man she barely knew. Making love was an act of giving. An offering. Something private and special and sacred. Why was she giving herself to a man she didn't care about?

Still, she hung on, letting him touch her, letting him remove her clothes and caress her, letting him invade her body. The bravest and the fastest and the strongest. . . . She'd set a goal for herself and she was going through with it, even though she had to bite her lip to keep from crying at how cheap and awful she felt giving herself to a man she didn't love.

Afterward he wanted to talk, but she told him she had an early meeting. As she jerked on her clothes, she saw that she'd hurt him. He'd been a considerate, unselfish lover, and she hadn't given him anything in return. By the time she left his apartment, her whole body was shaking. Everybody in the world indulged in casual sex. What was wrong with her? Why did she feel as if she'd just lost something precious?

Her spirits didn't improve the next morning when the *Daily News* announced that former Glitter Baby Fleur Savagar was back in New York working at the Parker Dayton Agency.

She had known that she couldn't remain anonymous forever, but she had hoped her luck would last a little longer. By keeping herself in jeans and staying away from anyplace trendy, it hadn't been as hard as she thought to avoid attracting attention. With the exception of an occasional call from Gretchen to see if she'd come to her senses, she might as well have lived in Topeka for all the contact she had with the fashion world. Until that morning.

When she reached the office, she found a stack of phone messages waiting for her. She closed her door and spent the rest of the morning politely returning the calls. She told them all that she wasn't giving interviews anymore and then hung up before they could ask her questions. The more aggressive showed up in person. They wanted the Glitter Baby back, signing perfume contracts, dating famous men, and talking about her rumored affair with Jake Koranda. All they got for their efforts was "No comment." They sent their photographers out for *couture* fashion and a whirling cloud of streaky blond hair. They got blue jeans and a Yankees cap. It was a one-week story, and then it died of boredom.

After her experience with Max Shaw, Fleur stopped dating. By Christmas time, Kissy was nagging her. "Your overachiever syndrome makes you vulnerable, Fleurinda. If you're not careful, you're going to end up like one of those hard New York

286

career women with money and power, but nothing else. You need a man."

Fleur glared at her. "That's absolutely medieval and the most unliberated thing I've ever heard you say."

"Liberation is more than a career, Fleurinda. It's an attitude."

"Thank you, Doctor. Now, butt out."

Fleur finally began dating actors again, but now that she understood uninvolved sex wasn't going to work for her, she kept the relationships casual. One day she'd meet a man she cared deeply about and sex would be right for her, but until then, she'd just have to keep busy and stop thinking about it all the time!

She directed more of her energy into her job, but as the months passed, she began to feel that Parker was holding her back. He wasn't doing it deliberately, but the longer she worked for him, the more evident it became that they saw almost everything from a different perspective. Olivia Creighton was a case in point. Olivia had spent most of the fifties as the queen of the B movies, specializing in torn dresses and being rescued by Rory Calhoun. With those days long gone, Parker and Olivia's personal manager, a man by the name of Bud Sharpe, had made the decision to capitalize on what was left of her name with commercial endorsements, despite the fact that their client still wanted to act.

"What do you have for me now?" Olivia sighed wearily after Fleur had identified herself on the telephone. "Laxative commercials?"

"Florida condominiums. They want a more glamorous image, and they know you'll give it to them." Fleur tried, but she couldn't manufacture any more enthusiasm than Olivia.

There was a brief silence on the other end of the line. "Did anything happen with that new Mike Nichols play?"

"It wasn't a lead, Olivia, and Bud wouldn't consider it for you. Not enough money. I'm sorry." She didn't tell Olivia about the argument she'd had with Bud and Parker over the whole thing. She'd almost had Parker convinced, but Bud wouldn't budge, and in that kind of battle, she'd quickly discovered that the personal manager always won out over the agent.

She was thoughtful for a few minutes after she hung up the telephone, and then she slipped her feet into the loafers she had kicked off under her desk and went to see Parker. After almost a year and a half working for him, their relationship was as rocky as ever. He needed her because she did a better job than any of his other employees, but she didn't think he was infallible and she wouldn't go to bed with him, both of which stung his pride.

The longer she worked for him, the more she saw what she would do differently. He concentrated too much of his energy on Neon Lynx and let his other clients slip, a shortsighted way to do business, as far as she was concerned. The last Lynx album hadn't done as well as expected, Barry was getting lazier all the time, and Simon had been talking about setting up a group of his own. It was axiomatic for rock groups to have a shorter life span than helium balloons, but Parker behaved as if Lynx would go on forever, and used Fleur to pacify his other clients. He also didn't always shoot straight with them, something she wouldn't have any part of.

"Parker, I've got an idea I want to talk over with you." She sat down on the couch across from his desk, noting that his squished-in face didn't register any particular pleasure at the idea.

"Why don't you send me another of your memos, Fleur?"

"I thought the personal touch might be more effective this time."

"I'm disappointed. I've started to look forward to your memos—all those bright college girl suggestions. They make great toilet paper."

It was going to be one of those days, she realized. He'd probably had a fight with his wife.

"What is it this time?" he went on. "More nonsense about computerization? A new filing system? A frigging newsletter for our clients!"

"The newsletter was a good idea, Parker, and I told you I'd do the work." She said it coldly, so he'd know his tantrum wasn't getting through to her. "Actually, it's something a little more fundamental this time."

Acting under the flies/honey/vinegar theory, she let her tone warm. "What happens when we negotiate a contract for one of our bigger clients?" One glance at his face told her he wasn't going to cooperate by jumping in with the answer, so she went on herself. "First, we have to clear everything with the client's personal manager. Then, after our legal looks it over, the personal manager studies it, passes it on to a business manager, who passes it on to another lawyer. Once the deal has gone through, there's a publicist . . ."

"Do you think you could get to the point, Fleur?"

She stood up and chopped columns in the air with her hand. "Here's the client. Here we are. We get ten percent for finding the client a job. The personal manager gets fifteen percent for directing the client's career, the business manager five percent for handling money, the attorney another five percent for studying the small print, and the press agent gets two or three thousand a month for publicizing. Everybody takes a cut."

Parker said, "Any client who's big enough to have that kind of team behind him is probably in the fifty percent tax bracket anyway, so Uncle Sam pays for half those commissions and nobody ends up in the poorhouse."

"But compare that to the way you operate with Lynx. You're their agent and personal manager. We do their tour publicity from our office, and the pie isn't split so many ways. With a little expansion, some more good people, we could make that kind of service available to your best clients, Parker. We could charge twenty percent commission, which is ten percent more than we're getting now, but fifteen percent less than the client is paying out to all those different people. We make more, the client pays less, and everybody is happy."

"Fleur, Lynx is a different situation. I saw that I had a gold mine from the beginning and I didn't let any of it get away from me. But an operation on the scale you're talking about would be too expensive to run. Besides, most clients wouldn't be willing to have all their business centralized like that, even if it cost them less. It leaves them open to mismanagement, not to mention embezzlement."

"You're right," Fleur conceded. "And that's why regular audits would have to be built into the package. But the current system leaves them open to mismanagement, too. Look, Parker, you know as well as I do how many of these managers are busier looking out for their own cut than for the interests of their clients. We've had good deals blown so many times by managers out for a fast buck. Olivia Creighton is a perfect example. She hates doing commercials, but Bud Sharpe won't let her accept any of the parts that are offered her because they

289

don't pay as much as condominium commercials. I happen to think Olivia has some good years left, and that's shortsighted management on his part."

Parker had started glancing at his watch, but she plunged on. "If it's handled properly, this is a more efficient system for the clients, and we can make money doing it. Obviously it means fewer clients, maybe only fifteen or twenty, but if we're discriminating about who we take on, it'll be a status symbol to be represented by Parker Dayton. We'll be a "caviar agency." Clients will be beating down the door."

"Fleur, I'm going to try this one more time with you, and this time I want you to watch my lips. I don't want to be William Morris. I don't want to be ICM. I'm happy with things just the way they are."

It was what she had known he would say, and she couldn't think why she'd wasted her breath, but as she headed back to her office, she tossed the idea over in her mind again and liked it even more. If she'd had someone taking care of her interests when she was nineteen, she wouldn't be out two million dollars right now.

She thought about the "caviar agency" all that day and on into the next week, considering it from every angle. There were definitely risks. Putting together an operation of that kind would be much more expensive than a standard agency. The nature of the project required a prestigious address and the kind of offices where the monthly rent could feed an underdeveloped nation. There would also be a larger staff involved, and they had to be the best, so salaries would be high. She estimated it would take almost a hundred thousand just to get started. Still, the more she thought about it, the more certain she became that the right person could make it work. Unfortunately, at that very moment the right person only had a little over six thousand dollars in her savings account.

That evening she met Simon for tandoori at the Indian Pavilion. "What would you do," she asked, when they had finished eating, "if you weren't already filthy rich, and you needed a big sum of money?"

"I'd clean apartments. Really, Fleur, it's impossible to find good help. I know I'd pay a fortune for someone who did a really great job on floors." He plucked a few fennel seeds from the bowl in front of him and popped them in his mouth.

290

"I'm serious, Simon. How would you go about it if you had, let's say, about six thousand dollars in the bank but you needed a lot more?"

"Assuming we eliminate peddling coke from the discussion, I'd say the fastest way would be to pick up our telephone and call that bitch Gretchen Casimir."

"That's not an option, Simon." It wasn't as if she hadn't thought about it, but she knew modeling was the one thing she couldn't do. This had to be all hers. Simon seemed to know it, too, because he didn't press the subject.

"Are we eliminating all forms of prostitution?" She glared at him and he held up his hand. "Just exploring the boundaries, pet; don't get in a snit. The best way would be to ask a filthy rich old friend for a loan, don't you think?"

She smiled fondly at him. "You'd do it, too, wouldn't you? All I'd have to do would be to ask."

He tilted up his head and pursed his lips. "Which, of course, you won't."

"Of course not. Any other ideas?"

"Mmmm. Peter, I suppose. He's your best bet, considering all these ridiculous artificial restrictions you've set up."

"Peter Zabel? How could he help me?"

"Tell me you're kidding, pet. You're the one who used to place all those phone calls for him. Peter knows more about making money than anyone I've ever met. He's made a fortune for me in precious metals and new stock issues. I can't believe he never gave you any tips."

Fleur nearly tipped over her waterglass. "Do you mean I was supposed to take him seriously?"

"Has anyone ever told you that you're an abysmal judge of character?"

"But he's such an idiot!"

"His banker would most definitely disagree."

Fleur called Peter the next day and laid out her problem. "I plan to pick up a little extra money doing some moonlighting—booking bands and working with promoters—that kind of thing, but it'll take a while. What do you think? Can I do anything with six thousand to start?"

"Depends on whether you're willing to lose it or not. High return means high risk, Fleur. You're talking commodities trading—currency, fuel oil, wheat. Sugar goes down a penny a pound and you lose your nest egg. Very risky. There's a chance you could end up worse off than you are now."

She thought about that for a moment. "I don't care. Six thousand dollars by itself isn't going to help me at all. Tell me what I have to do."

After that she spent every minute she wasn't working with her head buried in books and pamphlets that Peter had recommended on commodities trading. She read *The Journal of Commerce* on the subway and fell asleep with *Barron's* propped on her pillow. Following Peter's advice, she invested two thousand in July soybeans, bought a contract for liquefied propane, and after studying the weather forecasts, spent the rest on orange juice. Florida had a killer freeze, the soybeans rotted from too much rain, but liquefied propane went through the roof. She ended up with seven thousand. This time she divided it between copper, durum wheat, and more soybeans.

In April, Kissy landed the plum role of Maggie in a workshop production of *Cat on a Hot Tin Roof*. She flipped the overhead light on in Fleur's bedroom at two o'clock in the morning to tell her the news.

"I'd given up, Fleurinda. Really. I had completely given up! Then I got this phone call from this girl who was in a couple of my acting classes and she said she was directing a group that was doing workshops in this loft in SoHo and they were going to do *Cat* and she remembered a scene I'd done from it in acting class and . . . oh, God, I can't believe it! I just got back from meeting with her and it's all set. We start rehearsals next week! Of course, there's no money, and it's not really a big enough production to attract anybody important, but at least it's a part and I'll be acting again!"

Once rehearsals started, Fleur didn't see Kissy for days at a time, and when she did, Kissy was distracted and uncommunicative. No hunks passed through the apartment, and Fleur finally accused her of celibacy. "I'm storing up my sexual energy," Kissy replied.

By the time the night of the production arrived, Fleur was more nervous than Kissy. Somehow she couldn't see her little fluff ball of a roommate taking command of a heavyweight part like Maggie, and if she didn't like Kissy's performance, what was she going to say afterwards? She had already discovered that Kissy's claims of being "mildly psychic" weren't exaggerated. It was going to be practically impossible to lie to her.

A freight elevator took her up to an underheated loft with clanging pipes and peeling paint. The stage sat at one end, bare except for a big brass bed. She tried to tell herself that the bed was a good omen where Kissy was concerned and took a seat off by herself in a dented metal chair. Within a few minutes she found herself surrounded by a group of young men clad in blue jeans, all of whom looked like unemployed actors or artists. She noticed with disappointment that there wasn't a director or a casting agent in sight, even though she had called at least twenty and personally invited them. Not a very good sign, she thought glumly, for someone who wanted to start her own agency.

"So, are you a friend of the bride or the groom?" one of the men asked, leaning forward from the row behind her.

"Uh—the bride," she replied.

"Yeah, I thought so. Hey, I dig your hair."

"Thanks." It was past shoulder-length now, long enough that she could wear it up sometimes. It attracted more attention than she liked, and she had thought about cutting it, but she couldn't bring herself to do it.

"You think I could paint it sometime?" he asked. "I do wild acrylics."

"I don't think so."

He drew back, accustomed to rejection. "Hey, that's cool."

The play started. There was the sound of a shower running offstage. Fleur took a deep breath and squeezed her fingernails into her palms as Kissy made her entrance. She was wearing an antique lace dress, and her accent was thick as summer jasmine and tight with all the tension of Maggie the Cat. She stripped out of the dress and stretched, her fingers tiny claws in the air. One of the men sitting next to Fleur shifted in his seat.

For two hours she sat spellbound as Kissy prowled and hissed and scratched her way across the stage, telegraphing Maggie's sexual unfulfillment in everything she did. Her eroticism was dark and desperate, her voice like dime store talcum powder and backseat sex. It was one of the most riveting performances Fleur had ever seen, straight from the soul of Kissy Sue Christie, and by the time the play was over, Fleur finally understood Kissy's problem. If even her best friend hadn't taken her seriously as an actress, how was she ever going to be able to convince a director?

Fleur pushed her way through the crowd that had congregated around Kissy. "You were incredible!" she exclaimed, giving her a hug. "I've never seen anything like it!"

"I know," Kissy replied with a giggle. "Come tell me how wonderful I was while I change out of costume."

Fleur followed her to the makeshift dressing room where she was introduced to the other female cast members. She chatted with all of them, and then perched on a chair next to Kissy's dressing table and told her another dozen times how wonderful she had been.

"Everybody decent?" a masculine voice inquired from the other side of the door. "I need to pick up the costumes."

"I'm the only one left, Michael," Kissy called out. "Come on in. I have somebody I want you to meet. Fleur, you've heard me talk about our brilliant costume designer and future dressmaker for the Beautiful People? Fleur Savagar . . . Michael Anton."

It was one of those moments when everything seemed to stop, like a damaged frame of film frozen in a movie projector. He was wearing an antique purple satin bowling shirt and a pair of loosely cut wool trousers held up by suspenders, and he wasn't much taller than he'd been the last time she had seen him, perhaps six inches over five feet, with shiny blond hair that fell in long waves level with his chin. He had narrow shoulders, a small chest, and delicately carved features. She looked away from his eyes. Even a glimpse of that particular shade of blue made her ache inside.

"Hello, Fleur." He took several steps toward her, but he didn't extend his hand in greeting. She noticed that he carried himself with the languid grace that signaled aristocratic blood and old money. He moved just like Alexi.

It took a few moments before Kissy noticed that something was wrong. She looked back and forth between them. "Do you two know each other?"

Michael Anton nodded. Fleur recovered and fixed a pleasant smile on her face. She wasn't seventeen anymore, and she didn't have to let every one of her feelings show. "This is actually one of your better moments, Kissy," she said. "Michael is my brother Michel."

"Oh, boy." Kissy's gaze flicked from one to the other. "Should I play some organ music or something?"

Michel shoved one hand into the pocket of his trousers. "How about a few notes on the kazoo."

Fleur didn't like his hostility. It was her right to be hostile, not his. "Did you know I was in New York?" she asked.

"I knew."

She wanted to be composed and mature about seeing him again, but she couldn't make it. Grabbing her purse, she gave Kissy a quick peck on the cheek, and then she left the dressing room.

Kissy caught up with her just as she reached the street. "Fleur! Wait! God, I'm sorry. I had no idea . . ."

"It's all right, Kissy. It was just a shock, that's all."

"Fleur, Michael is really . . . He's really a terrific guy."

Fleur turned to her. "You think I'm terrible, don't you?"

"Of course not. I just think you should get to know him a little before you decide to write him out of your life."

Fleur spotted a cab and stepped out from the curb to hail it. "Go to your cast party, Magnolia, and have a drink for me. I'm going home to bed."

But it was a long time before she fell asleep that night.

In the weeks that followed, she tried to forget about Michel, but one evening she found herself walking along West Fifty-fifth Street and studying the numbers painted above the doors. It was nearly seven o'clock, and none of the shops were open, which was just as well, because if they had been open, she knew she wouldn't have been walking along that particular street.

She found the number she was looking for and saw that he wasn't much of a businessman. He had a good address, but the store front was unimposing, with windows that were too small and badly lit. They also contained the most beautiful garments she had ever seen.

Kissy had told her that Michel's designs were wonderful, but with Kissy, exaggeration was a way of life, and Fleur hadn't taken her opinion very seriously, especially since Kissy obviously wanted to see the two of them reunited. As she studied the garments on display, she realized that she should have listened more carefully.

He was obviously bucking the tide created by popular designers who wanted to make women look like men. The small window of his boutique held a quartet of outrageously feminine dresses that conjured up memories of everything from Renaissance paintings to Busby Berkeley musicals. As she gazed at the silks and jerseys and gracefully draped crepe de chine, she tried to remember how long it had been since she had worn a dress or pretty blouse. Too long. She hadn't bought anything more expensive for herself than lipstick and Tampax since she'd started putting all her money into the commodities market.

Spring drifted into summer, and then into fall. Kissy's theater group folded before she had a chance at a second big part, so she joined another group which, unfortunately, performed almost exclusively in New Jersey. Fleur celebrated her twenty-fifth birthday by talking Parker into another raise and then buying big into cocoa with it.

She was losing more often than she was winning, but she had learned that was normal in the commodities market. When the wins came for her, they came big. Peter gave her good advice, she studied hard to learn from her mistakes, and her initial six thousand turned into thirty-five. Unfortunately, the more money she made, the harder it became for her to sink it all back into the kind of risky speculations that were paying off so well for her. She forced herself to keep writing out the checks. Thirty-five thousand dollars was as useless to her as six thousand had been.

Winter settled in. She stopped relying on Peter so much and began to make her own decisions. Beef went up, pork fell. She developed an enchantment with copper and made almost twenty thousand dollars in six weeks, but she also started to get stomach pains. She kept going, cashing her paycheck each month and then putting every penny she could spare into the market.

On the first day of June, a year and a half after she had jumped on the financial roller coaster, she quit her job with Parker, sold everything she owned, and put it all into a nice, safe thirty-day certificate of deposit at Chase Manhattan. In eighteen months she had made ninety-three thousand dollars, and other than occasional stomach pains and a slight numbness in the tips of her fingers, she was no worse for wear. She started to look for an office, and three weeks later she signed the lease on a four-story town house on the Upper East Side.

The phone was ringing as she let herself into her apartment. Assuming it was Kissy, since they had made tentative plans to meet at the gallery that evening and then go to dinner, she tossed her purse down on the chair and picked up the receiver. "Hi."

"Hello, *enfant.*"

Despite the voice, despite the familiar endearment, it had been more than five years, and it took her brain a moment to register who it was. She tightened her grip on the telephone and made herself take a slow, steadying breath. "What do you want, Alexi?"

"No social amenities?"

"You have exactly one minute, and then I'm going to hang up."

He sighed, as if he were deeply wounded. "Very well, *chérie.* I called to congratulate you on your recent financial gains. Rather foolhardy, but then one doesn't argue with success. I understand you signed a three-year lease today on a house."

She felt a chill. "How do you know that?"

"I've told you before, *chérie.* I make it my business to know everything that affects those I care about."

"You don't care about me at all," she said coldly. "Don't play games with me, Alexi."

"On the contrary, I care about you very much. I've been waiting a long time for this, *chérie.* I hope you don't disappoint me."

"A long time for what? What are you talking about?"

"Guard your dream, *chérie.* Guard it better than I guarded mine."

CHAPTER 23

Fleur propped her heels on the rail of the deck and watched the dune grass bending against the breeze and changing color in the fading evening light. She was glad she had come. The house behind her was an angular sculpture of glass, weathered clapboard, and solar collectors overlooking the beach in the fashionable Long Island town of Quogue. At first, when Kissy had tried to talk her into spending the Fourth of July weekend at a beach party, she had refused, but then the heat and the fact that this would be her last chance to vacation for a while made her change her mind. She had also wanted a distraction from that small tape recorder in her head that kept replaying her conversation with Alexi. *Guard your dream,* he had said. It was a none too subtle warning, and she didn't have any trouble interpreting it. After all this time Alexi still wanted his revenge for the Royale, and he was threatening her agency.

She remembered how long it had taken her to get over the feeling that he would appear at any moment and drag her back to the house on the Rue de la Bienfaisance. She'd envisioned herself locked up in the attic room with the sagging parachute and Alexi's lust. But then, as one year had given way to the next and nothing had happened, she'd gradually stopped worrying about him. All that had changed with his phone call.

She tried to distract herself by envisioning her new home. She had spent the past week meeting with the decorator who was overseeing the interior design of the four-story town house that was going to serve as the new home of Fleur Savagar and Associates, Celebrity Management. The house had appealed to her because it was split vertically instead of horizontally, with the front half serving as three floors of office space and the rear making up her own living quarters. After putting up a token protest, the decorator had agreed to follow her instructions to the letter and promised that she could move in by mid-August, but before then she had to hire a staff and sign her initial batch of clients.

She had calculated that if there were no emergencies, and if a few breaks came her way, she should be able to keep herself afloat until February, but after that she knew she would be on her own, with no nest egg to fall back on if things weren't working out. She tried not to dwell too hard on the fact that a business like hers needed at least a year to get established. Since she didn't have a year, she would just have to work that much harder. And she couldn't spend any more time worrying about Alexi. Other than keeping her eyes open, there wasn't much she could do about him.

She told herself that she couldn't miss. Ever since she had introduced the concept of a "caviar agency" to Parker, she'd known it was a great idea—combining all the separate functions of celebrity management under one roof for a small roster of select clients. She'd made the decision not to confine herself to musicians and actors. She would represent artists, writers, sports figures—anyone who she thought had the potential to rise to the top. She already had three good clients including Rough Harbor, the rock group Simon Kale was founding now that Neon Lynx had faded; Olivia Creighton, whom she had stolen out from under Bud Shaw's greedy fingers, and Kissy. They weren't enough to keep her afloat past February, but all three had the kind of potential she was looking for.

She frowned at the thought of Kissy and slipped her sunglasses on top of her head. Other than a hypnotically restrained performance as Irena in a workshop production of *The Cherry Orchard* and a one-liner Fleur had gotten her on a CBS soap opera, nothing much had happened for her since *Cat on a Hot Tin Roof,* and she'd stopped going to auditions again. There had also been too many men lately, each one a little more muscle-bound and a little stupider than the last. Fleur blamed herself. Kissy needed a showcase, and she hadn't figured out yet how to arrange it. Not the best omen for someone who only had until February to prove herself.

The thought of Kissy and her men reminded Fleur of their host for the weekend. Charlie Kincannon was the backer of the workshop group's production of *The Cherry Orchard* and a man with painfully obvious hopes of being added to Kissy's hunk collection. Since he was short, intellectual, and the opposite of the kind of men Kissy preferred, Fleur had serious doubts that he'd be a contender, which she thought was unfortunate because she considered Charlie a much better match for Kissy than the hodgepodge of beefcake she had been associating with.

The patio doors slid open behind her, and she looked around to see her roommate stepping out onto the deck. Kissy was dressed for the party that evening in a one-piece pink and blue candy-striped romper, large silver heart-shaped earrings, and flat-soled pink sandals with beaded straps across her toes. She had threaded a ribbon through her curls and looked, Fleur decided, like a seven-year-old with breasts.

Kissy took a sip of her piña colada from the end of a lipstick-tipped straw. "It's eight o'clock and what's-his-name's guests are starting to arrive. Aren't you going to change your clothes?"

Fleur looked down at the pair of white shorts she had pulled on over the bottom of her black tank suit. They had a mustard stain shaped like Idaho on the front. She knew she should change them, and she had to do something with her hair, which was now pulled back into a ponytail, but instead she yawned and reached out for Kissy's piña colada. "I guess I'd better head for the shower. And I wish you'd stop calling him what's-his-name. Charlie Kincannon is a very nice man."

Kissy wrinkled her nose. "Then you date him."

"I just might. I like him, Kissy, I really do. He's the first man you've spent any time with lately who doesn't eat bananas and gaze longingly at the Empire State Building."

"Cute, Fleurinda. I give him to you with my blessings." Kissy reclaimed her piña colada. "He reminds me of a Baptist minister I used to know. He wanted to save me, but he was afraid if he did, I wouldn't put out anymore."

"I can't stand it when you do that!" Fleur exclaimed. "You're not 'putting out' for Charlie Kincannon, and you know it. If you have such an overpowering need to play the sexpot, do it onstage, where you can make us both some money!"

"Spoken like a true bloodsucker. You're going to make a great agent. By the way, all the unattached pieces of male flesh who've spotted you want introductions."

Fleur ignored her. If she listened to Kissy long enough, she'd believe that every man in the world wanted her. Several more guests walked out onto the deck, and she reluctantly got to her

300

feet, brushing the sand off her legs. After another sip from Kissy's drink, she headed inside.

The house was furnished in what she thought of as Long Island Beach Chic—tiled floors and sleekly minimalistic Japanese furniture, none of which bore any resemblance at all to the personality of the owner, who was at that moment sitting on the couch and ignoring his arriving guests by staring mournfully down into what looked like a double shot of bourbon. "Could I talk to you a minute, Fleur?" he asked when he saw her coming into the house.

"Of course." She moved aside his copy of *Rabbit Redux* and sat down next to him. Charlie Kincannon had always reminded her, both in looks and temperament, of a character Dustin Hoffman would play, the kind of man who, despite his money, always manages to be just a little bit out of step with the rest of the world. "Is something wrong?"

He regarded her seriously. "It embarrasses me to sound like an adolescent, Fleur, but how do you assess my chances with Kissy?"

"It's a little hard to tell," she hedged.

"In other words, no chance at all."

Fleur could have cheerfully strangled her roommate. "You have to understand that it isn't your fault, Charlie. Kissy's feeling a little self-destructive right now, and she doesn't do a very good job of seeing men as people."

He thought over what she had said. "It's an interesting role-reversal in a sociological sense, but rather uncomfortable on the receiving end. I realize I'm not a very good candidate for a sex object, but usually women overlook that because I'm rich."

And that, Fleur decided, was the kind of statement that could only have been made by Charlie Kincannon, which was exactly why she liked him. She made a sudden decision to give him a hand. "I don't have any idea if it will work or not, Charlie, but other than Simon, who doesn't really count, you're the only man in Kissy's life who has any idea how intelligent she is. Maybe you'd catch her attention if you ignored her body and concentrated on her brain instead."

He gave her a reproachful look. "I don't mean to sound like a chauvinist, Fleur, but it's a little difficult to ignore Kissy's body, especially for someone with a strong sex drive."

She smiled sympathetically. "Sorry, but it's my best shot."

Just then she heard a familiar voice and lifted her head in time to see Michel, resplendent in Madras blazer, yellow fishnet T-shirt, and shorts, step out into the living room from the kitchen. Her pleasure in the weekend vanished.

They had run into each other two or three times in the year since they'd met, and each time they had exchanged nothing more than cool nods, but even so, she'd found herself feeling edgy and out of sorts for hours afterwards. Why hadn't she realized he would be at Charlie's party with the other people in Kissy's group? She studied his companion, a muscular young man with dark hair that kept falling over his eyes. A dancer, she decided, as she watched his feet automatically open into the first position as soon as he stopped walking.

Although the house was filling with guests and she still hadn't changed her clothes, she quickly excused herself from Charlie and slipped back outside to walk on the beach. The moon was coming out, dabbing the foamy tops of the waves with phosphorescence, but she couldn't bring herself to appreciate the sight. Why did Michel have to show up? Until a few minutes ago she had been looking forward to the party. Charlie Kincannon had backed several off-Broadway plays, and in addition to Kissy's raggle-taggle theater group, there was the possibility that a few of the heavier hitters might be on hand. She should be back on the deck right now, sipping piña coladas with Kissy, and making some new contacts.

As her feet pressed into the cool, wet sand, she realized she had to stop letting herself get thrown off stride so easily. This kind of self-indulgence was a luxury she couldn't afford any longer, not if she intended to make her business a success before her money ran out. Stuffing her hands in the pockets of her shorts, she began the walk back to the beachhouse.

She was thinking about Kissy and Charlie when a man stepped out from the dunes about fifty yards ahead of her and turned to watch her approach. There was something about his stillness and the undeniable fact that they were alone on a deserted beach that made her immediately alert. He was silhouetted against the night sky, a tall man, bigger than anyone she wanted to tangle with, and he was watching her intently, not making any effort to disguise his interest in her approach. She looked toward the beachhouse, which was too far away for anyone there to hear her if she cried out for help.

Why would she need help? Living in New York was making her paranoid. He was probably one of Charlie's guests who'd drifted away from the party just like she had. But enough of her was still in doubt that she began to pick up her stride and edge closer to the water. From the corner of her eye she dimly made out a head of shaggy Charles Manson hair and an even shaggier moustache. The words to "Helter Skelter" skimmed through her brain.

He moved and she felt every muscle in her body tense. Abruptly, he threw down the beer can in his hand and began coming toward her, covering the space between them in long, swift strides. Paranoid or not, she didn't wait any longer. She dug her feet into the sand and sprinted past him.

At first the sound of her own breathing was so loud that she couldn't hear anything else, but then she heard the soft pounding behind her and realized he was coming after her. Her heart thudded in her chest. She knew she could outrun him; her muscles were strong and stretched out from her walk. All she had to do was concentrate on going a little faster than usual. Just a little bit faster.

She accelerated, staying in the hard-packed sand near the water and keeping her eyes on the beachhouse, which was still agonizingly far ahead. Should she take the risk of leaving the edge of the water when she got closer? If she headed toward the dunes, she was going to sink into that deeper sand and lose her speed. Maybe she should stay on the wet sand and keep going. She was an experienced runner, and he couldn't keep up with her forever. Sooner or later he would drop off.

But he wasn't dropping off. He was staying with her.

Fear made it hard for her to breathe, and she couldn't find her rhythm. She felt her lungs burning, and she sucked in air in short, ragged gasps. *Rape.* The word rattled around in her head and wouldn't go away. What had she read about rape? She remembered that you were supposed to try to talk your way out of it, but she didn't have any breath left to talk. And then she'd read that if talk didn't work, you were supposed to try to make yourself disgusting to the rapist by drooling or vomiting. That would be easy, except what did she say to everybody afterwards? *I made myself so disgusting that even a rapist didn't want me?* Jesus, that was crazy! What was wrong with her? *Why didn't he fall back?*

But instead of falling back, he was getting closer. "Leave me alone," she screamed. The words were garbled, little more than a collection of sounds, incomprehensible even to her, and she had lost precious air.

He shouted something. Near. Almost in her ear. She couldn't hear what he was saying. Didn't want to hear. And then she felt something on her shoulder. *What was on her shoulder?* Suddenly she was spinning around, and then she was falling with the sand rushing up to meet her, and he was falling with her. His hand bit into her shoulder, his body was pressed over hers, and she realized what she had heard. One word.

"Flower!"

Her chest heaved beneath his weight as she gasped for air. She tasted the grit of sand between her teeth, and with her last bit of strength, closed her hand into a fist and swung it hard against his back. She heard a sharp, angry exclamation, but his weight eased, and the ends of his hair brushed across her cheek as he raised himself on his arms above her. She felt his breath fan her face, and then she hit him again.

The blow forced him to pull further back, and she went with him, rising to her knees and punching at him again and again with her closed fist, not bothering to aim, just catching whatever she could reach—an arm, neck, chest, every blow punctuated with a small, choked sob.

He suddenly jerked her to him, making a vise from his arms that squeezed out her breath. "Stop it, Flower! It's me. It's Jake."

"I know it's you, you bastard!" she gasped against the soft fabric of his T-shirt. "Let me go!"

"Not till you've calmed down."

"I'm calm."

"No you're not."

"Yes I am!"

"Prove it."

"You son of a bitch!" She started to struggle again.

"Let me hear 'Thanatopsis,' Flower."

"You let me go, you son of—"

His grip tightened. "Let me hear the end of it. I'm not letting you go until you've calmed down."

"I don't know it."

"Don't you bullshit me, Flower. I mean it. 'Thanatopsis.' If you hit me again, I'm going to slap you, and I don't want to do that, so let me hear it."

"God damn it, Jake!"

"I'll get you started—"

"I know it, you bastard! 'So live, that when thy summons comes to join the innumerable caravan . . .'" She spit it in his face, one line after another, William Cullen Bryant delivered with snake venom.

When she got to the end, he slowly let her go. "If you hit me again, I swear to God, I'll deck you." He said it as if he meant it, and she sagged back on her heels.

Crouched on the sand, he had one leg under him, the other knee up, and he was looking at her in a distinctly hostile fashion. His hair, tangled and unkempt, fell nearly to his shoulders, and his moustache obscured all of his mouth except that impossible, sulky underlip. Dressed in a Nike T-shirt that didn't quite clear his waist and faded maroon shorts, he looked just as untidy as she remembered, but before his careless clothes had made him look friendly and now there was nothing particularly friendly about Jake Koranda.

"Why didn't you tell me it was you!" she shouted.

"It didn't occur to me that you wouldn't recognize me."

"You look like Charles Manson!" She struggled to her feet thinking that it wasn't supposed to happen this way. She'd dreamed about meeting him when she was dripping in diamonds, or coming out of the Casino at Monte Carlo with a disreputable European prince on one arm and Lee Iacocca on the other. She hadn't imagined white shorts with a mustard stain shaped like Idaho and a ponytail that was coming out of its rubber band.

Slowly he stood up next to her. "I'm making a new Caliber picture. Bird Dog goes blind, so I have to learn to use the Colts by sound. It's a piece of crap, but it'll probably make me another few million."

"How many women do you rape in this one?"

"What's the matter? Sorry you're not one of them?"

She sucked in her breath. He was deliberately antagonizing her. She knew it, and no matter how much she wanted to go after him, she wasn't going to rise to the bait. His eyes were openly insulting. They drifted down over her body, making her conscious of the fact that a nylon tank suit wasn't the best thing to have clinging to her chest when she was cold, but she forced herself to stand her ground. His gaze moved lower.

"Those chorus girl legs just don't stop, do they?" Somehow it didn't sound like a compliment. He came closer to her. Touched her shoulder. "How many times did we do it that weekend? Five? Six?"

"Stop it." She jerked away.

"You know what? I got shortchanged."

Fireworks went off in her head and she was once again standing in the rain on the front lawn of Johnny Guy Kelly's house finishing a conversation that had barely gotten started. "You really are a bastard!" she hissed. "You used me to get your picture finished—a stupid, naive kid who didn't want to take her clothes off. You took care of that, didn't you? You made me happy to take everything off. Did you think about that when they gave you your Oscar, Jake?"

He grabbed her arm. "You were your mother's victim, not mine, and don't you forget it! Don't push her guilt off on me! Between the two of you, I've had the best part of my life screwed up."

She didn't think about what he meant, all she thought about was trying to jerk her arm from his grasp.

"I think you'd better take your hands off her." A voice drifted over from the dunes, and both of them turned to watch a small figure coming toward them.

"This is a private party, so how about minding your own business?" Jake said, his hand loosening on her arm but not dropping away.

Michel came up next to them. "Let's go back to the house, Fleur."

She looked at her brother's face and realized that he had appointed himself her protector. She tasted the word, hugged it to her for a moment. Protector. . . . A head shorter than she was, certainly not as strong, dressed in his Madras and yellow net with wisps of blond hair blowing across his cheek, Michel was issuing a challenge to a man with an outlaw's squint.

"Why don't you take that cute ass of yours back where it came from," Jake drawled, "unless you want it kicked."

It sounded like a line from one of his worst movies, and she almost stopped it then. She could have stopped it; she knew she should, but she didn't. Michel, her protector. . . . She

306

wouldn't let Jake hurt him, but she had to see how far her brother was prepared to go to defend her. And it was easier to concentrate on Michel's gallantry than to think about how ugly Jake Koranda had become.

Michel's face showed no emotion. "I'll be happy to go away," he said softly, "but Fleur goes with me."

"Don't count on it."

Michel stuck his hands in the pockets of his shorts. He had obviously figured out that he couldn't physically remove her from Jake, so he was prepared to wait him out. Fleur glanced up and saw that Jake was getting uncomfortable. This wasn't the kind of villain Bird Dog was used to.

"A friend of yours?" he asked, looking from Michel to her.

"My brother, Michael An—"

Michel interrupted. "I'm Michel Savagar."

Jake studied them both and then slowly let her go. "I've made it a rule never to stay in the same place with more than one Savagar at a time. See you around, Fleur." He walked away down the beach.

Fleur looked at Michel for a moment, but neither of them said anything. They began moving toward the dunes, and when they reached them, he took her hand to help her over. She stopped walking. "Why did you do it, Michel? Jake could have broken you in two."

"You're my sister," he said simply. "It's my responsibility as a man."

Alexi would have given the same response, but Alexi would never have been capable of designing those beautiful clothes in the shop window on West Fifty-fifth Street. They walked back to the house, and neither of them let go of the other's hand until they got there. "Could we go someplace and talk?" she asked.

"I'd like that."

They drove in silence to a roadhouse in Hampton Bays where Willie Nelson was singing on the jukebox and the waitress brought them raw clams with french fries and a pitcher of beer. "I'm sorry I've been such a bitch about everything," Fleur said, needing his forgiveness. "I can't even explain . . ."

"Forget it." He leaned against the back of the scarred wooden booth and lit a cigarette. The neon sign outside the window flashed blue across his hair, and she found herself trying to explain anyway. She told him a little about the *couvent*

307

and how it had felt to be left behind. When she was done, he didn't say anything for a while, and then he told her about himself—his schooling, his homosexuality, Alexi. He spoke cynically about everything except his love for his grandmother, and she learned that Solange had left him the money that was supporting his business. When he fell silent, she told him about Belinda and about Errol Flynn.

He lit another cigarette. For a while he didn't speak, and when he finally did, his words weren't what she expected at all. "I want to design for you," he said. "I always have."

She woke up late the next morning and took the shower she'd never quite gotten around to the night before. After spending a few minutes fastening her hair into a loose knot on top of her head, she slipped into a bikini and a navy blue cover-up. The living room was deserted, but through the windows she could see Charlie, Michel, and several party guests lounging on the deck with coffee and the Sunday papers. She smiled as she took in Michel's outfit for the day, a pair of bermuda shorts and an emerald green shirt with ONE DAY DRY CLEANING emblazoned across the back.

She went into the kitchen and poured herself a cup of coffee, thinking about Michel and the fact that he seemed to care about her, even though she'd never given him any reason to. Last night, after they'd gotten back from the roadhouse, they'd stood outside on the front steps and hugged each other.

"How about making that two cups?"

Spinning around, she saw Jake standing in the doorway. She had already learned from Michel that her meeting with Jake last night hadn't been some sort of cosmic accident. He was one of Charlie's guests. He had heard she was at the party and had gone out looking for her.

"Get your own coffee."

He stared at her for a moment and then walked over to pick up one of the yellow mugs. Out of the corner of her eye she took in his clean T-shirt and a pair of faded swim trunks that she could have sworn were the same ones he'd worn a little over six years ago when Belinda had invited him for a backyard barbecue. Although she drank her coffee black, she busied herself with the cream and sugar so she could have a few seconds to steady herself. It was important for her to make Jake realize he wasn't dealing with a nineteen-year-old groupie anymore.

He reached out for the coffeepot, and his arm brushed against hers. She caught the scent of Dial soap and mint toothpaste. "I didn't mean to scare you last night," he said quietly. "I wasn't completely sober, and it hasn't been the best time of my life lately. I'm sorry, Flower."

She pulled as far away from him as she could and crossed her arms over her chest. "It must be hard to be miserable with all your millions, Jake. I think I'll save my pity for earthquake victims."

"Terrific," he muttered under his breath.

"What did you expect? I don't like being bullied. Macho theatrics haven't thrilled me since I was nineteen."

He leaned back against the counter and took a sip of his coffee. "Meaning?"

"Figure it out for yourself."

"You've toughened up over the years, haven't you, kiddo?"

"You bet I have."

He looked down into his mug. "You did okay in *Eclipse*, you know. Better than I expected."

"Gee, thanks," she replied sarcastically.

"Go for a walk on the beach with me?"

"No."

"Come on," he said. "Scared I'll bite or scared I won't?"

"Honest to God, Koranda . . ."

"Dare you."

She muttered an unladylike expletive and slammed the mug down on the counter. Jake grinned. It was the same old cocky, smart-ass grin that she remembered.

They slipped out the side door so they could avoid the group on the deck, and for a long time neither of them spoke. Fleur pulled off her espadrilles when they started to fill with sand, and Jake leaned over to pick up a shell. "I like your brother," he said. The wind tugged at his outlaw's hair and whipped it back and forth across his face. "We talked this morning. He's a nice guy."

She didn't want him sweet and polite, trying to melt years away with a handful of words. "A nice guy for a dress designer?" she asked sarcastically.

"Now what the hell do you mean by that?"

"I mean that I don't want you patronizing Michel."

He looked at her, disgust written all over his face. "Screw you, lady." He turned to walk away.

"Jake!" He didn't stop walking, but he slowed down enough so she could catch up with him without having to run, which was a good thing because she wouldn't have run after him for anything. Still, she knew she'd lost ground, and she had to recover. "Sorry," she said. "I had a late night."

He flopped down on the sand. "Call it even."

"Not a chance."

"Okay, Flower, let's have it out. Let's run the script through —beginning, middle, end—so we can put it away and get on with a new project."

She looked down the beach at a father and son flying a Chinese kite with a blue and yellow tail. "What's the point?" she said. "It's a little silly for two adults to discuss a nineteen-year-old's lost virginity. This is the age of sexual freedom, Jake. There've been a lot of men since you," she lied. "It's not that big a deal."

"Yeah?" He squinted against the sun. "Then why did you give up a career that was earning you a fortune? And why haven't I been able to write anything since *Sunday Morning Eclipse?*"

She felt a mean-spirited stab of satisfaction. "Is that true?"

"You haven't seen any Pulitzers running around with my name on them, have you?"

"You aren't writing at all?" she asked, lowering herself next to him in the sand.

"A concrete block. A concrete frigging writer's block." He threw the shell he was holding in his hand out toward the water. "And you know what, kiddo? I was writing just dandy before you and Mama came along."

"You're blaming me?"

"I don't like being jacked around."

"That's twice now that you've tried to play the martyr with me. I don't like it."

"In the immortal words of Rhett Butler . . ."

"Don't be a smart-ass," she snapped.

"Okay," he said. "Straight from the shoulder. What happened between us that weekend didn't have anything to do with *Eclipse,* and you damned well know it." He looked out toward the water. "I think you needed a convenient excuse to run home to Daddy."

She was furious. "Really? Then tell me something, Jake. If you don't feel any guilt, why the block? I can't pretend to see into the murky depths of your mind, but it doesn't take much to figure that one out."

"You don't know anything about it."

"All right," she said, "forget about *Eclipse*. Let's just look at the fact that I was a kid with an absurdly misdirected case of puppy love, and you were a grown man. I think the responsibility in a situation like that is pretty clear."

He jumped to his feet, spraying sand all over her. "Since when did I get nominated for sainthood? Don't you give me that 'kid' routine! Nineteen and looking the way you did wasn't a *kid,* damn you!"

He jerked off his T-shirt and ran down to the water. Throwing himself in, he dived under a wave and then swam out. His form was as lousy as ever, and she kept her eye on him to make certain he didn't drown. Big he-man movie star. Bastard. It pleased her that she had been able to make him lose control. But what did he mean, looking the way she *did?* What was wrong with the way she looked now?

As he came out of the water, she stood up, unfastened her beach robe, and let it drop to the ground. Underneath was a tiny tangerine bikini, and she made sure he got a front-row view. Without saying a word, she swept past him toward the water, performing a perfect runway walk with one foot planted directly in front of the other so that her hips swayed. When she reached the water, she turned in profile to him, lifting up her arms to fasten a tendril of hair that had come loose from the pins, casually stretching to make her legs look even longer, stealing a glance out of the corner of her eye to see if he was watching. He was. Good. He could eat his heart out.

She plunged into the water and swam for a few minutes, then came out and walked back to where he was sitting, her beach robe folded on his lap. As she leaned down for it, he grinned and moved it away. "Give a guy a break, Flower," he said, holding the robe just out of her reach. "I've been working with horses for three months."

"Thanks for the compliment," she replied sarcastically. "I'm glad to know that I look better than a horse." As soon as the words were out of her mouth, she wanted to kick herself for letting him get to her, and she decided right then that she wasn't going to get into a tug of war with him over her robe. Unfortunately, as she began to straighten up, she lost her balance and swayed slightly so that her breast brushed across his arm.

He leaned back on his elbows in the sand and grinned at her, a stupid sophomoric locker-room lecherous *male* grin. She glared at him, and then walked away.

Jake's grin faded as she headed toward the house. He felt as if he'd been hit in the stomach. He hadn't thought he'd ever see anything as beautiful as that nineteen-year-old kid who'd sent him into a tailspin, but now he knew he'd been wrong. That kid couldn't hold a candle to the woman walking away from him. It was purely a sexual attraction, he told himself, left over from six years ago. Even then, when she was an inexperienced kid, she'd knocked him out, and now that she looked like every man's fantasy, it was bound to be worse. Was it his imagination or was that pert little ass of hers sitting higher than ever on those knockout legs? She was definitely wiggling it more than necessary. He wished he'd given her back the robe so he didn't have to torture himself watching her body and that ridiculous tangerine bikini tied together with those little bits of string. He could eat that bikini off her in three good bites.

Definitely lust.

He walked down to the water to cool off, glancing over at the man flying the kite with his kid to make sure he hadn't been recognized. But the guy had somebody else on his mind at the moment. He'd spotted Flower as soon as she came over the dunes—almost let go of the string when he saw her—and now he was backing himself into the water to get a better view. It had always been that way with her—men stumbling all over themselves while she sailed past them, oblivious to the stir she was creating, the ugly duckling who wouldn't look into the mirror long enough to notice that she'd changed into a swan.

Jake went back to where he'd been sitting and picked up her beach robe. It smelled faintly of some light floral scent he couldn't identify, except that he remembered smelling it last night when she was struggling in his arms. He'd been a real prick last night, and she'd stood up to him. She always had, in one way or another. That was the trouble. Until she'd come into his life, everything had been going just fine for him, but she'd done a pretty good job of putting an end to that. She'd torn down walls that he didn't want down, and made him afraid to write for fear the rest would come down, too.

So if it's just lust we're dealing with here, a small voice whispered in his ear, How come you're so worried about walls? And how come Creedence Clearwater keeps playing in your brain everytime you look at her? Answer that one, boy genius.

CHAPTER 24

Fleur didn't see Jake again. He returned to the beachhouse shortly after she did and left without saying good-bye. When she got back to the city, she found herself jumping every time the phone rang, half expecting he'd call, almost hoping he would so she could tell him to go to hell. Dark, erotic dreams invaded her sleep, and when she awakened, her body was damp with perspiration. She had to find a lover. She couldn't keep on living like this—hungry for the touch of a man, denying her body's desires. Why couldn't she manage casual sex like other women? She felt trapped between her ridiculous Goody Two-Shoes sense of morality and a body that was burning up with sexual heat. Once again she submerged herself in her work and the plans for the renovation of the town house.

"Michel, I went over your books last night. They're a mess." She sat down on a straight-back chair next to the counter while Michel locked up the boutique. At first she and Michel had invented excuses to talk to each other. He had called to see if she had gotten stuck in traffic when she was coming back from Quogue, and then she had asked for his advice on an outfit she was buying Kissy for her birthday. Finally, they abandoned subterfuge and openly enjoyed each other's company.

She had just come from a conference with her decorator at the town house, and there was still a smudge of sawdust clinging to the sides of her jeans. She brushed it off and looked at Michel reproachfully. "How could you let your finances get so messed up? It's no wonder you're losing so much money."

He flipped off the front lights and walked back to her. "I'm an artist, not a businessman. That's why I hired you."

"My newest client," she smiled. "I'm excited about handling you, Michel. I really am. Your clothing designs are the most beautiful and creative this city has seen in years, and all I have to do is make people want them." She waved her hands over an imaginary crystal ball. "I see fame, fortune, and brilliant management in your future." As an afterthought, she added, "I also see a new lover."

He stepped behind her and pulled the pins from her hair. "Stick with fame and fortune and leave the lovers alone. I know you don't like Damon, but—"

"He's a whining little twit. Honest to God, Michel, your choice of men is worse than Kissy's. Her hunks are only dumb. Yours are neurotic." Damon was the dark-haired dancer who had been with Michel the night of Charlie's beach party, and Fleur had made no secret of the fact that she thought Michel could do better.

"Hand me your hairbrush," he said. "You look like bad Bette Davis. And those jeans are making me bilious. Really, Fleur, I don't think I can stand to look at your clothes much longer. I've shown you the designs—"

"Hurry up and finish my hair. I have to meet Kissy, and I just stopped by to invite you to dinner with us tomorrow night at the town house."

He shoved in the last pin. "At the town house? But you haven't moved in yet. Aren't you missing a few necessities for throwing a dinner party? Like walls and furniture?"

"It's informal." She hopped up, gave him a kiss, and left. As she stepped out onto West Fifty-fifth Street, she hoped he hadn't sensed how nervous she was about tomorrow night. She could have told him right then what she was going to do, but she'd wanted to make a small ceremony out of it. A ceremony made things official—and if she had second thoughts, a ceremony would make it harder for her to weasel out of what she had to do.

"No one's going to confuse this with La Grenouille," Michel said the next evening as he gingerly lowered himself into a folding chair set in front of the table Fleur had fashioned from two sawhorses and some sheets of plywood in what would someday be the center of her office.

Kissy looked pointedly at Michel's white clamdiggers and Greek peasant shirt. "They wouldn't let you in La Grenouille, so stop complaining." She surveyed the construction rubble around her. "If I were you, Fleurinda, I wouldn't get your heart set on moving in too soon. This place is really a mess."

"The decorator swore to me on his mother's grave that I'd be able to move in by mid-August. I figure that gives me a pretty good shot at September." Fleur ladled out generous helpings of lemon chicken and spicy Szechuan shrimp from paper cartons. "I really wish you'd reconsider, Kissy. Move into the house with me in September. Or if you want privacy, the attic is finished, and it has twice as much room as you have in the apartment. There's a modern kitchen, the plumbing works, and you'll even have a separate entrance off the front hallway so I won't be able to cluck my tongue over your playmates."

"Thanks, Fleurinda, but I like my place, I really do. And I've told you—moving makes me crazy. I never do it if I don't have to."

She knew she might as well give up. For all Kissy's teasing about Fleur's commodities money, she wasn't going to touch anything she didn't feel she had earned herself.

Kissy dabbed her mouth with a paper napkin. "Why the mystery, Fleurinda? You said you wanted Michel and me here so you could make an announcement. What's up?"

Fleur gestured toward the wine. "Pour, Michel. We're going to drink a toast."

"Beaujolais with Chinese? Really, Fleur."

"Don't criticize, just pour." The glasses were filled and Fleur lifted hers. "Tonight," she said, "we drink to my two favorite clients and to the genius who's going to put you both on top." She clicked her glass against theirs and took a sip.

The night she and Michel had talked in the Hampton Bays roadhouse she'd gotten the idea, but it had taken her a while to convince herself that she was ready to go through with it. Now she was as sure as she would ever be, which actually wasn't very sure at all, but she only had until February to get her agency off the ground, so she knew she had to go for it.

Setting down her glass, she looked at her brother. "Michel, why haven't you ever had a showing of your designs?"

He shrugged. "I had a showing my first year, but it cost me a fortune to put on and hardly anyone came. My stuff isn't like anything else on Seventh Avenue."

Fleur looked at Kissy. "And you haven't been able to get a shot at the kind of parts you're good at because you hardly ever get to audition for those parts, are we agreed?"

Kissy nodded while she consumed another shrimp.

Fleur went on, the food on her own plate growing cold. "What both of you need for your careers to take off is a showcase, and I've finally figured out how we're going to do it. A little luck, the right kind of publicity, and you two are going to make me a lot of money. Now. Of the three of us, which one stands the best shot at getting media attention?"

"Don't rub it in," Kissy grumbled. "You do."

Fleur shook her head. "I've been in New York nearly two years without getting much publicity. The newspapers don't want Fleur Savagar. They want the Glitter Baby." She handed them the evening paper, folded open to Adelaide Abrams's gossip column.

Kissy read it aloud.

> Guess what, celebrity watchers? Word has just leaked out that Superstar Jake Koranda was seen wandering the beaches of Quogue last Fourth of July weekend with none other than Glitter Baby Fleur Savagar. Koranda, taking a break from the Arizona filming of *Eyes That See Not,* the newest Caliber picture, was a guest along with the GB at the vacation home of millionaire pharmaceutical heir Charles Kincannon. According to friends, they were all eyes for each other. So far, no comment from either Koranda's West Coast office or the elusive GB, who has been quietly making a name for herself in New York these past few years as a talent agent on the rise.

Kissy looked up from the article, her face striken. "I'm sorry, Fleurinda. This is awful. Once Abrams gets hold of something like this, she won't let it go. I don't know who talked to her, but—"

"I'm the one who planted the story."

They stared at her, their surprise evident. "Would you care to let us in on the reason?" her brother asked.

Fleur took a deep breath and lifted her glass. "Drag out those designs you've been saving for me, Michel. The Glitter Baby's coming back."

Pain was harder to bear when you couldn't get drunk. It was something Belinda had discovered when she had forced herself to stop drinking. She slipped the cassette into the tape deck and pressed the button with the tip of her finger. As the room filled with the sounds of Barbra Streisand singing "The Way We Were," she put the crumpled newspaper aside and lay back against the satin bed pillows, letting the tears trickle down her cheeks.

All the rebels were dead now. First it had been Jimmy on the road to Salinas, and then Sal Mineo in that brutal murder—and now Natalie Wood. The three leading actors from *Rebel Without a Cause* had all died before their time, and she was afraid she was going to be next.

She and Natalie were almost exactly the same age, and Natalie's death scared her, especially because she, too, had loved Jimmy. They say he used to tease her when they were shooting *Rebel.* She was just a kid to him, and he played with her feelings. Bad Boy Jimmy Dean. And now Natalie was dead.

Death terrified Belinda, and yet she kept a secret supply of pills stashed in the bottom of an old jewelry box near the spinning gold charm Errol Flynn had given her. If only she knew for certain about heaven, she might be able to make up her mind whether or not to use them. She didn't think she could stand living her life the way it was much longer, but there was still a strain of optimism running deep inside her that said things might get better. Alexi might die.

Belinda missed her baby so much. Alexi told her he would put her in a sanitarium if she tried to contact Fleur. He said he would put her in a sanitarium for chronic alcoholics, and even though she hadn't let herself touch a drop of liquor for almost two years, she was afraid he might still be able to do it.

Although Alexi never left the house anymore, she hardly ever saw him. He conducted all his business from his suite of rooms on the first floor, working through a series of assistants who wore dark suits and somber expressions and passed her in the hallways without speaking to her. Almost no one spoke to her. Her days and nights blended together, stretching behind her and before her in an unending line, each one exactly like the last until there seemed to be no reason to go on living.

In the old days it had been different. When she walked into a ball or a restaurant on Alexi's arm, she became the most important woman in the room. People would seek her out to ask her opinion; they told her how beautiful she was. But now that

Alexi would no longer go with her, she felt invisible in crowds, and so she had stopped accepting invitations.

She remembered what it had been like in California when she was the Glitter Baby's mother. She had been charged with energy, luminescent, and everything she touched became special. That was the best time of all. . . .

The song finished playing. She moved the newspaper with the news of Natalie's death off onto the floor and walked back over to the tape deck, where she pushed the rewind button and began playing the song again. The music kept her from hearing the door open, and she didn't know that Alexi had come in until she turned around.

It had been nearly a month since he had visited her rooms, and she wished that her hair was combed and that her eyes weren't red from crying. "I—I'm a wreck," she said, nervously toying with the front of her robe.

"But always beautiful," he replied. "Fix yourself for me, *chérie*. I'll wait."

This was what made him so dangerous. It was not his terrible cruelties that gave him such power, but his awful tenderness. Both were intentional, and each, in its own way, completely sincere.

While he took a seat in the room's most comfortable chair, she gathered up what she needed and slipped into the bathroom. When she came out, he had turned off all the lamps except one, and he was lying on the bed. The dimness of the light hid the age creases and the unhealthy gray tinge of his skin from her. It also hid the network of fine lines at the corners of her own eyes.

As she approached him, she found herself remembering their wedding night when he had worn a robe in that same pale gold shade, and she had been dressed in a nightgown similar to the one she had on. But now her toenails were free of polish, her face scrubbed clean of makeup, and she had threaded a ribbon through her hair.

She lay back on the bed without speaking, and he came to her and pushed the nightgown to her waist. She kept her legs tightly closed while he caressed her. Then he slowly removed her underpants. When he pushed at her knees, she whimpered as if she were afraid, and he rewarded her for the whimper with one of the deep caresses she liked so much. She tried to push

319

her legs closed again to please him, but he had begun to kiss the insides of her thighs and her eyelids were slowly drifting shut. It was part of their unspoken pact. Now that the teenage mistresses were gone, she played the child bride for him, and he let her keep her eyes shut so she could dream about the times Jake Koranda had made love to her . . . and remember Flynn . . . and think about James Dean.

Usually he left as soon as it was over, but this time he lay still, a sheen of sweat visible on the flaccid skin of his chest. "Are you all right?" she asked.

"Would you hand me my robe, *chérie?* There are some pills in the pocket."

She quickly got the robe for him and then turned away as he pulled out the vial of pills. She no longer had any illusions about his illness. Instead of making him weaker, it seemed to have strengthened his power. Now, with his fortress on the first floor and an army of assistants carrying out his orders, he had made himself invulnerable.

She went into the bathroom to shower. To her surprise, he was still there when she came out, sitting in the chair and sipping a drink. "I ordered whiskey for you," he said, pointing with his glass toward a tumbler on a silver tray.

How typically cruel of him. The cruelty coming after the tenderness in a tightly woven pattern of contradictions that had controlled her life for more than twenty-five years. "You know I don't drink anymore."

"Really, *chérie,* you shouldn't lie to me. Do you think I don't know about the empty bottles your maid finds hidden in the bottoms of the wastebaskets?"

There were no empty bottles. This was his way of threatening her, of making certain she would do his bidding. She remembered the pictures of the sanitarium he had shown her, the small collection of ugly gray buildings set in the most remote part of the Swiss Alps. "What do you want from me, Alexi?"

"You are a stupid woman, do you know that? A stupid, helpless woman. I cannot imagine why I ever loved you." A small muscle ticked near his temple. "I'm sending you away," he said abruptly.

A chill shot through her. She thought of the ugly gray buildings that sat like great stones in the snow, and then of the pills hidden away in the bottom of her old jewelry box. All the rebels were dead now.

He crossed his legs and took a sip from his drink. "The sight of you depresses me. I do not wish to have you near me any longer."

Death from the pills would be painless. It wouldn't be like the saltwater that had closed over Natalie's head or the terrible blood when Jimmy had died. She could lie back on her bed and drift into sleep.

The hard Russian eyes of Alexi Savagar sliced through the layers of her skin like a razor. "I am sending you to New York," he said. "What you do once you are there no longer concerns me."

Baby
Resurrected

"I was now fair game."

Errol Flynn:
My Wicked, Wicked Ways

CHAPTER 25

The black velvet gown felt wonderful on her with its high neck, bare arms, and slashed skirt. She wanted to part her hair in the middle and wear it in a low Spanish knot like a flamenco dancer, but Michel wouldn't let her. "That big streaky mane of hair is the Glitter Baby's trademark. This time you have to wear it down."

Kissy stuck her head in the bedroom. "The limo's outside."

"Wish me luck," Fleur said.

"Not so fast." Kissy grabbed the purse from her hands and turned her toward the mirror. "Look at yourself, Fleurinda."

"Come on, Kissy, I don't have time—"

"Stop squirming and look in the mirror."

Fleur glanced at her reflection. The gown was beautiful. Instead of toning down her height, Michel had chosen to emphasize it with a lean design and the diagonal slash of skirt that started at midthigh and crossed over her body, revealing long glimpses of leg through the filmy black point d'esprit flounce that filled it.

Slowly she lifted her eyes. It was the same nineteen-year-old face, and yet different somehow. It had more character, and a certain maturity. She catalogued the separate parts—the wide-spaced green eyes, the marking-pen brows, the mouth that spread all over—and then, for an instant, all the parts came together, and her face finally seemed to belong to her.

The moment passed, the impression faded, and she turned away. "Just shows what good makeup will do," she said.

Kissy looked disappointed. "You never see yourself."

"Don't be silly." She picked up her purse and dashed downstairs past the Italian restaurant to the limousine, but just before she got in, she looked up at the window where Michel and

325

Kissy were both standing and gave them her very best grin. The Glitter Baby was back.

What she hadn't counted on was Belinda. . . .

Adelaide Abrams slowly dropped her hand from Fleur's arm and nodded toward the doorway of the Orlani Gallery. Belinda stood there, wrapped in golden sable, as fragile and beautiful as a butterfly. As her mother made her way through the guests, Fleur fought to control the whirlwind of emotions spinning out of control inside her. She had known this was the risk she was running. She took one deep breath and then another. No one was going to see that her insides had shattered into thousands of ice cold slivers.

Belinda extended one hand and pressed the other up against the bodice of her dress as if she were touching something hidden beneath. "There are people watching, darling," she said. "For appearances, at least."

"I don't play to the crowd anymore, Mother." Fleur turned her back and walked away. She walked away from the scent of Shalimar, and those delicately etched lines, like the veins of an autumn leaf, crinkling at the corners of her mother's blue eyes.

As she made her way across the floor of the gallery, she smiled automatically, exchanging a few words here and there with people she had known. She even managed to do a short interview with the reporter from *Harper's*. But all the time she was asking herself why it had happened tonight. For six years Belinda had left her alone. Why had she picked tonight to reappear in her daughter's life? Kissy and Michel were scheduled to arrive in less than half an hour. It was the point of the whole evening, and Belinda's presence was going to spoil it.

"Fleur Savagar?" A young man dressed in an olive-green messenger's uniform was standing in front of her. She nodded, and he held out a long florist's box. "The guy at the door said I could deliver this to you."

She reached in her beaded black evening purse for a tip and then took the box from him. Adelaide Abrams appeared at her side like magic. "An admirer?"

"I don't know." Fleur flipped open the lid of the box and pushed aside the nest of tissue paper. Lying beneath were several dozen long-stemmed white roses. . . . Her gaze lifted and

326

traveled across the gallery to lock with Belinda's. Slowly she pulled one of the roses from the box.

When Belinda saw what Fleur was holding, her fingers fluttered to the collar of her coat and her shoulders seemed to sag. For a moment she did nothing, and then she muttered something to the people she had been talking with and fled from the gallery.

Adelaide was poking around in the box. "There's no card," she said.

"I know who they're from," Fleur replied, her eyes fixed on the doorway through which her mother had just disappeared.

"His initials wouldn't happen to be J.K., would they?"

Fleur pulled her attention back and fixed a bright, phony smile on her face. "Really, Adelaide, secret admirers are meant to be secret. Especially ones who've made a career out of protecting their privacy."

"You're a good girl, Fleur, despite your occasional lapses." Adelaide gave her a sly wink and moved away.

Fleur shoved the rose she was holding back in the box with the rest. Let Adelaide think they were from Jake. He was a big boy, and he could take care of himself. Besides, it was a hundred times better than having her know that the roses were really a message from Alexi Savagar.

She had been waiting for something like this ever since Alexi's phone call. The smell of the roses was cloying, sticking in her nostrils and throat, making it hard for her to breathe. She pushed the lid back and set the box on a bench. She wanted to stuff it in the nearest trash can, but that was the kind of gesture she couldn't afford with Adelaide Abrams looking on. What had these roses meant to Belinda, and why had she left the gallery so quickly when she had seen them? Alexi was sending a message, but what was it? Another warning?

She was distracted by the sight of Michel and Kissy standing in the doorway. Michel, clad in a white tuxedo with a black nylon T-shirt, had dressed Kissy in a tiny pink and silver version of a prom dress, perfectly proportioned for her size. She clung to his arm, feminine, helpless, lips slightly pursed as if they were ready to expel a breathless boop-boopy-doop. It was no wonder, Fleur thought, that directors would only let her audition for sexpots.

Fleur brushed cheeks with each of them, whispering in Michel's ear that Belinda had just left. As they drew apart, she looked at him sympathetically. It had been his decision to stop hiding behind a phony name, and he was going to have to face the speculation the same way she had.

Kissy and Michel's entrance coupled with Fleur's greeting had attracted attention. *Women's Wear Daily* got to them first, and Fleur made the introductions. Both Michel and Kissy performed like champs, bored indifference on his part, a frothy cloud of pink and silver exuberance on hers. When they had finished with *WWD, Harper's,* and Adelaide Abrams, the three of them drifted around the room, stopping to chat with everyone they met. Michel kept himself aloof, Kissy chattered like a magpie, and Fleur was the Greek chorus interpreting for them both.

"I'm glad you like my gown," she said. "My brother designed it. He's really talented, isn't he? I'm trying to get him to take his work more seriously."

She responded to questions about Kissy's identity with a smile. "Isn't she outrageous? She's one of the Charleston Christies, of course. Michel designed her dress, too. What does she *do?* Nothing much, really. A little acting, but that's more of a hobby than anything else."

As the women looked back and forth between Fleur's incredible black velvet and Kissy's prom dress, she lowered her voice. "He's had so many women ask him to design for them, but right now he's only designing for Kissy and me. Confidentially, I'm hoping to change that."

Most of the crowd were too well-bred to pose the questions Adelaide had asked. Still, a number of people commented on Belinda's appearance, and the conversation became uncomfortably personal at times. Fleur answered as briefly as possible and then changed the topic. She told everyone about her new agency, and issued several early invitations to the party she was throwing to celebrate the official opening. A celebrity heart surgeon invited her to dinner the next evening. She took a deep breath and accepted. It would give her a chance to show off Michel's iris and blue silk sheath.

By midnight she was exhausted. As she sank into the back corner of the limousine, Michel picked up her hand. "You don't have to do this, Fleur."

"I know I don't, but I think this is something I need to do.

328

It's time I learn to live with who I am, and I guess that includes the Glitter Baby. I just wasn't prepared for so many ghosts to jump out at the resurrection."

As the limo pulled away from the curb, she thought of the roses she'd abandoned on the bench at the back of the Orlani Gallery, and she suddenly understood the message Alexi had been sending her. The roses were his way of telling her that he was the one responsible for Belinda. He had kept her out of Fleur's life, and now he was sending her back.

The phone calls began about a week later. They usually came late at night, sometime between eleven and two in the morning. If Kissy answered, the caller hung up immediately. If Fleur answered, the connection went unbroken. There was the occasional sound of a distant siren in the background or music that had been turned low—Barbra Streisand, Neil Diamond, Simon and Garfunkel—but the caller never spoke.

At first Fleur ignored the phone calls, but after a while she became convinced they were coming from Belinda. She had no evidence—no scent of Shalimar magically wafting through the telephone lines—but she felt it all the same. She hung up without saying anything, but the calls began to wear on her. She kept expecting Belinda to pop up everytime she turned a corner, and now that her mother had made herself so visible, she knew it wasn't all that remote a possibility.

In the space of a few weeks, Fleur and Kissy, wearing Michel's wonderful designs, had made themselves an integral part of the New York social scene. They had lunch at Orsini's or popped into David Webb to pick up an eighteen-karat bauble, which one of them later returned because it wasn't quite right. They stopped at Helene Arpels for a new pair of evening pumps and then danced until the wee hours at Club A or Regine's modeling silk dresses that floated like sea foam, a slim skimp of blue jersey with a gathered side seam, an evening gown that shimmered with tomato-red sequined panels. It didn't take long for every fashion-conscious social butterfly in New York to want one of Michel Savagar's dresses, and just as Fleur had predicted, when the women discovered the designs weren't available, they wanted them even more.

Sometimes Fleur and Kissy took Michel with them, but more often than not they went alone so they could gossip about him. "My grandmother ruined him with all the money she left him,"

Fleur would sigh from an Utrasuede banquette at Chez Pascal while she showed off a wrap dress made out of silk on which replicas of Monet's water lilies had been hand-painted. "People who don't have to work for a living get lazy."

Later that same week during a stop at Bottega Veneta for a new briefcase she couldn't afford, she confided to the gossipy wife of a department store heir, "He's afraid commercialism will stifle his creativity. Of course, he *is* working on something that does resemble a summer collection, and I do have some plans. . . ."

Kissy was less subtle. "I'm almost positive he's secretly putting together a collection," she told everyone. And then her candy apple mouth would form a little pout, and she'd pat the skirt of whatever sugarplum confection she was wearing that day. "I don't think it's right that he won't confide in me, his very dearest friend. I can keep a secret as well as anyone else."

As they gossiped about his idealism and indifference to commercial success, Michel was working sixteen-hour days overseeing every detail of a spring collection that was being paid for with the last of Solange Savagar's money. Meanwhile, the shop on West Fifty-fifth Street was closed for renovations. Fleur had hired the people who had done the Kamali boutique to set up better display areas and a more imposing storefront, with the name Michel Savagar embossed over the doorway in bold red script on a pearl gray background.

She began to feel as if she were back on tour with Lynx again, trying to survive on four hours of sleep a night. Every minute that she wasn't playing the social butterfly she was at the town house, dodging painters and wallpaperers while she fielded phone calls and dashed to meetings and tried to make certain everyone in New York knew that Fleur Savagar and Associates, Celebrity Management, was the hottest prospect for success in the city.

"You've got to slow down," Kissy said. "You can't keep up this pace much longer without getting sick."

"I'll slow down after February. I can't let up now, Kissy. I have too much at stake."

"You'd better make sure you know why you're pushing yourself so hard, Fleur Savagar."

Fleur ignored her and dashed to another meeting. After dozens of interviews, she hired two associates: Will O'Keefe, a cheerful redhead from North Dakota, who was an experienced publicist and talent agent, and David Bennis, gray-haired and professorial, to take charge of business and financial management and to give her agency an air of stability. She didn't have nearly enough clients to keep them both busy, but along with her beautifully decorated offices and couture wardrobe, they were part of the facade of success she knew she had to create.

"You've made the papers again," Will said, stepping around a paint-splattered drop cloth, "but I don't think you're going to be too happy about this one. It's not one of our plants."

Fleur didn't have to ask what he meant. Although she had not seen Belinda since the evening at the Orlani Gallery, Adelaide had been doing a good job of keeping her posted on her mother's activities. Over the past few months there had been a number of entries, but the cast of characters had stayed pretty much the same.

Belinda Savagar spent yesterday afternoon in Yves St. Laurent's men's boutique helping heartthrob Shawn Howell pick out a new set of YSL silk sheets. Word has it they ended up buying a second set at Porthault. Wonder what French industrialist hubby Alexi Savagar has to say about all that laundry?

Shawn Howell was nuzzled up with Belinda Savagar in the corner of the Elm Room at Tavern on the Green. Who says May/December romances don't work? Shawn and Belinda seem to be getting it just right. No comment from Glitter Baby Fleur Savagar, even though she and Shawn used to be an item.

Fleur glanced down at Adelaide's newest entry.

Belinda Savagar and constant escort Shawn Howell are being seen with everybody these days, except daughter Fleur. Old feuds die hard. Maybe Mom and the Glitter Baby will patch it up for Christmas. Peace on earth, girls.

She crumpled the column and pitched it into the wastebasket.

The army of decorators moved out of the town house with only five days to spare before the opening party, but after a leisurely inspection of the finished interior, Fleur decided the wait was worth it. The open design of the front half of the house was perfect for what she wanted to achieve, a look that was opulent, almost gaudy, with everything smelling of fresh paint and new money.

The offices were decorated primarily in white, with mother-of-pearl leather furniture, a soft steel-blue carpet curving up over the baseboards, and a few pale mauve accent pieces. The reception area and her own offices were on the main floor, while the other offices were set off from a balcony above. The balcony was bordered by a tubular ocean liner railing and black art deco columns with chrome collars. It could be reached by a curved stairway with carpet-wrapped open treads that looked as if they were waiting for Fred Astaire and Ginger Rogers to dance the Continental down them.

Fleur went into her own office and began arranging the contents of the drawers in her white marble-topped desk. Since the office was officially closed for the next few days, she'd substituted jeans and an orange Mickey Mouse sweatshirt for the executive wardrobe Michel had designed for her. As she pushed one drawer shut and slid open another, Will O'Keefe stuck his head into her office. "We've got a big problem, Fleur. I got a call yesterday from Olivia Creighton, chewing me out because she hadn't received her invitation to the open house. I sent her another one and didn't think anything more about it until a few minutes ago when Adelaide Abrams called with the same complaint. Fleur, I've checked around. No one's received your invitations."

"That's ridiculous!" she exclaimed, wiping her hands on her jeans. "They were mailed out ages ago."

"Apparently not. My secretary had them sitting in an open box on her desk. They were gone when she came back from lunch that day, and she assumed I'd mailed them. Unfortunately, she didn't bother to check."

Fleur sank down into her new desk chair and tried to decide what to do.

"Do you want me to call everyone?" he asked. "Explain what happened and issue the invitation over the phone? Or should we change the date? We only have four days. That's awfully short notice."

Fleur made up her mind. "No phone calls, and no explanations. Have new invitations hand delivered this afternoon with flowers from Ronaldo Maia." It would cost her a fortune, but it couldn't be helped. If she tried to explain what had happened, she would only look inexperienced and inefficient. As Will started to leave her office, she called him back. "Put my mind at ease and double-check the rest of the arrangements. Let's make sure there haven't been any other slipups."

He was back before she had finished the next drawer, and even before he spoke, she knew he didn't have good news. "I just talked to the caterer. Someone canceled all our arrangements weeks ago, and they've booked another party for our date."

Fleur didn't let herself stop to think. She spent the rest of the afternoon shopping for a caterer who could do the kind of job she needed on short notice, and for the next four days she was on edge as she subconsciously waited for disaster to strike again. Nothing out of the ordinary happened, but she still couldn't make herself relax, and by the afternoon of the open house, she felt as if her nerves had been tied into knots.

Telling Will she'd be back in an hour, she slipped past the caterers, who were covering long tables in white linen, and went out for a walk. He met her at the door when she returned, and as she took in the soot streaking his clothes and arms, she knew that the disaster she'd been waiting for had struck.

"Fleur, we've had a fire."

Her stomach pitched. "Is anybody hurt? How bad was it?"

"We got it in time," he said. "David and I were in the back hallway when we smelled smoke coming from the basement. We grabbed a couple of fire extinguishers and put the flames out before they could do much damage."

"Are you all right? Where's David?"

"We're both fine. He's cleaning up."

"Thank God."

"Fleur." He looked uncomfortable. "There's something I think you should see."

She followed him down into the basement, trying not to think about how close she had come to being ruined. What if the fire had happened tonight when the building was full of people? He pointed toward the window directly above a pile of charred wood scraps that marked the sight of the fire. It was broken, with triangular shards of glass sticking into the frame.

Fleur walked closer. "The window was broken from the outside," she said, pushing at the pieces of glass on the floor with the toe of her sneaker.

Will nodded. "I was down here this morning, and it was fine. Fleur, there were no combustibles in the basement, nothing that would start a fire. My guess is a couple of punks out for kicks broke the window and tossed something in on the wood."

It made sense except for the fact that it was five o'clock in the afternoon, not the time most punks were on the prowl. "Open the rest of the windows down here," she said. "I'll take care of the upstairs."

An hour later the charred wood was removed from the basement and the office sprayed with Opium perfume to camouflage what was left of the smoke smell. There was nothing else she could think of to do. As Will put on his coat to go home and get dressed for the party, she stopped him. "I really appreciate what you and David did," she said. "I'm only glad no one was hurt."

"All in a day's work." He fastened the last button and turned to leave. "Oh, I almost forgot to tell you. Some flowers arrived while you were out, and I put them in water. There was no card.

They were sitting in a tall chrome vase in the center of her desk.

One dozen white roses.

CHAPTER 26

Despite the late invitations and the fire and the fact that Fleur was a wreck, the party seemed to be a success. She took a glass of Dom Perignon from a waiter and sipped it while she studied her guests. They were a good mixture, with enough famous faces to keep all the reporters and photographers that Will had invited happy. Dina Merrill was in a huddle with Gay Talese. Kissy was pretending to listen to Olivia Creighton while she sized up Jim Palmer as he came in the door.

Earlier, Fleur had announced the date they were unveiling Michel's spring collection, and he was just breaking away from all the well-wishers. She watched as he made his way across the room, nodding at Simon as he passed. The two men had met for the first time that evening, and Fleur had been watching them with interest, but so far neither of them had paid any attention to the other.

Her dress for the evening was a long-sleeved ecru silk sheath shimmering with fat poppies picked out in brown and gold bugle beads. On Michel's orders, she had secured her hair in a low chignon at the back of her neck and speared it through with a jeweled hair ornament that looked something like a chopstick.

Kissy came up to her, one eye still fixed on Jim Palmer. "I've done my duty, but I can't stand another minute with Olivia Creighton. All she wants to talk about is her new part on *Dragon's Bay*. I mean, it's only for two episodes, and it's not even a lead."

"I think it could be before Olivia's done with it," Fleur replied. "That's one of the reasons I wanted to take her as a client. The nighttime soaps are hot now, Kissy, and Olivia's perfect for television. I think she could become another Joan Collins."

Fleur had been in Bloomingdale's, walking through the department that sold televisions, when Olivia's condominium

335

commercial had flashed simultaneously on dozens of television screens. As she watched, one middle-aged female shopper after another stopped what she was doing to look at Olivia Creighton. Fleur studied their reactions and realized that Olivia's mature, sexy beauty was conveying a subliminal message to them that had nothing to do with the good life in Florida. Olivia's beauty and bearing told them that the best was yet to come. It took Fleur almost a month to get the producers to listen to her, but her persistence finally paid off with a short-term contract. The money was unimpressive, something she intended to change the next time around.

Jim Palmer disappeared behind a group of women and Kissy turned her full attention to Fleur. "You look incredible tonight. A little intimidating."

"What do you mean by that?"

"Sort of like the 'other woman' in romance novels. The sophisticated blond bitch-goddess who tries to steal the hero from the rosy-cheeked heroine."

"My fingernails are too short," Fleur said, but she was secretly pleased. A blond bitch-goddess didn't have to worry about the little things in life—like the fact that Alexi Savagar was trying to destroy her.

Although she had told Kissy and Michel about the fire, she hadn't said anything about the roses, mainly because there was nothing they could do, and she didn't want to worry them. Alexi was playing a cat and mouse game with her that had begun when Belinda had walked into the Orlani Gallery. Then there had been the missing invitations to remind her that he was still bent on revenge. This afternoon he had gotten serious.

Kissy nudged her, and she forced her attention back to the party. "Have you watched Michel and Simon?" she asked. "They both have such bad taste in men that they haven't noticed each other, even though they both stand out in a crowd." Simon, with his shaved head and massive size, was probably the most conspicuous person in the room. He seemed to have talked to everyone at the party except Michel, who had been shadowed by Damon all evening. "Considering the fact that Simon and Michel are both pretty terrific," Kissy went on, "the temptation to do some matchmaking is almost irresistible."

"It's none of our business," Fleur said.

"You're absolutely right."

336

"Michel doesn't interfere in my personal life, and I'm not going to interfere in his."

"You're a good sister."

Michel laughed at something Damon had said, and Fleur leaned closer to Kissy's ear. "How about an intimate little dinner party?"

"Perfect."

With that piece of business out of the way, Kissy took a sip of champagne. "Didn't you tell me you invited Charlie Kincannon?" She tried to make the inquiry sound casual, but Fleur wasn't fooled.

"Uh-huh."

"Did you get the impression that he was coming?"

"I really don't know. Do you want me to ask Will?"

"No, it's not important.'"

"Problems?"

Kissy shrugged. "I guess he's gay or something."

Fleur arched an eyebrow. Kissy knew darned well that Charlie Kincannon wasn't gay. What kind of game was she playing with herself? "I heard he was dating Christie Brinkley," she offered in a deceptively casual fashion. It was a rotten thing to do to her best friend, but in this particular case, the end justified the means. Charlie Kincannon was a perfect match for Kissy, whether she knew it or not.

"Christie Brinkley! She has to be a foot taller than he is."

"Charlie's pretty self-confident beneath that scholarly facade. I don't think he worries too much about the externals."

"Personally, I've never found Christie all that attractive," Kissy sniffed.

Fleur nodded solemnly. "Definitely a dog."

"You think I deserve this, don't you?"

"Divine retribution, Magnolia."

Kissy was working herself up to deliver her most scathing retort when Will gestured Fleur over to meet with the reporters. She gave Kissy a quick, affectionate hug and then went to pose for the photographers and answer questions about her agency and about Michel's showing. When she was finally done, she turned away only to bump into someone who had come up close behind her. It was Shawn Howell.

"Hello, gorgeous." He bypassed her cheek for a direct shot at her mouth. She felt the flick of his tongue on her bottom lip before she could draw away. "You don't mind a couple of gate-crashers at your party, do you?" he asked.

A strobe flashed next to them. "It's a little late to mind." She noticed that Shawn's boyish teen idol face didn't suit him as well at twenty-nine as it had at twenty-two, and from everything she had heard, neither did his career. He reportedly owed the IRS a quarter of a million dollars and was having a hard time finding enough work to repay them.

"Hey, it's business, right?" He grinned and rubbed his hand up and down her spine like a high school boy checking for a bra. "I hear you're in the market for clients and I'm looking for a new agent, so maybe we can talk."

"I don't think so." She started to push past him, and then she realized what he had said. "What did you mean by a couple of gate-crashers, Shawn? Who else?" Even as she asked the question, she was afraid she knew the answer, but she hoped with all her heart that she was wrong.

"Belinda's waiting in your office. She asked me to tell you."

Not tonight, she thought. No more tonight! For a moment she was tempted to leave her own party, but then she knew that this was something she couldn't put off any longer.

Belinda was standing with her back to the door looking at a Louise Nevelson lithograph that Fleur had bought with the profits from a March delivery of palladium. As Fleur stared at the small, straight line of her mother's spine, she felt tears stinging her eyes. A stab of sharp yearning pierced through her, and she remembered how she used to throw herself into Belinda's arms when her mother appeared at the front door of the *couvent* and bury her face in the crook of her neck. Belinda had been her only champion, defending her against the nuns, telling her that she was the most wonderful baby in all the world. . . .

"I'm sorry, baby," Belinda said, still staring at the Nevelson. "I know you don't want me here."

Fleur quickly pulled out her chair and sat behind her desk, using its authority to protect herself from the flood of painful feelings that made her want to rush across the room and hold tight to the person she used to care about more than anyone in the world. "Why did you come here?" she asked.

Belinda turned. "I tried to stay away."

She was dressed in an ice-blue suit draped at the shoulders in petals of white mink. Her shoes were satin with French heels and pale blue ribbons that tied around her ankles. They were too youthful and too frivolous for a woman of forty-five, but somehow they managed to look perfect on her. "Ever since that night at the Orlani when I saw the roses I've tried to stay away, but I couldn't help myself any longer."

"What did the roses mean to you, Belinda?"

She fumbled with the jeweled clasp on her evening bag, and then reached inside for a cigarette. "You should never have destroyed the Royale," she said, pulling out a gold lighter and flicking it with unsteady fingers. "Alexi hates you."

"Why shouldn't he?" Fleur looked down at the desk, hating herself for the catch in her voice. "Alexi's not my father."

For a moment there was silence between them. "I wanted to tell you," Belinda said softly. "You'll never know how many times I wanted to tell you about your real father." With a faraway look in her eyes, she gazed across the room. "We lived together for three months at the Garden of Allah. Errol Flynn was a great star, Fleur. An immortal. You look so much like him."

Fleur slapped her hand on the desk. "How could you lie to me! All those years! Why couldn't you have told me the truth instead of letting me torture myself wondering why my father sent me away?"

"I didn't want to hurt you, baby."

"Hurt me? Your lies hurt me more than the truth ever could. All those years I thought it was my fault that Alexi banished me from the family! Don't you understand that?"

"But, baby, if I'd told you the truth, you would have hated me."

Her mother looked fragile and helpless, and Fleur couldn't stand to hear any more. She eased back in her chair, fighting for control. "Tell me about the roses. Why did Alexi send you to me? He did send you, didn't he?"

Belinda gave a soft, nervous laugh. "He thinks I'm no good for you. Isn't that silly, baby? I didn't realize he felt that way until I saw the roses. I knew he wanted me to go to you, so I stayed away."

"Until tonight."

"I did my best. I'm sorry, but I couldn't manage it any longer. I had to see if we could start over. I miss you so much, baby."

Fleur held herself stiffly in her chair, saying nothing, staring at Belinda until her mother gradually wilted. "I'll go now," she said, walking over to the door. "Watch out for Alexi and remember that I still love you. I didn't mean to hurt you."

Fleur rubbed her temples. Belinda didn't understand. Even after all this time, she still didn't see that what she had done was wrong. The tears she could no longer hold back slipped down her cheeks. "You pimped me," she said.

Belinda looked confused. "The man was Jake Koranda, baby. I would never have given you to anyone else." She hesitated for a moment and then slipped out the door.

The party was an unequivocal success, but Fleur was exhausted by the time the last of her guests had left. She slipped out into the front hallway, where she unlocked the door that led to the back part of the house and her own home. It smelled of eucalyptus piled in wicker baskets, the only decorating touch her bank account permitted for the time being. Walking into the living room, she flicked on the lights and collapsed on her second-hand couch, its shabbiness only marginally disguised by a fringed paisley shawl. The peacefulness of the room began to ease the jagged edge of tension inside her.

From the couch she looked down through the two-story expanse of metal-paned windows that had come from an old New England textile mill to the small, sunken garden. Even in the winter, the garden delighted her with its lacework of tree branches and evergreen shrubs and the bright orange berries of pyracantha climbing the high brick walls.

She envisioned the nearly empty room as it would look someday, a warm combination of rich, dark walnut furniture and oriental rugs that would provide a haven from the showy opulence of the offices. There would be loose pillow chairs and couches upholstered in deep green fabric sitting next to antique tables holding brass lamps and Waterford bowls.

The living room was actually an open loft set into what used to be the second floor of the town house, and it was fronted with a wooden railing that overlooked the brick floor of the kitchen and dining area below. Fleur wandered over to the railing in her stocking feet and looked down the expanse of windows to the weathered brick floor and the antique cherry harvest table Michel had given her as a housewarming gift. Now it was surrounded with mismatched chairs, but someday she would have beautiful old ladder-backs and a nubby handwoven rug.

Flicking off the panel of lights for the garden and the living room, she climbed the stairs to her bedroom, unzipping her dress and stepping out of it on the way. Dressed in her bra and a pair of tap pants with lace on the edges, she walked across the bare wooden floor to her closet. The irony of the closet hadn't escaped her. She had the most beautiful couture wardrobe in New York stashed away in a bedroom that held only a second-hand chest of drawers with chipped orange paint, a creaky chair, and a double bed without a headboard. As she switched on the closet light, she saw something in the periphery of her vision and spun around with a small, frightened gasp.

Jake lay asleep on her bed.

"That you, Flower?" he asked groggily.

With an angry exclamation, she dropped the dress and dashed over to the bed. "What are you doing in my bedroom? Get out of here, Koranda! How did you get in? I swear—"

"Your secretary spotted me in the hallway and let me in before she left the party." He yawned. "She thinks I'm a better actor than Bobby DeNiro."

"You're not! All you know how to do is snarl and squint! And I want you out of here! This is my house. You have no right to barge in like this and turn that cheap charm of yours loose on my secretary." She knew she was babbling, but it was better than stomping her feet or throwing something, which was what she really felt like doing. Why tonight? Was there some kind of conspiracy against her? Why couldn't they all leave her alone? Why couldn't Jake—

He reached over, flipped on the light next to the bed, and her body—the same body that refused to wake up for any of the men she dated—sprang to full, agonizing attention. Not now! she wanted to scream, but it was too late. She could feel the heightened sensitivity in her skin, the warmth creeping through every part of her. Although his moustache and the Manson hair were gone, Jake didn't look much more civilized now than the last time she'd seen him. He looked rough and male and infinitely desirable. She suddenly realized he was performing his own inspection and that she was standing in front of him in a cut-out bra and a pair of vanilla satin tap pants.

341

"Does all your underwear look like that?"

"None of your business."

He sat up, swinging his legs over the edge of the bed. "Could you maybe put on a robe? Something flannel that smells like bacon grease."

"No." She told herself that he was the interloper and that she wasn't going to do anything to accommodate him, but it was more than that. She liked the way his mouth had begun to tighten in that hard, unfriendly line. It showed that his control wasn't all that much better than hers.

"Are you pissed because I didn't make your party?" he asked. "Sorry, but it's not my scene. I told your publicist that on the phone. Still, it was nice of you to invite me."

She almost cried with frustration. Jake hadn't been on any invitation list that she had seen. Will had overstepped his boundaries, and the two of them were going to have a long talk. Picking up her robe from a chair next to the bed, she shoved her arms into the sleeves.

Jake said, "Is it too late for me to change my mind about the bacon grease?"

"Forget it and tell me what you want." That's the way to do it, she told herself. Play the cool blond bitch-goddess. And whatever you do, don't let him see how shaken you really are.

He stood. "I've got a business deal for you, but I can see that you aren't in any mood to talk. You can fix me breakfast in the morning."

A business deal. She felt a pang of disappointment. Damn him! Why did he think he could walk back into her life like this? She turned toward him and began taking the pins from her hair. "What kind of business?" she asked. He watched her hair fall to her shoulders. She shook it out and then combed through it with her fingers.

"In the morning," he said, his gaze traveling down over the open neck of her robe. "Where do you want me to sleep?"

"At a hotel!"

He sat back down on her bed. "Thanks, this'll be just fine. Nice, firm mattress . . ."

"No!" She was suddenly afraid to spar with him any longer. "Take the room at the end of the hall. There's a twin bed in there, but it's too short for you, so don't say I didn't warn you."

He stood. "Are you sure you're not going to be lonesome in here by yourself?"

"Actually, I'm looking forward to having my bed to myself for a change." God! What had ever made her say that?

His expression tightened as he walked toward the door. "Sorry to spoil your track record."

She stomped into the bathroom and flipped on the shower. As the hot water ran over her body, she tried to distract herself from her ridiculously adolescent body urges by figuring out what kind of business deal Jake wanted to discuss with her. Was it possible that he wanted her to represent him? Just the thought of what that would mean to her agency made her stomach queasy with excitement. She tried to tell herself not to get her hopes up. An established superstar wasn't going to turn himself over to new management just because that new management happened to be an old lover.

Maybe he felt guilty. Maybe he was going to let her represent him to make up for what had happened. She picked up the cake of soap and thought about how stupid that sounded. Jake hadn't shown any signs of remorse. On the contrary, he seemed to blame her for something she didn't have anything to do with. But what other kind of business could they have together? She rinsed off and let herself think about what it would mean to have Jake Koranda's name on her client roster. Once the word got out that she was representing him, she'd have all the high-powered people she wanted to choose from as clients. She could complete her magic dozen and then close the doors on the most exclusive agency in the city.

Her eyes drifted shut at the thought. She'd be able to do everything she dreamed about. Fleur Savagar and Associates would become a model for what celebrity management should be. The bravest, the fastest, the strongest. . . .

She awakened after nine the next morning, and in the light of day her dreams of the night before seemed foolish. Once again, she had let herself get carried away where Jake was concerned. The smell of freshly brewed coffee drifted up from the kitchen. She pulled on her oldest pair of athletic gray warm-ups and fastened her hair into a ponytail. She was almost out her bedroom door when she went back and added a touch of lipstick and then a dab of blusher. Her hair looked terrible. After combing it out, she changed into charcoal slacks and a soft gray sweater. It was a very old sweater, she reminded herself.

Jake was drinking coffee at the harvest table in the kitchen, his legs stretched out in front of him. She walked past him to the refrigerator and poured herself a glass of orange juice. "I'll make the toast if you make the eggs."

"Are you sure you can handle it?" he replied. "As I remember, cooking isn't your strong point."

She ignored him and began collecting dishes, eggs, and a skillet. Then she pulled a grapefruit out of the refrigerator and cut it in two.

"Don't do anything weird with that," he said, as he moved over to the stove and began cracking the eggs into a bowl.

"Do you have something specific in mind?"

"You know—putting it under the broiler or frying it in olive oil or something. I think food should taste like what it is."

"You can be absolutely certain," she said, "that I won't do anything subversive to your grapefruit."

They settled themselves across from each other at the harvest table, and the scene suddenly seemed so cozy and full of Saturday morning domesticity that she was afraid she couldn't swallow the bite of toast she had just put in her mouth. "I thought you had a penthouse in the city," she said quickly.

"I do, but too many people bother me there. After a while, I can't handle it, so I disappear. Actually, that's one of the things I wanted to talk to you about."

"Oh?" She held her breath, waiting to hear what was coming. The thought flashed through her mind that she would have to be very careful to keep her distance if they were going to do business together. Jake was the very last complication she needed now that everything was finally coming together for her.

"I wanted to see if we could work something out with your attic," he said.

"My attic?" She couldn't believe what she was hearing.

"I asked your secretary to show it to me last night. It's a great place—private, self-contained. I need a place where I can hide out and work."

Her hopes crashed in on her. She wanted to jump across the table and strangle him. Jake didn't want her as an agent—he wanted a landlady! Throwing down her napkin, she yelled at him. "Are you crazy? Tell me why you think that I'd even consider something like that! Are you so used to having people kiss the ground you walk on that you actually think I'd let you live in my house?" She jumped up from her chair and pointed toward the door. "Get out of here, Koranda. I'm sick of looking at you! I'm sick of listening to you! I'm sick of everything about you!"

He crossed his arms behind his head. "Should I take that as a definite no?"

"Don't you be cute with me! I mean it, I—"

"Maybe you'd better let me finish before you decide. Actually, I had something in mind to make it worth your while."

"So help me God, Koranda, if you offer me money . . ."

He held up a hand. "Sit down, Flower. I told you last night that I had a business deal to talk over with you. Now drink your coffee and pay attention."

She sat back down, but she didn't touch her coffee.

"I have to start writing again," he told her. "If I don't work through this block now, I never will. I've decided to take six months off from acting and use the time to write. I want you to represent me."

She tried to swallow her excitement. Jake as her client—she'd been right all along! It was a little difficult to play the cool professional after having lost her temper, but she did her best. "I'd be glad to represent you, and I think you'll see that I can make your life a lot easier." She leaned back in her chair, laying out the facts for him as she always did when she was trying to sell her agency. "As you know, I'm offering total celebrity management to a small group of clients. That means that I can handle all your business and legal affairs and, of course, negotiate future film deals for you—"

He interrupted. "I have good people handling all that. They've been with me for a long time, and I won't fire them."

She felt like a balloon that had just lost all its air, and her anger came rushing back. "Then, exactly what are you offering me?"

"I want you to handle everything I write."

She stared at him. "Big deal."

"You get my name on your client roster, and all you're risking is a small piece of real estate."

"Jake, you haven't written anything in six years! Your name

as a writer on my client roster won't get me anything but snickers."

"You're the one who blocked me, kiddo. All you have to do now is unblock me."

She picked up her plate and took it to the sink, where she jerked on the faucet. "Why do you keep saying that? Why do you keep blaming me?"

"Like I said, I was writing just fine before you came along."

"That's no answer, and you know it."

She heard his chair scrape against the floor, and then he came up beside her. "Maybe it's all the answer you're going to get for now," he said tightly.

She couldn't quite hide her bitterness. "And how am I supposed to unblock you? On my back?"

"Is that wishful thinking?"

Her hand clenched the edge of the skillet. "You bastard."

He caught her by the shoulders and spun her around, his eyes angry. "You know me better than that!"

"I don't know you at all!"

"I need some help! Is that so hard for you to understand? Whatever went wrong happened that spring when we were making *Eclipse,* and I want to work it through."

"Why is it so important? You don't need the money. You don't *have* to write."

"Writing is what I do!" His hands tightened on her shoulders. "Acting is satisfying and it's made me rich, but writing lets me breathe." He said it defiantly, as if confessing so much had compromised him.

The same old Jake, she thought. He dangles little bits of himself in front of me and then snatches them away before I can get a good look.

"Listen," he said, his arms dropping to his sides, "I don't intend to live in your pocket and maybe I just need some privacy, but this is something I have to do. I don't need to tell you that if I can start writing again, your agency is going to pick up a fat piece of change."

Their exchange grew angrier before Fleur finally gave in. She had to take a chance on him, and he knew it. Still, it was a real risk for her—not only personal, but professional. When word of their deal leaked out and people learned that she had committed herself to representing a writer who didn't write anymore,

346

the gossip would spread like wildfire. Everyone would say that Jake was letting her use his name because they were sleeping together—that he didn't trust her enough to handle his film deals, just a writing career that had gone sour years ago. She suddenly wished she hadn't planted all those stories about the two of them, because now she was going to have to pay the price. She had worked hard to project the image of a confident, knowledgeable professional, but as soon as people heard about this, she was going to look like a woman trying to build a business from her bedroom.

But what if she *could* get him to start writing again? What if she really *could* break through that block and get him to produce another Koranda play? If Jake started writing again, she wouldn't have to worry about gossip, or about February, for that matter. It was a gamble she couldn't pass up, and she refused to let herself dwell on the personal price she would almost surely pay for once again involving herself with a man who tore down all her defenses.

But when the gossip did begin, it didn't have anything to do with Jake Koranda. She learned about it Monday morning, two days after she and Jake had made their deal and long before it could become common knowledge. As she was leaving the office to meet a Brazilian soccer star she hoped to woo, she received a phone call from a network vice-president she'd known for several years. "I've been hearing some gossip floating around about you lately that I thought you should know about," he said. "Somebody's been reminding people of those broken modeling contracts from a few years ago."

She tried to sound unconcerned. "Isn't there anything better to gossip about? That's old news."

"Not when you're trying to start your own business. It's lousy PR, Fleur."

He didn't need to spell it out for her. She'd broken contracts before, and the implication was that she might do it again. But why were these stories starting up now, after all this time? It was almost as if someone had deliberately— Then she realized that Alexi had made his next move.

The soccer star didn't show up for lunch, a message that didn't need much in the way of interpretation, and she returned to the office in time to take a call from Olivia Creighton. Just the week before, Olivia had sent her a half-dozen antique Baccarat goblets and a case of Pouilly Fuissé to celebrate the signing of her contract for *Dragon's Bay*. Now she was clearly upset. "I've been hearing some terrible stories about you, Fleur," she said. "Of course, I'm sure none of them are true, and you know how I adore you, but after what happened to poor Doris Day and all her money, you can't be too careful. I'm just not comfortable with instability."

"Of course you're not," Fleur said soothingly. "No one is." She thought quickly and then made a date for Olivia to meet David Bennis for lunch the next day. With his leather elbow patches and his smelly pipe, he radiated stability better than anyone she knew, and she hoped he would reassure Olivia, but as she climbed the open stairway that led to David's office off the balcony, she felt a small wellspring of anger inside her. She had thought she was all through with using someone else to solve her own problems.

That evening she had her hand on the telephone to place a call to Alexi when she changed her mind. What was she going to gain by accusing him directly of having started the stories? It would be better to let him wonder how she was handling his attack, perhaps keep him a little off balance.

She leaned back in her chair and forced herself to look at the situation logically. By the time the gossip about the broken contracts died down, news of her arrangement with Jake would be all over town and an equally damaging sort of gossip would arise, this time without any help from Alexi. She could see his delight, envision him mentally toying with the pieces of her life while she contemplated his next move. It wouldn't take him long to understand how important Michel's collection was to her. He knew that she was responsible for the collection being shown, and he would realize that its success would go a long way toward restoring her professional reputation. On the other hand, if the collection failed . . . It didn't take a crystal ball for her to figure out what Alexi's next move was going to be, and she knew she couldn't put off telling Michel what was happening any longer.

She located him in his workroom on the second floor of a converted factory in Astoria, where weary Italian seamstresses were putting the final touches on his garments. He was exhausted from the strain of trying to get everything together so quickly, and she wished she didn't have to add to his worries.

"That bastard!" he exclaimed after she had finished telling him everything. "What are we going to do, Fleur? How are we going to stop him?"

"We're not," she said. "I'm the one who's responsible, and you're going to leave it to me. As of tonight, I've put this workroom under twenty-four hour guard. There'll be guards on the boutique, too, but my guess is that he'll go after the samples."

Michel looked physically ill. "Do you really think he'd do that? Do you really think he'd try to destroy my samples?"

"I'm sure of it, Michel," she said gently. "It's the way he could do the most damage. I don't think even Alexi would try to burn down the hotel ballroom while we're showing the collection, so getting to the samples ahead of time is the next logical choice."

He automatically straightened the scarf she had tied at the neck of the white cashmere sheath he had designed for her. He had to reach up to do it because she was wearing the stiletto heels that had become a standard part of her business wardrobe ever since she had realized that her height sometimes worked to her advantage. "Alexi won't stop," Michel said. "If we make it through this, there'll be something else. You know that, don't you?"

"I know." She shrugged. "I have to take it one step at a time, and hope he gets bored. There's not much else I can do."

Jake had settled himself into the attic, and Fleur sometimes heard his footsteps late at night as she was falling asleep. Occasionally, she heard the sound of water running or a toilet flushing, but it didn't take her long to realize that she never heard a typewriter. The silence infuriated her. Just as she had feared, the stories of their business arrangement had surfaced on top of the other gossip. A Broadway actor and a singer she had been close to signing had both backed off, and Olivia was getting more skittish every day. She found herself straining for the sound of the typewriter as soon as she walked into her house and had to force herself not to charge up the stairs to the attic and confront him each time she came home to silence. She couldn't *make* Jake write. All she could do was encourage him, and she wasn't exactly sure how to go about doing that.

Acting on the theory that exercise improves almost everything and would at least get him out of bed in the morning, she began leaving notes under his door inviting him to join her on her daily runs, and one crisp October morning, a few days before Michel's collection was to be unveiled, she came outside to find him sitting on the front step waiting for her. He was wearing a gray UCLA sweatshirt, navy sweatpants, and a pair of beat-up Adidas. As he gazed up at her, his pouty bottom lip curled in a smile.

Her heart gave one of those ridiculous jumps that made her feel as if she were nineteen again. She took the three front steps in one leap and ran past him. He laughed and came up behind her.

"Think you can keep up with me, cowboy?" She tossed over her shoulder.

"Ain't met a woman yet who could outrun me," he drawled, all full of sagebrush and buffalo chips.

"Are you sure about that? It seems to me you've been leading a pretty indolent life lately."

"Playing basketball three afternoons a week with a bunch of black kids who call me Mister isn't exactly taking it easy."

"I'm surprised you can keep up at your advanced age."

"Who said I can? My knees are shot, and I can't jump anymore, so I usually get pulled from the game before the third quarter is over. They only put up with me because I bought the uniforms."

As they crossed over into the park, Fleur smiled and thought about how much she liked Jake's self-deprecating sense of humor. Next to his body, it was the best thing about him. His body and his no-nonsense masculinity. And his face. God, she loved his face! She was suddenly furious with herself. How about his two-bit morality? Did she love that, too? And his manipulations, his betrayals—the fact that he'd taken her to the top of the mountain and then shoved her off without a moment's remorse.

"I haven't noticed a typewriter banging away over my head," she said sharply.

"Ever hear of pencils?"

She remembered the paper-littered floor beneath his typewriter in the library of his house in California, and didn't believe him for a moment. "I've heard of pencils. Pretty useful

350

things for people who feel the urge to put words down on blank sheets of paper."

"Don't push me, Flower. Okay?" His face closed up, and she decided she'd better not go any further for the moment. But only for the moment. If Jake thought he was going to destroy everything she was working for by indulging himself like this, he was in for a surprise. She just had to figure out how to get him started without getting herself burned in the process. Impulsively, she invited him to the dinner party she and Kissy had planned for that weekend so that Michel and Simon could get to know each other. Maybe being around congenial people would loosen Jake up.

"Sorry, Flower, but formal dinner parties aren't my thing."

"It's not exactly formal," she said. "The guests cook. It'll just be Michel and Simon Kale and Kissy. I invited Charlie Kincannon, but he's going to be out of town."

"Do you really know somebody named Kissy?"

"I guess you didn't meet her at Charlie's beach party. She's my best friend. Although"—she hesitated—"it might be a good idea not to walk into any dark rooms with her."

Jake apparently thought that was an interesting comment for someone to make about her best friend, because he pressed her to elaborate. Fleur told him she had work to do and that he'd better pick up the pace.

They ran for a while without talking, and then Jake looked over at her. "My office sent me a pile of clippings in the mail. It seems you and I were a pretty hot item a while back in the New York gossip columns."

She tried to sound nonchalant. "You just heard about it? Don't you read the papers, Koranda?"

"Front page, sports, and Ann Landers. There's nothing else worth reading."

"You're kidding. You don't read *Doonesbury*?"

"Not if I can avoid it."

She sidestepped an ice-slicked puddle in her path. "How can you go through life without *Doonesbury*?"

"Why do I get the feeling you're trying to change the subject?" He reached out and caught her arm, pulling her to a stop. For a moment he stood there, chest heaving, studying her. Finally, he shook his head, his expression incredulous, "I don't frigging believe this! You planted those stories, didn't you? They were coming from your office!"

She thought about lying, but then she decided not to. Still, she tilted up her chin so he would know he couldn't intimidate her. "At the time, I needed the publicity. It won't happen again."

"You know how I feel about my privacy!" he exclaimed.

"I know."

"I don't like cheap tricks."

"That's funny," she snapped. "I thought you invented them."

He shoved his hands on his hips. "What's with you, anyway? Do you want success that bad? Is money so important to you that you'll do anything to get it?"

"Very touching, especially coming from someone who's worth a cool five million."

His jaw tightened. "You want some of it? You want me to write you a check? Is that what I have to do to keep my name out of the newspapers?"

"Go to hell! I said I was sorry."

"As a matter of fact, you didn't."

"Good, because actually I'm not!"

He studied her for a moment and then shook his head in disgust. "You know what? I liked you a lot better when you were a kid."

She stood alone on the path watching him walk away from her. Of course you liked me better, she thought. When I was a kid, you could pull all my strings, you could make me melt just by looking at me, make me forget everything except how much I wanted you. Now I'm grown up, and now—

Now it was just as bad.

CHAPTER 27

Saturday Fleur went shopping for her dinner party. After she had put away the groceries, she placed a pot of amber chrysanthemums in the center of the table and then set several bottles of Mexican beer in the refrigerator to chill, even though she didn't really expect Jake. She hadn't heard from him since the morning they had gone running, and she assumed he had returned to his penthouse, or even left town for all she knew. What did *he* care? She was the one who had to deal with the sly gossip, the innuendoes, the bank balance that was dipping lower by the day.

To her surprise Jake was the first to arrive, knocking on her door at precisely nine o'clock. He made no reference to their last argument, and she didn't bring it up. They chatted for a few moments, and then his eyes skimmed down over the ivory wool pleated trousers and dusty rose silk blouse she had chosen for the evening. "Don't you ever look bad?" he asked, thrusting a gift-wrapped package into her hands.

She unwrapped it to find a copy of *The Joy of Cooking*. "Tacky, Koranda," she said, turning to set the book down while she took a deep breath and told herself that she absolutely wasn't going to make a fool of herself tonight just because King Movie Star had condescended to show up for her party.

"Uhm," he sighed. "You're probably right. Definitely tacky."

She heard him coming up behind her, smelled his clean shirt, his toothpaste. And then she jumped as his hands lifted the back of her hair. "What are you—"

"Relax! Jeeze, you're jumpy." He touched her neck just beneath the collar of her blouse, and something small and cold settled between her breasts. She looked down and saw that he had fastened a thin gold chain around her neck. Suspended from it was a trumpet-shaped flower picked out in blue and green enamel, with tiny diamonds forming beads of dew on the blossom.

Holding the flower in her fingers, she turned to him. There was something soft and unguarded in his expression, and the old lump settled back into its familiar place in her throat. For a moment they gazed at each other, and the present seemed to slide away until they had returned to the time when things were easy between them. "It's beautiful, Jake. You didn't have to—"

"It's a morning glory. I've noticed that's not your best time of day."

"It was so sweet of you—"

"No big deal, for chrissake." Abruptly, he shattered the softness of the moment. Turning away, he slammed the door on her pleasure, and headed for the kitchen.

The morning glory charm slipped from her fingers. Why had she let her guard down, even for a moment? She should have learned by now.

"How come I don't smell any food?" he called out. "I consider that an ominous sign."

"The cook hasn't arrived yet," she replied as lightly as she could manage. Just then the front buzzer rang, and she opened it to admit Michel.

"I've brought my own knives," her brother announced, heading for the kitchen, where he set a grocery bag on the counter, "and this wonderful garlic you can only buy at a little hole in the wall off Canal Street. Did you get the clams at the fish market I told you about?"

"Aye, aye, sir." She saw how tired he looked and was glad she had planned this evening for him.

Simon arrived shortly afterwards, and she performed the introductions. As luck would have it, he had seen every Caliber picture Jake had ever made and barely noticed Michel, who was standing at the kitchen counter unpacking his grocery bag. And Michel was too busy treating Fleur to a long list of mishaps that he was absolutely convinced were going to ruin his collection to pay any attention to Simon. As she handed her brother a cutting board, she thought that this wasn't working out exactly the way she had planned it.

Kissy arrived. "Sorry I'm late," she said as Fleur opened the door, "but Charlie called me from Chicago just as I was leaving."

"Congratulations. Things must be improving."

Kissy stepped down into the kitchen, her expression glum. "I think I've lost my touch. It's just like—" And then she saw Jake leaning against the counter. . . .

Fleur performed the introductions. Jake gazed down at Kissy, and a grin spread like butter over his face. Kissy looked like a kindergarten snack. She stared up at him, all gumdrop eyes and wet red candy apple mouth, and Fleur felt something like a snake coiling in the pit of her stomach, something ugly and awful that made her feel as if she were thirteen again, taller than everybody else, gawky and awkward with bruised elbows, bandaged knees, and a face that was too big for her body.

Kissy smiled her dippy, gooey, what's-your-name-sailor-boy smile, and Jake's chest puffed up like a rooster's. Their lips were moving, so Fleur knew they were talking to each other, but she hadn't the faintest idea what they were saying. All she could see was Jake's face, split wide open in a ridiculous adolescent grin, and Kissy looking like a teenager's wet dream. And then Kissy was back by her side, murmuring something stupid about borrowing a book, and dragging Fleur from the room by her wrist.

Kissy took her into her bedroom. After she had shut the door, she leaned back against it and closed her eyes. "That one," she sighed, "belongs in the Hunk Hall of Fame."

"His teeth are crooked," Fleur snapped.

"I'll bet the rest of him isn't."

"Just what do you mean by that?"

Kissy slowly opened her eyes. "I mean that you'd better get that whipped puppy look off your face right now, or I swear to God, Fleurinda, I'm going to go back down to that kitchen and take back all the dishes I loaned you."

"I don't know what you're talking about."

Kissy looked at her with disgust. "I'm about ready to give up on you, do you know that? You've just had your twenty-sixth birthday. That's too old not to know yourself better." Unlocking the door, she slipped out of the bedroom.

With the exception of Fleur, everyone seemed to have a wonderful time. Michel prepared linguine with white clam sauce for them, while Kissy and Simon made the salad and Jake acted as bartender. At first, Michel and Simon ignored each other, but before long they got into a heated argument over the relative merits of cooking with mesquite or corn cobs. That led to a

355

discussion of their favorite restaurants, and they were soon making cautious plans to go to a trendy place they had both heard about that specialized in wild game. Kissy tried to catch Fleur's eye for a congratulatory salute, but Fleur pretended she didn't notice and soon Kissy turned her attention back to Jake. They acted as if they had known each other for years, laughing together and telling off-color jokes. Why don't they just go to bed and get it over with? Fleur thought.

When it was time for dessert, she unveiled a *gâteau marjolaine,* with layers of nuts, buttercream, and chocolate. It had taken her most of the afternoon to make, and it was a little crooked, but it was delicious and everyone complimented her. She could barely force down a bite.

Afterwards, they went up to the living room with cups of Irish coffee. When Kissy sat down on the couch, Fleur deliberately took a seat on the floor pillows, feeling petty and miserable. What was wrong with her? Wasn't this what she wanted? Nobody walking in here would ever believe that Jake had any ulterior motives for asking her to represent him. It was too bad she couldn't invite the entire city into her living room right now. She could kill those rumors in thirty seconds flat!

Her unhappiness settled into a lump in the pit of her stomach along with the *gâteau marjolaine.* She looked up and caught sight of Kissy's face. Her best friend sent her a sympathetic smile, and Fleur suddenly realized what she was doing.

She managed to drag Kissy back up to the bedroom while the men were arguing over the five best rock and roll groups of all time. "I'm sorry," Fleur said. "I was acting crazy, and I don't even know why. God knows, he's the last person I want in my life right now. I mean, I've practically lost Olivia, and the only clients who want me to represent them are ones I don't want to represent, and he's not even writing—"

"You were green-eyed jealous, Fleur Savagar, and I think it's about time you take a hard look at your feelings for that gorgeous piece of male flesh sitting in your living room."

"My feelings for him are made up of old habit and frustrated hormones, nothing more. I'm sorry, Kissy. I was really acting terrible toward you. Forgive me."

"I have to. I feel exactly the same way every time I see you and Charlie together."

"Charlie and me! I don't believe you."

356

Kissy sighed. "He likes you so much, and I know I can't compete with you when it comes to looks. Everytime I see the two of you talking, I feel like the Pillsbury Dough Boy."

Fleur didn't know whether to laugh or cry. "It seems like I'm not the only one who doesn't know herself very well." She gave Kissy a swift, awkward hug, and then glanced at her watch. *"Butch Cassidy* is on television tonight. If I have the time right, we should be able to take a peek and then get back downstairs before we're missed. Should we indulge ourselves?"

"You bet." Kissy walked over to the black-and-white portable that was sitting on Fleur's dresser and flipped it on. "God, I love Redford. Do you think we're getting too old for this?"

"Probably. We'll make a promise to give it up for Lent."

At first they paid little attention to the action on the screen, chatting about Michel and Simon instead, while the Hole-in-the-Wall gang robbed the Overland Flyer and then Paul Newman's Butch and Robert Redford's mustachioed Sundance Kid sat drinking on the balcony of the whorehouse. Finally they grew quiet as the schoolteacher Etta Place climbed the steps to her small frame house and lit the lamp inside.

She unfastened the top buttons of her shirtwaist and shut the front door before she moved into her bedroom, pulling off the shirtwaist and hanging it in the closet. And then she turned and screamed as she saw the chiseled features of the Sundance Kid staring menacingly at her from across the room. "Keep going, Teacher Lady," he said.

Her eyes were wide and frightened as she stared at him. Slowly he picked up his gun and leveled it at her. "That's okay. Don't mind me. Keep on going."

She hesitantly unfastened the long undergarment and then stepped out of it, clasping it modestly in front of her to try to hide the eyelet-trimmed teddy she was wearing from the outlaw's eyes.

"Let down your hair," he ordered. She did as he asked, quickly dropping the undergarment and then pulling out the hairpins.

"Shake your head."

No woman was going to argue with the Sundance Kid when he had a pistol trained on her belly, and the schoolteacher did as she was told. All that was left was the teddy, and Sundance didn't have to talk. He raised his pistol and cocked the hammer.

357

Etta slowly opened the teddy, her fingers moving down the long row of buttons until the garment parted in an open V. Sundance's hands moved to his waist, where he unfastened his gunbelt and pushed it aside. He stood and walked forward, stopping just in front of her and slipping his hands inside the open garment.

"Do you know what I wish?" Etta asked.

"What?"

"That once you'd get here on time!"

As Etta threw her arms around Redford's neck, Fleur got up to turn off the set. She sighed. "It's hard to believe it was written by a man, isn't it?"

Kissy gazed at the blank screen. "William Goldman's a great screenwriter, but I've always had the feeling his wife wrote that scene while he was in the shower. God, what I wouldn't give . . ."

"Uhmm. It's the ultimate female sexual fantasy. All that unleashed male sexual violence, coming from a lover you know perfectly well would never really hurt you. They don't make men like that anymore."

Jake stood unseen in the hallway outside the partially opened door and listened to them. He hadn't meant to eavesdrop, but Fleur had looked funny all evening, and they were gone so long he wanted to check up on her. Now he was sorry. This was exactly the kind of conversation that a man shouldn't hear. What the hell did women want anyway? In public the rhetoric was all male sensitivity and equality and Alan Alda for President, but in private, here they were, two intelligent women having orgasms over caveman macho. Christ.

He didn't want to admit that part of him was jealous. He was one of the biggest box office draws of the decade, and he was living right on top of Fleur Savagar's head, but it didn't seem to mean anything more to her than a chance to take verbal potshots at him with that wiseacre mouth of hers. He wondered if Redford had to put up with this kind of crap and decided that if there was any justice in the world, he was sitting in front of his television someplace in Sundance, Utah, watching his wife go all melty-eyed over one of Bird Dog Caliber's rough-'em-up love scenes. The thought gave him a small moment of satisfaction before he slipped away from the door. Anyway you figured, it wasn't the easiest time to be a man.

The next morning Jake showed up to run with Fleur, but he hardly spoke to her as they made their way around the park. When they returned to the house, she impulsively invited him in for breakfast, and he declined so abruptly that she was offended. "Pardon me," she said sarcastically, "I know your schedule's been a real killer lately. All that time at the type-writer has to be exhausting."

"Just shut up about it, will you?"

"Are you even trying to write, Jake, or are you just kidding yourself because you don't want to face the facts?"

"What facts?" He jerked open the zipper of his sweatshirt. "For your information, I've been writing every day." She gave him a look that told him she didn't believe a word of it. He scowled and brushed past her into the house.

She took her time in the shower and then slipped into a pair of jeans and her favorite cable-knit sweater, finding herself getting angrier by the minute. She was counting too much on the success of Michel's collection and not doing anything about the cause of her most recent problems—the fact that Jake Koranda had made a deal with her to start writing again, and now he was welshing, making her look like an incompetent fool!

At ten o'clock, she went out into the front hallway, paced back and forth twice, and then unlocked the door that led to the attic apartment. There was no answer when she knocked at the top of the stairs. She hesitated for only a moment before she inserted her key.

The attic was a large, open space lit by a skylight and a series of small, rectangular windows. It was the first time Fleur had been there since Jake had moved in, and she saw that he had furnished it sparsely with a few comfortable chairs, a long couch, and an L-shaped arrangement of desk and table that held a typewriter and a ream of paper still in its wrapper.

He was sitting at the desk with his feet propped up, idly tossing a basketball back and forth from the palm of one hand to the other. "I don't remember inviting you in," he said.

"You didn't."

"I told you I was going to be busy. I don't like interruptions when I'm working."

"I wouldn't dream of interrupting the creative process. Just pretend I'm not here." She walked over to the small kitchen set behind a curve of counter and opened the cupboard doors until she found a can of coffee. Then she began to make a fresh pot.

"Go away, Fleur. I don't want you here."

"I plan to. But first you and I are going to have a business meeting."

"I'm not in the mood for meetings." The basketball passed from one hand to the other.

She plugged in the coffeepot, walked over to the desk, and perched on the top near his chair. "Vacation time is over, Jake," she said. "When you signed a contract with me, in effect, you made me your boss. I don't like dead wood, especially when it's pulling me under. Everyone in this town thinks you signed with me because we're sleeping together, and there's only one thing that's going to put an end to the gossip, and that's another Koranda play."

"Then tear up the contract."

"Stop being such a crybaby!" She swiped at the basketball with her hands and sent it flying across the room, where it bounded into the wall.

His expression hardened, and the easygoing, wise-cracking Jake Koranda faded from sight, leaving her face-to-face with Bird Dog. "Get out of here," he snarled. Doors slammed shut, shades flew down, shutters banged closed. "This isn't any of your goddamn business."

She didn't move. "You'd better make up your mind which it is. First you tell me that I'm the one who blocked you, and now you say it's none of my business. You can't have it both ways, Jake!"

"Don't push me!" His feet slammed to the ground, and he stood up, grabbing her arm and taking her with him. "Get out of here!"

She was suddenly furiously angry, not just because he was manhandling her or because of what he was doing to her agency, but because of the waste of his wonderful talent, because of the plays that were not being written. "Big hotshot playwright!" she shouted. "That typewriter has an inch of dust on it!"

"I'm not ready yet!" He pushed her away from him and stalked across the room, grabbing a jacket that hung near the door and jerking it on.

"What's the big deal, Jake?" He shoved his arms into the

jacket, and she reached across the desk for the ream of paper, ripping off the wrapper, and shoving the top piece into the typewriter. "Anybody can put a piece of paper into a typewriter! See. I just did it. It's no big deal!" She threw herself in the chair he had just vacated and flicked on the switch. The machine hummed to life. "Watch how it's done. Act One . . . Scene One." She picked out the words on the keyboard. "Where are we, Jake? What does the stage set look like?"

"You goddamned little bitch."

"You goddamned . . . little . . . bitch," she repeated, typing out the words. "Okay, we'll start there. Typical Koranda dialogue—tough, realistic, and antifemale. What comes next?"

"Stop it, Fleur!"

"Stop . . . it . . . Fleur. Bad name choice. Too close to someone you know."

"Stop it!" His hand crashed down on top of hers, jamming the keys, and stinging her fingers. "This is all some big joke to you, isn't it! You think this is all pretty goddamned funny!"

She looked up at him and saw that Bird Dog's face had slipped away, giving her a good, long look at the pain underneath the anger, and suddenly she was ashamed of herself. She turned her hand palm upward beneath his, and impulsively dipped her head to touch her lips to his knuckles. "I don't think it's funny," she said softly.

He stood very still, and then she felt him touch her hair for a moment before he pulled away. She heard a kitchen cupboard open, the clink of dishes, the sound of coffee being poured. Slowly she pulled the paper from the typewriter, her fingers shaking. As Jake came toward her, mug in hand, she slipped in a fresh sheet.

"What are you doing?" he snapped.

She took an unsteady breath. "You're going to write today. I'm not letting you put it off any longer. This is it."

"Our deal's off, Fleur. I'm moving out of the attic."

"I don't care where you move. I've got a contract and the deal sticks."

"You've really turned into a first-class money-grabbing bitch, haven't you? You don't care about anyone or anything except your two-bit agency."

"You're going to write today," she said, refusing to give him any explanations.

361

He stepped behind her, set down his coffee mug, and settled his hands lightly on her shoulders. "I don't think so."

She sat without moving as he lifted her hair and leaned down to press his mouth to the side of her neck just beneath her ear. His breath felt warm on her skin and the soft touch of his lips made every one of her senses come alive. For just a moment, she let herself relax. What was the harm? For just a moment . . .

Her eyes drifted shut and she gave in to the sensations he was arousing. His hands moved down over the front of her sweater and then slipped beneath to touch her skin. Almost immediately they rose again, sliding up over her ribs to the lacy cups of her bra and toying with her nipples through the silk. She could hear her own breath coming in short, uneven gasps. It had been so long, and he felt so good. He unfastened the center clasp of her bra and then pushed aside the fabric. . . .

Part of her knew that something was wrong, but as he slipped up her sweater and bared her breasts, all she could think about was the wave of heat spreading through her body. He pushed her shoulders back in the chair so that her breasts were tilted upward and then he began to tease the nipples with his thumbs. Leaning over her from behind, his lips caught her earlobe and then trailed up and down her neck. He was a master seducer playing with her body, going from one erogenous point to another as if he were following a chart in a sex manual. She suddenly realized that she was being bought.

"No!" Shoving Jake's hands away from their calculated seduction, she sprang from the chair, jerking her sweater down as she did. Her eyes stung with tears as she rounded on him. "You're a real bastard, Koranda, do you know that? A real twenty-four-karat bastard! Was sex the only way you could think of to shut me up?"

He stared at a point just past her head. "I don't know what you're talking about."

"Like hell you don't!" She was furious with him, furious with herself for giving in so easily.

His hand clamped down on her arm for the second time, pulling her toward the door. "You've overstayed your welcome, kiddo. Now get the hell out of here."

"Don't you touch me!" She tried to jerk away, but he was holding on too tight, his face full of hostility. "The circle's complete now, isn't it?" she exclaimed. "You've played Bird Dog for

362

so long that he's finally taken over! Don't you realize that everything good about you is being eaten up by him? You can't write
plays anymore, but I notice you don't have any trouble making
those crappy movies!"

"Shut up!" He grabbed the doorknob.

"Mister Tough Guy! Mister Hot Shot Tough Guy!" She
swung her hand in frustration and caught him hard in the side.
He dropped her arm, more out of surprise, she guessed, than
because she had done any real damage. She took advantage of
her temporary victory and threw herself back down in the
chair, putting her hands on the typewriter keys even though she
was shaking so hard she could barely push them. "Act One,
Scene One, damn you!"

"You're crazy," he shouted. "You're out of your frigging
mind!"

"Come on, you know what the play's about! Let's get it
started!"

"It's not a play!" In one harsh motion he stalked over to her,
his expression so full of fury that she winced. "It's a book!" he
exclaimed. "I have to write a book! A book about 'Nam."

She took a deep breath and shook her head in disgust. "A
war book. That's right up Bird Dog's alley, isn't it?"

His voice grew quiet. "What a judgmental little bitch you are.
You don't know a goddam thing about it."

The force of his pain hit her like a slap, and she was suddenly
ashamed. Reaching out, she gently closed her hand over his.
"I'm sorry. You're right. I don't know anything about it. Explain it to me."

He jerked away. "You weren't there. You wouldn't understand."

"You're one of the best writers in the country. Make me
understand."

He turned his back to her and silence fell between them. She
heard the distant sound of a police siren, the noise of a truck
passing below. "You couldn't tell them apart," he finally said.
"You had to regard everybody as the enemy."

His voice was quiet and controlled, but it seemed to be coming from far away. He turned and looked at her, as if he wanted
to make certain she understood. She nodded her head, even
though she didn't, and slipped her fingers back to the typewriter
keys.

"You'd be walking next to a rice paddy," he went on, "and spot a couple of little kids—four or five years old. Next thing you knew, one of them was throwing a grenade at you. Shit. What the hell kind of war is that?"

Numbly, she began to type, trying to get it down, hoping she was doing the right thing. He didn't seem to notice the sound of the keys.

"The village was a VC stronghold," he went on. "The guerillas had cost us a lot of men. Some of them had been tortured, mutilated. They were our buddies . . . guys we'd gotten to know, even though we shouldn't have. We were supposed to go in and waste the village. The civilians knew the rules—God, don't think they didn't know! If you weren't guilty, don't run. *Don't for chrissake run!* Half the company was stoned or doped up—it was the only way you could make it." He took a ragged breath. "We were airlifted to a landing strip not far away, and as soon as the strip was secure, the artillery opened up. When everything was finally clear, we went in. The peasants were all herded together in the middle of the village. They didn't run— they knew the rules—but some of them were shot anyway. . . . A little girl . . . she had on a ragged shirt that didn't cover her belly and the shirt had these little yellow ducks on it. And when it was over, and the village was burning, somebody turned Armed Forces Vietnam on the radio and Otis Redding was singing 'Sittin' on the Dock of the Bay' and the little girl had flies all over her belly."

For the first time since he had begun, he seemed to notice what she was doing. "Did you get that part about the music? The music is important. Everybody who's been in 'Nam remembers the music."

"I—I don't know. You're going so fast."

"Let me in." He pushed her aside, ripping out the sheet that was in the typewriter and inserting a new one. He shook his head once as if he were clearing it and then he began to type.

Fleur walked over to the couch and slumped down on it, feeling numb and drained. The pictures he had drawn in her mind kept coming back—the village, the peasants, the shirt with the little yellow ducks. She watched him for nearly an hour, punching at the keys, cursing under his breath, his forehead beaded with sweat even though the room was cool, never taking his eyes off the pages that were moving like magic through his typewriter. And all the time he worked, she tried to understand his pain. If what had happened to him in Vietnam was blocking his writing, why did he insist on blaming her? But the only person who could answer that question was Jake, and he didn't even notice when she finally slipped out of the room.

She spent the rest of the afternoon working on the arrangements for Michel's collection and then changed to meet Kissy for dinner. When she returned shortly before midnight, the sound of his typewriter was still faintly audible above her head. She went to the kitchen to fix a sandwich and then cut off a slab of the *gâteau marjolaine* she had made for the dinner party. This time she didn't bother to knock before she used her key.

He was hunched over the typewriter and his face was lined with fatigue. Coffee mugs, some still half full, and sheets of paper littered the desk top. He grunted as she set the tray down and collected the cups, which she took to the sink and washed. Then she cleaned out the coffeepot and set it up so it was ready to be plugged in again. While she worked, she thought about the massacre he had described. Was it possible that Jake could have— Her brain pushed away the thought.

Later that week she received her first phone call from Dick Spano. "I've got to find Jake."

"He never calls me," she said, which was literally true.

"If he does, sweetheart, would you let him know we're looking for him."

"I really don't think he will."

That evening, she went to the attic to tell Jake about the call. His eyes were red-rimmed, his jaw stubbled, and he looked as if he hadn't slept. Not for the first time, she found herself doubting the wisdom of having forced him to write. "I don't want to talk to anybody," he said. "Help me out, will you, Flower?" She told him she would, even though she suspected it wasn't going to be easy.

By the middle of the next week, she had put off his West Coast agent, his business manager, and all of their secretaries, but when she realized that his people were becoming genuinely alarmed, she knew she had to do something, so she called Dick Spano. "I've heard from Jake," she said. "He's fine. He's started writing again and he wants to hide out for awhile."

"No good, sweetheart. I've got a deal that won't wait, and I have to talk to him. Tell me where he is."

She hesitated for only a moment. "I think he's someplace in Mexico. He wouldn't say exactly where."

Dick swore and made some generally accurate comments about Jake's character; then he bombarded her with a long list of things she was to tell him if he called her again. She wrote them all down and then shoved the list to the back of her desk drawer.

October slipped into November to the muffled sounds of a typewriter. Fleur lay awake listening to it, and in those dark hours she worried about Jake and her agency and Michel's collection, which had so much riding on it, and she worried about herself. Then she was up early in the morning for a quick run before she dressed for the office. Although she and Jake seldom spoke, she made a habit of checking on him in the evening, and after awhile it became difficult to tell which one of them was looking the more haggard.

The day before Michel's fashion show she remained at the hotel, scurrying around between the carpenters and technicians as they set up the runway and driving all of them crazy with her insistence on security passes and guards at the door. Even Kissy lost patience with her, but Fleur paid no attention. Alexi had less than twenty-four hours, and this time he wasn't going to catch her unprepared. She called Michel twice at the factory in Astoria to make sure all the guards were doing their jobs. When she finally left the hotel late that afternoon, she could almost hear a collective sigh of relief go up from everybody there.

Willie Bonaduce burped and reached into the pocket of his uniform for a roll of Tums. He liked the taste of Tums, and sometimes he chewed them one after another, even when he didn't need them. It helped to pass the time until the daytime shift took over. They had been working this job for a month now, and tonight was the last night. Willie thought it was a lot of trouble to go to for a bunch of dresses, but as long as he got his paycheck, he minded his own business.

There were four of them working each shift, and they had the place sealed up tighter than a drum. Willie was seated just inside the front door of the old Astoria factory while his partner Andy was at the back and two of the younger men were outside the doors of the workshop on the second floor where the dresses were locked up. In the morning the boys on the day shift would accompany the big dress racks as they were driven to the hotel, and then the job would be over.

Willie leaned back in his chair and picked up a copy of the *Daily News*. A couple of years back he'd guarded Reggie Jackson. That was the kind of job he liked. When his brother-in-law came over for Sunday dinner and they were sitting around watching the Giants and shooting the bull, he liked to talk about guarding payrolls and Reggie Jackson, not a bunch of dresses. Willie Bonaduce went back to his Tums and the *Daily News*. As he absorbed himself in the sports' page, a battered orange van with BULLDOG ELECTRONICS painted on the side drove past the front entrance. Willie didn't notice.

The man driving the van turned into an alley across the street without even glancing at the factory. He didn't have to. He had driven by every night for the past week, each night in a different vehicle, and he knew exactly what he'd see. He knew about Willie Bonaduce, although he didn't know his name, and he knew about the guard at the back entrance and the locked room on the second floor with the guards stationed outside. He knew about the day shift that would come on in a few hours, and the fact that the interior of the factory was kept dimly lit at night. Only the last piece of information was important to him.

The warehouse across the street from the factory had been abandoned for several years, and the rusty padlock at the back gave easily beneath the jaws of the bolt cutters. He returned to the van and pulled out an equipment case. It was heavy, but he had carried it many times before, and the weight didn't bother him. When he was safely inside the warehouse, he switched on the small flashlight he held in his hand and shined it at the floor as he walked toward the front of the building. The flashlight annoyed him. Its beam of light spread out in a pool that became larger and less defined the further away he directed it. The beam had no clear boundaries, no precision. It was sloppy light.

Light was his specialty. Pure beams of pencil-slim light. Coherent light that didn't spread out in undisciplined pools like a flashlight beam.

It took him almost an hour to set up. Normally it didn't take so long, but he had been forced to modify his equipment by adding a high-powered telescope, and the mounting was difficult. He didn't mind, however, because he liked challenges, especially ones that paid him so well.

When he'd finished setting up, he cleaned his hands on the white rag he carried with him and then wiped a circle in the dirty glass of the warehouse window. He took his time sighting and focusing the telescope, making certain everything was exactly the way he wanted it. He could pick out each of the tiny lead plug centers without any difficulty; they were clearer to him than they would have been if he were standing in the center of the second-story room.

When he was ready, he gently pulled the switch on the laser, directing the pure beam of ruby red light at the plug of lead that was farthest away. The plug needed only a hundred and sixty-five degrees of heat to melt, and within seconds he could see that the hot ruby light of the laser had done its work. He picked out the next plug and it, too, dissolved under the force of the pencil-thin beam of light. In a matter of minutes, all the lead plugs were melted, and the heads of the automatic fire sprinkler system were drenching the racks of dresses with water.

Satisfied, the man packed up his equipment and left the warehouse.

Fleur

"What do you know about yourself, Flynn?"

Errol Flynn:
My Wicked, Wicked Ways

CHAPTER 28

The phone call from the security company woke Fleur at four in the morning, and she listened to the lengthy explanation from the man on the other end of the line. "Don't wake my brother," she said just before she hung up. And then she turned onto her stomach and pulled the covers up over her head.

She had finally drifted back to sleep when her doorbell started to ring. Squinting at her clock, she wondered if florists delivered white roses at six in the morning and decided she wasn't going to get out of bed to find out. The ringing eventually stopped, only to start up again a few minutes later. She stuck her head under the pillow and tried to go back to sleep, but before that could happen, the pillow was abruptly jerked off her head. She screamed and bolted upright in bed.

Jake towered over her in his jeans and a zippered sweatshirt that he'd thrown on over his bare chest. His hair was shaggy, his jaw unshaven, and his eyes had an empty, haunted look. "What the hell is wrong with you?" he yelled. "Where have you been? Why didn't you answer the door?"

Fleur grabbed the pillow out of his hands and hit him in the stomach with it. "It's six thirty in the morning!" she screamed. "You scared me!"

"You run at six o'clock! Where were you?"

"In bed!"

"What are you so grouchy about? How was I supposed to know you were sleeping?" He shoved his hands into the pockets of his sweatshirt. "When I didn't see you from the window, I thought something was wrong."

She threw back the covers, facing the fact that she couldn't postpone the day any longer. He didn't even pretend not to notice that her gown was bunched up around her thighs. She stretched out to push off the button on her electric blanket and then switched on the light, casually rearranging her legs like the girl in the mattress ad, with her toes pointed and her arches delicately curved. It wasn't the greatest reflection on her character, she decided, that with the problems that lay ahead that day all she could think about was giving Jake Koranda the best view of her legs.

She pushed out of bed without looking at him and went into the bathroom, totally disgusted with herself. How could she even think about sex at a time like this? But it was too early in the morning to lie to herself, and she knew that she had been thinking about it in one way or another ever since Jake had popped back into her life. If she wanted to go to bed with him, she decided, she should come out and say it instead of demeaning herself by playing archaic female games. She should start her own hunk collection, just like Kissy, and sample all the attractive men that came her way. No strings, no attachments, just good, dirty sex. And she should start right now with Jake Koranda! Wasn't that what real liberation was all about? Women didn't have to play games anymore. They *shouldn't* play games!

As she squeezed toothpaste on her brush, she decided that what she was going to do was walk back into the bedroom, exactly like any reasonably aggressive male would do, and look Jake right in the eye and tell him that she wanted to—. She hesitated. What words would she use? "Go to bed" was too wishy-washy, "make love" was full of implications, "screw" was tacky, and "fuck" was just plain awful.

She tried to make herself think; she wasn't going to buckle under just because of a language barrier. How would a man do it—an experienced, seductive man? How would Jake do it? Why wouldn't Jake do it? she wondered. She rinsed out her mouth and returned her toothbrush to the rack. He'd looked so angry. Maybe he wouldn't even want her. Or was she just trying to cop out? She told herself to go back in the bedroom and kiss him. She would stand in front of him and put her arms around him and start kissing him. Then she'd let nature take its course.

She slipped off her nightgown. Naked, she wrapped herself in a robe, took a deep breath, and opened the door. Jake was gone.

Actually, he wasn't gone; he was in the kitchen, but she didn't know that until she'd pulled on her jeans, a pair of argyle socks, and an old ski sweater. He glanced up from the eggs he was cracking into a skillet as she stepped down onto the brick floor. Standing over a stove, he looked taller than ever, with his shoulders straining the seams of his sweatshirt in a way that was aggressive and indisputably male. She knew then that she wasn't going to take the lead. When it came right down to it, it really didn't matter whether her reluctance was rooted in cultural conditioning or biological instinct, because women's lib got all tangled up when it hit the bedroom door. If he wanted her, he was going to have to come get her—it was that simple.

Something else occurred to her. "How did you get in?" she demanded. "I know the doors were locked because I double-checked them before I went to bed last night."

"You want your eggs scrambled or fried?"

"Jake . . ."

"Look, Flower, I'm not the world's greatest cook, okay? I can't talk and make breakfast at the same time. You could help, you know, instead of standing there like the Queen of Sheba."

It was a typical male counterattack, but she let him get away with it because neither of them was going anywhere for the moment. They finally settled at the table. "You got to my secretary again, didn't you?" she accused him. "You had a duplicate made of her key." He picked at the eggs, looking uncomfortable. "Come on, admit it. There's no other way you could have gotten in. My secretary has a key, I have one, and Michel has one. How else—"

He had stopped eating and was looking at her. "Your brother gave me the key," he said. "The night of your dinner party he told me what your father's been up to. He's worried about you, Flower, and I can't say I'm exactly calm about the whole thing. When you didn't go out to run this morning and there was no answer when I rang the bell . . ."

She slammed down her fork. "Alexi won't hurt me physically; Michel should know that. It's not his game. He wants me alive and suffering, and none of this is any of your damned business! Don't you have enough to occupy yourself with right now?"

"I don't like it, Flower." He ignored her anger, temporarily deflating her.

"I'm not exactly crazy about it myself," she admitted.

They ate in silence for a while, and then Jake asked if she always wore jeans and sneakers to work.

"I'm riding with the crates over to the hotel," she said, "and the men aren't due here to pick them up for an hour. That's why I wanted to sleep this morning. It's going to be a long day for me. Besides, I couldn't leave while all this was in the house."

Jake gestured toward the narrow wooden machine crates that were taking up most of the kitchen floor. "Do you want to tell me what's in them, or should I guess?"

"The dresses in Michel's collection," she said. "His samples." And then she told him about the factory in Astoria and the phone call she'd received in the middle of the night. "The security people aren't exactly sure how the sprinkler system was set off, but all the dresses hanging on the racks were waterlogged."

Jake nodded toward the crates. "I thought you said the dresses were in there."

"They are. I had thrift shop stuff hanging at the factory." As she stood up, she tried to feel some sense of satisfaction for having outwitted Alexi, but she couldn't quite manage it because she knew she was only going to have to start worrying all over again and trying to anticipate his next move. "If you'll excuse me, I have to call Michel before he heads over there and has a heart attack."

"Wait a minute," Jake interrupted. "Didn't you tell Michel that you were moving the stuff here?"

"It's not his problem, Jake. I'm the one who chopped up the Bugatti, and I'm the one Alexi's after. Besides, Michel has enough to worry about."

Jake was furious. "Suppose your father sent one of his thugs here? What would you have done then? You want to tell me that?"

"Why should he? The factory was crawling with guards. There was no reason for him to suspect the samples were here."

"You know what your problem is? You don't think!" He stood up abruptly, and as he did, the pocket of his sweatshirt bumped into the edge of the table with a solid thunk. His hand slipped inside, and for the first time she noticed that the right side of the garment was hanging further down than the left. Maybe she wouldn't have thought any more about it if he hadn't darted a quick, wary glance at her before he took his plate and started toward the sink.

She set the receiver back on its hook. "What's in your pocket?"

"Forget it."

She could feel a sharp prickle at the base of her spine. "I want to know."

"Leave it alone, will you?"

"Tell me, Jake."

At first she thought he was going to walk away, but then he shrugged. "It's a twenty-two automatic."

She looked at him blankly. "A what?"

"A gun."

"Are you crazy?" she exclaimed. "How could you do that? How could you bring a gun here? My God, this isn't Vietnam, or—or one of your movies. This is my house!"

He shrugged off her anger. "Your father isn't exactly an Eagle Scout, and I didn't know what I was going to find when I walked in here this morning."

He held her gaze as she stared at him, and once again she had the feeling she was looking at his screen image. She turned away because it made her think about massacres and a little girl with yellow ducks on her shirt—things she absolutely could not yet face.

He walked out of her house without speaking, but within fifteen minutes he was back again, dressed in a parka and a pair of corduroy trousers. By then the white roses had arrived, so it was clear that Alexi didn't know his plans had gone haywire, but that didn't make any difference to Jake. He interrupted her phone call with her brother, pulling the receiver out of her hand and growling into the mouthpiece, "Michel, I'm riding over on the truck with Wonder Woman. After that, you're on your own."

He stayed with her while the truck was unloaded, standing off in a corner with a baseball cap pulled down over his eyes, trying his best to look inconspicuous. Still, it wasn't long before one of the men recognized him, and he was quickly surrounded by fans shoving packing slips and dry cleaning receipts at him to autograph. She knew how much he hated it, but he stayed where he was until she went inside with the crates. When she came back to thank him, he was gone.

Between the backstage chaos and Michel's near hysteria over the rumpled condition of some of the gowns, it was hard for her to keep calm, but she forced herself to smile and exude confidence. Too much depended on what would happen within the next few hours. Despite the overwhelming demand for invitations, they had decided to show the collection only twice, once in the afternoon and again in the early evening. As with any *couture* collection, each of the models was assigned a separate dress rack, where all of the pieces she would wear were arranged in order, along with the proper accessories. Customarily, the racks were set up the day before, but Fleur had refused to let the dresses out of safekeeping until that morning. As a result, the racks had to be organized in very little time and there were last-minute hunts for missing accessories and a nearly disastrous mix-up with shoes, all of it accompanied by dark glances in her direction. In the meantime, a camera crew was setting up its equipment to videotape the collection so it could be shown later in boutiques and department stores.

When it finally looked as if everything would get done on time, Fleur changed into the dress she had brought with her, fumbling with the zipper because her hands were shaking. The dress was one of the first pieces Michel had designed for her, and as soon as she had seen it, she had decided to save it for today. It was a lacquer-red sheath with a center slit that ran from her neck to below her breasts, and another that climbed from a mid-calf hem to her knees. Beaded jet butterflies were embroidered on each shoulder and duplicated in miniature version on the toes of her red satin heels.

Kissy appeared at her side, looking pale and tense. "This was a terrible idea, Fleur. I don't know why you ever thought it would work. I must have the flu. I think I'm running a temperature."

"It's just butterflies. Take a few deep breaths. You'll be fine."

"Butterflies! These are not butterflies, Fleur Savagar. My stomach has been taken over by giant turkey buzzards."

Fleur laughed and gave Kissy a careful hug so she wouldn't disturb her makeup. "Break a leg, Magnolia."

She went out to mingle with the crowd that was filling the ballroom and found herself surrounded. By the time she had finished chatting with dozens of people, talked to reporters, and posed for photographers, the ends of her fingers had gone numb from nervousness. She took the small gilt chair that had been reserved for her near the front of the runway and squeezed Charlie Kincannon's hand.

He leaned over and whispered, "I heard them talking, Fleur.

The other designers don't like your brother. They were calling his designs *froufrou,* whatever that means."

"It means they're jealous as hell because he makes women look like women." She wished she felt as confident as she sounded, but the truth was that any new designer who thumbed his nose as impudently as Michel had at current fashion trends was in danger of being slaughtered by the powerful fashion arbiters. Michel was the new kid on the block in an overcrowded, territorial neighborhood. She glanced across the room toward the *Women's Wear Daily* reporter, noticing that she looked hostile, and suddenly understood what Kissy meant about turkey buzzards.

Sad, bluesy music began to play, and new worries absorbed her attention. Complicated theatrics had gone out of style with *couture* showings; the trend was simplicity—just the runway, the models, and the clothes. Once again, they were bucking the tide, and this time it was her fault. This was her idea. She was the one who had talked Michel into it.

Slowly the chatter in the ballroom died away and the music grew louder. The house lights dimmed and the lights on the stage behind the runway came up on a moody *tableau vivant* set behind a gauze curtain that made the scene filmy and dreamlike. The scenery—a wrought-iron railing, a lamppost, the shadow of palm fronds and broken shutters—suggested a shabby New Orleans courtyard on a steamy summer night.

Gradually, figures became visible. Models in filmy dresses draped the set, their breasts, elbows, and knees jutting out in exaggerated angles like the figures in a Thomas Hart Benton painting. Some of them had their heads thrown back and an arm extended, holding palmetto fans frozen in midair, one was bent forward, her hair trailing toward the floor like the branches of a willow, a hairbrush poised in her hand. There were whispers from the audience, sidelong glances to see how others were reacting, but it was obvious no one was anxious to commit until it was evident which way the tide was turning.

Suddenly one figure moved away from the others, growing visibly more and more agitated as she stepped forward into a pool of blue light. She looked at the audience for a moment, blinking her eyes as if she were trying to make up her mind whether or not to confide in them, and then she began to talk. She told them about Belle Reve, the plantation she had lost, and about Stanley Kowalski, the subhuman her dear sister Stella had married. Her voice was agitated, her face weary and tortured. Finally she fell silent and lifted her hand toward them, wordlessly begging for understanding. There was a moment of absolute silence, and then the bluesy music began again. Defeated, she silently faded back into the shadows.

There was a stunned silence and then the applause started to build, slowly at first and then gradually increasing in volume. Kissy's monologue as Blanche DuBois had been extraordinary, and everyone there recognized it. Fleur could feel Charlie sag with relief next to her. "They love her, don't they?" he whispered.

She nodded and then she held her breath. If only they loved Michel's designs as much. No matter how good Kissy's performance had been, the afternoon was ultimately about fashion.

The tempo of the music picked up and one by one the models broke their poses and moved out from behind the gauze curtain to walk down the runway. They wore filmy summer dresses that called up memories of scented flowers, hot southern nights, and old streetcars with names like Desire. The lines were soft and feminine without being fussy, delicately fashioned for women who were tired of looking like men. New York hadn't seen anything like it in years.

Fleur listened to the murmurs around her, the scratch of pens on notepads, the whispers. The applause was polite for the first few dresses, but as one followed another and the members of the audience slowly began to absorb the beauty of Michel's designs, the applause began to build, growing louder and more enthusiastic until the sound engulfed the great ballroom. She felt her fingers cramp and suddenly realized she had been digging them into Charlie's knee.

As the final dress cleared the runway, Charlie let out his breath in a long, tortured sigh. "I feel as if I've lived a lifetime in the last fifteen minutes."

Fleur planted a cool, confident smile on her face and joined in the applause. "Only one?" she whispered.

Two more *tableaux* followed, each one greeted with more enthusiasm than the last. A steamy *Night of the Iguana* rain forest showcased Kissy in a second monologue and then served as a background to a group of wildly colorful jungle blossom prints for informal wear. Finally, Kissy performed her dazzling

Maggie the Cat against the shadowy outline of a huge brass headboard as an introduction to an exotic collection of feathered and beaded evening gowns that evoked delicious decadence and brought the house to its feet.

When the show was over, Fleur watched as Michel and Kissy took their bows, and she knew that life was never going to be quite the same for either one of them. As she hugged Charlie, she realized it wouldn't be the same for her either—she could stop worrying so much about February—although that didn't seem very important at the moment. She owed this public recognition of their talents to both of them—to Kissy for her unwavering friendship, and to Michel for all those years she had hurt him with her misplaced hatred.

The audience began to leave their seats, people were coming toward her, and as she turned, she caught sight of an unexpected face at the very back of the ballroom near the door. Just before he slipped out, Jake Koranda gave her a silent thumbs up.

The next few days passed in a whirlwind of telephone calls and interviews. *Women's Wear Daily* did a cover story on Michel's collection, calling it "The New Femininity," and fashion editors lined up for news about his future plans. Michel sailed through the press conference Fleur scheduled for him with flying colors and afterward took her to dinner at Tavern on the Green. They sat alongside a glass wall in the Crystal Room and grinned at each other over their menus.

"The Savagar brats haven't done too badly for themselves, have they, Big Sis?"

"Not badly at all, Little Brother." Both of them smiled self-consciously before Michel turned his attention back to the menu.

"I think we'll order the turkey in aspic," he said.

"I won't eat anything that wiggles."

"Cold salmon, then."

"Warm sirloin?"

"Really, Fleur, you have the taste buds of a cocker spaniel." He sighed dramatically. "I suppose we could compromise on veal."

Ever since the night they had eaten raw clams and french fries in the Hampton Bays roadhouse, it had become a tradition for them to order the same meal—a practice that usually entailed at least ten minutes worth of spirited argument, although their tastes were not quite as dissimilar as Michel believed. Once, when Fleur had been distracted, she had given in to Michel's first entrée suggestion and he had looked so crushed that she'd vowed never to make the same mistake again. Now she didn't disappoint him. "I'll eat no cow before its time," she declared. "Forget the veal. How about capon?"

He shook his head. "Too Freudian. Trout?"

"Yuck. Those eyes—"

"Lamb?"

"They're so cute. I know," she exclaimed, "pork chops!"

He shuddered. "Capon."

She laughed and touched the poplin sleeve of his safari jacket, worn for evening with a burgundy silk shirt, French commando sweater, and Swiss Army necktie. "I love you, Michel. Big heaps. I always forget to tell you."

"Me, too. Even bigger heaps." He was quiet for a moment, then he cocked his head to the side so that his hair brushed his shoulder. "Does it bother you that I'm gay?"

"I hope you're not asking me this because I suggested the capon?"

He smiled. "Purely coincidental."

"If I could wave a magic wand," she said, "I'd rather see you live happily ever after with someone who could give me a small tribe of nieces and nephews, but since I'm not going to have that, I want to see you in a stable relationship with someone who's worthy of you."

"Someone like Simon Kale?"

"Now that you mention it . . ."

He set down his menu and looked at her, his eyes sad. "It's not going to work, Fleur. I know that you've been counting on it, but it's not going to work."

She was embarrassed. "Look, Michel. Let's forget it, okay? I've stepped over the line. This isn't any of my business."

He smiled at her. "Yes, it is. You love me, remember? Do you know how much it means to me to finally have somebody care whether I'm happy or not?"

"Careful, Michel. It sounds like you're giving me free license to interfere in your life."

"I'll risk it." He started to cross his arms over his narrow chest, and then uncrossed them. She could see that he was nervous. "Simon is a special person," he said, "and we've developed a friendship that's important to both of us, just like you and Kissy. But that's all it'll ever be—a wonderful friendship. Simon is strong and so am I. We're both independent and self-sufficient. Simon doesn't really *need* anybody."

"That's important to you, isn't it? Being needed."

He nodded his head. "I know you don't like Damon. And you're right—he can be selfish, and he's not the smartest person I've ever met. But Damon loves me, Fleur, and he needs me."

Fleur pushed aside her disappointment. "I never said Damon didn't have good taste."

Michel gave her a mischievous smile. "I noticed sweetbreads on the appetizer list. Okay with you?"

In addition to Michel's success, word of Kissy's performance had spread like wildfire, and four different producers wanted her to audition for them. Fleur also noticed that several people who had been dodging her for months suddenly found the time to return her phone calls, and she suspected that her days of being a pariah were over—at least until Alexi made his next move.

For the next few weeks she concentrated on Kissy, scheduling her for auditions and then a screen test. By Thanksgiving, the dust had settled and Kissy was signed to appear in a limited run of *The Fifth of July,* after which she would fly to London for a supporting role in a big-budget action-adventure film Fleur was convinced would make her career. Their schedules kept them too busy for more than a quick snatch of conversation on the telephone or a hurried lunch together, and it was late one Friday evening before they were able to settle in for a catch-up visit. Kissy appeared at the door with a pizza and a large bottle of Tab. "Hurry up and take the phone off the hook."

"I already did." Fleur put on an old Eagles tape and went down to the kitchen to get glasses, while Kissy settled the pizza box on the new living room coffee table.

"Just like old times, huh, Fleurinda?" she called out over the sounds of "Tequila Sunrise." "Except now that we're rich and famous, maybe we should switch to beluga, although I can't honestly imagine trading in an all-American pepperoni pizza for commie fish food."

Fleur called up from the kitchen, "We'll drink our Tab out of Baccarat; that way we can have the best of both worlds." She appeared at the top of the steps with two ice-filled goblets and a stack of paper napkins. "Do you think we're hypocrites because we drink diet soda with pizza? I mean, it seems like we should commit ourselves one way or the other."

"You worry about philosophy while I eat. I haven't had anything since breakfast, and I'm starved." She bit into the piece she had just pulled from the box, and the cheese stretched like a rubber band out from her mouth. "I don hink I've eber been az happy az I am now," she mumbled.

"God, you really do love pizza."

" 'S not the pizza." Kissy sank her teeth in for another bite, but this time she chewed before she spoke. "It's the play, the movie, everything. Bob Fosse said hello to me yesterday. Not 'Hi, kid' but 'Hello, Kissy.' Bob Fosse, for God's sake!" Between bites, she began to fill Fleur in on the events of the last few weeks.

As Fleur listened to Kissy's description of the first week of play rehearsals and her wildly contradictory assessments of her own performance, she felt a bubble of pleasure growing inside her. Despite Kissy's enormous talent, none of this would have happened if it hadn't been for her. Without warning, the image of Belinda's face flashed into her mind, and her pleasure slipped away as she wondered if this was the way her mother had felt.

The subject switched to the film Kissy would be making in London. She was nervous about the project, and she began pumping Fleur for her own experiences during the making of *Eclipse*. Eventually, the subject switched to Jake. "You haven't said much about him lately," Kissy observed.

Fleur shrugged. "I don't see him very much. He works all the time, and when I go upstairs to check on him, he doesn't see me."

"Translated that means that you're not sleeping together."

"God, Kissy, there's more to a relationship than sex!"

"Spare me, Fleurinda. This is your best friend you're talking to."

"Look, I won't lie to you. I'm still attracted to him—I probably always will be—but that's as far as it goes. I was burned by him once, and I won't ever be burned again. He's bad for me."

"Are you really sure about that?"

"For God's sake, he was my mother's lover!"

"That's none of your business, you know. Belinda may be a little warped, but from what I've seen, she's also beautiful and seductive. Jake was attracted to her. The two of you weren't lovers at the time, and whatever he and Belinda were doing in bed didn't have anything to do with you."

"She had to know how I felt about him," Fleur exclaimed, "but she jumped into the sack with him anyway!"

"And what does that have to do with him?" Kissy shifted her body further around on the couch and tucked her legs beneath her. "Look, you don't still believe that old garbage about Jake seducing you for the sake of his movie, do you? I've only met the man a few times, but even I could see that wasn't his style. I'm sure he has his faults, but I don't see blind ambition as one of them."

"He has his faults, all right. He's the most emotionally dishonest person I've ever met!"

"How do you mean?"

"He evades anything or anyone who comes too close to hi He gives little glimpses of himself and then slams the door shu It's fine for casual friendships, but it's rough for somebody who really loves him."

Kissy set down the pizza crust she had just picked up and stared at her. Fleur could feel her face growing hot. "I was talking generally, for Pete's sake, not specifically. Not about me. I'm not in love with him, Kissy. I mean, there are things about him that I love—he's smart, and he's funny, and when I'm with him, I feel like myself— See what I mean? Being with Jake is like being with you."

"Except not as safe."

"No. Not as safe." A long silence fell between them. Fleur finally said, "I can't afford him. I've had too many impermanent, dishonest people in my life, and I don't need another one. I'm not begging anybody for love ever again. I've done enough of that to last three lifetimes. I'm proud of what I am, Kissy. I've made something of myself. I don't have to beg anybody to love me."

"Of course you don't."

Kissy saw how upset she was and mercifully changed the subject. They chatted about Olivia Creighton's latest neurosis, and what clothes Kissy should take with her to London. Eventually Kissy seemed to run out of things to say, and Fleur finally realized that there was something different about her, a sense of suppressed excitement. It suddenly occurred to her that the name Charlie Kincannon hadn't crossed her friend's lips all evening. "Okay, Kissy, cough up. You're dying to tell me, so spit it out."

"Spit what out? Really, Fleur, such a vulgar expression."

"Don't you go all Southern Belle on me. What's up? It's Charlie, isn't it?"

Kissy hesitated, and then tucked her feet beneath her. "Uhmm. . . . Well, I haven't really said anything because I was afraid you'd think it was silly." She twisted a curl around her finger, and then looked up at Fleur, awaiting her reaction.

"Kissy, we have to be at work on Monday morning. How about telling me before then?"

"Actually," Kissy said in a rush, "I think I might be in love."

"Now, why would I think that's silly?"

"Isn't Charlie sort of an unlikely companion for me, considering my past history?"

Fleur smiled. "As a matter of fact, I've always thought you and Charlie were the most likely of companions. You were the one who didn't agree."

Now that Kissy's news was out, it was as if she had to tell everything before she lost her nerve. "I feel like such a fool, Fleurinda. He's the most wonderful man I ever met, but it had been so long since I'd met a man who wanted me for something other than sex that I didn't know how to handle him. I kept trying to seduce him, but he wanted to talk about Kierkegaard instead, or dadaism, or the Knicks, for God's sake. And listen to this—no matter what we were talking about, he never once tried to dominate the conversation. He didn't talk *at* me like other men do. He genuinely wanted to hear what I had to say. He *challenged* me. And the more we talked, the more I remembered how smart I really am." Kissy's eyes suddenly filled with tears. "Fleur, it felt so good."

Fleur found her own eyes stinging. "I'm so glad for you, Magnolia. Charlie's a special person, and so are you."

"The funny thing was that at first all I could think about was trying to get him into bed—my territory. I'd push myself up against him or tell him my muscles were aching and ask for a back rub, and when he'd come to the door, I wouldn't quite have all my clothes on. But no matter what I did, he never seemed to notice. And then I started to forget about seducing him and just settled down to enjoy his company. That's when I realized he wasn't quite as unaffected by me as he pretended to be. But it still took him a long time to get serious."

At Kissy's dreamy expression, Fleur grinned. "Knowing Charlie Kincannon, I'll just bet it was worth the wait."

Kissy grinned back. "I didn't let him touch me."

"You're kidding!"

"Fleur, it was so nice being *courted.* And then two weeks ago he came over to the apartment one night after rehearsal. He started kissing me, and I was really enjoying it, but I started to feel afraid—you know, afraid that after everything that had gone on, I might disappoint him. I could tell by his face that he knew how I felt, because he just smiled that sweet, understanding smile of his. And then he said we ought to play Scrabble."

"Scrabble!" There was such a thing as carrying restraint too far, and she was disappointed in Charlie.

"Well, actually, not regular Scrabble. Sort of—strip Scrabble."

Good for you, Charlie, Fleur thought. And then she inquired, "Might one ask how this particular perversion is played?"

"It's pretty simple really. For every twenty points your opponent gains over you, you have to take off one item of clothing. And you know, Fleur, as much as I wanted to go to bed with him, I really did like being courted, and I happen to be a truly exceptional Scrabble player, so I had no intention of losing." She swept a dramatic arc in the air with her hand. "I started out strong with *klepht* and *pewit.*"

"I'm impressed."

"Then I hit him right between the eyes with *whey* and *jargon* on a double word score."

"That must have taken his breath away."

"It did. But he came back pretty well. *Jaw* off my *jargon* and *wax* off *pewit*. Still, it was pretty obvious that we weren't in the same league—I *never* do three-letter words unless I'm pressed to the wall. By the time I made *viscacha,* he was down to his briefs and one sock, while I still had on a slip and everything under it." Her forehead puckered in a frown. "That's when it happened."

"I'm breathless with anticipation."

"He hit me with *qaid.*"

"There's no such word."

"Oh, yes there is. A Northern African tribal leader, although generally only world-class Scrabble players and crossword addicts know it."

"And?"

"Don't you see? The son of a bitch was hustling me!"

"Dear God."

"To make a long story short, he laid *zebu* in on a horizontal and then capped it with *zloty* on the vertical. My *quail* looked pretty pitiful after that, but worse was to come."

"I don't know if I can stand the tension."

"*Phlox* on a triple word score."

"That devil."

CHAPTER 29

Instead of cutting back and enjoying her successes, Fleur extended her hours at work, driving herself and everyone around her until they were all snapping at each other. The unqualified success of Michel's collection had brought with it an avalanche of publicity, and she felt secure enough to begin turning down clients, although she was still short of the magic number of twelve she had set as her initial goal. Rough Harbor's first album was coming out in a few weeks, and it showed every indication of being a winner. Kissy's play premiered; she got rave reviews and more requests for interviews than she could handle in the time before she left for London. Fleur was faced with the sudden realization that she had nearly everything she wanted. Alexi had made no moves against her since he had tried to sabotage Michel's collection, the old stories about her broken contracts had been forgotten, and although there was still gossip about her relationship with Jake, her other successes had taken away the sting. All in all, her agency was doing better than she had any right to expect, so why wasn't she happy? She backed away from the question by working harder than ever.

One Friday night just after New Year's, something awakened her and she stirred. "It's okay, Flower," a soft voice whispered. "It's just me."

The draperies that she had shut before she went to bed were open now, so the room was dimly illuminated by the streetlight. Jake was sitting in a chair not far from her bed, shirtsleeves pushed up to the elbows, his rangy legs stretched out in front of him.

"What are you doing?" she asked.

"I've been watching you sleep." His voice was as soft and dark as the night room. "The light's like a paintbrush in your hair. Do you remember how we wrapped your hair around us when we made love?"

Her pulse began to pound, and the blood rushed through her body. "I remember."

"I didn't want to hurt you, Flower. You got caught in the crossfire."

She wasn't going to think about the past, only the present. "That was a long time ago, and I'm not that naive now."

She had spoken more sharply than she'd intended, and now his voice developed an edge. "For somebody who wants me to believe she's been making a career out of promiscuity, your bedroom seems to have been pretty empty lately."

Why did he have to bring that up now? Why couldn't he have stayed soft and sweet, talking about paintbrushes and the light in her hair? She wanted to punish him. "Do you think I'd bring men back here with you living over my head? We go to their places."

"Is that so?" He crossed his arms, and she realized he didn't believe a word of it. Slowly he uncurled from the chair and began unbuttoning his shirt. "If you're passing it out for free, I guess it's my turn."

She bolted up in bed. "I'm not passing it out for free, and you know it! I'm not passing it out at all—not that it's any of your business! What are you doing?"

He stripped off his shirt. "This could have happened between us months ago, but you didn't have the guts to ask."

"Me! Since when does a woman have to ask?" His hand went to the snap on his jeans. "Stop right there, Jake."

"Since you accused me of wanting to unblock my writing with your body, that's when." The zipper fell open in a V revealing his bare stomach. He planted his hands low on his hips, just inside the waistband. "Knowing the twisted way your mind works, I couldn't afford to touch you until the book was done— that way you couldn't make any more accusations. Well, the book's done now, so let's stop playing games."

She wanted him. God, how she wanted him, even though she could see that something was terribly wrong. Why did she feel like this when he refused to commit himself to her in even the smallest way? Her emotions tangled into a knot. She thought about the fact that his book was finished and what that would mean to her agency, and then she realized that she no longer cared. All she cared about was the haunted look in his eyes, and finding out what had put it there. "Zip your pants, cowboy," she said quietly. "We need to talk first."

"The hell we do." He kicked off his shoes, then whipped away the blankets covering her, gazing down at the ice-blue nightgown twisted high on her thighs.

"Jake, stop it. You're being ridiculous."

"Shut up," he muttered, peeling his jeans down off his hips and taking his briefs with them. "Just be quiet, will you?"

Before she knew what had happened, he was naked and reaching for her gown. "No!" She scooted across the bed, away from him. "No, Jake, I want to talk first."

"We can talk later." He snared the skirt of her nightgown in his hand, preventing her escape.

"Tell me what's wrong. You have to talk to me."

"I don't have to do a goddam thing!" he exclaimed, his face taut with anger.

"I'm not into recreational sex!" she cried.

Without warning, he slammed his fist against the wall above her head. "How about mercy fucking? Are you into mercy fucking, Flower, because if you are, you've got yourself a hell of a candidate!"

Her heart broke apart at the pain he couldn't hide. "Oh, Jake. . . ."

The shutters banged shut. "Forget it!" He grabbed his jeans from the floor, shoving his legs into them. "Just forget it! Forget I was ever here!" Snatching up his shirt, he headed for the bedroom door.

"Jake, wait!" She ran after him, the skirt of her nightgown flying behind her, but he was already running down the steps into the living room. "Stop a minute. Let's talk about it!"

"You know what you can do with your talk!" He slammed the door behind him.

She stepped down into the empty living room feeling lost and guilty. Guilty? Why should she feel guilty when he was the one acting like a caveman? What was she supposed to do—let him climb into her bed after all these years and use her body as some sort of handy convenience? She heard the harsh pounding of his feet on the steps leading to the attic and remembered the tension in his body, the deep shadows under his eyes, the sense of desperation emanating from him. Without thinking about what she was doing, she ran out into the hallway and up the stairs to the attic only to find the door at the top locked. "Open up!"

Nothing but silence came from the other side. She slapped the wood panels with the palm of her hand. "I mean it, Jake. Open this door right now!"

"Go away!"

"If you don't open this door I'll break it down."

She heard his harsh laughter. "Sorry, Scarlett, but Rhett needs his beauty sleep."

She swore under her breath and ran back down the stairs to get her key. By the time she finally got his door unlocked, she was shaking.

Jake sat on the unmade bed, leaning against the headboard, with a bottle of beer propped on his bare chest and his jeans still unzipped. "You ever heard of tenant's rights?" he asked, his hostility crackling in the air like dry ice.

"You don't have a lease." She walked toward him, stepping over his shirt, which lay crumpled on the floor. When she reached the side of the bed, she looked at him for a moment, trying to read his mind, but all she saw were the harsh lines of exhaustion around his mouth and the desperation that had etched itself even deeper into the shadows of his eyes. Finally she spoke. "If anybody needs mercy," she said quietly, "it's me. It's been a long time."

His expression tightened, and she understood right away that he wasn't going to make it easy for either of them. He'd revealed too much of his own need, and now he wanted compensation. He took a swig of beer, looking at her as if she were a roach who'd just crawled across his floor. "Maybe some poor slob would take you to bed if you weren't such a ballbuster."

She clenched her teeth, wanting nothing more than to take a swing at him but realizing that it was up to her to stay in charge, that right now he was only capable of self-destruction. "It's not like I haven't had plenty of offers," she replied as calmly as she could manage.

"I'll just bet you have," he sneered. "Let me guess. City boys with Cuisinarts and BMW's."

"Among others."

"How many?"

She wondered why he couldn't just tell her he needed her. There was nothing wrong with one person needing another.

Why did he have to put them through all this? "Dozens," she replied. "Hundreds."

"I'll bet," he scoffed.

"I'm legendary."

He took another slug of beer and then swiped at his mouth with the back of his hand. "And now you want me to take the edge off your sexual frustrations. Play stud for you."

The man was shameless. She wondered how he could look her in the eye when he was spouting such garbage? "Do you have anything better to do?" she inquired.

He shrugged and kicked the blankets away from his feet. "I guess not. Take off your nightgown."

"No way, cowboy. You want it off, you take it off. And while you're at it, slip off those jeans so I can see what you've got."

"What *I've* got?"

"You bet, buster. Consider this an audition."

He couldn't even manage a smile, and she knew then that he was close to the breaking point. "On second thought," she said, "why don't you just lie there; I'm feeling aggressive." Without giving him a chance to reply, she reached for the hem of her nightgown and peeled it over her head, but as she pulled it off, one of the straps caught in her hair. She stood naked and vulnerable in front of him, trying to untangle her hair, but her fingers were trembling, and she only succeeded in making the snare worse.

"Lean over," he said softly.

She did as he asked, still pretending to be working at the strap so she wouldn't have to look at him looking at her. His hand closed over her arm, pulling her down to the side of the bed. As the mattress dipped, her bare hip brushed against the denim covering his thigh.

"There," he said, the nightgown slipping free. "That's got it."

And then nothing. He made no move to touch her. She sat with her back to him, spine stiff, hands crossed in her lap, and knew she couldn't go any further. He seemed to know it too, because the mattress moved, and she heard him sliding off his jeans. Why did it have to be like this? she wondered. So awkward and difficult. Maybe he wouldn't even kiss her. Maybe he'd just pull her back on the bed and have sex with her without even kissing her. Wham, bam—nice knowing you, kiddo, but I'll be moving on now. Dammit, and wouldn't that be just like him? He was such a sonovabitch. Playing on her sympathies. Refusing to talk except to insult her. Getting ready to run out on her again!

"Flower?" His hand touched her shoulder.

She spun on him. "I won't do it if you don't kiss me! I mean it, Jake! If you don't kiss me, you can go to hell!"

He blinked.

"And don't you think for one minute—"

He caught her by the back of her neck and dragged her forward over his bare chest. "Just shut up, okay?" he whispered, "I need you, Flower. I need you real bad."

His mouth closed over hers in a deep, sweet tongue kiss. She floated through the kiss, bathed in it, drank it and ate it, and didn't want it ever to stop. He grabbed her hair and rolled her onto her back, where he pressed her into the mattress with his weight. The kiss changed dimension and lost its sweetness, becoming dark and desperate. His breathing grew more ragged, and she arched her back, pressed her hips closer. Sweat broke out on his body, mingling with her own, and suddenly his hands were all over her. Rough, clumsy hands at her breasts and waist, on her hips and buttocks, pushing inside her.

She could have stopped him, but she didn't. She was frightened for him, frightened for herself. All the frustration, all the years of denial, formed a fiery ball deep in her chest. She wrapped her arms around his shoulders, meeting his fierceness with her own. "Love me, Jake," she whispered. "Please love me."

His fingers dug into the soft skin of her thighs, pushing them farther apart as his weight settled between them. Without warning, he thrust himself deep and hard within her. She cried out. He grabbed her head between his hands and covered her mouth with his own, kissing her desperately, driving inside her. She came at once, breaking apart in a joyless orgasm. He didn't stop. He stayed with her, tongue in her mouth, hands in her hair, pushing harder . . . faster . . . letting out a harsh, anguished cry as he spilled himself deep within her.

He pulled away as soon as it was over, and she lay staring at the ceiling, fear gnawing at her insides. His book was done. She thought of his desperation, his silence, the dark hurt of his lovemaking, and couldn't shake the feeling that he had been saying good-bye. The words she had spoken in the throes of lovemaking came back to her. *Love me, Jake. Please love me.* The echo of those words left her cold inside.

They lay side by side in the bed with not even their hands touching. Nothing.

"Flower?" She kept her eyes closed, pretending she was asleep. In her mind she saw a long stretch of sun-scorched sand spreading bleak and empty before her. Ridiculous. She had so much—her job, her friendship with Kissy, Michel.

"Flower, I want to talk to you."

She turned her back to him, burrowing her face into the pillow. Now he wanted to talk, now that it was all over. Her head ached and her mouth felt as dry as that arid stretch of sand she kept seeing in her mind. His hand touched her shoulder, and she jumped.

"Dammit," he exclaimed, "I know you're not asleep!"

The mattress creaked and she felt him leaving the bed. "What do you want?" she asked.

There was the click of a switch as he turned on the light. She rolled over to face him. He stood next to the bed, totally unself-conscious about his nakedness, and said, "Do you have anything going this weekend that you can't get out of? Anything important?"

He wanted to play out the final scene, the great good-bye. She glared at him, hiding her anguish. "Why? Are you going to ask me for a date? Do you want me to go to the movies with you? Let me reach under the pillow and check my appointment calendar to see if I'm free."

His eyes were angry. "You always do that to me! Anytime I ask you a serious question, you slap me in the face with your sarcasm. I'm sick of it."

She didn't know what to say. It was as if someone had tilted the room at a crazy angle, so that nothing looked quite the same. She felt edgy and defensive. "I don't do that! You're the one. You're the one who always backs away."

He shrugged. "Forget it. Just forget it."

"See! See what I mean! You're backing away now."

"God damn it! Go downstairs and throw some things in a suitcase. I'll get you in half an hour."

Two hours later they were in a chartered jet flying to God-knew-where, and Jake was asleep in the seat next to her. Was there some basic flaw in her makeup that made her fall in love with a man who couldn't love her back? Did she have some sort of death wish? She closed her eyes, but sleep eluded her. She couldn't slide around it anymore—she loved Jake Koranda. She had fallen in love with him when she was nineteen years old, and she had never really fallen out of it. He was the only man she had ever been with who seemed as if he belonged to her. It was funny when she thought about it. Jake, who closed himself off from her, also seemed to be a part of her. My better half. She had always thought that was such a strange expression. But Jake was her better half—and her worse half, too. He didn't *give* anything. Every time they were together, he left her emotionally stranded at the gates of the *couvent* while he drove away. He wouldn't talk to her about anything that was important to him—the war, his first marriage, Belinda, what had happened to them when they were making *Eclipse.* He deflected her with accusations, put her off with wisecracks, distanced himself from her whenever she got too close. And if she were honest with herself, she would have to admit that she did the same to him. But it was different with her. She did it because she had to protect herself. What did he have to protect?

It was seven in the morning California time when they landed in Santa Barbara, although Fleur didn't know it was Santa Barbara until they were walking across the Tarmac and she saw the signs. Jake had the collar on his leather jacket turned up against the early chill, or maybe the prying eyes of any fans who might be lurking around—she wasn't sure which. He carried an attaché case in one hand and guided her by the elbow toward the parking lot with the other. They stopped next to a dark maroon Jaguar sedan, where he unlocked the door and slung his case along with her overnight bag into the back. "It'll be a while before we get there," he said. "Why don't you try to get some sleep."

The cantilevered glass and concrete house looked almost the same as she remembered it. What a perfect spot for the great good-bye they still had to play out. "A return to the scene of the crime, Jake?"

He pulled up to the front of the house and turned off the ignition. "I don't know that I'd exactly call it a crime, but we have some ghosts to put to rest, and this seemed like the right place to do it."

She hadn't been able to sleep any better in the car than she had in the plane. She was tired and scared, and she couldn't help sniping at him. "Couldn't you find a root beer stand? As long as we're dealing with the business of lost innocence, it seems like that would have been more appropriate." He ignored her, pulling their cases from the back seat and climbing out of the car. She remembered how he had accused her of putting him off with sarcasm and wished she'd kept quiet.

While he took a shower, she changed into the suit she had brought with her and wrapped herself in a warm robe to go out to test the water in the pool with her toes. It wasn't heated enough to combat the January chill, but she shed her robe and dove in anyway. She stretched out her body and glided in swift laps up and down the length, but the tension that was coiled inside her refused to unravel. She got out, wrapped herself in an oversized bath towel, and lay down on one of the chaises in the sun, where she instantly fell asleep.

A small Mexican woman with a gold front tooth awakened her to announce that dinner would be ready soon if she wished to change first. She deliberately avoided the big bathroom with the sunken tub where they had once made love, choosing one of the smaller guest bathrooms instead, and by the time she had finished her shower and pulled her hair back from her face with a set of combs, her grogginess had disappeared and she felt better. She changed into her ivory wool slacks and an open-necked lime-green blouse. Just before she stepped out into the living room, she fastened the chain with the flower Jake had given her inside the collar of her blouse, but then she secured the button between her breasts so he wouldn't see that she was wearing it.

He was clean-shaven and dressed almost respectably in gray cords and a navy sweater, but none of the lines of exhaustion around his mouth had eased. As they picked at the food that was set before them, she could feel his tension. The meal was a nightmare. They barely spoke, yet she knew everything that had passed between them was leading to a climax, that tonight it was going to be resolved one way or another. And then she caught herself. There weren't any happy endings. Loving Jake was a one-way street.

Eventually the housekeeper appeared with coffee, setting the pot down harder than necessary to protest the injustice that had been done to her meal. Jake dismissed her and sat without moving until he heard the back door close. Then he pushed himself away and disappeared from the room. When he came back, he was carrying a fat manila envelope. She stared at it, and then at him. "You really did finish your book."

He nodded. "I'm going out for a while. Maybe you'd like to read this while I'm gone."

She took the envelope gingerly. "Are you—are you sure you want to do this? I know I pushed you into it, and maybe I was wrong. Maybe I—"

"Don't sell the serial rights while I'm out." He tried to smile, but he couldn't make it. "This one's just for you, Flower. Nobody else."

She watched him leave the room and felt a sickness growing in the pit of her stomach. He had spent the last three months nearly destroying himself over a manuscript that only she would read. A manuscript that couldn't be published. Was the material that private, or were the contents simply too incriminating? The image of a little girl and a shirt with yellow ducks flashed through her mind yet again.

Picking up her coffee, she took it over to the window and stared out into the lavender evening as she tried to push back the ugly suspicions that had plagued her since Jake had first told her about the village. He had written about massacres twice, first in *Sunday Morning Eclipse* and now again in those pages sealed inside the manila envelope. She thought about the two faces of Jake Koranda. She only wanted one face, the one she understood, the one that could never harm an innocent person. Her easy cowboy. Only that.

It was a long time before she could make herself walk back to the table and pull the manuscript from the envelope. She settled herself in a chair near the windows, turned on the light, and began to read.

Jake dribbled toward the basket on the side of the garage and went in for a quick dunk, but the leather soles of his boots slipped on the concrete and the ball hit the rim and then bounced off the wire cage around the floodlight. For a moment he thought about going back inside for his shoes, but then he knew he wouldn't. He couldn't watch her reading.

His old '68 Chevy pickup was still in the garage, and he remembered a stale pack of Winstons left in the glove compartment by some long-forgotten passenger. He hadn't smoked since he was a kid, but now he took the cigarettes out and, with the basketball tucked under his arm, walked around the garage to the stone wall that kept the hillside from falling into his house. As he sat on the ground and leaned back against the rough stones, he wished he had a six-pack of Mexican beer sitting at his side, but he wasn't going back into the house to get it. He wasn't going to watch her disillusionment a second time.

Closing his eyes, he thought of other ways he could have ended everything between them, ways that would have put him someplace else where he wouldn't have to see her disgust. The pain grew too sharp, and he tried to distract himself by listening for the sounds of the crowd in his head. . . . He envisioned himself in center court at the Philadelphia Spectrum, wearing a Seventy-Sixers uniform with the number six on his chest. *Doc . . . Doc . . . Doc . . .* He tried to make his mind form the right images, but they wouldn't take shape.

Standing up, he ground out his cigarette and carried the ball back around the garage to the hoop. He began to dribble. He was Julius Erving, a little slower than he used to be, but still a giant, still flying. . . . *Doc . . .*

It didn't work. Instead of the crowd, a different sort of music was playing in his head.

Inside the house, the hours slipped by and the pages of the manuscript were scattered over the floor near the chair where she was sitting. Her hair fell from its combs, her neatly pressed slacks became wrinkled, and, as she reached the end of the final page she found she was crying again. . . .

> Now when I think of Nam, I still think of the music that was always playing. Otis . . . the Stones . . . Wilson Pickett. Most of all, I think of Creedence Clearwater and their bad moon rising over that badass land. Creedence was playing when they loaded me on the plane in Saigon to go home, and I knew as I filled my lungs with that last breath of monsoon-heavy, dope-steady air, the bad moon had blown me away. Now, fifteen years later, it's still got me.

CHAPTER 30

She found him by the garage, sitting on the ground just outside the reach of the floodlights. He was leaning up against a stone wall, a basketball propped in his lap, cigarette butts scattered around him, and he looked as though he'd walked through the fires of hell, which wasn't far from the truth.

As she knelt beside him, he stared up at her, his face hard, the shutters drawn and tightly locked, daring her to pity him. She felt the sting of tears. "You scared the hell out of me," she said. "I forgot about you and your damned metaphors. All that talk about massacres, and the little girl in the shirt with the yellow ducks. . . . I saw you wiping out villages full of innocent civilians. I thought you'd deliberately killed her. You scared me so bad . . . It was like I couldn't trust my own instincts about you. I thought you'd been part of some obscene massacre."

"I was. The whole frigging war was a massacre."

"Metaphorically speaking, maybe, but I happen to be a literal-minded person."

"Then you must have been relieved to learn the truth," he said bitterly. "That John Wayne ended his military career in a psychiatric ward pumped full of Thorazine because he couldn't take the heat."

There it was—the secret that haunted him; the reason he had erected such indomitable walls around himself. He was afraid the world would find out he had broken apart. She wiped her cheeks with the sleeve of her blouse. "You weren't John Wayne, buddy. You were a twenty-one-year-old kid from Cleveland who hadn't had many breaks in life and was seeing too much."

"I freaked out, Flower, don't you understand that? I was screaming at ceilings!"

"You can't have it both ways. You can't write beautiful, sensi-

398

tive plays that look into people's hearts and then not expect to be torn apart when you see human suffering."

"A lot of guys saw the same things I saw, but they didn't freak."

"A lot of guys weren't you."

She reached out for him, but he stood up and turned his back toward her. "I managed to arouse all your maternal-protective instincts, didn't I?" he said bitterly. "I made you feel sorry for me. Believe me, that wasn't what I wanted to do."

She stood, but this time she didn't make the mistake of trying to touch him; this time she didn't want to. "Why are you so angry with me? You gave me the book to read, but you didn't tell me I wasn't supposed to react to it. Did you expect me to respond to your book the same way I'd respond to one of your stupid Caliber pictures? I can't do that, Jake. I hate them. I don't like watching you shoot up people and bash heads in. I liked you a lot better curled up on that cot in the hospital, screaming your insides out because your best friend had had his legs blown off by that obscene booby trap. Your pain made me cry, Jake, and it made me suffer with you, and if you can't handle that, then why did you give me the book?"

"You didn't understand a goddamn thing!" he shouted, and then walked away.

She went around the house to the pool, where she stepped out of her shoes and then her clothes until she was standing, shivering with cold, in her bra and panties looking down at the lights, wavy and blurred under the water. She dived in, gasping against the chill, and swam to the deep end before she turned over on her back and floated. Her position in the water was pretty much the way she felt—cold, suspended, waiting.

She wasn't angry with him for walking away from her again. How could she be angry after what she'd read? She felt a deep, wrenching pity for the boy he'd been, raised without any softness by a mother who was too tired and too angry over the unfairnesses of her own life to give any love to her child. He'd looked for a father in the assortment of men who frequented the neighborhood bars and sometimes found one, sometimes not. Then there was the irony of the college scholarship he had received, not for his fine, sensitive mind, but for a ruthless slam dunk.

As she floated in the water, she made herself think about his marriage to Liz. He had loved Liz long after it was over, and she thought how typical that was of him. Unlike the way she had behaved with the important people in her life, Jake didn't give his love easily, but once it was given, he hadn't withdrawn it easily either. Numb with pain, he had enlisted and then tried to distract himself with war and death and drugs.

He hadn't really cared if he survived, and it frightened her to realize how reckless that lack of caring had made him. Then, when he could no longer outrace himself, he had broken apart, and despite all those long months in the VA hospital, she knew that he had never really recovered. As she lay back in the water and looked up at the night sky, she thought she understood why that was.

"The water's too cold to swim. You'd better get out." He stood at the side of the pool, his posture neither friendly nor unfriendly, an orange beach towel in one hand, a bottle of beer in the other.

"I'm not ready yet."

He shrugged and took the towel and the beer over to a chair, where he sat down.

"Why did you blame me for the block, Jake?"

"I never had any problem writing until I met you," he said harshly. "Before you came along, everything was just dandy."

"Got any ideas about that?"

"A few."

"Care to toss them out?"

"Not particularly."

She laughed bitterly. "I'll tell you why you couldn't write. I was storming the fort. Breaching those walls. You'd built them thick and strong, but this funny nineteen-year-old kid, who ate you up with her eyes every time she looked at you, was tearing them down as fast as you could build them, and you didn't know what to do about it because you were scared to death that once those walls took their first shot, you'd never be able to build them up again."

"That's ridiculous. You're making it more complicated than it was. I couldn't write after you left because I felt guilty, that's all. You made me feel guilty!"

"No!" She jerked her knees under her and began to tread water, her throat tight and painful. "You didn't feel guilty! That's just the name you're putting on it! You didn't feel guilty

400

because you didn't have anything to feel guilty about. You made love to me because you wanted me, because you even loved me a little." She could feel the tears coming and she fought them back. "You had to, Jake; I couldn't have generated all that feeling by myself."

"You don't know anything about what I felt!"

She swam to the shallow end of the pool and stood shivering in the water, the wet bra clinging to her breasts, the flower necklace stuck to her skin. Suddenly she saw it all so clearly that she wondered why she hadn't understood it before, wondered why he couldn't fully understand it now. "This is about macho, Jake. That's all it is. With *Sunday Morning Eclipse,* your writing had become too self-revealing, and then I came along at the same time and all your warning flashers went off. You stopped writing because you didn't want to peel off any more layers. You didn't want everybody to know that the tough guy on the screen was pretty far removed from the real man."

"You sound like a goddam shrink, you know that?"

Her teeth had begun to chatter, so that her words came out in short, broken bursts. "Even when you joke about your screen image, it's as if you're winking your eye. 'We know it's just acting, don't we folks, but I'm still a hell of a man.'"

"That's bullshit!"

"You bought that guy on the screen probably before you even had your first acting job, probably the day you saw your first John Wayne movie." She climbed up the steps, shivering as the air hit her. "That's macho, Jake. You're not Bird Dog! Bird Dog is a fantasy of the kind of man you'd like to be—a man who's emotionally dead, who never feels pain. A man who's *safe.*"

"You're full of crap! You hear me?" The beer bottle slammed down on the table.

She gripped the railing, her shoulders hunched against the cold, her chest tight with pain. "Bird Dog's not half the man you are! Can't you see that? Your breakdown doesn't mean a thing. It doesn't matter to me!"

"You're so full of crap it's pitiful!"

She could no longer hold back her tears. They welled in her eyes and spilled down her cheeks. "If you want to heal yourself, go inside and read your own book—"

"Fucking unbelievable, you're so stupid!"

"Read your book and try to feel some compassion for that poor, brave kid who'd had his nerves burned raw—"

He jumped up from his chair, his face white with fury. "You're so goddamned stupid you've actually managed to miss the whole point! Christ, you're stupid—too dumb to see what should be obvious to a fucking moron! Too dumb to see that this isn't about pity!"

"Read your book!" She threw herself at him, digging her fingers into his arms, desperate to touch him, to make him face the truth. "Read about the kid who didn't have a single person in the world who gave a damn about him!"

"Why can't you understand?" he cried, shaking her off. "This isn't about pity! This is about disgust!" He kicked away a chair that stood in his path and sent it crashing into the pool. *"I want you to feel disgust so you'll get out of my fucking life!"*

As he stormed toward the house, the gates of the *couvent* slammed shut for the thousandth time. He walked away like they all did, shattering that sense of confidence she had felt and leaving her stranded, cold and alone, trying to think why she'd ever believed it would be any different. She fell down on the concrete shivering and crying, sobbing like a baby for all the things she couldn't have, and the sound was carrying over the night stillness and mingling with the old cedars until it sounded more like an owl than a human voice. Numb with cold, she crawled over to the orange beach towel and wrapped herself in it. Then she lay down, resting her head on the pillow of ruined clothes she had taken off earlier, crying until there were no tears left.

Jake stood next to the window in the darkened living room and looked down on her crumpled at the side of the pool. His heart twisted at her pain, and something swift and sharp, like the claws of a cat, kept tearing at the backs of his eyelids. But he didn't go to her—wouldn't let himself go. He had given her the book—had written it for her so she would understand why he couldn't offer her everything he wanted to, everything she deserved. But she'd dismissed the shame of his nervous breakdown as if it were nothing, oversimplified it with her pseudopsychoanalytical bullshit.

She said his breakdown didn't matter to her, but he remembered the night he had walked in on her when she and Kissy were watching *Butch Cassidy*. What a hypocrite she was. He'd seen her drooling over Redford's strong arm. Christ. Redford wouldn't have ended up lying on a cot curled up like a fetus. The Doc wouldn't have cracked up. Neither would've Bird Dog. How could she love a man who'd ended up like that?

He turned away from the window. He wished he hadn't brought her here, wished he hadn't let her back into his life at all, wished he didn't love her so goddamned much. If he'd learned anything from his relationship with Liz, he'd learned that he wasn't cut out for love. Love made him vulnerable, and he was already vulnerable enough as it was. Why couldn't she understand that? He was weak. *Weak*. The other guys hadn't cracked up, and he had. . . .

For the first time, he noticed the manuscript pages scattered on the floor near the chair where she'd been reading, and in his mind he could see her sitting there, those long legs tucked up under her, that beautiful big face puckered in concentration. He walked over to the chair and knelt down to stack the pages. He would build a fire and burn them tonight before he went to bed. They were like a live grenade lying around, and he couldn't relax until he had destroyed them, because if anyone else ever found out what was in them, he might as well put a pistol to his head and blow out his brains.

When the pages were together in a neat stack, he laid them on the chair where she had been sitting and walked back over to the window. She was quiet now. It looked as if she had fallen asleep. He walked back over to the chair and his eyes fell on the top page. He picked it up, glanced at it, studied the layout, the quality of the type, the fact that he'd run the right margin too close to the edge. He took in all those separate, unimportant facts, and then he began to read. . . .

Chapter One

Everything in Nam was booby-trapped. It was a fact of life, and we all accepted it. A pack of cigarettes, a lighter, a candy bar wrapper—all of those things could blow up in your face. But we didn't expect anything other than another small, dead body when we saw the baby lying at the side of the road outside Quang Tri. Who could have imagined that even the Cong would booby trap the body of a baby? It was the ultimate rape of innocence. . . .

It took her a few moments after she opened her eyes before she realized she was in the guest bedroom, and then she remembered that sometime during the night Jake had come to get her from the side of the pool and carry her inside. He bumped her head trying to get her through the door and cursed under his breath. She had muttered something into his sweater about Rhett Butler and he had said that Scarlett O'Hara wasn't six feet tall so she could just shut up about it. But there hadn't been any animosity in his voice, not like earlier. Instead, there had been a tenderness beneath his words that was so horribly typical of him that she had closed her eyes and refused to look at him when he laid her on the bed. Emotionally dishonest, she had told Kissy, and she had been right. He was just like Alexi—sweet one moment and stabbing you in the heart the next. She'd had enough of it in her life, and she was bailing out. The pain of loving a man who was batting her around like one of his basketballs had grown too awful to bear.

She remembered the hateful words he had flung at her the night before. They were his final smokescreen against facing something about himself that he didn't want to look at—the fact that he wasn't invulnerable. The words hadn't had anything to do with her; he had been like a child kicking out in anger against the easiest target he could find. But she couldn't be his target any longer.

He was asleep on one of the couches, his mouth slightly open, his leg dangling over the side into the pool of manuscript pages scattered on the floor beneath him. She set down her overnight case quietly so she wouldn't wake him and then began looking for the keys to the Jag, finally locating them beneath his wallet on the bedroom bureau.

The car started for her right away, and as she slipped it into reverse and backed it around in the drive, the sun struck her in the eyes. They were still swollen from the night before. She reached into her purse for her glasses. The drive was steep and badly rutted, and she crawled down it slowly so she wouldn't damage the car. Damn Jake and his insecurities. He'd made sure the road was practically impassable to everything but rabbits. His precious, stupid privacy. She glanced at the speedometer and couldn't understand why it was so hard for her to read and then she realized that she was crying again. Ten miles an hour. She could walk faster—

A blurry movement in the rearview mirror caught her attention, and she looked up to see Jake running after the car. His shirttail had come undone beneath his sweater, his hair was standing up on one side of his head, and he looked as if he were ready to commit murder. He was yelling something, but she couldn't tell what it was—probably just as well. She hit the accelerator, took the next curve too fast, and felt the car bottom out on one of the ruts. She overcompensated by jerking the steering wheel to the right and the Jag swerved. Before she could correct it, the front wheel was hanging over the ditch on the right side of the road.

She turned off the ignition and folded her arms over the top of the steering wheel, waiting for Jake and his anger, or Jake and his wisecracks, or whatever other smokescreen he was going to throw up between them. Why couldn't he have let her go? Why couldn't he have let her take the easy way out?

The door next to her jerked open, but she didn't move. She heard the sound of his breathing, heavy and ragged like hers had been that Fourth of July night on a deserted Long Island beach. Her nose was running. She sniffed and then thought, the hell with it—it didn't matter anymore—and dabbed it on the cuff of her sweater.

"You didn't take your necklace." His voice was higher-pitched than normal, and it didn't sound angry at all, but she wondered why he kept clearing his throat. "I want you to have your necklace, Flower." The morning glory pendant slipped into her lap. She felt the warmth of it seeping through the fabric of her slacks from where he had clutched it in his hand.

She didn't ease her grip on the top of the steering wheel. "Thank you."

"I—I had it made especially for you. This guy I know. I did a pencil drawing for him."

"It's beautiful," she said, as if she were receiving it for the first time.

She could hear his feet shifting in the gravel, but still she wouldn't look at him. "I don't want you to go, Flower. All that stuff last night . . ." Again the gravel scraped. He cleared his throat and then said, "Look, I'm sorry, okay?"

Her nose was running, and some of her tears were seeping

through her lips. "I can't take anymore," she said brokenly. "Let me go."

There was a long pause, a raggedly drawn breath. She heard him brace his hands on the hood of the car. "I read the book. You were right. I—I've been locked up inside myself too long. Afraid. But when I went to get you by the pool last night, I suddenly realized that I was a hell of a lot more afraid of losing you than I was of anything that happened to me fifteen years ago."

She finally turned her head and tried to look at him through her tears, but his head was turned to the side, and he wouldn't meet her eyes. She pulled off her sunglasses and heard him clear his throat again and then she knew that she wasn't the only one who was crying.

"Jake?"

"Don't look at me, God damn it!"

She turned her head away, and then suddenly his hands were on her arms, pulling her from the car, squeezing her to his chest so tightly she could barely breathe. "Don't leave me, Flower." He choked the words out. "I've been alone for so long . . . all my life. God, don't leave me. Jesus, I love you so much. Please, Flower."

She felt him crumbling, felt his need for her. She finally had what she wanted—Jake Koranda with his emotions stripped raw, all the protective layers pulled away. Jake letting her see what he had never let anyone else see. And it broke her heart.

She turned her head and covered his tears with her mouth, swallowing them, making them disappear, trying to heal him with her touch. She had to make him whole again, as whole as she was. Except she wasn't whole. He was the strong one now. He had looked at himself and faced his own humanity, but she had never had that kind of courage. She couldn't even look into a mirror.

"It's all right, cowboy," she said through her tears. "It's all right. I love you. Just don't shut me out. I can take anything but that."

He finally drew back and looked down at her, his eyes red-rimmed, all the cockiness stripped away. "What about you? How long are you going to keep shutting me out? When are you going to let me in?"

"I don't know what you—" She stopped herself, and leaned

her cheek against his jaw. She thought of his smokescreens and knew they were no different from her own. All her life, she had tried to find her personal value in the opinions of others—Belinda, Alexi, the nuns at the *couvent*. More recently, it was her business. Of course she wanted the agency to succeed, but if it failed, that didn't mean she was any less a person. There was nothing wrong with her. She'd been a victim just as much as Jake.

Try to feel some compassion for the kid you were, she had told him. Maybe it was time she felt some compassion for the frightened child she had been.

"Jake?"

He muttered something into her neck.

"You'll have to help me," she said.

He pulled her to him and they kissed long enough to lose track of time. When they finally moved apart, he looked down into her eyes and said, "I love you, Flower. Let's get this car out of here and then drive down to the water. I've got a real urge to look at that ocean and hold you close to me and tell you everything I've been wanting to say for a long time. And I think you have some things to tell me, too."

She thought of the *couvent* and Alexi, of Belinda and Errol Flynn, of the years in France and her own ambitions. She nodded her head.

They got the car back on the road without too much trouble. Jake drove, and as they began their slow crawl down the drive, he picked up her hand from its resting place on his thigh and kissed the tips of her fingers. She smiled at him and gently pulled away. Opening her purse, she took out a pocket mirror and began to study her face. It was an unsettling thing to do, vaguely embarrassing, but she didn't turn away as she'd done for so many years. Instead, she stared at her reflection, trying to look at her features with her heart instead of her brain.

Her face was part of her. It might be too big to fit her personal definition of beauty, but there was intelligence in her reflection, sensitivity in her eyes, humor in that wide mouth. It was a good face. It belonged to her, and that made it good.

"Jake?"

"Hmmm?"

"I really am pretty, aren't I?"

He looked at her and grinned, a wisecrack ready to slip from his mouth, because when it came to stupid questions, that one ranked at the top of his list. And then he saw the expression on her face, and his grin disappeared. "I think you're the prettiest woman I've ever seen in my life," he said simply.

She sighed and settled back into her seat, a satisfied smile on her face. . . .

The Jag pulled out of the drive and onto the highway, where it disappeared around the bend. For a few moments everything was quiet. Then a dusty motorcycle moved out from behind the scrub on the far side of the road. The driver lifted his helmet, looked up and down the road, and then headed up the rutted drive that led to the cantilevered house.

CHAPTER 31

A week later as the city of Santa Barbara slipped away beneath her, Fleur looked out the window of the plane and felt as if she were leaving the biggest piece of her heart behind. "We have to get used to separation," she had told Jake the night before. "It's going to be a fact of life for us."

"That doesn't mean I have to like it." He tugged on her earlobe with his teeth and then whispered, "Do you know that you have a little mole right next to your—"

She smiled at the memory. Only three weeks, four weeks at the most, and Jake would have all his neglected business settled so he could come back to New York to start work on a new play. She thought about that first day when they had returned, shivering with cold, from their rambling walk along the ocean. Jake had lit a fire and they had huddled next to it, wrapped naked in a comforter, and made a ceremony out of burning his manuscript. As one page after another caught fire, Jake seemed to grow visibly more relaxed. "I think I can forget it now."

"Don't forget too much," she said. "It's part of you. In some strange way, it may be the best part."

He picked up the poker and pushed several loose pages back into the flames, but he didn't say anything, and she didn't push him. Jake needed time. They both did. It was enough for now that he was ready to write again, that he could talk to her about what had happened, and she could talk to him.

Their happiness seemed almost iridescent, their lovemaking tender and passionate, filling them both with a sense of wonder, and yet when he broached the subject of marriage, a yellow caution light flashed in her head. "All this is pretty new," she said, "so let's not rush ourselves. We need some time to learn to be together. Neither of us can stand to fail at this—we bruise too easily—so let's see how we handle the separations, and two careers, and all the other rough spots that are going to come our way."

"God, Flower, you sound so analytical about it. I thought women were supposed to be romantics. What happened to impulse and passion?"

"They're opening in Las Vegas for Engelbert Humperdinck."

"Jesus, you've got a smart mouth." He lowered himself over her and began nibbling at her bottom lip. "Only one cure for that. . . ."

What she didn't tell him was that she had to be absolutely certain that she was marrying him, and not some twisted version of Bird Dog Caliber that lingered inside him. Still, she almost gave in the day she told him that she wanted to go horseback riding. She was still in bed wearing nothing but a T-shirt when he came out of the bathroom, a towel wrapped low on his hips. "There's no good place to ride around here," he told her.

"What do you mean? There's a stable not three miles from here. We passed it yesterday when we went out. Come on, Jake, let's go. I haven't been on a horse in months."

He picked up a pair of jeans and uncharacteristically began inspecting them with concentration. "Why don't you go by yourself. I need to catch up on some work. I have to ride all the time; it'd be a busman's holiday."

"It won't be fun without you."

"It's like you said, Flower. We have to get used to the separations."

He took two steps forward and stumbled over her sneakers. She looked at him more closely. He was actually fidgeting, and she was suddenly struck with an outrageous suspicion. "How many westerns have you made?" she asked.

"I don't know."

"Take a guess."

"Seven . . . eight. I don't know." He seemed to have developed a sudden reluctance to drop his towel in front of her. Snatching up a pair of briefs along with his jeans, he carried them back into the bathroom.

"How about—ten?" she called out brightly.

"Yeah, maybe. Yeah, I guess that's about right." She heard him turn on the faucet and then the sounds of an elaborate and noisy toothbrushing. He finally reappeared—bare chest, jeans still unzipped, a dab of toothpaste at the corner of his mouth.

She offered her most polite smile. "Ten westerns, did you say?"

He fumbled with his zipper. "Uh-huh."

"A lot of time in the saddle."

"Damn zipper's stuck."

She nodded her head thoughtfully. "A *lot* of saddle time."

"Shit. I think it's broken."

"So tell me? Have you always been afraid of horses, or is it something recent?"

His head shot up. "Yeah, sure. Yeah, right," he scoffed.

She didn't say a word. She merely smiled.

"Me? Afraid of horses?"

Not a word.

Another jerk on the zipper. "Lot you know."

He was determined to gut it out. He even managed an appropriately belligerent expression, although she thought she detected a hint of a pout beneath it. Her smile passed from sweet to saccharine, and he dropped his head. "I wouldn't exactly say I was afraid," he muttered.

"What exactly would you say?" she cooed.

"We just don't get along, that's all."

She let out a whoop of laughter and fell back on the bed. "You're afraid of horses! Bird Dog's afraid of horses! Oh, God, you'll have to be my slave forever. I can blackmail you with this for the rest of your life! Backrubs, cooking, kinky sex—"

He looked hurt. "I like dogs."

"Small ones, I bet."

He didn't deny it.

She almost said right then that she'd marry him.

Success breeds success, she was to think more than once over the next few weeks as she renegotiated Olivia Creighton's *Dragon's Bay* contract, tripling the money the actress was getting per episode, and then signed one of the most promising of Hollywood's new wave of actors as her tenth client. Now that it didn't matter so much, everything she touched seemed to turn to gold. Rough Harbor's album was getting the kind of airplay that signaled a big hit, there were good reports on Kissy's performance coming from England, and to ice the cake, Fleur came back from a meeting one afternoon to find a long mail-gram on her desk, the crux of which read:

ELOPING AT HIGH NOON TOMORROW STOP WILL PHONE
AFTER HONEYMOON STOP CHARLIE JUST TOLD ME HOW
RICH HE REALLY IS STOP AINT LOVE GRAND

Fleur laughed and leaned back in her chair. Ain't love grand, indeed!

She talked to Jake at least twice a day. He called her as soon as he woke up in the morning, and she called him before she went to bed at night. Both of them looked forward to these times when they could exchange the news about the days they spent apart and count the days until they would be together again. Their telephone conversations, she informed him with just the right amount of pedantry to set his teeth on edge, were good for their relationship because physical contact was impossible; therefore, they had to learn to relate on a more cerebral level.

He told her to cut the crap and tell him what color panties she was wearing.

Later, Fleur was to wonder why she hadn't realized that it was all going too well. She came back a little after one o'clock from a housewarming party that Michel and Damon had thrown to celebrate moving into their new co-op, and as she stepped out of her dress and hung it in her closet, the phone rang. She smiled as she picked up the receiver and deepened her voice into a husky whisper. "Did you think I'd forgotten you, lover boy?"

"Fleur? Oh, God, baby, you've got to help me! Please, baby—"

Her fingers tightened around the receiver. "Belinda?"

"Don't let him do this, baby! I know you hate me, but, please, don't let him get away with this!"

"Where are you?"

"In Paris. I—I thought I was rid of him. I should have known—" Her words grew muffled, and she began to sob.

Fleur spoke harshly. "Belinda, you can indulge in hysterics later. Tell me exactly what's happened."

"He sent two of his henchmen to New York after me. They were waiting in my apartment when I came home yesterday, and they forced me to go with them. They're going to take me to Switzerland—I know it. He's going to lock me up, baby! He's threatened me for years, but now—" There was a sudden click, and the line went dead.

Fleur slumped down on the edge of her bed, the receiver still clasped in her hand. As the minutes ticked by, she told herself that she didn't owe her mother anything. It had been Belinda's choice to stay married to Alexi. She could have gotten a divorce years ago, but she'd been too attached to Alexi's limelight to give it up. Whatever was happening to her now was her own fault. Except—

She was her mother.

Fleur set the receiver back on the cradle and finally let herself examine the relationship that she'd avoided looking at for so long. As the memories of their times together slipped before her like the pages of Jake's manuscript, she saw with new eyes what she had not been able to see before. She saw her mother as she was—a weak, frivolous woman who wanted the best from life but didn't have the faintest idea how to get it on her own. And then she saw her mother's love—selfish, self-serving, laced with conditions and manipulations, but love nonetheless. Love that was so heartfelt, Belinda had never been able to understand how Fleur could ever doubt it.

She had told Jake that she might be back too late from Michel's party to call, so she didn't phone him that night. Instead, she booked herself on the next flight to Paris, one scheduled to leave at least three hours before he would try to reach her in the morning. She'd leave a note telling her secretary that she had to make an emergency trip to London and that she would call Jake as soon as she could—anything to hold him off for a few days. The last thing she needed was to have him show up in Paris with a twenty-two, or brass knuckles, or some other weapon of his choice and make everything worse than it was already going to be. Because even as she threw her clothes in her suitcase, she knew that it would be bad. There was no doubt in her mind that Belinda was once again being used as a piece of human bait cast out by Alexi Savagar to bring his daughter back to him.

The house on the Rue de la Bienfaisance stood gray and silent in the Parisian twilight. It looked as unfriendly as she remembered it, and as she gazed out the window of the limousine she thought about the first time she had seen the house. She had been so frightened then—worried about the way she was dressed, afraid to meet her father, aching to see her mother. Some things never seemed to change. At least this time she wasn't worried about her clothes.

Beneath her satin and velvet evening cape, she was wearing the last gown Michel had designed for her, a wine velvet sheath with tight-fitting sleeves and a deeply slashed bodice embroidered at the edge with a web of tiny burgundy beads. The dress had the uneven hem that was becoming Michel's trademark, knee-high on one side, dipping to midcalf on the other, with beadwork emphasizing the diagonal. She had put her hair up for the evening, arranging it more elaborately than usual, and then added garnet earrings that winked through the tendrils fanning her ears. At seventeen she might have thought it wise to appear at Alexi's door in slacks and a blazer, but at twenty-six she knew differently.

A young man in a three-piece suit, who was most definitely not a servant, answered the door. One of the henchmen Belinda had referred to? She decided he looked like a mortician with a degree from Harvard Business School, although his French accent somewhat spoiled the effect. "Good evening, Mademoiselle Savagar. Your father has been expecting you."

Of course he was expecting her; not for one moment had she imagined differently. Stepping inside, she handed over her evening cape. "I'd like to see my mother."

"This way please." She followed him into the front salon, a little surprised at how easily he had given in to her wishes, until she saw that the room stood cold and empty. She couldn't quite suppress a shiver at the white roses that were arranged on the mantelpiece like a funeral spray.

"Dinner will be ready momentarily," the mortician said. "Would you like a drink first? Some champagne perhaps?"

"I would like to see my mother."

He turned as if she had not spoken and disappeared down the hallway. She hugged herself against the chill of the room and wished it weren't so dark. The few lamps that were lit did little more than cast shadows on the gruesome frescoes of the ceiling, and she shivered again.

Enough of this, she thought. The mortician had closed the

door to seal her in, but now she opened it and went out into the hallway, where she slipped past the great tapestries of Gobelins and Aubusson and made her way to the staircase. The heels of her pumps clicked against the marble, and she kept her head high as protection against any invisible eyes that might be watching her.

Just as she reached the top of the staircase, another young man with neat hair and a dark suit stepped out to block her from going farther. "You have lost your way, mademoiselle." It was a statement, not a question.

She realized that she had made her first mistake, and she quickly cut her losses with a few inane remarks and a dignified retreat back to the salon. The mortician was waiting to lead her to the dining room, where the huge mahogany table was adorned with another spray of white roses and a single place setting of china and crystal laid for her at the end. Everything had been carefully orchestrated, she realized, to make her feel as powerless as possible. It was going to be a war of nerves. She turned to the mortician. "I hope the food is as well prepared as the table setting. I'm hungry."

She had the satisfaction of watching surprise flicker briefly across his face before he nodded and excused himself. Who were these men, she wondered, with their dark suits and officious manner? And where was Belinda? Where was Alexi for that matter?

A liveried servant appeared to attend her, the first she had seen since she had entered the house. She sat alone in her wine velvet gown at the end of the table, garnets and beads winking in the candlelight, and concentrated on eating her dinner with every appearance of relish, even asking for an additional helping of a chestnut soufflé. She took her time, ordering a second cup of tea and then a brandy that she had no intention of drinking. Alexi could only dictate how he would play his portion of their game, she thought; he had no control over the way she would play hers.

The mortician appeared while she was toying with the brandy. "If Mademoiselle would please come with me . . ."

She took another sip, then dipped into her purse for compact and lipstick. The mortician was not trained to be a servant, and he made his impatience known. "Your father is waiting, mademoiselle."

"You've misunderstood me," she said. "I came here to see my mother, and if I can't do that, I'll leave. I don't have any business with Monsieur Savagar until I've seen my mother."

This was obviously something that hadn't been anticipated. He hesitated, and then he nodded. "Very well, I'll take you to her."

"I'll find my own way." She swept past him into the hallway and then up the staircase. The man she had encountered earlier appeared at the top, but this time he made no effort to stop her and she walked past him as if he were invisible.

Almost seven years had passed since she had last been in the house on the Rue de la Bienfaisance, but she saw that nothing had changed. The fifteenth-century Madonnas still rolled their eyelids heavenward from their gilded frames; the Persian carpets absorbed her footsteps so completely it was as if she had never walked on them. It was the kind of house where time was measured in centuries, and decades slipped by unnoticed.

As she walked the opulent, silent hallways, she thought of the house she wanted to share with Jake—a big, rambling house, with doors that banged and floorboards that squeaked and banisters that children could slide down. A house that measured time in noisy decades. She saw herself on Saturday mornings standing at the top of the stairs and calling down to them. "Be quiet, kids! Daddy's still sleeping."

Daddy. . . . It was like looking through a mirror from the opposite side. She had never thought of Jake that way, as the father of her children . . . their children. When he got mad, he would yell at them, like Alexi never had, and he would hug and kiss them and fight the whole world if necessary to keep them safe.

She suddenly wondered why she had ever hesitated. Marrying Jake was what she wanted to do more than she'd ever wanted anything. If it meant she had to accept both sides of him —well, she was wise to most of his tricks by now, so it wasn't going to be that easy for him to shut her out when something was bothering him. And he wasn't getting such a bargain himself. She wouldn't give up her career, for one thing, and nothing was going to make her work up any real interest in housekeeping. Besides, he wasn't the only one who was good at shutting people out. She suddenly experienced a sense of relief so overwhelming that she felt her knees go weak. There was no other man on earth she would trust to be the father of her children, and she was going to call him that night and tell him so.

She realized she had reached Belinda's room, and she forced herself to set aside her dreams of Jake and noisy kids to knock on the door. It took a few moments before she heard movement inside, and then Belinda's face peered through the crack. Her voice quivered as if she hadn't used it for some time. "Baby? Is it really you?" She pushed aside a lock of pale blond hair that had fallen forward over one side of her face, and then her hand went to her cheek, fluttering there like a captive bird. "I—I'm a mess, baby. I didn't think—"

"You didn't think I'd come."

"I—I didn't want to count on it. I know I shouldn't have asked you."

"Are you going to let me in?"

Belinda suddenly seemed to realize that she was standing in the way and let her in. As the door shut, Fleur noticed that her mother smelled like stale cigarettes instead of Shalimar, and she thought of the bright bird of paradise who used to arrive at the *couvent,* carrying a fragrance so sweet it instantly dispelled the musty scents of chalkdust and her own lost prayers.

Belinda's makeup had long since worn off, leaving only an oily tracery of blue eyeshadow in the creases of her eyelids. Her face was too drained of color to hold its own against the saffron silk of her rumpled Chinese robe. Fleur noticed a stain on the bodice and the sag of a front pocket that looked as if it had been forced to carry too many heavy cigarette lighters. Belinda's hand once again went to her cheek. "Let me go wash my face. I always liked to be pretty for you, baby. You always thought I was so pretty."

Fleur caught her mother's hand; it felt as small as a child's inside her own. "I still think so. Please stop fussing and sit down in that chair over there and tell me what's happened."

Belinda did what she was told, an obedient child bowing to a stronger force. She told Fleur about Alexi's threats to put her in a sanitarium, despite the fact that she hadn't been drinking. "He uses it as a sword over my head. As long as I please him, he leaves me alone, but as soon as I displease him, he threatens me." She dipped into the pocket of her robe, pulled out her cigarettes and her lighter. "He didn't like what happened between you and me in New York. He thought I'd try harder to be

417

with you. He expected me to embarrass you, but all I did was embarrass him."

"With Shawn?"

Belinda nodded. "Shawn left me for an older woman, did you know that? Funny, isn't it? Alexi closed off all my accounts, and the other woman was rich."

"Belinda, Shawn Howell is a cretin."

"He's a star, baby. It's just a matter of time before he makes a comeback." She looked at Fleur with her old reproach. "You could have helped him, you know. Now that you're a big agent, you could have helped an old friend."

Fleur saw the reproach in her mother's eyes, and waited for all the old guilt to wash over her, but it didn't come. Instead, she found herself experiencing the tolerant exasperation of a mother confronted with an unreasonable child. "I'm sure I could have helped him," she said patiently, "but I didn't want to. I don't think he has any talent."

Belinda lit her cigarette, and as she exhaled, her lip settled into a pout. "It's not very fair, Fleur. I don't understand you at all."

Fleur suddenly heard the echo of a child's voice in Belinda's words. *That's not fair, Mommy! You're not being fair!* She shrugged. "Life isn't always fair. We just have to do the best we can."

Belinda took another drag on her cigarette and then scanned Fleur's dress. "Michel designed that, didn't he?" Fleur nodded. "It's beautiful. I never dreamed he could be so talented. Everyone in New York was talking about him." Her eyes narrowed vindictively, and Fleur understood she was about to be punished for refusing to help Shawn. "I went to see Michel, did he tell you? Such a beautiful boy. He looks like me, everybody says so."

Fleur felt a flash of pity. Michel had not told her about the visit, but she could imagine his reaction.

"We had a wonderful time," Belinda said defiantly. "He told me he was going to introduce me to all his famous friends and design a wardrobe for me." The child's voice sent out its echo. *And you can't play with us!*

"I'm glad to hear the two of you got along so well. Michel's a special person."

Belinda couldn't hold the facade together any longer, and her face suddenly crumpled. She bent forward in her chair, shoving the fingers of her left hand through her hair. "He looked at me just like Alexi does. Like I'm some sort of insect. You're the only one who's ever understood me. Why does everybody have to make things so hard for me?" *It's not my fault, Mommy. Nobody likes me, and it's not my fault!*

"It would probably be easier if you stayed away from Michel."

"He hates me even more than Alexi does. Why does Alexi want to lock me up, baby?"

Fleur put her hand on her mother's shoulder. "What's happening with Alexi right now doesn't have very much to do with you. He's used you to bring me here. He wants to settle old scores."

Belinda's head shot up, and her petulance fell away. "God, why didn't I think of that. Of course!" She stood abruptly. "You have to leave right away. Alexi's dangerous. I won't let him hurt you. Just let me think for a minute."

Fleur sat on the edge of Belinda's bed and looked up at her mother pacing the carpet, one hand pushing her hair back from her face, the other holding the cigarette as she tried to figure out how to protect her child . . . and all Fleur could think about was how simple it was. Why hadn't she realized before what it was all about? When mothers and daughters got older, their roles became less distinct, the edges got blurred. *It's my turn to be the mommy. No, you be the baby. No, I wanta be the mommy.* . . . At a certain point, it seemed as if daughters had to get used to the idea of reshaping themselves into the parent. Even now, as Belinda paced the floor, trying to think how to shelter her daughter, Fleur knew that the time of being Belinda's baby was forever behind her. Belinda no longer controlled the way she viewed the world or the way she viewed herself. She also knew that she could be kind enough to protect her mother from the knowledge of just how far apart they really were.

She stood. "I'm going back to the hotel to get some sleep; I'll visit you in the morning. Try not to worry." She wanted to tell Belinda she'd take her with her, but she suspected the mortician and his cohorts would make that impossible, and she wasn't going to weaken her position by waging an argument she couldn't win. She also had no intention of telling Belinda that she was going to confront Alexi before she left.

Belinda gave her a swift, desperate hug. "Don't come back, baby. I should have realized it was you he wanted all along. I'll be all right. Please, don't come back."

Fleur looked into her mother's eyes and saw that, for the moment at least, she was sincere. "Don't worry," she said, returning her hug. "I'll be fine."

She let herself out and made her way back through the maze of hallways to find the mortician waiting for her at the bottom of the staircase. "I'll see Monsieur Savagar now," she said.

"I'm sorry, mademoiselle, but you'll have to wait. Your father is not ready to see you at the moment." He indicated the rococo chair that sat outside the library doors.

So the warfare dragged on. She had little choice but to grant Alexi his victory for the moment, but as soon as the mortician disappeared, she made her way to the front salon, where she plucked one full-blown rose from the mantelpiece and pushed it into the deep V of her bodice. It gleamed against the gown, white velvet against wine, and she carried its heavy fragrance with her as she left the salon and went back to the library doors.

She stood in front of them for a moment, not quite able to repress a shudder. Alexi's presence seemed to seep through the heavy paneling. She could feel it grasping onto her, clinging to her as tenaciously as the scent of the rose, leeching into her skin. He was waiting on the other side, malicious and confident, marking off the minutes as he played his war of nerves to the end. Slowly she turned the knob.

A lamp burned in the corner of the room, throwing a dim light over the center, but leaving the periphery in shadow. Even so, there was enough light for her to see that the vigorous man she remembered seemed to have shrunk in size. He was sitting in a chair behind his desk, his right hand resting on the top, his left hand hidden from her in his lap. He was dressed as immaculately as ever—a dark suit with impeccably cut lapels, a platinum collar pin at the neck of his silk shirt—but everything seemed as if it was slightly too big. There was a small gap at the neck of the shirt, a looseness across the shoulders. She told herself not to place any consequence on these signs of frailty, because even in the shadows of the room, she could see that his narrow Russian eyes missed nothing. They slid over her, taking in her face and hair, then swept along her dress, and finally came to rest on the rose between her breasts.

"You should have been mine," he said.

CHAPTER 32

"I wanted to be yours," she replied, "but you wouldn't permit it."

"You are a *bâtarde*. Not *pur sang*."

"How could I forget?" She stepped closer to the desk, wishing she could see his features more clearly. "All that Irish Flynn blood is a little too uncivilized for you, isn't it?" She had the satisfaction of seeing him stiffen. "I understand one of his ancestors was hung for stealing sheep. Definitely bad blood, Alexi. Then there was all that drinking and whoring." She paused deliberately. "His young girls . . ."

The hand resting on top of his desk curled in upon itself. He said, "You are foolish to play games with me that you have no hope of winning."

"Then let's end the game. Stop terrorizing Belinda."

"What if I told you that I intend to institutionalize your mother? Lock her up in a sanitarium for incurable alcoholics."

"I think that might be difficult, considering the fact that she no longer drinks."

Alexi chuckled. "How naive you still are. Nothing is difficult when one has money."

The day had been too long, and she could feel her own weariness catching up with her as her head began to ache. She wanted to go back to the hotel and call Jake so she could feel that life was sane again. "Do you really think I'd sit by and let you do that? I'd scream so long and so loud that the whole world would hear."

"Of course you would. I don't know why Belinda has never realized that. I'd have to silence you first, and that would be impossible without resorting to barbaric methods that are quite out of the question."

Fleur thought of Jake with his blazing Colts and ready fists—Jake, who was so much more civilized than the old man sitting

422

in front of her could ever hope to be. She took a chair across from him and wished that the lamp on the desk were lit so she could see his expression more clearly. "Not really much of a dilemma, is it? Especially since you've never had any intention of locking her up at all."

"You've become a worthy opponent. But then, you've been that from the beginning, *n'est-ce pas?* I expected you to discover the fire in the basement, but the substitution of the dummy dresses was quite clever."

"When you've been around a snake long enough, you learn to crawl in the dirt. Now tell me what you want."

"How very American you've grown. Direct and to the point, with no patience for *nuance.* It must be those vulgar friends with whom you keep company."

Fleur felt something inside her grow cold. Who was he talking about? Kissy? Michel? Jake. . . . Alarms jangled inside her, warning her to keep Jake tucked safely away, well hidden from Alexi's ruthless calculations. He might know that Jake had lived in the attic above her, or even about her trip to his house, but he could never know how deeply she felt about him, and she had to keep it that way.

She crossed her legs and launched her counterattack. "Actually, I'm happy with my friends," she said, "especially my brother. You made a mistake with him, you know. Michel's talent is extraordinary, and he has a brilliant career ahead of him. He's very bad at business, of course, but I happen to be very good, and I'm making sure that he earns both of us a lot of money."

"A dress designer," Alexi said contemptuously. "How can he hold up his head?"

She laughed. "Believe me, he has no trouble at all. Half the city is courting him, and the other half is standing in line. People feel privileged to be with him. He's very much like you, do you know that? The way he walks, his mannerisms. He has a habit of looking at someone he doesn't like the same way you do, narrowing his eyes, lifting one brow until you can practically watch the person shrinking. It's very intimidating. Of course, he also has the humanity that you lack, which makes him a far more interesting person."

"Michel is a *tapette!*"

"And your mind is too small to see beyond that, isn't it? Poor

423

Alexi. Maybe sometime I'll actually be able to pity you." She heard his sharp intake of breath and concentrated on keeping her gaze even with his.

"Do you ever feel remorse for what you did?" he asked abruptly. "Are you ever sorry that you destroyed an object of such remarkable beauty?"

She thought for a moment. "The Bugatti was a work of art, and I'm not proud of having destroyed it. But that's not really what you're asking, is it? You want to know if I'm sorry." She pressed her hands over the beadwork on her skirt, making small indentations in the tips of her fingers. Alexi leaned slightly forward in his chair, and she heard the soft creak of leather as he shifted his weight. "Not ever," she said. "Not for one moment have I ever been sorry."

"Bitch!" he spat.

"You've made yourself emperor of your own private kingdom, a man who's above the law, just like Belinda's movie stars. 'He's a star, baby. He doesn't have to follow the rules like everybody else.' I grew up hearing that, and do you know what—it's wrong! Nobody is above the law; everybody has to follow the rules. And people who don't follow them should be punished. What you did to me was horrible, and I punished you. Civilized people have to protect themselves against barbarians or they lose their own humanity. You can keep fighting me for as long as you want, Alexi. You can threaten Belinda and keep on trying to ruin my business, but you'll *never* make me regret what I did. I think I've grown too strong for you to ruin me now, but if I've miscalculated—if you somehow manage to destroy my business—then so be it. I don't regret what I did, and I'm willing to take the consequences. You don't have *power* over me any longer."

The leather sighed as Alexi settled back into its depths. "I said I would destroy your dream, *chérie,* and that is what I intend to do. The score will finally be even between us."

"You're bluffing. There's no longer anything you can do to hurt me."

"I never bluff." He slid a small envelope across the desktop. She looked at it for a moment before she reached out to take it. It was heavy. "A keepsake," he said.

Her heart seemed to rise into her throat. She slit open the envelope, and a battered piece of metal fell out into her lap. The letters embossed upon it were still visible: BUGATTI. It was the red metal oval from the front of the Royale.

She looked back up and saw that he had pushed something else across the desk toward her. In the dim light it was a moment before she recognized it.

"A dream for a dream, *chérie.*"

She could feel a trembling begin deep inside her as she picked it up. It was a tabloid newspaper—an American paper with that day's date—and the headlines leaped out at her:

NEW KORANDA BIO REVEALS CRACK-UP

"No." She shook her head, willing the ugly words to disappear. Alexi had read her mind, pried into her heart, practiced black magic on her thoughts. "Dear God . . . no. . . ."

> Thirty-six year old actor/playwright Jake Koranda, best known for his portrayal of the renegade cowboy, Bird Dog Caliber, suffered a nervous breakdown during the fall of 1968 while serving in the United States Army in Vietnam. Fleur Savagar, the actor's literary agent and recent companion, revealed in a press release today that Koranda was hospitalized for a post-traumatic stress syndrome following the death of a friend. According to Savagar, details of the breakdown will be revealed in the actor's new autobiography. "Jake has been honest about his emotional and psychological problems," Savagar says, "and I'm certain the public will respect him for that honesty and look upon his terrible experience with compassion."

The article went on, but Fleur could read no further. There were photographs—one of Jake as Bird Dog, another of the two of them taken when they were running in the park, a third of her alone, with a sidebar to the main story: GLITTER BABY SCORES BIG AS AGENT FOR THE STARS. She put the tabloid on the desk and slowly stood up. The battered Bugatti oval fell to the carpet.

"I have been patient for seven years," Alexi whispered from across the desk. "Now the score is settled. Now you, too, have lost what you care about most. It wasn't your business that was the real dream, was it *chérie?*"

Tears glittered in her eyes, and her heart seemed to have contracted into a small mass of frozen tissue that would never again pulse with life. All the time she had thought it was the agency he was after, but Alexi had known better; he had known, perhaps even before she did, that Jake Koranda was as elemental to her life as food and water. Jake was the dream.

But there was something in her that refused to give Alexi his victory—something that still had the will to fight him and prove that the rules were the same for everyone. "Jake will never believe this," she said, her voice little more than a whisper, but calm. Calm as the center of a storm.

"He's a man accustomed to the betrayal of women," Alexi replied. "He'll believe it."

"How did you do this? The book is gone. We destroyed it together."

"I understand there was a man with a special camera. Such things have been possible for years."

"You're lying. The manuscript was never out of Jake's—" She stopped. It had been. When he had come running after her, and they had gone to walk on the beach. "The facts in the article are wrong," she said. "Jake will realize that. He knows I'd never do anything like this to him."

"The facts are meaningless when one has been betrayed. I know this better than anyone. And Koranda understands how important your business is to you. You have used his name before for publicity purposes; he has no reason to believe you wouldn't do it again."

Every word he spoke was true, but she wouldn't let herself think about that now. "You've lost," she said. "You've underestimated Jake, and you've underestimated me." She reached out quickly—so quickly that he could not anticipate her movement —and snapped on the desk lamp.

With a harsh exclamation, he jerked up his arm and smashed the lamp to the floor where it rocked crazily from side to side, casting cruel, moving patterns of light and shadow over him. She stared at him, but it took a moment to realize what was wrong. He lifted his hand and covered the side of his face, but by then she had seen . . .

Someone who did not know him well might not even have

426

noticed. The slackness on the left side of his face was so subtle that if he had not been turned with his right side visible for comparison, even she might have missed it. There was an extra fold of skin beneath his eye, a looseness in his cheek, a slight dip at the corner of his mouth. Another person with the same malady might have given little thought to it, but for a man as proud and obsessed with perfection as Alexi, even so slight an imperfection was intolerable. She understood—she even felt a flash of pity—but it didn't make any difference.

"Now your face is just as ugly as your soul," she said.

"Bitch! Sale garce!" He tried to move so he could kick at the lamp. But the left side of his body was not as responsive as the right, and the motion was awkward. The light patterns from the rocking lamp flashed back and forth across his face.

"You've made a fatal mistake," she said. "Jake and I love each other in a way you could never comprehend. You have no heart, Alexi. The only thing you can feel is the desire to control. If you understood about love and trust, then you'd know that all your schemes and all your plots are worth nothing. Jake trusts me with his life, and he'll never believe this."

"No!" he cried. "I've beaten you!" The weak side of his face had begun to quiver, as she saw his first flicker of doubt.

"You've lost," she replied. And then she turned her back on him and left the library, walking down the hallway to the front door and stepping out into the cold January night. Her limousine was gone—Alexi had probably planned to keep her there—but it didn't occur to her to reenter the house. She walked down the drive toward the gates that led to the street, and the tears dripped down her cheeks. Every word she had spoken to Alexi was a lie. He had gone for the weakest part of her defenses, and he had calculated correctly. This was something Jake would never forgive. She could try to explain it to him—he might even believe that her father was responsible—but he would still blame her. A dream for a dream. Alexi had finally beaten her.

He stood at the window, the fingers of his right hand clutching the edge of the drapery, and watched her tall, straight figure grow smaller as it disappeared down the drive. It was a cold night, but even though she wasn't wearing a coat, she didn't huddle into the chill, or hug her arms, or in any way acknowledge the temperature. She was magnificent.

The leafless branches of the old chestnut trees formed a skeletal framework over her head, and he remembered how the trees looked in blossom and how years before another woman had disappeared down the same drive into those blossoms. Neither woman had been worthy of him, he told himself. Both had betrayed him. Yet, even so, he had loved them. . . .

A great feeling of desolation filled him. For seven years he had been obsessed with Fleur, and now it was over. He no longer had any clear idea how he would fill his days. His assistants were well trained to handle his business affairs, and the hideous deformity of his face since his last stroke meant that he could no longer appear in public. A dull ache throbbed in his left shoulder, and he kneaded it with his hand. Her walk was so straight and proud, and tiny fires lit themselves on her dress as the beads caught the headlights of the distant cars. He watched her lift her hand in front of her, and then something fell to the ground. It was too far away for him to see, but even so he knew at once what she had thrown away. A white rose.

It was then that the pain hit him.

Belinda, frantic with worry about Fleur, found him on the floor next to the window, his body curled into a comma. "Alexi?" She knelt beside him, speaking his name softly because she knew his henchmen couldn't be far away, and she wasn't supposed to be here.

"B-Belinda?" His voice sounded distorted, thick and guttural. She picked up his head to cradle it in the lap of her saffron robe, and then gave a startled cry as she saw that the side of his face was grotesquely twisted. "Oh, Alexi," she moaned, pulling him to her. "My poor, poor Alexi. What's happened to you."

"Help me. Help—" The agony in his voice horrified her, and she had the sudden urge to slap him on the wrist and tell him to *stop that this very minute.* She felt a damp spot on her thigh, saw that saliva had leaked from the side of his mouth through her robe, and knew then that it was too much for her. She wanted to be back in her room with her records and her magazines, and she could barely stop herself from jumping up and running from the library. Instead, she forced herself to think of Fleur and stay where she was.

His mouth worked for a moment before he could form the words. "G-get help. I—I need help."

"Hush. . . . Save your strength. Don't try to talk."

"Please . . ."

"Rest, my darling." His suitcoat was gaping open and one of the lapels was turned over. They had been married for twenty-six years, and she had never seen him with his suitcoat untidy. She straightened the lapel.

"H-help me. . . ."

She leaned back a little so she could look down into his face. "Don't try to talk, my darling. Just rest. I won't leave you. I'll hold you until you don't need me any longer."

She could see the fear in his eyes then, at first the merest spark but gradually growing more intense until she knew he finally understood. She stroked his thin hair with the tips of her trembling fingers. "My poor baby," she said. "Poor, poor baby. I loved you, you know. You're the only one who ever really understood me. If only you hadn't taken my baby away from me."

"Do not—do this. I beg you—" The muscles in his right side tensed as if he were trying to lift his arm, but he was too weak, and soon abandoned the movement. She could see the blue tinge to his lips and could hear his breathing grow more labored. His suffering was terrible, and she tried to think how to comfort him. Finally, she opened her robe and cradled him against her bare breast as if he were a baby being put to nurse.

Eventually he grew still. As she gazed down at the face of the man who had shaped her life, a pair of tears balanced perfectly on the bottom lashes of her incomparable hyacinth-blue eyes.

Jake felt as if all the air had been knocked out of his lungs. A basketball whizzed past his arm and bounced into the empty bleachers, but he didn't notice. Even the noises of the game going on behind him faded away. He felt cold seeping through the sweat-drenched jersey into his bones, and he struggled for breath.

"Jake, I'm sorry." His secretary stood next to him at the side of the court, her face pale, her forehead knitted with concern. "I—I knew you'd want to see it right away, so I brought it over. The phones are ringing off the wall. We'll have to issue a statement—"

He crushed the newspaper in his fist and pushed past her, heading for the scarred wooden door with the wire cage over its glass. The sound of his breathing echoed off the chipped plaster walls as he fled down the steps to the empty locker room. He pulled on his shirt, shoved his legs into his jeans, and raced from the old brick building where he'd played basketball on and off for ten years, knowing as the door slammed shut behind him that he'd never be back.

The Jag's tires squealed as he peeled out of the parking lot and onto the street. He had the sudden, idiotic thought that he'd buy up all the newspapers. Every copy. Send planes all over the country. All over the world. Every store, every newsstand. Buy them and burn them and—

He remembered the day he had come home and found Liz. He'd been able to fight then, smash his fist into that bastard's face until his knuckles bled. He remembered how Liz had clutched at his legs, wrapping her arms around them like a poster from *A Hatful of Rain*. She'd cried and begged him to forgive her while that poor bastard lay on the linoleum floor with his pants down around his ankles and his nose pushed to the side of his face. It hadn't been as bad then. His rage had had a target.

Sweat dripped into his eyes and he blinked it away. Christ. How many times could he be so fucking stupid? He'd written the book for her, spilled out his guts. . . . She'd set out to destroy him six years ago, but he hadn't learned his lesson. Instead, he'd let her back into his life and helped her finish the job.

He clutched the steering wheel more tightly and envisioned her lying on the floor at his feet, her arms wrapped around his legs, her face streaked with tears, begging him for forgiveness. He envisioned himself pulling her up by the hair—smashing her, hurting her, killing her.

And then he tasted that old familiar gun metal in the back of his mouth. The taste of fear. Cold metal fear.

CHAPTER 33

Belinda gazed at the suitcase that lay open on Fleur's bed as if it were the first time she had seen such a strange object. "But you can't leave me now, baby. I need you."

Fleur checked her purse for her airline ticket, thinking that it was just as well Belinda couldn't see the destination printed inside. "We've gone over this a dozen times before. It's been two weeks since the funeral, Belinda, and I can't spare any more time. Besides, you're doing beautifully. You don't really need me."

"That's not true. I could never have handled everything without you. And you know that all this legal nonsense makes my head spin. I can't cope."

Fleur struggled to hold herself together. Only a few more minutes. . . . "I don't expect you to. That's why I've taken care of everything for you. Alexi's staff is yours now, and they'll do what you tell them to. I'll work out the problems in New York, so you'll hardly be bothered."

Belinda's mouth formed the same pout that she had launched in Fleur's direction dozens of times over the past few weeks whenever she didn't get her way. "It's not right," she said pettishly. "I hate this house. I can't spend the night here."

"Then move to a hotel."

"You're cold, Fleur. Do you know that? You've gotten very cold with me."

"Belinda, you're a grown woman with the right of free choice —not to mention a generous yearly income. If you don't want to live here, move. I've offered to go apartment shopping with you more than once, or to get you settled into a hotel, but you kept putting me off."

"Well, I've changed my mind. Let's go tomorrow."

"I'm sorry. I won't be here."

431

"But, baby!" Now it was a wail. "I'm not used to being alone."

Knowing Belinda's penchant for male celebrities, Fleur doubted that she'd be on her own for very long, but she kept that thought to herself. "You'll do just fine," she said as she shut the latches on her suitcase. "Remember what I told you. I'm going to be tied up for a while so I won't be able to call every day. David Bennis will be in touch with you and help you with anything you need."

Tears filled Belinda's eyes. "I can't believe you're deserting me. After everything I've done for you."

Fleur gave her mother a quick, reassuring hug. "You'll be just fine."

As she rode to the airport, she tried to make herself relax, but she was strung too tight. The burden of Alexi's death had fallen entirely on her. A massive stroke, the doctors had said after one of Alexi's assistants had found him lying on the floor next to the front window. It had happened not long after she had left him, and Fleur couldn't help wondering if he had been standing there watching her when he collapsed. She felt neither triumph nor grief over his death, only a vague sense that an important force in her life was no longer there.

Although Michel called every day to offer moral support, he had refused to fly over, even for the funeral. "I can't do it, Fleur," he had told her. "I know I'm a coward with lemon Jell-O for a spine, but I just can't handle Belinda looking at me with those calf eyes of hers now that people know my name."

And what makes you think I can handle it? she'd wanted to say, but she'd understood his feelings and kept silent. Besides, it was probably for the best. It had taken all her energy just to make it through the hours of the day, without adding to it the complications of Michel and Belinda's relationship. There had been the problems with Alexi's assistants—who hadn't been all that anxious to take orders from a woman until she had made it clear that their jobs were in jeopardy—along with Belinda's constant manipulations, and her own weakness every time there was a telephone call for her. It was the reason she had decided to spend some time on Mykonos before she went back to New York. She needed a chance to heal herself, and she couldn't do that as long as she was waiting for a telephone call that wasn't going to come. The memory of her humiliation with Jake's secretary came flooding back.

The efficient voice on the other end of the line had said the same thing each time she phoned. "I'm sorry, Miss Savagar, but he isn't taking any calls. . . . No, there're no messages for you." Fleur tried the house in California and received a recording that the phone was disconnected, and there was no answer at his penthouse in New York. With each failure, she called his secretary back, begging to be put through to him. After three days of frustration, she accused the woman of not passing on her messages.

There had been a cold silence at the other end of the line and then a small, deadly explosion. "Haven't you done enough harm? Jake gave me specific orders not to put through any phone calls from you, and I'm following those orders. You've humiliated him; he's being hounded by reporters and television crews. Why don't you get the message and stop bothering him? He doesn't want to talk to you!"

That had been ten days ago, and Fleur hadn't tried to call him since.

The limousine stalled in traffic, and she stared blindly into the shop windows until a Cityrama bus pulled up and blocked her view. The limousine crawled forward another thirty feet, swung in front of the bus, and she found herself abruptly confronted with Jake's blown-up face on a billboard advertising *Eyes That See Not.* The flat brim of his hat shaded his eyes. His cheeks were grizzled, and he had a cheroot clamped in the corner of his mouth. She willed herself to look away, but she couldn't seem to turn her head. Staring into that hard face was like staring into her worst nightmares. Bird Dog Caliber—a man without a trace of weakness, a man who didn't need anybody in the world. What had made her think that she could beat him when no one else had ever been able to?

The cottage on Mykonos was made of white stucco and set in an olive grove at the desolate end of the island. She toasted herself in the sun during the day and took long, barefoot walks along the ocean at night, patiently waiting for the healing to begin. But instead of feeling better, she merely felt numb, as if all the color had seeped out of her life. It was ironic—on Mykonos of all places, where the whites were so white they hurt the eyes, and the turquoise of the Aegean so bright it redefined the hue—color had lost its meaning. All her sensations seemed blurred. She didn't feel hunger when she forgot to eat, or pain when her heel mashed down on the sharp edge of a rock. She walked along the ocean—saw that her hair was blowing—but couldn't feel the touch of the breeze on her skin, and she wondered if the terrible emptiness would ever go away.

At night, she tortured herself with memories of Jake's mouth —the crooked tooth, the bottom lip that she liked to catch between her own when they made love, his smile. She invented fantasies in which he came to her and took her in his arms and said he still loved her. Fantasies. Just like the ones she'd invented as a little girl about Alexi coming to get her and take her home with him.

She pushed the fantasies away and looked in the mirror, seeing herself clearly. She wasn't a little girl anymore, and she wasn't going to beg for anyone's love, not even Jake's. She was numb and griefstricken, but she wasn't broken. What had happened wasn't her fault. He should have known that, but his vision of himself was too narrow, too easily threatened. He was weak. It was what she had been afraid of, the reason she had hesitated when he asked her to marry him. He hadn't loved her enough to stand strong.

Eventually, she forced herself to accept the fact that Mykonos held no magical healing powers for her. She knew that she had already neglected her business for too long and burdened David and Will beyond what she could reasonably expect. It was time to return to New York. Still, she lingered another few days before she could make herself call David and tell him when she was returning.

The trip was long and uncomfortable, and by the time she got off the plane at Kennedy, she was exhausted. Her wool slacks itched her thighs where they were peeling from the sun, and her stomach was queasy from two hours of turbulence over the Atlantic. A light dusting of snow combined with heavy airport traffic made getting a cab even more arduous than usual, and when she finally found one, its heater wasn't working. It was well after midnight when she slipped the bolt on her door to let herself into her living room.

The house was damp and nearly as cold as the cab. Dropping her suitcase, she pushed up the thermostat and then sat on the couch to kick off her shoes. Finally, she pulled off her slacks and scratched her legs. They still itched. Without removing her coat, she walked down to the kitchen, filled a glass with tap water, and then tossed in two Alka-Seltzers. As the tablets fizzed, she shifted back and forth to escape the cold that was seeping through her stockings from the brick floor. She was going to get into her bed, she decided, turn up the electric blanket, and not move until morning. But first, she was going to take the hottest shower she could stand and then rub herself all over with lotion.

Not until she was in her bathroom did she take off her coat, along with her sweater and her underwear, and turn on the shower. Taking time only to pin her hair on top of her head, she slid open the shower doors and let the hot water wash over her. In six hours she was going to get out of bed and run in the park, no matter how badly she felt. This time she wasn't going to crumble in on herself. Every day she would go through the motions, and before long, things would be all right again. Time would heal her. That's what everyone had told Belinda at Alexi's funeral.

After she had dried herself, she opened the bathroom door a crack to let out the steam and pulled a lace-trimmed beige satin nightgown from a hook next to the shower. She remembered that she had forgotten to turn on her electric blanket, so she slipped into the matching robe. The temperature change after Mykonos was too much for her, she decided. She was already getting cold again, and the sheets were going to feel like ice.

Stepping over her pile of discarded clothes, she pushed open the bathroom door, fumbling behind her for the sash that held the waist of the robe shut. Funny. She thought she'd flipped the light on when she'd come into the bedroom. God, it was freezing! The windows were rattling, and a blizzard had started up outside. Why hadn't the furnace kicked— She screamed.

"Stay right where you are, lady, and don't move."

A whimper caught in her throat.

He was sitting in a chair on the far side of the room, with only his face visible in the patch of light from the open bathroom door. His mouth barely moved as he spoke. "You do what I say and nobody gets hurt."

She put her foot behind her, took one step backward toward the bathroom . . . then another . . . He lifted his arm, and she found herself looking down the long, silver barrel of a gun. "That's far enough," he said.

Her heart jumped into her throat. "Please . . ."

"Let go."

At first she didn't know what he was talking about, and then she realized he meant the sash she was clutching in her damp hands. Quickly, she dropped it.

"Now the robe."

She didn't move.

He lifted the gun so that it was aimed at her chest.

"You're crazy," she gasped. "You're—"

The hammer clicked. "Take it off."

Her hands jerked to the front of the robe. She opened it and slipped her arms out. The fabric made a soft, hissing sound as it dropped to the floor at her feet.

He lifted the barrel ever so slightly. "Let your hair down."

"Jesus . . ." Her hands fumbled with the pins. As her hair came down, stray drops of water from her shower splattered on her bare shoulders.

"That's nice. Real pretty. Now the gown."

"Don't . . ." she pleaded.

"Pull down the straps slow. One at a time."

She slipped down the first strap and then stopped.

"Go on." He made a sharp gesture with the gun. "Do what I tell you."

"No." She shook her head.

He sat up straighter in the chair. "What did you say?"

"You heard me."

"Don't push me, teacher lady."

Fleur clamped her arms over her chest.

Shit, Jake thought. Now what was he supposed to do?

CHAPTER 34

"Just hold me for a minute, okay?" she asked.

He set the pearl-handled Colt on the table next to the bed, and walked over to where she was standing. Her skin was like ice. He opened his parka and put it around them both, cuddling her against his flannel shirt. "You're no fun; do you know that?"

She gave a choked little sob.

"Hey, are you crying?" He felt her head nod against his cheek. "I'm sorry, sweetheart. I didn't mean to make you cry. I guess my timing wasn't too good, was it?" She shook her head, not even attempting to figure out how he knew about *Butch Cassidy* and her fantasy.

"It seemed like a good idea at the time," he said, "especially when I couldn't decide what I was going to say when I saw you."

She spoke against his shirt front. "You can't let Bird Dog resolve this for us in bed, Jake. We have to settle it ourselves."

He tilted up her chin. "You've got to learn to separate fantasy from reality, kiddo. Bird Dog's a movie character. I like playing him—it gives me a chance to act out all my aggression—but he's not me. I'm the one who's afraid of horses, remember?"

She stared up at him.

"Come on, you're freezing." Leading her over to the bed, he pulled back the covers. As she climbed in, he took off his parka and his boots, then he slid in next to her, still wearing his shirt and jeans. "The pilot must be out on your furnace. It's colder than hell in here."

She reached over to flick on the light. "Why wouldn't you take my calls? I went crazy . . ."

"I'm sorry, Flower. The press was everywhere, and I felt like I was suffocating. A lot of old stuff came back and grabbed me. I wasn't feeling too charitable."

"You knew it was Alexi, didn't you?"

"I wish I could say yes, but it took me a couple of days before I calmed down enough to figure it out. I still don't know how he managed to do it."

"Someone photographed the manuscript while we were walking along the ocean that first day. I found the negatives after he died."

His head jerked around toward her. "What did you do with them?"

"Burned them, of course."

"Dammit!"

She looked at him, unable to believe what she was hearing.

"I wish you'd talked to me first," he muttered, "that's all."

She couldn't help it. She slumped down in the bed, jerked the comforter over her head, and screamed. For a moment there was silence, and then he pulled the comforter back to a point just below her chin.

"It's going to be a lot of rewriting." His bottom lip was sulkier than ever. "I mean, you can't expect me to be exactly happy about that, can you?"

She nodded toward the Colt. "Is that thing loaded?"

"Of course not."

"Too bad." She suddenly realized he'd distracted her. "If you knew it was Alexi, then why—"

He pulled her close against him and buried his lips in her hair. "You forget what an old pro I am at blaming you for anything I can't handle."

"What made you change your mind?"

"Kissy will tell you it was her—she flew back from her honeymoon. God, can that woman cuss. . . . Simon threatened to go to the newspapers and tell everyone I was gay. Michel hit me." Fleur looked at him sharply, and he threw up his hands. "I didn't touch him. Honest to God." He pulled her back into his arms. "Even some cretin named Barry Noy got hold of me."

"You're kidding."

"God is my witness." He stroked her hair. "Do you have any idea how many people love you?"

She started to cry again, but he just kept talking and petting her hair. "I was pretty ragged by the time Belinda found me. She has a way about her, that mother of yours. She looked at me with those blue eyes and told me I was the most exciting star in Hollywood and that I was throwing away the only woman in the world who was good enough for me." He shook his head. "But listen to this, Flower. Not one—not one of those interfering sons of bitches had any idea at all where I could find you!" He shuddered. "Until David Bennis called me yesterday I thought I'd lost you for good this time. Mykonos, for chrissake. Who the hell goes to Mykonos? Honest to God, if you ever run off again like that—"

"Me!"

He crushed her to his chest so hard she thought her ribs would crack. "I'm sorry, Flower. I'm so sorry, babe. When that story broke, I went crazy. It was like waking up from a terrible nightmare only to find out that it wasn't a nightmare at all. I felt as if I'd been raped. Everybody was trying to get to me . . . peel off my skin . . . pick at my bones. I'm telling you, the press is a bunch of goddamn vultures, and the only person I could blame it on was you. But all the time I was blaming you, I needed you so bad it was like part of me had died. That's when I knew I'd do anything to get you back."

Fleur wiped her face on his flannel shirt.

"And then the letters started to arrive. Flower, they came in from all over the country. Guys who'd been in Nam and couldn't get it out of their souls—they wrote me about what had happened to them. Teachers, bankers, garbagemen, a lot of guys who couldn't hold on to a job. Some of them are still having nightmares; others said Nam was the best time of their lives, and they'd do it again if they had the chance. Guys told me about broken marriages and good marriages, about their kids. Not all of them were patting me on the head, either. Some said I was 'perpetuating the myth of the crazed Vietnam vet.' Shit. We weren't crazed. We were just a bunch of kids who'd seen too much. But as I read those letters, I knew that I had something the whole country needed to see. I'm going to write my book again, Flower, and I'm going to include those letters."

"Are you sure about this?"

"I'm tired of living in shadows, Flower. I want to walk in the sun for a while. But I can't do that without you."

She put her arms around his shoulders and buried her face in his neck. "Do you have any idea how much I love you?"

"Is it enough to start talking about station wagons and two-career marriages?"

She nodded her head. "And kids, Jake. I want babies. Lots and lots of little Koranda babies running around."

He grinned that crooked-tooth grin that drove her crazy and slid his hand up under her nightgown. "Want to start now?" He didn't wait for an answer but settled his mouth over hers. After a few moments, he drew back. "Flower?"

"Uh-huh?"

"I'm not enjoying this kiss."

"S-sorry." She tried to force her teeth to stop chattering, but it was no use. "I'm just s-so *cold*. I can see my breath in the air!"

He groaned and pulled back the covers. "Come on. You'll have to hold the flashlight for me."

With his parka wrapped over the top of her satin gown, and her feet encased in wool sweatsocks, she followed him to the basement. While he kneeled on the concrete floor to light the pilot, she stuck her free hand under his shirt. "Jake?"

"Yeah?"

"After the house heats up—"

"Hold that flashlight steady, will you? I almost have it."

"After the house heats up, what would you think about—I mean, would you think it was silly if—"

"There, that's got it." He shook out the match and straightened up. "What were you saying?"

"What?"

"You were saying something. Would I mind if—"

She swallowed. "Nothing. I forget."

"Liar." He put his hands inside the parka and slipped them around her waist so he could draw her up against him. "Don't you know that there's nothing I'd rather do?" His lips caught her ear lobe, then traveled down along the curve of her neck and over her jaw until he could whisper against her mouth. "But you'll have to put your hair back up again with those pins. That was my favorite part."

EPILOGUE

Belinda watched the young man's body form a perfect arc as he dived into the turquoise water of the pool behind her Bel-Air home. His name was Darian Boothe—the final *e* had been her idea—and when he came to the surface, she blew him a kiss. "Wonderful, darling," she called out. "I love watching you."

He gave her a smile that she suspected might not be totally sincere, then pulled himself out of the water, his biceps knotting as they supported his weight. She watched his tiny red nylon trunks ride up into the crack of his rear as he walked back to the diving board, and found herself hoping that the network would buy his pilot. If they didn't, he'd be miserable, and she'd have to expend all her energy trying to cheer him up. Of course, if they did buy it, he would probably move out, but that was all right, too. It wouldn't be difficult to find another handsome young actor who needed her help.

She moved her legs farther apart so the sun would reach the insides of her oiled thighs and pulled her sunglasses back down over her eyes. She was tired. It hadn't been easy for her to fall back asleep last night after Jake's phone call; it wasn't every day that your daughter gave birth to twin boys. They had known about the twins ever since the sonargram, so it wasn't a surprise, but still it was hard for her to get used to the fact that she was now a grandmother of three. It was also embarrassing. Fleur and Jake had been married for three years and they already had three children, and didn't plan to stop there. Her beautiful daughter had turned into a brood mare.

Not for the first time, Belinda admitted to herself that Fleur was something of a disappointment. It wasn't like all those years when they had been apart; at least now she was certain her daughter still loved her—Fleur sent thoughtful gifts and called her several times a week—but she didn't really *listen* to

441

her anymore. She didn't pay attention! Belinda tried to be fair. With the opening of Fleur's West Coast office last year, not even the most dedicated skeptic could say that her agency wasn't a success, and she *had* been photographed for *Vogue* wearing Michel's new line of executive maternity clothes, but it was still clear to anyone with eyes that Fleur was not living up to her potential. All that beauty gone to waste—God knew, she didn't need it to sit behind a desk—and if she wasn't at work, she was buried away at that godforsaken farmhouse in Connecticut instead of staying in Manhattan where she and Jake could be the brightest, most sought after couple in town.

Belinda remembered her last visit to the farm two months ago. It had been early July, just after the Fourth. The summer heat settled over her as she stepped out of the air-conditioned limousine directly into a pile of dog refuse from one of those dirty animals Fleur insisted upon keeping. A quick glance told her that her new Maud Frizon pumps were ruined. She rang the front door bell. No one answered, so she let herself into the house.

The interior was cool and fragrant with kitchen smells, but certainly not her idea of what the inside of the house of two such famous people should look like. Instead of thick carpeting in a rich color that would complement the wood, the wide-pegged floors were covered only by a braided rug, a *rag* rug they had called it in Indianapolis. A basketball was shoved into one corner of the foyer, along with a copper urn full of some rather ordinary garden flowers and something that looked suspiciously like the Peretti evening bag she'd once given Fleur, except now the handle was broken and Big Bird's fuzzy yellow head was sticking through the opening. A book was propped between the banister railings, and a riding helmet hung on the newel post. Belinda couldn't believe that Jake was permitting Fleur to ride horses this late in her pregnancy.

Wishing that she'd called first to let them know she would be arriving earlier than she'd planned, she removed her soiled pumps and padded through the silent downstairs, ending up in the dining room. There was a manuscript sitting on the sideboard, but Belinda wasn't tempted to look at it, even though she knew there were many people who'd give anything to get an early peek at a new Koranda play. Despite all his awards and honors, Jake's writing didn't interest her much. And that book about Vietnam that had won him his second Pulitzer was the most depressing thing she'd ever read. Actually, she'd only made it through the first two chapters, but that had been enough.

She still liked his movies much better, even though he didn't make many anymore. There had been only one Bird Dog picture in the last three years, and Fleur had had a fit about that. They'd argued for days, but Jake wouldn't budge. He told her he liked playing Bird Dog, and she could just put up with it every few years. She ended up going on location with him and spending all her spare time with the horses.

Just as Belinda turned to leave the dining room, she heard Fleur's laughter drifting through the open window. She walked over to it and pushed back the lace curtain.

There her daughter lay—her head in her husband's lap, both of them sprawled underneath a gnarled cherry tree that was probably insect-infested and should have been removed years ago. She was wearing a pair of faded navy maternity shorts and one of Jake's shirts with the bottom buttons unfastened to make room for her stomach. Belinda wanted to cry. Her daughter's beautiful blond hair was pulled back with a rubber band, a long scratch ran along the calf of one sunburned leg, and a mosquito bite marred her ankle. Worst of all, Jake was popping cherries into her mouth with one hand while he stroked her stomach with the other.

Fleur tilted her head to the side, and Belinda saw the sheen of cherry juice on her chin. And then she watched as Jake's hand slid under the hem of her shirt and rose to cup her breast. He dipped his head to kiss her, letting long moments pass. Embarrassed, Belinda moved to turn away, but a car door slammed and the late afternoon stillness was pierced by a high-pitched, happy shriek. Belinda could feel her pulse quicken, and she leaned to the side to catch the first glimpse of Meg she'd had in weeks. Meg. . . .

Fleur and Jake looked up as the child came running around the side of the house, dashing past a green plastic wading pool and launching her chubby two-and-a-half-year-old body at them. Jake caught her before she could reach Fleur and pulled her into the crook of his arm. "Whoa, Cookie Bird. You're gonna bounce on Mommy's tummy and make her pop."

"Great start to her sex education, cowboy." Fleur reached

out to tug down the elastic leg on Meg's cotton sunsuit, and then lingered there for a moment. "You're wet, baby. Did you forget to ask Nanny to use the potty?"

Meg plopped her index finger into her mouth and took a contemplative suck, then she turned to her father and gave him her biggest grin. He laughed and pulled her close to bury his head in the soft skin of her neck.

"Con artist," Fleur smiled. She leaned forward and closed her mouth over a chubby thigh, almost as if she were tasting her daughter's skin rather than kissing it.

The diving board banged, and Darian Boothe somersaulted into the pool, bringing Belinda back to her own house in Bel-Air and the reality that her daughter now had two more babies. As she lay in the sun, the scent of chlorine filling her nostrils, she thought of how contemptuously Alexi would have regarded Fleur's childbearing. Poor Alexi. They had done terrible things to their children. But she didn't like to think about Alexi because it made her remember that terrible night when he had died, so she thought about Darian Boothe instead and whether or not the network would buy the pilot. And then she thought of Fleur, who was still so beautiful she made her heart ache. And Meg. . . . It wasn't much of a name in her opinion—far too plain for a beautiful little girl with her father's mouth and her mother's eyes and Errol Flynn's gleaming chestnut hair curling in ringlets around her dear little face. But still, any name with Koranda after it was going to look good on a marquee, and blood would tell.

More than thirty years had passed since the night James Dean died on the road to Salinas. Belinda stretched in the California sun. All in all, she hadn't done too badly for herself.

Lose yourself in fabulous, old-fashioned storytelling— the triumphant *Lavette Family Saga*

_____	#1 THE IMMIGRANTS	14175-3	$4.50
_____	#2 SECOND GENERATION	17915-7	4.50
_____	#3 THE ESTABLISHMENT	12393-3	4.50
_____	#4 THE LEGACY	14720-4	4.50
_____	#5 THE IMMIGRANT'S DAUGHTER	13988-0	4.50

from HOWARD FAST

You're invited to a reunion well worth attending

College classmates Emily, Chris, Daphne, and Annabel will be there. Friends from their days at Radcliffe in the 50s, they found glamorous careers, married "perfect" men, and expected to have "perfect" children. They played by the rules —sort of—but the rules changed midway through their lives.

You'll meet them first in Rona Jaffe's wonderful **Class Reunion.** And catch up with these remarkable women 25 years after graduation in **After the Reunion.**

R o n a   J a f f e

_____CLASS REUNION	11288-5-43	$4.50
_____AFTER THE REUNION	10047-X-13	4.50